Manufacturing Artificial Intelligence Agency (M.A.I.A.)

WD Shipley

For Heather,

Whose love and support
illuminates every page of our story

Love you.

I am immensely grateful to Masheri Chappelle, whose keen insight and unwavering patience helped transform this manuscript. Her ability to see the potential in my story and guide me through countless revisions has been nothing short of transformative.

Special thanks to editor Keera Luposiewicz for her sharp eyes and skill in finding all the little things, and Dan Pouliot for his guidance on design.

Published by PortalStar Publishing llc
www.portalstarpublishing.com
ISBN: 979-8-218-42025-3 (pbk)
ISBN: 979-8-218-42025-0 (digital)

Story Guide : Masheri Chappelle
Editor : Keera Luposiewicz

First Printing, 2024

First Edition Published by Page Publishing Inc, NY
Date of 1st Publication March 09, 2016
ISBN: 978-1-68289-406-4 (pbk)
ISBN: 978-1-68289-406-0 (digital)

Manufacturing Artificial Intelligence Agency (M.A.I.A.)

Prologue

Manufacturing Artificial Intelligence Agency
M.A.I.A.
By W.D. Shipley

Production Floor

Tom pinched the clear chip and brought it up to the light. Squinting through his glasses, he read the number out loud and scribbled down the digits.

"Okay."

Tom pressed his thumb to the fingerprint scanner. A tray slid out from the tablet, and he placed the nanochip into it. A hologram keyboard beamed out from the bottom of the tablet. He hovered his hands over it to the traditional keyboard next to it. His fingers pitter-pattered on the keys and found the boy's sperm donor's profile and social security numbers. Although useless for anything else, it was an effective serialization. He poked at the screen and swiped. The digital outline of the chip swiveled around in a full 360-degree motion. He cracked his fingers.

"Infantry ... good to switch it up ... I've been programming female chips all morning ... basic skills ... yada, yada ... all right ... got that ... and that."

His fingers banged on the keys. His eyes scrolled down the line. All the basic math skills—science, logic, everything you could learn in years of high school and college decades before—now completed in a programmer's ill attempt at milking an hour. He checked off basic programming for syncing to the M.A.I.A. monitors—much like the flat screen computer that overlooked the white room.

"Okay, got program 19-84.... Just military programming left. "

Binary code filled the lower half of the screen, and the upper half of the screen spread a series of equations and boxes. He loaded in basic military logic for an infantryman, thousands of years of military strategy crammed into one upload.

"Another drone for M.A.I.A. He'll be counting his kills soon enough."

Tom pressed the finger pad, and the tray slid out. He placed the chip in and checked off the social security number as completed.

"Ah, one more for the day." Tom's shoulders twitched as the door to the lab slid open.

"Talking to yourself is the normal down here. It's part of the wear and tear on the human mind from being isolated." The doors slid shut behind Albert.

Tom cut a side look at Albert. *Pompous, pain in my ass.*

Tom turned his back on Albert, pinched the clear chip, held it up to the light, and squinted to read the next social number to program.

"You know, they have surgery for vision. It doesn't hurt and you'll see better than the eyes you were born with. You might want to try it." Al placed a cup of hot coffee between Tom's bicep and rib cage and then pressed Tom's arm against it to hold the coffee in place.

"Why do you have to be such an asshole?"

"It's my nature," Al replied with a smirk.

"Al, destruction of M.A.I.A. property is a serious offense. If I dropped this chip in the coffee or drop this coffee, on the floor, or within this sealed room, that you deliberately, and with malice, tucked under my arm, I will pull the surveillance video and rat you out. They will take the loss of this chip out of your pay."

"What a little whiner," Al spat as he removed the coffee cup, and placed it safely on a freestanding tray with cup holders.

Tom placed the chip onto the tray and opened the donor's profile. He reached for his coffee and sipped it.

"I brought you a coffee, because I was afraid you were going to fall asleep on the job."

"Never," Tom replied without looking at him.

"You should owe me at least a week's pay for all the sludge you make me retrieve for you. You do realize I'm smart enough to do your job."

"They didn't hire you for that. You're my assistant. You're here to help me."

"I'm a glorified gopher."

"No matter how small, everyone makes a contribution to the cause," Tom said, moving his eyes between the keyboard and screen.

"One day, I'm going to be the one in charge," Al said. "I'll outlast all of you."

Tom stopped and looked at Al. "You do have an active imagination. I need you to imagine yourself going through those folders I sent you. Separate the cadets from the medics. I will be starting a new batch of cadets, and you haven't prepared the list for me." He tastes the coffee and grimaces. "The coffee is getting worst every day."

"I heard they're running out of real coffee supplies. Everyone will be on coffee in a cube."

"I can't survive on those rations."

"This is all I need to make it through a day." Al nibbled on a brown cube.

"Al, I'm sixty years old. It's nothing but a bitter candy bar."

Al snickered, held his ration, and inspected it. "Candy bar? When's the last time you had a candy bar? This doesn't taste like anything, and it gives you half of the day's nutrients, carbs, and vitamins in less than thirty seconds. I'm around the same age as you, Tom. I always wondered why you're so full of piss and vinegar. You're cranky because you haven't eaten in over ten years. When I become the Supreme Reader, I'll have them create gourmet flavors like lasagna."

"Supreme Reader? You expect to be the Supreme Reader?"

"Yes, I'm just as smart as any of you. Why are you staring at me like that?"

"I'm trying to figure out who you are going to blackmail to get that position."

"I have the brains for it. Where there's a will, there's a way," Al shot back.

"Right now, I need you to find your way to the folders and get me the new cadet list."

Tom inserted the chip into the tray and focused his eyes on the serial number that appeared on the screen. The serial number was the social security number of the sperm donor. It was a number issued at birth; a number that promised life, liberty, freedom, and the pursuit of happiness. People used to strive to receive a social security number to be considered part of the greatest nation world history had ever known. There was a time when that number sealed one's identity as an American citizen.

As Tom's eyes scanned the serial number again, his stomach twisted, and its contents swished around like he was on a slow-moving ship. He read the serial number again on the vial to make sure. He couldn't remember the last time he had seen it. The blood drained from his hands, his face heated, but his brain froze.

"You all right?" Al's neck craned forward.

Tom looked down at his watch—a Rolex his father gave him on the last day of his dad's life. When he received it, the diamond for the five had been missing for years. Before going to M.A.I.A., he never thought of replacing the diamond. Instead, he made a posthumous private pact with his father to use that time to think of him. Tom never planned anything for 5 a.m. or 5 p.m. because that time of day was given to memories of being with his father. Tom's work, and the breakdown of life above ground didn't permit Tom to marry or have kids. The title of father had eluded him until now. He wiped his eyes and looked at the serial number again. He looked at his EED, his pulse and heart beats per second were elevated.

"Al, can you read me this number? My eyes are getting tired. It's the end of a long day."

Al confirmed the number.

The chip trapped in a M.A.I.A. soldier would technically belong to his child from a sperm donation of the past. His child would be in the M.A.I.A. army. He fluttered through documents that belonged to the chip. His child would be trained as a sniper! Tom thought about all the files for the sniper, all the advanced math that had to be done on the fly to make a shot from nearly two miles away.

"Tom, are you sure you're feeling well?"

"The coffee is upsetting my stomach." Tom's fingers spread across the keyboard.

"I just have this last chip to program to meet my quota for the day, and I really want to get out of here."

"Should just switch to ration strips." Al turned around in his glass cubicle, which faced the opposite direction.

Tom scanned through the programs, and checked anything he thought might be necessary for the extreme success of a young sniper. His throat ached from the strain of his emotions. The sniper's list seemed extensive—not so extensive it might be put aside for audit, but did a sniper really need to understand four languages?

His fingers paused. He read the last program. The flat screen overlooked their hologram cockpit. He stared down at the tray only large enough to hold the day's quota of programmable mind chips. A blue wave flowed across the screen. Were they watching him? If he had one of these chips in his head, could they really read his mind or control what he knew or thought he knew? He stared down at the keys. This was the first time he had ever questioned Program Number 19-84—the Vanishing Sequence—the ability for M.A.I.A., the quantum supercomputer, to dictate what someone knows. Tom stared at the protocol and then at the monitor, back at the protocol and then at the little chip that would be put into his son's head. Minds are not meant for controlling.

He typed, *Delete 19-84. Do not allow access for the Vanishing Sequence.*

1

Nineteen Years Later...

Alix Basil stared down at his hand. The helicopter jolted and shook, but his hand remained still. His body pulsated, and his mind raced; but his hand remained still. His other hand gripped his rifle. He was molded for perfect accuracy.

"Atten-hut!" Captain Milligan yelled over the deafening hum of engines and propellers. His steel-studded boots scraped on the metal paneling beneath his feet. A Smith & Wesson revolver hung from his right hip. "Listen, boys! First attack! You're all green, and none of you have a story to tell! Today it starts! Right here! Right Now! Your first day on the field! Now strap up, ladies! ETA—two minutes!"

The eight soldiers put on gray camouflage vests and tightened their black boots with clicks and clinks. Pistols strapped to their thighs, knives tucked in a holster near their ankles, their primary weapons dangled from their shoulders, and their secondary, semiautomatic guns strapped to their backs with a crossbody holder.

Alix's eyes locked on Hayden who sat directly across from him. Their knees bumped together with every jolt of the helicopter.

Hayden's jaw clenched, and the muscles on his shaved head tightened. When their knees bumped again Hayden looked directly at Alix. "Why the dim eyes? This is what we live for, Alix."

"I'm thinking."

Hayden shook his head. "No time for that. It's already been thought up."

Alix smirked and pulled his mask over his face. The world brightened through yellow lenses, and he inhaled his first, bitter, audible breath.

Captain Milligan held the support straps dangling from the helicopter's ceiling and looked over each pair of yellow eyes. His forearms tightened to hold him in place. Through Alix's mask, Milligan's orange beard glowed, and his freckles appeared like luminescent dots on his face.

"ETA—thirty seconds! Hayden, Wes, Phil, Eli, Matt, and Adam, you're Team Alpha. Alix and Victor, you're Team Echo. Don't forget your training! Keep your masks on! And remember, if you find yourself out of contact of M.A.I.A. and surrounded by the enemy, do yourself a favor and turn the gun on yourself after taking a few of those bastards down with you."

The top of a pine tree scraped under the helicopter's steel belly. Snow and ash puffed into a swirling cloud of jet fuel and exhaust. Captain Milligan spun and caught his balance.

"Sorry, Captain!" A girl's voice called out in their earpieces. "Closing in."

The helicopter vibrated. Sweat dripped under Alix's vest.

"Ready for deployment maneuver!" the female pilot announced.

The helicopter jolted and banked backwards. Eli and Phil closed their eyes and held in their stomachs as the chopper dropped. Matt and Adam pressed their feet to the floor and their heads back against their seat. Victor hung his head low and braced his feet. Alix stared forward and let his eyes blur in unfocused laziness, and the chopper descended faster than gravity. The sound of metal pings of bullets engulfed the small, armored cabin. The odor of burning fuel, and the dank air, filled the cabin, elevating their anxiety as the helicopter descended down into the war below.

The soldiers' shaky hands released their shoulder straps.

"Three!" the pilot uttered. "Two!"

The straps tangled Matt in. He broke one to get loose. The helicopter hovered over the ground. Their bodies were forced forward.

Captain Milligan caught himself by hanging off a strap.

"Deploy!"

The plated floor door flopped open, and the heavy, steel rattle echoed in their helmets. The floor shook. Hayden lifted his assault rifle, screamed, and barreled out the chopper's cabin. Hayden's gun fired left. Like a sneeze, the helicopter emptied the remaining soldiers. The earth vibrated beneath the soldiers' boots. Gravity felt like it pulled harder here. Smoke lifted in twisters from burning, fallen buildings against a backdrop of white-tipped mountains. Remains of disintegrating structures tilted and shook as they ran. The smell of decay clogged the air.

Machine-gun sputter hogged the sound of Hayden's scream. Blood pelted out the back of Hayden's vest as bullets thudded into his body and drew him down.

Silence.

Pebbles mushroomed out and sandblasted nearby broken, stone walls as the helicopter lifted. The smoldering chopper shrank behind the pines and restored the sound of war that surrounded them. A small missile launched from over the burning horizon and left a streak of smoke across the sky. The soldiers' heads followed the missile over the tips of pines, in pursuit of the chopper. Wes dropped his eyes first. "To the wall!"

Everybody veered left after him and slammed against the crumbled, stone wall. Anxiety and fear tugged their boiling hearts. Alix watched a wave of dust crawl over Hayden's dead body and drown him in the shredded street, just another piece of debris among broken boards, glass, loose trash, carcasses, and rusted cars.

"Don't look at him!" Wes slugged Alix's vest and drew a finger to his face. "Don't!" He grabbed Alix by the strap and pulled him down as a wave of bullets poured over them. Bits of rock rained down.

Alix stared into yellow, metallic bubbles that were the eyes of Wes's mask—his breaths filtered and robotic.

"Focus." Wes angled his rifle over the wall and stared through the video display built into his helmet. "Do an infrared scan on the building across the street. We might have a shot at this guy." A burst of bullets skimmed the top of the wall. Wes swiped his rifle back to his chest.

Adam pointed his rifle at the building and scanned it for body heat. "One possible on second floor. I'll keep him tagged. If he moves, you'll know about it."

Wes turned to Adam. "Keep it in your sights." He turned to the rest. "We're going to provide cover fire. Alix and Victor, go over to that old coffee shop across the street, clear the top floor, and take out that gunner!"

Wes swiveled and tossed his gun over the wall. "Suppressing fire!"

The sound of a million bags of popcorn amplified and moved Alix's legs for him. He slung his massive rifle over his shoulder and stumbled. Victor clasped Alix's arm and shoved him forward into the disheveled street.

Alix and Victor dashed across the devoured road. Bullets sputtered on the concrete behind them. Holes the size of grapefruits trailed them across the pavement in a game of connect the dots neither wanted to finish. Victor aimed his pistol midstride at the wooden door of the shop. His gun spat. The door splintered around the knob. Alix and Victor split the door in two, crashed into the room, and slid into a counter that held a busted cash register. Machine-gun rounds sprayed the doorway, wooden walls, and shelves. The room fell to pieces around them as coffee beans, utensils, pieces of porcelain, glass, wooden shards, and shredded paper rained down. Alix lifted his head and shook dust and debris off his helmet. He checked left. Victor checked right.

Victor hunched against the counter, breaths sifting hard through his mask as he drew his assault rifle. "Adam, how's that body looking?"

"All clear, hasn't moved yet."

Alix's radio rang. "Echo, take 'em out! We're pinned!" He pulled his sidearm out of his side hostler.

They hopped the sticky counter, cleared the small rooms behind it, and rushed up old, creaking stairs in six heartbeats. In times like these, Alix counted in heartbeats. Victor kicked the door off its hinges, veered left, and checked his corners, searching for the source of heat radiating in Adam's infrared scanner. Alix pulled right, checked his corners, nothing.

Victor pointed his gun down at a ball of two people. A partial halo of white hair topped the man's head, and he clutched a quivering girl under him. White lace trimmed the outside of her blue dress and poured out from under the old man.

"Please, allow me to live. Por favor! Por favor!"

"Shut the fuck up!" Victor kicked the man in the ribs.

"Por favor! Por favor!"

Victor stomped on him again.

"Argh! Por favor."

Again. Again.

The quivering, smothered girl yelped.

Victor lowered his assault rifle.

Alix twitched, turning his head away as Victor's bullets tore through the man's arched body and into the dress beneath him. The man's scream blended into the thick, purple blooming of the dress. Blood sifted through cracks in the splintered planks.

"Room clear!" Alix declared, keeping his view away from the bodies.

Victor shoved two cups of dirty water and a checkerboard off the table. Red and black pieces skidded across the floor and rolled into blood, stalled on the girl's dress, and clinked down the stairs. Alix dragged the table toward the broken window. He propped up his rifle on its bipod and prepared to fire. He aimed from the shadows of the room to the clamoring machine gun that was outfitted on the back of a pickup outside of their window and down the street.

Victor tossed a motion detector down the stairs. Invisible beams when broken would ring in their ears. Victor drew his scope, a mirror image to Alix's. He focused on the gunner, a human figure but only human in form. He breathed hard between words. "Target: ... gunner ... fifty cal. ... Distance: ... one hundred ... fifty meters ... Wind: ..." Victor checked the embedded screen on his wrist. "Ten kilometers per hour south ... southeast. Walk in the park on this one." He dug his eyes back into the scope.

Alix zoomed in on the gunner, cranked his scope two clicks counterclockwise, and set crosshairs on the target's forehead. The gunner's ripped, raggedy clothes hung off his shoulders. His goggles glowed red. His teeth gritted in a nest of beard, and his arms jiggled from the massive machine gun strapped to the back of a broken-down pickup truck.

Victor whispered, "Fire. Shoot."

Alix exhaled and squeezed the trigger. The gun kicked. Air and sound were sucked from the room.

Blood sprayed the brick wall behind the gunner, and he disappeared behind the truck. Victor didn't pull his bubble eyes away from the scope. "Echo to Alpha, target down. Clear to advance."

"Copy that! Alpha advancing. Cover us until we get to the end of the street."

Wes's voice trailed in Alix's ear. He lifted his eye from the scope to watch Wes lead the team down the narrow road, crouched down as they hugged the outside embankment.

Alix returned his eye to the scope and saw her. Dark hair fluttered out from the grille of the truck. She stood, and Alix used the crosshairs to explore her body. She wore a dirty smock over a tank top and ripped denim pants. Smudges of ash and dirt smeared her smooth face and high cheek bones. She stepped over the body behind the truck, dripping tears onto the dead man. The streams cleared clean paths down her cheek. Her skinny body sprang for the gun.

Victor spotted her. "Echo to Alpha, not clear. I repeat. It is not clear to advance!"

The girl climbed onto the bed of the truck.

Wes yelled into their radio, "Too late, Echo! Cover us!"

Victor glared through his binoculars. "Target: gunner. Distance: same. Wind: same. Fire. Shoot. Fire. Shoot, dammit!"

Alix zoomed in on the girl's face. He felt his pulse increase.

She grabbed the gun like her arms weren't hers anymore but robotic add-ons; her face froze in fright and shock, but her arms moved the gun into position from instinct. Alix shifted the crosshairs across her cheek, to her forehead, to her brown eyes.

Through the scope of his rifle, he gazed into the girl's brown, outlined pupil. Hundreds of distorted images fluttered in his mind. His trigger finger softened. The weight of his rifle overpowered him. The laws of M.A.I.A. compelled him to play the role of judge. Guilty or not, a question held his finger in place.

"Anna?" Alix's whisper focused him. "It's Anna."

"What?" Victor nudged Alix's foot without pulling his eyes out of the binoculars. "Alix, fire! Shoot, dammit!"

The girl pulled the trigger on the mounted gun.

Alix held his breath and felt his heart in his throat.

Victor watched bullets tear through Team Mantis, the regiment torn apart, ripped open by smoldering metal, the soldiers piling on top of one another. Victor chucked his binoculars to the side, gripped Alix by the throat, and thrust him backwards. Victor set the gun into his shoulder and aimed at the girl.

Alix leaned back on his elbows. His hand landed in a trail of blood that led back to the soaked, blue dress of the young girl. When his eyes landed on her, he found himself suddenly there again, a painful numbness; doing things for reasons he couldn't understand. He attempted to pull his eyes away from the dress and the man's blank stare, but a dead face had never looked so real. His eyes shined like a doll's, but his skin had already lost its complexion. The man's mouth hung open. Alix couldn't tell whether his ears didn't hear the man's scream or if sound just wasn't coming out.

Victor's shot erupted in Alix's ear. He closed his eyes and pictured the brown eyed girl: blood splattering, her toppling over, loose limbs bouncing off dirt, the red-and-black hole in her dirty face, and her eyes—her brown eyes—wasted, sunken in, and lost forever.

Victor pulled back his fist and fell onto Alix. He ripped Alix's helmet off, and the first, muffled breath of putrid air clogged Alix's lungs. Alix's face burst into fire, and his head thumped off the floorboard. After the third punch, Alix felt smoldering blood ooze from the crack in the back of his head and down his neck. He saw sounds swirling, blue and yellow, and heard colors, birds screeching and bellowing thunder. His vision sprinkled back.

Victor raised his fist again.

2 |

"Enough! Turn the simulator off!" Captain Milligan's voice came from a dream-like place, far away yet close enough to hear the echo.

Alix lifted his helmet's shield. The desolate world in which he'd just existed,-disappeared. The fluorescent lights on the rounded ceiling above him flickered, and the door alarm cranked and echoed. Alix squinted. His pupils shrank fast. He undid the chinstrap and lifted his helmet. The hard pads inside stuck a checkered pattern of red, irritated regions on his shaved head. The battle simulator powered down to a low hum.

"What happened, Alix?" Hayden ripped the strap off his arm and plucked sensors from his elbow.

"You didn't see her?"

"Her?" Victor tossed his helmet. It rolled and twisted on the metal floor at the foot of his simulator lounge chair. "You gave up your team for a bitch?"

Hayden shook his head. "Who? What woman? All I saw was my leg barely on. I could move my toes though."

Wes pulled his feet from the boots in the chair and rubbed his heels. "Alix blew it! He's fried. His chip's tapped."

Alix sat up. He clenched his teeth and ripped a strap off.

"He fell in love with that little brunette behind the gun," Victor smirked.

Alix's head snapped sideways. "Pound sand, Victor!"

Victor reached for his helmet. "Here, take my helmet and go-ahead back in. We'll leave you two alone." He dropped his helmet at Alix's feet. "I killed her, but maybe there's a little life left in there."

Laughs from the rest of the team swirled around the curved room. Phil's deep laugh held over the others.

"Shut up!" Alix boiled.

Captain Milligan entered the room outlined in simulator beds. "Atten Hut!"

They scrambled to get into line.

Captain Milligan eyed them and scratched his orange frizz. "You all suck!

Victor pulled a strap off.

"Did I say at ease?! You stand there at attention with your mouth and your sphincter shut until I give you permission to move! My office, all of you, in two hours—except for you, Victor. You will do five miles before coming to my office." The room hushed. Captain Milligan left, leaving the echo of his steel boots ricocheting off the hall's walls.

Victor jerked the rest of the straps off. "Alix gets nearly all of us killed, and I get five miles. This is bullshit! You got a virus in that little chip of yours. Next time shoot, Citi!" He shoved Alix, who stumbled back onto one of the chairs.

The word burned—to be called a Citi, a citizen of the country that lay in desolate condition hundreds of feet above their military bunker, was worse than being called a bastard.

"I'm no Citi!" Alix sprung up and shoved Victor back.

Helmets skidded and twirled as Victor and Alix tussled. Eli launched himself between them, shoved them apart and looked to Alix.

"I won't spot for a Citi! Find another spotter!" Victor spat. Adam shoved Victor and they exited.

Eli stood over Alix. "You good?"

"Thanks for having my back." Alix turned and ran his hand over the bristles of his shaved head.

"Always." Eli extended his hand to Alix to pull him up. "I heard Captain Milligan say that the love of a good woman, can drive you crazy and make you do things you'd never do."

Alix walked into the common room. Four squads and a unit of infantry looked up from billiards, darts, military video games, and weight benches. The eyes of each soldier fell fast. Alix passed the billiard table, and a large cadet smirked, eyed his partner, and nodded toward Alix. More insulting glances landed on him, but his squad's eyes weighed the heaviest.

Alix sat alone in one of the five empty chairs that surrounded a large screen on the wall. He leaned back. A faint, blue wave rippled across the screen. Ancient pool balls cracked and clacked into each other as they rolled around the green felted table. The squads' whispers blew on the back of his neck. His failure was now a virus that spread throughout the regiment. He focused on the flat screen and couldn't stop thinking about Anna. Knowing the impossibility of seeing her, he looked for her during the walk from the simulator, past the worker's quarters, past vehicle bunkers full of tanks and armored all-terrain vehicles, past the weapons bunker, and past the hallway leading to the Reader's offices.

Everyone else's face turned toward the screen at the same time. The blue soundwave grew and shrunk. "Good evening. I'm bringing you the latest information on our progress and goals. I have determined there to be only two weeks before we start seeing efficient sunlight in sector 320 E for possible Conservation of the city. The increase in sunlight will provide energy needed to power the other half of the island. Reader Albert Rankin predicts entering the mainland for Conservation before autumn. With 92 percent efficiency against Citizens on the mainland, I predict only 500 deaths in the first week and only 1,300 deaths in the first six months with complete control of islands within a five-mile radius."

"Alix, you want to vote who goes and who lives?" someone called out. Chuckles from over Alix's shoulder pricked his spine.

Eli walked up and stood behind Alix.

"I also intend on introducing the first training on *new* military technology. Security of the mainland is inevitable. Anyone captured will have the ability to have a new, updated level-3 chip installed and will join you at the front lines or be terminated."

"I wonder what the level-3 chip is." Eli asked as he leaned into Alix.

Alix raised his eyebrows and shrugged his shoulders. "Probably just another crazy ability for the computer to get inside your head—Like M.A.I.A. doesn't have enough power already to take the world over five times."

Eli sat down next to Alix, held his pool stick in between his legs, and stared at him. He passed his pool stick back and forth between his hands.

"Alix, what happened to you today?"

"I don't know. I couldn't shoot." Alix checked over his shoulder to Hayden and Wes, who were huddled in the corner.

"Alix, if you don't—"

"I know," Alix sighed, banging his fists lightly on the end of the chair. "Next time."

Eli looked away and scratched his dark stubble on his head. "You better hope there is a next time. Captain was pretty pissed."

"Yeah, I don't think Captain is done with me."

The sound wave bounced on the screen and a picture of an old, bald man appeared in the corner of the screen.

"In other news, Lead Programmer, Dr. Thomas Ethex died yesterday at age eighty. Dr. Ethex was born in the Commonwealth of Massachusetts of the former United States of America when M.A.I.A. was only a Fortune 500 company on the Island, formerly Governors Island. He served in the most top-secret technology production center. Dr. Ethex remained a top programmer for M.A.I.A.

"Dr. Ethex programmed cerebral M.A.I.A. chips for military personnel—from the fall of the United States of America until the end of his life. His cerebral chip and memory have been requested to be stored in the archives."

Eli smiled. "I hope my chip is stored after I die."

"Humph," Alix snorted.

"Alix, when we get back, and we are genetically paired up with the medics and pilots, who do you hope to be conjoined with?"

Alix's face flushed. "I don't know. We don't really have a say in who M.A.I.A. genetically matches us with. She puts us all into a pool and matches us up based on compatibility."

"Come on though, if you *could* choose."

"I really don't know, Eli." Anna's name burned his tongue.

Eli leaned in closer. "Come on, I can't talk to any of the other guys about this stuff. They look at me crazy ... like I got a virus or something."

"We don't have a choice."

"Alix? Come on. Who would it be ... if it could be anybody? Sid? Beth? ... Anna? They have to be the three best-looking in the regiment. We've had the most time in simulation with them."

Alix's eyes twitched and he melted in his chair.

"I knew it!" Eli sat on the edge and laughed.

"Knew what?

"You were about to say Anna," Eli prodded.

"I wasn't ... no ...not Anna. I don't know who."

"If you don't think you'll be conjoined with Anna, I think I'd like to be."

"I didn't say I wouldn't be compatible with Anna!"

Eli dropped his pool stick, retrieved it, and leaned in closer. "Why is that?"

"I told you. M.A.I.A. decides."

Eli's eyebrows narrowed, "Anna is who you would like to be conjoined with. Just admit it. I'm telling you now: I'm going to hope Sidney and I are paired so hard M.A.I.A. will have a migraine if she tries to access my head."

"... And good luck, new cadets. Have a good night and remember—train hard." The screen flicked off and everyone's EEDs emitted two quick chirps.

"Ah! I hate that sound." Eli bowed his head and squeezed his temples.

"I think my EED is malfunctioning. It doesn't beep with everyone else's." Alix tapped his EED. It didn't chirp.

Eli squinted. "You're lucky then. Like Captain said *if it ain't broke don't fix it.* Trust me, you don't want to get that low humming before and after the screen prompts. It's stronger if you miss a broadcast. It's over now."

"Hey, what were you doing this morning? You almost missed Captain's briefing."

Eli checked over his shoulder and leaned in. "I didn't get too far, but I was trying to use the simulator on one of those nonmilitary scenes. I heard when you graduate and pass, you can use rations to create your own time in the simulator for whatever you want."

Alix smirked and leaned further back in his chair. "You're lucky you didn't get caught. You remember what happened to the last guy, right?"

"No."

"You don't remember?" Alix gestured.

"No, who?"

"I forget the guy's name, but he's nowhere to be found."

Eli leaned in. "I'm going to do it though. I can't wait. I want to see the sun, Alix. Aren't you curious how it feels, or used to feel? Imagine a bright sun over the ocean, and the colors it creates over a blue ocean with more water than you can ever think to drink."

"You can't drink ocean water."

"That's not the point! Imagine how amazing it must feel to have the wind tickle your neck. I can't wait to be up on the surface for the Conservation. I bet the mainland is unbelievable. It can't be as bad and toxic as they say."

"They say it's pretty bad. I heard the smell is unbearable. The bombs did a number on the ozone around this part of the world."

The bright glee in Eli's eyes darkened. "Alix, you have to believe there is more to life than what goes on down here."

Alix pictured Anna and knew what Eli said carried an air of truth. He also knew to keep his mouth shut and his thoughts to himself. He hoped Eli was right. Alix's mind wondered what time it was, and it appeared in the blue, hazy screen on his skin: 19:55:38.

"We should get going," Eli checked over his shoulder. "Captain's ready to scrap us all. I have a feeling we're going to get stuck below in the gun cages cleaning weapons all month."

3

Captain Milligan stared into the eight pairs of eyes. The cadets stood erect and frozen in a tiny room. Milligan glanced at the gentle, blue wave on the screen that hovered on the wall behind his cadets. He leaned over his desk. A hologram map of sector 320 E lay before him. His elbows planted firmly on the desk; he rubbed his eyes.

"Gentlemen..." The room shrank with his gravelly voice. "We had a problem today, didn't we?"

Victor raised his chin. "Permission to speak, Captain."

"Denied. Shut up and listen." Captain Milligan eyed Victor.

Victor clenched his jaw.

The captain swiveled in his chair and pulled his boot up to his knee. He swirled his finger around a small glass globe on the desk. "Some of you believe there is one person in this room responsible for your deaths today, a failure that, by the way, gentlemen, is on your military record for the rest of your lives. Today, you were supposed to take all that you've learned in your ten years of schooling, all the strength and physical ability of your training, all the tactical maneuvering you've learned, and apply it all into a beautiful symphony of a perfectly executed mission."

Eight pairs of eyes fell to the floor.

Captain gripped the small, glass globe. "Now, the problem today was not only your sniper and spotter. Hayden, how long were you alive in simulation?"

Silence.

"Hayden! You with us?" Captain Milligan snapped his fingers. "I asked you a question, boy."

Hayden raised his chin. "One minute, sir."

"You were in *simulation* for one minute. How long were you on the field?"

"Seconds, sir."

"How long?!" Captain Milligan slammed his fist over the Eastern Seaboard on the map and stole all the breath in the room.

Hayden's throat thinned. "Approximately three seconds, sir."

"You charged out of the helicopter with no suppression fire. The covering fire from the chopper couldn't have been sufficient. There is one of two things wrong with this scenario, boys." Captain Milligan held his fingers in the shape of a gun and pointed at Hayden. "Either you charged out too quick, or your team didn't come out fast enough." Captain Milligan dropped his hand. "What was the first thing I told you about this squad?"

No one responded.

"What was the first thing I told you?!"

Phil gulped. "Move as a unit, sir!"

"You don't take a damn breath if the person next to you isn't ready for it." Captain Milligan sat back. "Victor?"

"Yes, sir?"

Alix held his breath in the firing line. He felt the blindfold coming over his eyes. He was next.

Captain's eyes glowed a soggy red. His thick, worn finger aimed at Victor. "The man in the building that you executed; do you know who he was?"

Victor's eyes shot sideways, and he thought. "No, sir."

"Of course not. May I ask you what in that little chip of yours says that beating down this eighty-year-old man and his daughter and killing them is more important than taking out the gunner that has your team pinned?" Captain Milligan held in his breath. "What are you wasting time for?! You see a man, you shoot. If you have time to realize he is not going to kill you…" Captain Milligan slammed his hand down. "… Restrain the bastard and report it for clean-up crew, so we can get some damn information out of the bastard and his daughter! Your team is pinned, and you're worried about this old, unarmed man. Think! You killed potential intel."

Victor sniffed and spoke through his teeth, "Yes, sir."

Captain held out his arms, "The team, after you secured him, took out the gunner, and then interrogated him. You know what they found out?"

Victor shook his head.

"Exactly, because he was too dead to talk! He's eighty! Weigh your damned options, Victor. You're lucky I only gave you five miles for that." Captain stopped and waved his hand. "Now, I have to go to the Readers and listen to the reasons M.A.I.A. thinks you failed, and how I could have prevented it. I can't stand to look at you. Dismissed!"

Victor shot a glance at Alix then back at the captain. "Sir?"

"There's an old expression we used to use, and it's 'shit rolls downhill,' and right now you're at the bottom. Get ready for a double session tomorrow. Back to step one, boys, learning how to work, and run—a lot, and as a team. I said, get out of here. Get out!" Captain Milligan studied his map.

The cadets turned to leave, but Victor held his footing. "Sir? Permission to …"

The captain whipped a pen at Victor. "Permission for nothing! Out, or you'll be running until the Conservation starts!"

Victor dodged the pen, which bounced off the wall, and rolled toward the doorway. Silence followed him down the hall as he trailed behind the pack.

"Alix!" Captain Milligan's voice had cooled to a rigid temperature. "Get back here."

Alix stalled in the hall. He turned slowly back to the office, and Victor banged his shoulder hard into his shoulder as he passed. The door swished shut behind Alix and trapped him in the room he'd just escaped.

"Take a seat." Captain Milligan pointed to the old computer chair in the corner.

Alix sat and waited for the captain's rain of condemnation. Captain Milligan stared at him for a moment, swayed back and forth in his chair with his leg pulled up onto his lap and his fist pressed to his lips.

"Alix, I have my theories about what happened today, but I want to know what you think happened today in simulation."

Alix's lips were chiseled out of a single piece of unmovable rock. He stared at the captain as if he spoke an incomprehensible language.

"Alix?"

Captain picked up the glass globe. Flickering sprinkles floated weightlessly. In the clear dome, a functioning, miniature clock tower stood within a protective casing.

"It's funny, you know, they still call it a snow globe even though it has sparkles in it."

Alix swallowed.

"That's what they call these things, snow globes. It's some scene; usually something related to a holiday we used to celebrate. They would fill it with ground rice, which made it look like snow. When you shook it," Captain Milligan flicked his wrist, and the sparkles exploded within the globe, "it looked like it was snowing inside the globe. They replaced the white rice with sparkles, but they still call it a snow globe. You might need one of these someday."

"Sir, I froze."

"And ..." Captain Milligan drummed his fingers on the top of the globe.

Alix wiped the sweat from his palms on his knees. "Captain, before I pulled the trigger, I thought—"

"Correction, before you *squeezed* the trigger. And you can't think."

"Sir?"

"Alix." Captain Milligan's stare ripped through Alix. "You, more than anyone out there, can't think. The thinking is done for you. But for the others, it's easier. The others shoot their enemy, and it's often a blind shot filled with adrenaline. A figure falls, and they move to the next target." Captain Milligan leaned forward. "You, on the other hand, have to stay composed. You can't have adrenaline running through your veins. You are supposed to be completely still, hidden from the battle, accurate, steady, composed." He held his hand flat and still. "Furthermore, you're often hundreds of meters away from the battle. But here's the hard part, Alix, and I think you know this from all the way back there, from hundreds and hundreds of meters from the battlefield. Sometimes, you get to look into their eyes, don't you?"

Alix swallowed.

Captain Milligan leaned in over the desk. "Something *they* don't have to do. You have to look into this thing's eyes and end its life. You get to see the grit on their face, their missing teeth, their zits on the side of their cheek, and the missing pieces of ears and noses. You are an assassin; you get to know them and then blow them away. Alix, you are the most important person on this team, because you are far more dangerous to the enemy, and if you can't do this, if you can't shoot, you won't have the opportunity to. If you're going to be on this team, then you must squeeze the trigger."

Captain lifted the small, glass globe and twisted the knob on the bottom.

"I don't care if you see *me* down there with a machine gun shooting at your team. You see someone threatening M.A.I.A., you shoot. If you find yourself threatening M.A.I.A., blow your own brains out. No matter what, defend M.A.I.A. That quantum computer is your life." Captain finished twisting the knob. Twinkling music played from the globe.

The screen above Alix flickered, and the blue wave stilled and faded into a line. Alix's mind rested to the music. He felt relaxed, strange, different, a breath of air before drowning, water before dehydration, flame before hypothermia. The music freed him.

Captain's eyes darkened, and his voice deepened. "Listen to me, you don't want to see what happens to the ones who can't shoot, who can't Conserve and defend M.A.I.A., to those who *think*. It's an empty bunk. People are forgotten overnight, Alix. Existence can be erased for your generation. I made a promise to a man who just passed away; don't make me break it, Conserve M.A.I.A."

The music stopped. The screen flickered, and the blue wave continued.

Alix's head tightened. He felt shriveled up, dead, drowned, depleted, and burned. He stared at the globe and wondered at its ability. The second hand within the globe hit twelve.

"Dismissed."

Alix didn't check the room for more permission to leave.

"And Alix…"

Alix forced his head to turn to the captain's as if their faces were the repelling ends of a magnet.

"Who was the girl behind the gun?"

The flush of Alix's face failed to conceal a truth buried beneath his tongue.

"The day will come when you will be forced to ask yourself, 'Is she worth it?' In the real world, there is no compromise in war." Captain squeezed the globe and looked down at his blue outlined map. "You better get some sleep. There will be no resting tomorrow."

Alix stood up, saluted Milligan, spun on his heels and disappeared through the door into the hall. The door swished closed.

The captain's phone rang. He picked up the clunky, rotary phone connected by a spiraling cord. "No, sir, everything is fine here. I think there was only a glitch …"

#

Alix lay in his cold bunk. He listened to the electronic static of the screens. He watched the waving, blue light through a helix of thin, vertical bars holding bunks on top of bunks, thick enough to support Eli above Alix's bed.

He thought about the girl behind the gun, her brown hair and eyes, the curve of her hips and body, and her sad face. Alix recognized her, which wasn't the scary part. The true eeriness lay in the facts. Simulation was programmed. It could not have been a mere coincidence. Anna was placed in that simulation for Alix to see, but how could anyone know about Anna and what they'd been doing? For that reason alone, he could not meet her tonight. The thought of using the simulation tonight to see Anna brought a shocking wave of blackness to his stomach. Hopefully she would understand—too risky tonight.

"People can disappear overnight. *Conserve M.A.I.A*," he mumbled to himself, turned over to force himself to sleep.

#

Anna lifted her head at the same time as Alix close his eyes. She looked left to right. It'd been days since she'd seen him. Her heart bumped in her throat, and she felt her pulse in her ears. Her anxiety was cured only by her sweet surrender to him; the calmness of her skin against his, and the tranquility of his arms around her. The door had slammed shut an hour ago, and she couldn't wait any longer. Beth, in the bunk above Anna, breathing heavily as she slept, was Anna's cue.

Anna slid the sheets off. Her bare feet met the cool polished cement floor of the girls' barracks. Twenty-two steps to the right, and she could barely make out the silhouette of the door to the hallway. She did not dare close her eyes again. Last time, it took what seemed like a half hour to orient herself and make it back to the barracks. One-hundred-and-five steps toward the door, and she could make her move.

"Step back! Get back to where you were!" the voice bellowed out from Anna's three o'clock.

Anna's senses heightened. Her blood became lava boiling through her veins. She turned and froze. She pictured Dr. Susan Maynard storming down the hall, tackling and holding her down for a M.A.I.A. robot to seal her eyes shut, wipe her brain, and store her in a medical box until after the Conservation.

"Shut up, Tracy!" the voice echoed. "I can't stand when she talks in her sleep."

The lights remained off.

"Shh."

She was safe. She crept to the door. Through a small line of light, she saw the booth with two nurses talking and staring down at a boxed computer. Anna raised her wrist. The time appeared on her EED, two minutes thirty-five seconds. She and Alix had rendezvous so many times. Anna knew the nurse at the computer would blink nine times before she signed out. It took the nurse's replacement forty-five seconds to log on, which provided Anna with the thirty-two seconds she needed to slide down the hallway and slip into the solo simulation room to meet Alix in their virtual world.

She remembered how to disengage the flashing light over the door that alerted staff the room was occupied. Alix taught her well. She held her breath and waited for the replacement nurse to sit down at the computer. Anna's eyes followed the nurse's hands as they rearranged a stapler and a short stack of papers. The moment the nurse's fingers touched the keyboard, Anna advanced quickly and quietly down the hall. She got to the simulation room door, eased the handle down and slipped inside. In the darkness of the room, her heart pounded hard against her chest. Ten more seconds and she could disengage the flashing light. Seven... six... five... four... three... two...

The light snapped on inside the room, blinding her. Anna recognized the voice before she could make out who was standing in front of her.

"Go back to bed Anna. And don't ever do this again," Dr. Maynard admonished.

_Light filtered through Alix's eyelids at the same time a horn pierced his eardrums shortly after he felt he'd fallen asleep. He sprang up, stood at attention at the end of his bed. Despite two-hundred-and-fifty steel-framed bunk beds, which held five hundred cadets, Alix felt strangely alone. His right eye did a quick peripheral check of the bunk over his. The top bunk was neatly made and unslept in.

Captain Milligan's boot's clomped on the polished cement floor as he made his way down the aisle of bunk beds. "Squad Twenty-Eight, you ready to pay?!"

"Sir, yes, sir!"

"Good, get dressed, take your tabs, and let's go! The rest of you run six miles before your half-day off." Captain Milligan's announcement sucked the air out of the room.

"Squad Twenty-Eight, Vomit Room at o-five hundred!" the captain called out as he placed his hands behind his back and marched away.

Alix yanked up his running shorts, dove into a black t-shirt, and zipped up his vest. When he pulled two blue tabs and two red tabs from the column next to his bunk to put into his vest pockets, he noticed two extra red and blue tabs stacked on top of his. Alix checked over his shoulder.

Why would he get extra tabs?

He pulled the extras and shoved them under his pillow.

"Alix, don't bail on us today. Can't have you forget how to run, too." Victor zipped up his vest.

Alix turned and smiled. "Victor, try and keep up."

"Pick up the pace ladies!" Captain Milligan's voice bellowed through the loudspeaker in Track Room 401.

Physically exhausted, the captain's voice shook their brains. Their stomachs replied to his command with a throat burning acid reflux that they struggled to keep down. Vomiting would not be a reason to stop. They had to keep running. If one of them stopped, they would all have to start over again.

Milligan stared down on them from the glassed Observatory Room above. Squad Twenty-Eight's legs churned like gears; their pores pumped wells of sweat. Their backs were soaked, and their faces drenched from their sweat, blurring their vision as they ran around the circular track like lab rats.

Alix led the group, with his legs red from fiery exhaustion.

The Vomit Room had earned its moniker legitimately. It was the room that pushed body and mind further than they ever wanted to go; a room that often led to puking in mid stride, but demanded you keep running, keep pushing your body to an almost robotic, inhumane existence. There was only the first step, first push, first thrust, then another and another until your body pleaded for mercy. When mercy arrived, it came in the form of another physical challenge. The Vomit Room deteriorated humans and created soldiers in their place. It was designed to erase the cadet's mind's ability to object to the captain's demands, even if it meant personal sacrifice. According to the cadet's folklore, the Vomit Room had delivered several cadets near death's door. There was a rumor that the Vomit Room did claim a life, but the name of the cadet was never spoken of. It was as though the cadet never existed.

Alix felt his throat constrict from lack of oxygen. He couldn't slow down. Wes's strides were on his heels. Victor's and the other four were behind Wes with the same burning, same tingling and straining of the muscles. Alix breathed through his nose, ignored the sweat streaming down his face and stinging his eyes, the numbness of his muscles, the strain in his legs, the ache in his knees, and tried to forget the number of times they had circled the track—easily triple digits. He knew better than to hope Captain Milligan would allow them to stop running because waiting for the command made the tortuous run longer. It was as though Captain Milligan knew what they were thinking.

"That's enough!—for now," Captain's voice echoed in the chamber.

The damp, ripe air held the stench of their sweat. Wes took four more steps and came to a halt. His hands planted on his knees. His breaths sputtered out of rhythm.

Alix halted. He paced in a small circle, breathed deeply through his nose, felt his pulse, and checked his EED.

"Why did we let Alix lead?" Wes wiped sweat from his forehead. "Whose dumb idea was that to have the fastest one out front?" He straightened his neck, his eyes widened, and his mouth opened wide as it gasped for air.

"Mine." Phil squeezed his eyes together and breathed through his teeth.

Wes ran to the nearest bucket and stuck his head inside of it. The echo of his retching and the splatter of his vomit into the bucket invoked an empathetic retching reflex in the rest of the squad.

Alix winced, turning away, while Victor closed his eyes, sucking air and propping himself up on his knees.

Captain stormed through the side door. He grabbed Hayden's and Matt's vests by the back of the neck and yanked them straight up.

"Don't bow your damn heads! What the hell are you praying for?" He moved on to Wes and grabbed his shoulders, pulled him up from the bucket as brown fluids dripped back into the pail and onto the floor. "Stand up straight!"

Captain looked in the seven pairs of eyes begging for mercy. "Look at you all. You're as sad as the first day we started physical training. Have you learned anything?" Heavy panting was the only response. "I'll be happy to put you boys back in the classroom. Want to sit through some more programming? You want to watch those five-hour strategic videos again? Learn more about those savages outside?"

"Sir, no, sir!"

"You want to be first on the mainland?"

"Sir, yes, sir!"

"Well, what the hell are you waiting for? Eight more laps, go!" Captain kicked Wes' pail, its contents smearing over the rubber track mats.

The squad resumed their run. Each time they came to Wes's vomit on the rubber mat, they dodged it with a move Captain Milligan coined the 'Vomit Room Hop.'

Alix reached for the thirty-pound dumbbells and stood in front of the full wall mirror. He raised them to his shoulders. A stampede of runners' sneakers on the track pulled his attention off his own rubbery legs. Alix watched the younger cadets race around. He remembered the first time he ran around the track and looked down into the weight room, at an older generation of soldiers. He set the bars down and waited for Matt to move to the next station, bench-press.

Phil picked up the forty-five-ounce dumbbells next to Alix. He focused on his movement in the mirror and curled the thirty-five-pound weights. Every other curl, Alix caught Phil's eyes darting away from a hostile stare. Getting into a fight in the weight room was not smart. There was too much ammunition.

After the tenth curl, Phil finally spoke. "Lifting these weights isn't going to keep you alive out there." Veins strained out of his arms, and they bulged every time he brought the iron to his pectoral. "And running will get you shot in the ass."

Phil gritted his teeth and ripped his cheeks back into a scary smile, breathing through his teeth. He slammed the iron dumbbells down on the steel shelf. "If I get shot again because of you, bullet in the brain or not, I'm coming after you."

Alix gripped his weights.

Matt moved onto the bench press, giving Alix a peaceful escape from Phil.

Phil pointed to Hayden. "Hayden, will you spot me?"

"Sure."

At the bench press, Alix kept a roving eye on Phil as he and Hayden tossed two big plates on each end of the bar suspended across a bench. Alix lay down beneath the bar and pressed the weighted bar above his chest.

"Come on, you got one more in ya. Come on!" Hayden coached. "Three more ..."

The bar suddenly froze in midair. Phil stood over him and gripped the middle of the bar.

"Do another set for me for getting me shot."

Phil released the bar, and it dropped unevenly across Alix's chest.

"Hey!" Wes stopped working out and took a step toward them.

Alix gritted his teeth and shoved the bar up onto the hooks and sat up.

"What are you doing?" Wes appeared in Phil's face.

"I'm making sure he can carry his own weight. If he can't carry his own weight, he'll take us all out," Phil shot back.

"He just outran you. You barely broke into a sweat. If you want to challenge him, do it on even terms. Otherwise, you come off looking like a weak pathetic coward who can only come at someone if they're vulnerable. Captain Milligan would say, 'That's not a soldier, that's a punk,'" Wes spoke directly in Phil's face. "Unlike you, he's not expendable. You threaten Alix, you threaten all of us."

"You're no fun." Phil turned away and moved to a leg press machine.

Alix caught his breath and checked the mirrored office windows that overlooked the weight room.

"You all right?" Wes asked Alix.

"I don't know." Alix bit his bottom lip.

"Did the weight hit you in the chest? You need to see a medic?"

"No, something's off," Alix said. His eyes roamed the room. "Wes, don't you feel like something's missing today?"

Phil added weights to the leg press. "Yeah, our day off."

Alix got up from the bench. "I'm telling you, something's not right. Something's missing."

Wes looked to Hayden, "Did the weights strike his head? What's wrong with him?"

Hayden shrugged. "Wes, I don't know. I swear the weights didn't go near his head."

"Alix, look at me?" Wes motioned. "Let me check your eyes."

"My eyes are fine, but I'm telling you something's missing..." Alix checked over his shoulder.

Phil pushed all the plates on the leg machine up. "I'll tell you what missin.' Real action. I'm sick of simulation. We are trained from the time we're born, and I don't think simulation is enough. It's making us soft. Let me put a notch on my belt for God's sake."

"Eli..." the name escaped from Alix's mouth.

"Who?"

Captain Milligan watched his team play musical chairs with different weights. His mind faded, to a better place. He rubbed his beard and remembered his father surrounded by hay, driving a metal mallet down on a horseshoe an eternity ago. It was a mallet he needed all his strength to carry let alone swing. Each metal-on-metal clink made his ten-year-old eyes blink. He wondered how his father could see where he was hitting. How? His father stopped, put the mallet down on the workbench, and wiped sweat from his head with the bottom of his shirt.

"A Virginian farm can cause you no harm." His father looked up at little Milligan sitting on the fence by the horse stall. "But the heat's only cure is Virginia's Beach."

"Where's Virginia Beach?" The horse stirred, neighed, and looked toward Little Milligan.

"It's about a five-hour drive from here. I'll bring you again someday. Ya see, you were too little to remember the last time your mother and I brought you."

Milligan pushed the dirt beneath his feet into an arc spread before him.

"Why don't you run over to the house and ask Mamma to get us some lemonade, or iced tea, or something?"

Milligan hopped the fence and pushed the heavy door aside, plowing dried hay from its path. He stared across the field of the biggest farm in Virginia. The house appeared small and hazy, grown out of the rows and rows of corn, and further away than what he wanted to run in this heat. Milligan reached in his pocket and pulled out the small cell phone his mother got him. He dialed his mother with his tiny fingers and held the receiver to his ear.

"Robby, honey, where are you calling from?" her voice sang to him.

He watched as a curtain shifted to the side in the kitchen window of the large colonial in the distance. Suddenly, the phone lifted from his hands and pulled up to the sky. He jumped up to grab it, but huge, callused hands had already fastened around it in a steel grip. His father brought the cell phone over to the workbench faster than Milligan's lips could scream.

"Hello? Robby?" his mother's melody echoed in the barn. "Robby, is everything OK?"

His father lifted the mallet and drove it down. Pieces of screen, plastic, and components erupted from the bench. The metal mallet came down repeatedly.

Milligan's mouth hung open. His eyes locked on the destruction of his first cell phone.

"Close your mouth, Robby. No need to bother your mamma on the cellular phone just to bring us some drinks. Now run over across the yard to your mamma and get us some lemonade." His father's six-foot two frame loomed over eclipsing the sun and cast Robby into his father's shadow.

"Yes, sir." Robby wiped away the tears before they could settle on his cheeks.

"Dreaming of me again?" Albert Rankin's voice pulled Captain Milligan from his memory. When Captain Milligan's eyes refocused, the silhouette of Rankin floating on what Captain Milligan deemed Rankin's floating pedestal, was before him. Rankin's shadowy appearance was like an old-fashioned film noir villain, who needed to be rubbed out.

"Captain Milligan, how's Squad Twenty-Eight looking after the terrible performance yesterday?" Albert Rankin's voice lingered in the dimness of the office. He floated into the room, arms connected at the wrists, wrists behind his back. His medals and badges decorated his long navy-blue coat. His smile pulled far back. His bald head shined, and his

T-Port set too high to pass through some centers of the facility without hunching. "At the last M.A.I.A. Reading, Squad Twenty-Eight was favorable to be the first deployed. Statistically, they had the best chance. I can't say that's still the case; M.A.I.A. will have to do another analysis of the Squad. Did you see Squad Fifty-Three?"

Captain Milligan stared down from the mirrored, windowed office as the seven cadets lifted weights one floor below. "Yeah, they scored a 97.7. That's the new course record if I'm not mistaken. Isn't it, Reader Rankin?"

"I never would have thought your favored squad would get a 23.8 on their final battle simulation test. They've fared so well in past practice simulations. That Alix is quite a shot."

"I know. I'm not entirely sure what happened."

Rankin's T-Port electronically whined around the stretched glass table and swiped one of the swivel chairs, turning it around. He rolled up next to Captain Milligan. They stood side by side, overlooking the Vomit Room and weights.

"How are they taking it? Not just the failing, I mean the recent change."

Captain Milligan looked down at his men and stiffened his jaw. "The physical reprimands they can handle. The loss of a team member if they actually knew, immeasurable. But so far, there are no signs of them realizing. It does not appear that any of them have any clue. Astonishing really."

Rankin's voice dominated. "Do you propose that the Vanishing Sequence of Private Eli Williams was not a sound decision and that keeping him on the team was actually beneficial to the Conservation of M.A.I.A.?"

Captain Milligan looked Rankin in the eyes. "That's a decision for M.A.I.A., not an old war junkie like me." Captain Milligan looked away. "My expertise is in military strategy, not societal discipline."

"You know the crimes he committed. Why can't you accept the punishment? I sensed your bitterness but did not think it would affect your judgment. We caught him sneaking into the simulators, M.A.I.A. property…"

Captain Milligan shook his head and faced Rankin. "Don't give me that shit about M.A.I.A. property. Everything is M.A.I.A. property." He turned his back to the glass. "This team was just starting to come together."

"From my understanding, Captain, Squad Twenty-Eight just failed simulation," Rankin hissed. "I don't want my lead squad to be *just coming together'* just weeks before our commencement of Conservation of the mainland. They need to be ready—quickly. Once we get enough sun to power…"

"Sir, with all due respect, I've already…"

Rankin's face turned hot. "Keep your respect, Captain, and bite your tongue. Hold it until it bleeds, it doesn't matter. The boy snuck out of bed during system hibernation hours and used a two-billion-dollar piece of equipment to run a simulation on how to swim in the ocean and run naked on the beach! M.A.I.A. has configured the most logical punishment. Don't doubt M.A.I.A.'s analysis of the recommended reprimand. The Vanishing Sequence was required to erase his cerebral chip and start over, repress old memories, and create new, fabricated ones. The Vanishing Sequence was created for a reason. We didn't kill him. Eli is not dead."

Captain Milligan clenched his jaw. He looked down at the steel supports that held Rankin's knees locked and his boots in place. He wondered if Rankin's short little body could get out of the high T-Port, and if the machine held his prick for him while he pissed.

Rankin eyed the screen in the corner.

Captain Milligan sighed. "What about the girl they caught? Anna? Wasn't she caught doing the same thing?"

"M.A.I.A. is going to decide her fate later this evening. She's one of the best medics we have. I think that is why M.A.I.A. is taking longer to decipher. The girl is none of your concern."

Captain Milligan cleared his throat. "Sir, requesting permission for Squad Twenty-Eight to have another chance at simulation."

Rankin stared at Alix below, who looked up to the booth. He turned to Phil, said something, and looked back up at the mirrored office.

"How's Alix been after simulation? Did you discuss his performance with you?"

"I had a conversation, sir."

Rankin smiled. "I know. I watched the recordings of the simulation, and your meeting. You didn't go too hard on Alix until after the rest of the squad left, but even then, it was hard to tell because your screen's signal cut off suddenly. I found that peculiar." Rankin knotted his fingers in front of him. "I'll send someone in to check out your server."

"As you wish, sir."

Rankin smiled. "We'll see what the other Readers think about giving your squad another chance, but as for first deployed, I don't see that happening." Rankin pulled away.

Captain Milligan listened to the electronic strain of the T-Port as it stopped to realign the swivel chair to a right angle to the glass table.

"And Captain, don't feel bad. Your team doesn't miss Eli. They don't even remember him." The door closed.

#

"Come on! Push yourselves!" Captain Milligan's voice chased them around the gym, but his body paced back and forth across the middle of the floor, wrists locked behind his back as the rush of Squad Twenty-Eight swished by him. They crouched down and touched the painted line on the north end of the gym, raced to the other side of the gym and touched the painted line on the south end. They did it repeatedly.

Alix loped over to touch the line, craned himself back up, and jogged across the court to the other line. Sweat leaked from his depleted body. He could not feel his knees. He accepted that his toes might not be there.

"Down!"

The teammates, scattered throughout the floor, dropped to their hands, pushed up, and continued running.

"All right! Stop and breathe!" Captain smiled. "Good, let your damned self breathe."

Alix held his breath. He heard his pulse. He felt his stomach heating up and rising to his chest. His knees throbbed and kept buckling under him. He strained to stand.

Victor's knees hit the floor. His palms slapped it, and it left him on all fours. He spat. Strings of saliva dangled from his dry lips. He spat again. He stared into the floor and looked for resolution for his body dysfunction as if laying his head down on the floor would fix all the muscle destruction.

Captain Milligan shook his head and listened to their huffing and wheezing, a symphony of weakness.

"Must be a generational thing. If my captain could get his hands on you for two minutes, you'd be praying for these little sprints."

Deep body odor blended and hovered over the group. Sweat rained down Alix's face, and he stared at Captain Milligan through a stinging pain that emerged in his joints. In the humid, hazy room, Alix felt a chill that crawled up his spine and into his head. That panicked sensation of something missing seized him again.

"Get up. You're embarrassing me. Let's move." Captain Milligan pinched the bridge of his nose.

Thud!

Phil collapsed.

Gravity pulled Alix down to the gym floor. On his knees, black dots sprinkled his vision. A pulsing sound entered his ears followed by waves of colors. Deep blues waved in large, slow arches, and reds radiated in little, rapid ones. Alix breathed heavier.

Matt fell next to him.

"I said get up. Now!"

Alix planted his foot on the ground and pushed against his knee to stand. He wanted nothing more than to disappear. His next thought began as a calm rain that transformed into a raging storm of thoughts and emotions. He wondered about Captain Milligan's words from his office and what they really meant. They rang in Alix's ear behind like a throbbing pulse. Sweat covered him and seeped into his shirt, his vest, and his pants, but his body felt cold, abandoned. *People can disappear overnight.* Who had disappeared?

Flashes of scenes of his life became clear. His mind twisted and wrung out what energy he had left. His eyes widened. His hair on his arms stood straight up.

"Eli," Alix whispered.

Captain Milligan angled his eyebrows and sharpened his eyes. He moved in close, looking into Alix's hazy pupils. "What did you just say?"

Oxygen deprived, light-headed, and hunched over, Alix swayed before Captain Milligan. The room became small. The walls pushed in. The doors grew large. Color enzymes flicked on and off in his pupils. His brain became heavy along with his eyelids, and the world Alix saw swirled.

"Alix?" Wes gulped for air and grabbed Alix's shoulder. "Alix, you all right?"

Captain Milligan tilted his head to the side and watched Alix's body waver. Alix's eyes circled around back into his head, and the color in his face fell the moment his eyes flickered. His head tilted back, and he collapsed. Everyone gathered around Alix's sprawled-out body. "Victor, go get a medic!" Captain Milligan yelled.

Alix floated in the deep sea of a dream. His body felt pressure like a giant fist was squeezing him like a stress ball. A massive shadow floated in the distance and consumed his world. His ears popped and a familiar voice echoed underwater. *"You better hope there is a next time. Captain Milligan was pretty pissed ... I hope my chip is stored after I die ... Come on. Beth? Anna? Sidney?"* The sentences formed from memory like he had heard them before. But something buzzed in Alix's head, in his mind, or maybe his chip. Somehow, Alix believed the words had never happened, like finding a downed tree and saying it never fell.

A face welded to the voice: a round, male face with a freckle above his lip and dark stubble on his head. He looked at Alix and said, "*It's stronger if you miss a broadcast. You were about to say Anna?*"

The face drew closer.

"*You have to believe there is more to life than down here.*"

Alix recognized the face. His mind and his chip struggled as he strained to piece together memory, fact, and truth.

"Eli, wait!" Alix reached out for him, but the walls of the dream closed in and squeezed Alix out.

6 |

The monitor lit up the room and the blue wave took the screen. "Good evening, Captain Milligan."

"Yes, M.A.I.A., run a surveillance file on Alix from this morning to now." Captain Milligan sat in the dark booth of the security center. He needed evidence before he took action. The tail end of an hourglass always seemed to drain faster whenever he needed an answer.

Years ago, he received a warning about Alix's differences and he shrugged it off. He wished he took that warning seriously and kept a closer eye on him. He hoped it wasn't too late.

The grains of sand created a conical pile as M.A.I.A collected a digital pile. Somewhere in that stack of information was confirmation of a secret shared years ago at a urinal from an unlikely source.

Captain remembered how the old programmer shuffled into the restroom. He swayed on old legs and a limber back in front of the urinal. He'd used his index finger to hold his glasses on his face to assist with his aim.

"Captain Robert Milligan." The old man did not break the aim of his weak stream.

Milligan's orange beard reflected in the white tile. "If I were Captain Milligan, what would a programmer want with an officer?" His gravelly voice bounced off the tiled walls.

"Dr. Thomas Ethex." He jiggled himself and stepped away from the urinal.

"What brings the brains to the muscle? You seem to be quite far from your computer."

Dr. Ethex stepped slowly, caught his balance in each step toward the sink, and waved his old, swollen knuckles under the faucet's motion sensor. "A man in his old age can't always regard bathroom designations. Slow steps and a small bladder sometimes require one to ignore rules. Your bathroom was closer."

"Sometimes rules are meant to be broken," Captain Milligan laughed, jiggled, zipped, and approached the sink. As the tepid water rained washed over his hands, Captain Milligan surreptitiously studied Dr. Ethex's wrinkled face, and translucent skin.

Dr. Ethex continued to scrub his hands under the water even though they were clean. "Are you going to report me?"

"No, can't report a man for pissing. It's not like you wandered into the ladies' room." Captain Milligan shook the excess water off his hands and grabbed a towel. He offered a towel to Dr. Ethex. The sweat in the creases of his forehead, and an anxious look in his eyes, alerted Captain Milligan's senses this was no chance meeting.

"Private Alix Basil," Dr. Ethex said flatly.

Captain Milligan raised his brows. "Yeah? What about him?" The stiff towel scraped his knuckles as he dried his hands.

"He's on your list of cadets coming from education to training next week. He's a sniper. They say he could be one of the best." Water outlined Dr. Ethex's eyes.

"I know. I read his file. What about Private Alix Basil?"

"He's different."

"His programming is special ops. Of course, he's going to be a bit different from the rest, Dr. Ethex. One out of ten take the time to be programmed for special ops. You should know that. You could have programmed him."

"I did program him. Are you familiar with the program 19-84?"

"Yeah." Captain Milligan's eyes flicked to the corners of the bathroom, searching for a monitor.

"Don't worry, we're safe in here. This is one place where the microphones are kept muted. No one in Security wants to listen to the sounds of bodily fluids and such. It's the one human behavior that remains intact despite our obsession with technology. You'll find Alix a bit different in regard to program 19-84 meaning he doesn't have it."

The memory felt hazy, far away yet so close. The computer blinked and flickered and then beeped and returned Captain Milligan's mind back to the present. He squinted in the dark to see the bright screen. The thought of that day dissembled time and direction. The captain shook his head and pinched his eyebrows to stay awake.

"One moment please." M.A.I.A.'s voice hummed.

Alix appeared on the screen before his bunk, standing next to no one, where Eli should have been.

"Computer, run speed times two."

The footage sped up and flicked between camera angles following Alix and the team to the Vomit Room. Like cartoon characters, Alix and the team zoomed around the track, then around the weight room, and back to the court where they did sprints.

"Computer, slow speed to real time."

Captain Milligan watched Alix sway and collapse to the floor. He squinted as he watched himself drop to his knees in the video to hold Alix's head up. Two medics rushed in with a stretcher. They lowered the gurney, hoisted Alix onto to it, and wheeled it out through the double doors.

The monitor switched to a view from above the long hallway, as the medics moved to the elevator. With the sound muted, Alix's mouth twisted from his screams as he shook his head back and forth and tried to break free from the straps.

"Computer, increase volume."

"Eli, No! Eli! Eli?" Alix's screams echoed down the hallway.

Two men in black suits emerged from the elevator, took the stretcher from the medics, and swiftly stepped back into the elevator with Alix

The screen blackened: **Data not receivable.**

Captain Milligan stood. "Computer, where is Alix Basil?"

The message blinked: **Data not receivable.**

"M.A.I.A., my credentials grant me access to these files. Where is Alix Basil?"

Data not receivable.

A drop of sweat ran down the side of Captain's face. He paused and looked down to the right. He looked up. "Computer, where is Private Matthew?"

The monitor blinked and brought a live view that overlooked the barracks and bunk that Matt slept in.

"Private Phillip."

The computer switched angles to a massive lump under a sheet.

Captain Milligan angled his head down in thought and then lifted it. "Private Eli?"

Data not receivable.

"Private Alix."

Data not receivable.

Captain Milligan punched the screen.

#

Eleven M.A.I.A. Readers sat around a polished oak meeting table. Their eyebrows furrowed as they pondered in large, engulfing leather recliners. They scratched their heads, pinched their chins, and stared off into space.

"It's physically impossible," a white-haired man slapped the table in front of him.

"Hold your comments. We must wait for Rankin."

"I can't believe we are here again already."

The door swished open. Rankin rolled in on the whine of the T-Port and circled the table. He lowered himself to a seat level, braces holding his bent knees.

The room hummed. "M.A.I.A. Reading number 784 commencing." A blue hologram screen sprung up and opened like a book in front of each reader.

Rankin cleared his throat. "OK, gentlemen, we all know why we're here. Let's get to it." His words sprang up on the screen in front of them as a transcript of the discussion. "As you all know, earlier today, a cadet collapsed during a drill. Although not all that uncommon, it is what happened after his collapse that brings us back to this table so soon.

"Private Alix Basil, in a delusional state, has relinquished memories that, according to M.A.I.A. Reading number 783, should not exist. As stated by the Vanishing Sequence section nineteen line thirteen, 'All memory of a cadet that is vanished by the M.A.I.A. Central Computer is to be erased from all cerebral chips.'

"'Additionally, the chip is to work as a suppressant against any other acknowledgment of the individual that is vanished.' But, somehow, gentlemen, as you have seen in recent surveillance, Private Alix Basil at 17:47, has in a dreamlike state, spoken the name of a vanished individual. This is a violation of code six forty-five, section eight, line three stating as such, 'Any cadet that is subject to required action of Vanishing Sequence must not return to existence in any shape or form including, but not limited to speech, both written and vocal, photography, videography, media of any kind, thoughts, memories, or gestures of any kind leading to the thought of the Vanished.' It says on line four that, 'Any cadet in violation of remembrance of any sort of the latter shall be subject to the Vanishing Sequence in thyself.' Are there any initial questions before we get started?" Rankin said flatly.

A blinking box appeared on the screen. The message inside read: "Are we going to Vanish another one of our boys?" The text on the screen never held a label, name, or an attachment. Anybody in the room thinking that could have posed that question or even M.A.I.A. had the ability to comment.

Rankin looked over at Reader Elmer Washington and his white hair parted to one side. Rankin stared at the screen. The glare from the screen entered his eyes, a direct route to his brain. He pictured the words, and they appeared on the screen as a silent debate: "We are going to do exactly what M.A.I.A. statistically says is orthodox."

Washington's eyes avoided the screen. "Statistically, at this rate we will not have a fighting force against the Citizens. Two cadets in a week? Does anyone else think this could potentially be too much?"

"Elmer, look at the damn screen and use M.A.I.A. to present your comments and objections, so they can go on record," Rankin demanded.

"Why? We all have minds to remember what is being said here. I will look you dead in the eye and ask you—demand you tell me how this could have happened." Elmer's jowls shook with his words.

A chair squeaked. No one's eyes moved.

Rankin watched them all. "Let's leave it up to M.A.I.A. like we have been all along, shall we?"

Washington's eyes narrowed. "The question raised here should be whether Alix can remain in the armed forces or not. We cannot determine the extent of Alix's condition yet until further analysis. I think M.A.I.A. and the rest of the Readers will agree."

The screen and chat box became green. M.A.I.A. projected Washington's statement in a highlighted green font. M.A.I.A. agreed.

Rankin eyed the screen as M.A.I.A. delivered another proclamation. "We will determine today if it is worth having Alix fight for M.A.I.A. or if he is a threat. We will notify his officers and return in twenty-four hours for a Rereading of the Alix situation and possible Vanishing Sequence. Dismissed."

"I guess that is the end of our meeting," Elmer declared and stood up.

Rankin watched the room clear out. His head twisted slightly to deliver an angry glare at M.A.I.A.'s screen. A green wavy line scrolled quietly across the screen like a discreet snicker. Rankin floored his T-Port, its motor making a high-pitched whine as he sped out of the room.

7

Dr. Susan Maynard stared up into Rankin's old eyes. "You just got back from a M.A.I.A. Reading about erasing another boy's memory and existence, but you want to cover it up? I don't understand."

"You don't need to understand. It's above you."

"Everyone will find out."

Rankin looked down at her from his T-Port. He checked over the cubicle walls. She was alone. "You don't have to understand, Susan, but you will follow the directions that I'm given by M.A.I.A."

"Why would M.A.I.A. order...?"

"Be grateful M.A.I.A. determined there is nothing about Anna that warrants a review by the Reading Board; that's why I'm staying with M.A.I.A.'s plan. While I don't always understand my orders, I must abide by them."

"What do you want me to tell the other girls? Anna's sudden disappearance will make the others think..."

"You are the head of our medic department. You don't have to explain yourself to them. They are cadets."

"But Al..."

"Remember your rank. Don't ever refer to me as Al. I'm sick and tired of being cooped up down here like animals. You will follow orders."

"I don't care about what you're sick of. I only care about Anna."

Rankin grabbed her arm. "As do I. That's why Anna will be the one to monitor Alix. It's the only way I can keep her safe and from being detected. Once I reset the whole system, no one will know who Eli, Alix, or Anna were."

"But we will."

"It's for the best."

Susan looked away, bit her lip and fought back tears. "Our own daughter ... a Vanishing Sequence?"

"Don't push me. I'm doing everything I can. If we had programmed her correctly, she wouldn't be sneaking out. You said you had her under control, but you didn't. I can't depend on you. I have to do everything myself." Rankin wheeled away.

#

Crusted gook and old tears sealed Alix's eyes together. He forced them open. A dim monitor severed the blurry darkness. Alix blinked to break his eyelids free and lifted his hand to dig it out of the corners. His arm stopped short with a metal clank. He looked around. Several boxes glowed green in the dark, jagged lines brought forth by the blackness, and slow and steady beeps. Old computers surrounded him and flowed a dim, aquatic light over the room. Alix twitched his nose and moved the hoses pumping oxygen into him. He followed the tubes to the glimmer of a reflection on the metallic oxygen tank and more tubes from his wrist to a bag of clear fluid that clung to the side of his bed. His eyes could not focus.

The name Eli and a face stood vividly in his mind now. The back of his head tingled. His chip worked overtime to repress thoughts and words but failed miserably.

A silhouetted, slender figure in a white overcoat stepped into the room. "Alix? You're awake?" Her voice was older but warm and comforting.

Through the slits of his eyes, he followed her as she went to the nook next to the bed, opened the drawers, and pulled out two rubber gloves and a stethoscope. "Is this all I have to work with?" she mumbled. Her warm breath fell on his face. The familiar vitamin and bullion scent of a protein tab wafted into his nose. She picked up several medicine plugs for his intravenous port.

"What's going on?" Alix opened his eyes fully. He lifted his restrained arm as far as it would go.

Her hands never stopped moving. "You caused quite a fuss today. Do you remember anything?"

Her blonde hair rested on her shoulder as she turned her head, pulled the plug out of his intravenous tube, and snapped another tube in place. A squirt of blood hit the back of the test tube. She lifted the sample to the ceiling and squinted.

Alix strained to make out her shadowy features.

"You trained the medics..." His voice was soft, and his throat scratchy from screaming.

Sue stopped and looked down at him. "You remember me?"

"I remember a lot of shit I'm not supposed to."

Sue froze, and then put her face in his. "No, you don't remember anything," the heat of her words blasted his face. She withdrew her face and lifted his right shoulder to remove the johnny and expose his chest. She pressed the cold stethoscope against his skin. "OK, breathe for me."

Alix inhaled and let it out slowly. "I remember getting dizzy after sprints."

"Deep breathe, please."

She unlatched his armband on her side and leaned over to unlatch the other. "You should try to go to the bathroom; this could be your only chance for the next several hours." She undid his ankle restraints.

Alix swiveled to the side of the bed, pulled the johnny up over his shoulders, and hung his head. He cupped the back of his neck and rubbed. His head felt top heavy. "What did you give me?"

"I'm sorry. Your information is classified exclusively to M.A.I.A."

"Did I die or something?" Alix checked his embedded screen. *Analyze blood*. His thought was clear and instinctive.

"I can assure you that you're very much alive."

Alix tapped his wrist. "What's wrong with my EED?"

"Your Embedded Electronic Device has been temporarily disabled."

"Temporarily disabled? Is that possible?" Alix stood up. The cold floor bit his toes. He swayed back and forth, stepping toward Sue. He reached out his hand to grab her arm to steady himself.

She stepped back, and raised a small, handheld device.

Alix eyed the small piece of metal in her hand. A blue light lit.

He slapped her hand away. "I could kill you in…"

Sue pressed the button and held it.

Alix's body jolted as a current went from the top of his head to the balls of his feet. His knees buckled, and he flopped to the floor, smacking his cheek hard against the tile's coldness. He couldn't move. His eyes and ears worked, but drool trickled out the left corner of his mouth.

Sue released the button.

Alix's body softened. He gasped for air and moaned.

"We all have one of these. If this button is pressed, you hit the floor. There is an armed agent right outside this door."

Alix pushed himself up onto one knee, wiped the drool, and exhaled.

"Go use the restroom." Sue pointed to the narrow door. "You have two minutes."

Alix hoisted himself and stumbled into the door. He looked around the ceiling of the dark room and waited for light, waited for motion sensors, or the heat sensors, or something to light the room. Nothing came.

Sue glanced above the labels she read on the intravenous plugs. "You have to turn on the light. There's a switch to your right." She shook her head. "This generation is doomed."

Alix reached for the switch and fingered it until the light flickered on. He stared at the grit between the cracks of ancient tiles. It smelled of damp copper and musty porcelain. As he urinated, he swayed back and forth. He walked away from the toilet, but it didn't flush. He looked back. Condensation dripped from the metal handle attached to the pipes of the toilet. Alix stared at it. He yanked the handle up and then down. The toilet flushed, and he wiped his hand off on his johnny.

Alix checked himself in the mirror. His pale skin appeared stretched over his face, pupils dilated almost to the width of his irises. When the toilet stopped gurgling, he turned the handle on the old faucet. It sputtered, and then brown water flowed. He let it run until the water cleared. He scooped up a handful of the water and brought it to his face. It smelled of metal and sulfur. He sipped it, spit it out, and splashed his face. In the mirror, he watched a drop roll down his forehead, sink into an eyebrow, slide to an eyelid, and then dangle on his eyelashes. He blinked. The drop fell.

Sue tapped on the door. "Alix, time to come out."

Alix exited the bathroom.

A second figure stood in the room, a medic. She had dark hair and her back was towards him. She studied the labels of the intravenous plugs as Alix laid down. His eyes traced the medic's curvy silhouette, a natural attraction. He looked where her eyes would be if sufficient light filled the room.

Sue grabbed his wrist and pulled it to the side.

Alix withdrew. "Are these restraints necessary?"

"Yes." Sue held down his wrist and clasped the buckles. She looked over to the medic. "Anna, can you do his legs?"

"Yes, ma'am."

Alix's heart popped and his head snapped up. His chest burst inside, and love poured into his veins.

Sue pushed his head back down. "Down. Eyes to yourself. Other hand." She tightened the clasps around his wrists.

Alix craned his head to stare at the Anna, who was at the foot of his bed. Her delicate hands clasped around his ankle. The white, hallway light painted one side of her body from the waist up. It illuminated her shoulder, skidded across the wrinkles of her lab coat, and glowed on her face.

Alix felt his pores tighten; his hair straightened. A familiar profile. *Anna...*

He felt Anna grab his toe and twisted gently. His body grew excited. *Anna!*

Sue attached three medicine plugs to the intravenous ports. She leaned over Alix and tightened the other strap. "Are those buckled tight?"

"Yes, ma'am."

Alix wondered if this was all simulation. Was he being tested? Did someone find out about their visits to the simulation rooms and was using her presence to get a confession?

Sue tossed the empty medicine plugs into a biological waste barrel and left.

Anna turned her back and tugged on Alix's leg hair. She ran her finger up his bare foot and offered him a coy surreptitious smile.

Alix's toes curled. He smiled. It was no simulation. Anna was there to get him out of there.

#

"Good job, Anna." Susan didn't lift her head from her paperwork.

"Thanks, Ms. Sue," Anna sniffled.

"What's wrong?" Sue turned from her report.

"Nothing." Anna's broken breaths sputtered in every pull of air she made. She leaned her head on her hand and moved her stylus across her tablet screen.

"Anna?" Susan watched a teardrop fall onto the tablet screen. "Anna?"

"I'm sorry, Ms. Sue. I just... It's nothing." Anna dabbed her nose.

Sue approached her.

Anna stiffened and clenched her teeth and braced herself for a tongue lashing. The display of emotion was not allowed, but she couldn't help herself.

Sue put a warm hand on Anna's shoulder and squeezed.

Anna froze.

"I'm not going to hurt you, Anna." Sue's voice softened.

Anna erupted into sobs, which melted her into a child. Her arms wrapped around Sue. "What are they going to do to us? Ms. Sue, I'm sorry. I'm so scared."

"Us?" Sue tilted her head.

"Alix and I. Are we going to be able to return to our teams?"

"Shh." Sue wrapped her arms around her. This was the second time she held her daughter. She glanced upward at the old camera. It was still inactive. No doubt, Rankin kept the camera offline to hide his actions.

Sue took a breath and released a big sigh. The freedom to love was a valued commodity. This moment was worth more than five-thousand rations. "If they don't know, say nothing," she whispered.

"But you knew. You caught me..."

"But I didn't say anything. I didn't report you. You're safe." She pulled Anna in for another hug. "Continue on like everything is normal. We'll wait for our orders."

Sue's eyes glanced upward at the camera, still no movement or red light. She squeezed her daughter tighter.

8

Alix snapped his eyes open. A white bulb glared above. A tall, bald figure blotted out a portion of eye stinging light. He strained to see Rankin.

"Alix, feeling better today?" Rankin smirked.

Alix squinted at the towering man above his bed. The light reflected off his head, his few strands of white hair, and dust that circled the room. "Where am I? What are you doing to me?"

"We need to run a few more tests." An electronic whine emitted as Rankin floated around the room. "This may sting a little." He stood above Alix, withdrew a silver bullet-shaped object, and a red line beamed from it into Alix's EED.

Alix's eyes burst open. His limbs jerked at the chains that claimed his freedom. A boiling stream floated up his arm and into his shoulder. "Stop! It burns!" Electrical charges spider-webbed their way up his arm.

"Hold still! This will only take a minute!" Rankin clasped Alix's forearm and placed the bullet-shaped device close to the small, embedded screen. His T-Port rolled back and forth.

"Stop!" A burning circle of pain encompassed Alix's wrist and followed the initial shot of pain under his skin to his elbow, to his shoulder, and then up the back of his neck. He gritted his teeth, and the muscles from his neck to his jaw tightened and pushed through his skin. He jerked his other arm and clenched his right fist toward Rankin, but his fist stopped short like a leashed junkyard dog charging full speed to the end of its chain. A monitor next to Alix's bed wailed, a flat-line whine. Beeping and malfunctioning computers filled the room.

Anna burst in the doorway. "Stop! What are you doing to him?!"

The old man's head snapped toward the door. His eyes narrowed. "Leave us!"

"You're hurting him!" Anna screamed.

Sue stood beside Anna wide-eyed and torn between fear and rage. "Please!" Sue cried out.

"Get out of here, or she's next!" Rankin yelled.

Sue pulled Anna back and closed the door.

"Argh." Alix's eyes rolled up into his forehead. His tense jaw popped open. His tongue protruded. A wild scream swirled off its caked dryness, and foam formed at his lips. "Stop! Ah, stop!"

Alix jerked his right knee up. The chain tightened. He tried his left knee; it was weaker. He tried twisting his body, but Rankin's hands held him steady as the beam jumbled around his brain. His ears popped like a semiautomatic gun. "Stop! Stop!" Alix's head slammed back; his body slackened.

"There!" Rankin dropped Alix's limp arm.

Alix's breath sputtered in and out, tears streaming down his face. He looked down to his wrist as the pain retreated toward his EED, a receding tide of torture. The red finger imprints faded on his wrist like memory foam regaining its form. Sweat matted his back, arms, forehead, and legs. He shook his head and glared at Rankin.

"What," Alix breathed, "was that?"

"I just got a program analysis, that's all. I need to see what's on your chip to best treat you. I know how much that must have hurt." Rankin dropped the silver bullet into a pouch and shoved it into his pocket.

"Where's Captain Milligan?" Alix jerked on his restraints repeatedly. "Let me out of here!"

"In time," Rankin replied with a smirk and rolled to the exit.

Alix tried to launch off the bed, but his restraints held him in place. "You motherfuc..."

His body jolted and then deflated. Paralysis.

Rage twisted his stomach. He wanted to remember every detail about his persecutor: cold, dark eyes; shit eating grin with crooked teeth and soul; wild bushy gray eyebrows; large nose pointed and filled with unmitigated arrogance. Alix pictured Rankin's face in crosshairs.

Alix's body softened. He wiggled his fingers and felt his toes. The function of his body returned. The throbbing in his head subsided, and allowed his mind to alert him of the true identity of the man who dealt him a painful blow. Alix now remembered his black suit and the medals across his right breast. His torturer was a Supreme M.A.I.A. Reader, a protected and powerful man that represented M.A.I.A. Attacking a Reader meant attacking M.A.I.A and certain death. Someone had stopped him from threatening the Reader and committing suicide.

Sue and Anna entered the room, Anna rushing to his bedside. Her eyes were red from tears. She gripped his hand, and then pretended to take his pulse.

"Sorry," she mouthed, and showed him the paralysis device that was in the pocket of her lab coat. She surreptitiously placed her finger to her lips to silence him. She nodded her head to the door, and stepped aside so he could see that Rankin, his torturer, was still there.

Rankin showed his veneers of pearly teeth. "Make sure the monitor in Alix's room is properly functioning. Play one of the educational documentaries on the civilians and their way of life and track his emotional and thought patterns. I want the readings in the morning. I'm retiring for the night. Have Dr. Harrison send the records directly to me."

"Yes, sir." Sue glanced over to the monitor on her desk, which carried only the view of the patient's bed and a portion of Anna's body. Sue was grateful for the limited view. "May I make a request?"

Rankin stopped and turned to her.

"Could we bring down more proficient equipment than this?"

"Negative. I put Alix here for matters of discretion. There are no cameras down here, and I need to keep things under M.A.I.A.'s radar. A request for equipment will create a paper trail that M.A.I.A. and the other Readers will track. He will remain on U40 until he is diagnosed, and I have complete control."

"I can't remember the last time we used this facility…"

"Enough, Susan. Get to work. Stick to the privacy protocol. Don't tell him anything, and don't tell anyone else anything. He could be a threat to M.A.I.A."

Susan's eyes shifted to his pocket where Alix's data sat on the extractor.

Rankin's shoulder dipped as his right hand dove into his pocket to grip it and assure himself it was there. "I know there are easier ways to obtain a program list, but we don't have time. I need to see what is on his mind chip." His T-Port emitted a soft mechanical whine as he turned and sped off towards the elevator.

#

Alix looked down at small sensor patches connected to his fingertips, arms, chest, stomach, legs, feet, and head. Black, red, and yellow, thin wires ran from his head and over his body. Each patch of wires led to a single, thinner, black wire which was fastened to the wall console.

Compared to M.A.I.A.'s standard testing equipment, the patch and wire testing program was archaic, but it was the only way Susan could get the information Rankin demanded without detection from M.A.I.A. or the other Readers. Susan diligently shaved thin patches of hair to create contact spots for the sensors. She paused, shook her arms, and sighed.

"That's a lot of work." Alix scanned the wires. "What are these things going to do?"

"This is an older way of tracking emotional patterns of the brain and body," Susan said without taking her eyes off the screen. "These little circular tabs are sensors. They just give us information about your body. They won't hurt."

"I didn't think the psycho was going to hurt me through my EED either." Alix raised his head. "I've been blown up, shot, stabbed, and even hit by a truck in simulation, and I never imagined anything more painful than what that guy did to me."

"He wasn't supposed to do that."

"Is this what happened to Eli?"

She opened her mouth and then clamped it shut. She hid behind her blonde hair and fiddled with the wires around Alix's feet.

"You know. Is this what they did to Eli?" Alix lifted his head to watch her. "You do know. That's why you're not answering me."

"I'm not at liberty to discuss patient files with other patients."

Alix let his head fall back. "Patients? Eli and I are patients now? Is he still a patient?"

"Enough!" Sue grabbed the batch of unused tab sensors and tossed them in the drawer of a nearby cart. She stood and glared at him.

A dark stillness settled between them. His eyes locked on her dry lips. When they parted to speak, he focused on her eyes. Her chest heaved several times. Alix craned his neck to maintain eye contact.

She took a step forward and then spun on her heel to turn on a nearby monitor. She picked up a remote aimed at the monitor, the screen on the monitor. "Here's a video. Watch it."

"Oh, thanks. That's going to make me forget all about these restraints, wires, and the fact that *Eli* and I are hidden in this hole of a place. Do you have any popcorn?"

She flicked the lights off and disappeared into the outer office.

The monitor flickered. The video started. A camera panned high in the air above a snowy city surrounded by water. A deep, apologetic man's voice came from behind the screen, accompanied by a gentle, instrumental jingle.

"Manufacturing Artificial Intelligence Agency was not always the great, strong, advanced company we know it as today." The camera zoomed in over the island. "This world-changing organization we know as M.A.I.A. owes its life and birth to the once-great nation formerly known as the United States of America."

A map of the world appeared on the screen with the country highlighted. It flicked to programmers in lab coats, checking their clipboards in the foreground while two black-suited men stood in the background.

"Before the war, this island we now reside in used to be referred to as Governors Island, which is just outside of Manhattan, but also part of New York City. New York City was home to ten million civilians before the invasion."

"I've seen this one before," Alix bellowed.

Sue responded by pulling the shade down on the windowed door between the office and his room.

He looked away from the screen. He only cared about Anna. The Conservation mission came in a distant second to her. Unbeknownst to M.A.I.A., Anna gave him more purpose to his life than the mission he was created for. Had Rankin and Sue learned about their secret simulation missions? They had been so careful.

With the video's narration droning in the background, Alix drifted off.

9

Alix remembered being incredibly careful as he lifted the sheets in the darkness. He listened to the deep snores that resonated throughout his cadet container.

Take three light steps forward and fifty steps to the right.

The door latch to the main hall had to be cranked open perfectly; too slow and it squeaked, too quick and the door slammed like a sledgehammer on a tin can. Alix closed his eyes and unlatched the door. In less than a breath, he'd swung the door open, entered, and closed it. Perfect.

Alix moved down the hallway, his back against the wall. His heart raced. He held his EED to the simulator. It unlatched and echoed. He strapped up, attaching his sensors and electronic equipment. He closed his eyes and hoped it was a night that Anna made it out, too.

He selected simulation number thirteen. No matter how gruesome, or disgusting, or difficult, they both entered simulation thirteen and awaited the fate of the scenarios. Alix checked the description and whispered it out loud. "M.A.I.A. intelligence detected Citi leader protected in the penthouse of an old hotel complex. Infiltrate the heavily patrolled infrastructure and kill the terrorist leader."

He pulled the shield over his eyes. The shield zipped him through a world of colorful waves of revolving shimmers, whooshing him through a rainbow. The sound of glass tinkled and shrank into a complete and solid, tangible world. Alix lowered his binoculars from his eyes. The dark hotel's windows glowed. He spotted yellow lit rooms. White flakes drifted lightly from the sky at dew point. His breath was noticeable, a sniper's nightmare. No long shots tonight. Got to stay in cover.

Alix checked his six. A team of seven hunkered behind him and was awaiting a plan. He searched each of their eyes and painted faces, all black clothes, none of them Anna.

"All right, men, let's get some practice." Alix returned his eyes to the binoculars.

"Getting started without me?" Anna hurried in and tucked in her shirt under her tactical vest. "Sorry I'm late."

Alix's body jolted in excitement. "Babe!"

"Shh!" One of the digital men held his finger to his lips.

Alix and Anna embraced, their lips met, and they breathed each other in.

"What do we have?" Anna slouched down and snagged the binoculars.

"We have a target in on the top floor suite, snipers on the roof. If they have thermal or see our breath, we're smoked. My rifle won't be getting much use tonight."

"You're right." Anna squinted and stared through the binoculars. "Plus, they know we're coming. Look at the guard at each doorway. Don't look like much, but by the bump in their jackets, I bet they have semi-autos at least."

"Agreed. They would stand clear of the windows for sure."

Anna shouldered Alix. "Looks like we're getting a room."

Alix smiled. "Did you pack a dress? We could go undercover."

"Hold on. Let me pull a red dress and heels out of my ass, Alix. No, I don't have a dress. Did you bring a tux in your rifle bag?"

"Actually, I did. First, you're late and now unprepared?"

Anna chuckled. "Bullshit you packed a tux, and if you did, you forgot your shoes."

"That was one time."

"The only time we needed them."

"Okay," Alix smiled, "Let's try the back and see what that looks like."

Anna shook her head. "That's a waste of time. You and I flank that side of the building. We take out those two guards on the west side quietly, disable the elevators, and take the stairs to the top floor. When we are in position, let's pull a full-frontal assault with what we have from these guys. Leave one perched with a rifle to cover us."

"Not a bad plan." Alix huffed. A deep, cool cloud left his lips. "Let's move."

Alix and Anna screwed on silencers and snuck down and around the left side of the building. The rifleman watched both of them blend in like chameleons to their surroundings. Like wolves, they approach the east entrance, which had the least protection.

Two guards heard crunching snow and a broken branch, drew guns, and approached Anna's position behind a bush. Anna appeared in a white tank top, no vest, no guns, no gear, just a low-cut shirt and well-defined cleavage. She appeared disheveled as the two men stepped toward her. She fell to her knees with her hands up. Her lips moved, and she looked up helplessly toward the men, innocent and sexy through a long, dark strand of hair.

Alix hopped behind the men, pulled a zip line around one's neck, and pulled him back and out of view.

Anna sprang up, disarmed the other, kicked his legs from under him, and drew a blade down into his throat. She dragged him out of view.

"Holy shit, that was close." Alix tossed the guard's body into a large trash bin and helped Anna lift and depose of the other body.

"I thought the night was going to end early. That would have sucked." Anna wiped her hands off. She drew her gun and peeked around the corner. "The elevator controls are downstairs in the control room. Let's move."

"All units, report!" the radio from the bin bellowed in French.

"Shit. Let's go. No time to disable elevators. They will know in the next couple of minutes." Alix handed Anna her vest and took off his black overthrow which left him in only a white tee, bulletproof vest, and tactical pants.

"Agreed. Let's get in position." Anna kicked the door. Her pistol pointed as she checked each corner.

Alix and Anna bolted down the colorful, carpeted hallway. Mirrors hung every ten paces, which meant they could be seen if not careful. Old paintings stood perfectly between doors, and end tables held single roses Classical music chimed throughout the facility.

Alix lowered his chin to whisper into his radio clipped on the collar of his t-shirt. "Foxtrot to Fairview, what is your position and possible ETA?" He pressed his earpiece as they entered the stairwell.

"Fairview to Foxtrot. Waiting for the signal to infiltrate. ETA will be twenty seconds," a husky voice replied.

"And the black horse?" Alix spoke with his hand shielding his mouth and microphone.

"The black horse is in the corral- Ye haw!" the husky voice added with a country twang.

"Roger that." Alix looked to Anna. "The team commandeered the limousine."

Anna and Alix bolted up the stairs. Anna watched Alix's eyes scan the stairwell above. She studied the veins and muscles on his right hand that held his pistol. Sinewy muscles protruded through his skin. His triceps, flexed, showed chiseled rock-hard muscles that bulged below his t-shirt sleeve. He was her modern Achilles and she had to be mindful not to become his heel of vulnerability. She had to be better in combat than his team, because together, they were endgame and ultimately, in the end, it was just them.

Alix stopped on the fourth-floor platform, peeked at her, and the echo subsided. He shook his head. "What?"

"Sh." Anna approached him, a nervous look in her eyes. "You hear that?"

"No, hear what?" he asked. Only their whispers sank and rose through the stairwell.

Anna closed in on him. "Come here." She grabbed him by the V-neck and jerked him into her.

Alix's teeth fought through his lips. "Anna," he peeked through the thin, vertical glass on the door and peered down the hallway, "Here?"

Her teeth clamped around his earlobe, her nose breathing heavily in his ear. She reached down and unbuckled her belt. He unsnapped his vest in the front as Anna pushed him hard into the corner of the stairwell.

Alix eyed the long corridor through the thin glass window of the stairwell and shrugged.

Anna dug her nails into his white t-shirt and separated the fabric, his definition lit by the single light bulb above. She wiggled and tugged her pants off her hips, down her legs, tore one boot off, and kicked the other off.

Alix's pants lowered halfway down his butt, just enough to allow himself out of his zipper. He spun and lifted her effortlessly as her cool legs parted and wrapped around his warm waist.

Anna dragged her lips along his neck and clung onto the back of his vest as they connected. Her muffled moans and his light grunts bounced off the cement walls and stairs, tangled with their heavy and audible breaths. His belt jingled like Christmas bells and his elbows knocked the wall each thrust.

"Oh, my God, Alix," she whispered in his ear, and her lips circled his entire lobe.

He lifted his head off her shoulder and pressed his lips hard into hers, a loud groan from deep inside his body infusing her.

She smelled their sweaty skin rubbing. Her arms squeezed the straps on the back of his vest as hard as her fingers would clasp, and she closed her eyes. Her body released, and a long high-pitched, uncontrolled moan left her lips.

Alix smothered her mouth hard and pushed her head sideways into the corner. She lifted and shifted her head, nipped his palm hard.

Alix groaned and bite prints appeared on the side of his hand, and he shook his wrist. He revolved his hips heavier as she pulled him closer by the back of his short, wet, dark hair, and mashed their lips together. He felt his pelvis twitch. His breath stuttered.

Anna bit his lip hard, her body relaxing fully. She tilted her head back and dragged her wet hair across the cement wall. She saw the black suit in the corner of her eye.

The door popped open. "What are you two doing here?!"

Anna, from her hoisted position against the wall, pulled Alix's pistol out of his holster as both guns went off.

A bullet smacked Alix in the back as the suited guard's head snapped back and revealed the blood spatter behind him.

Alix let Anna collapse. He arched his back and held his ears. He breathed through his teeth as if stung by a bee. "Dammit!" He snatched his pistol from her. "Right near my ear too."

Anna scrambled to pull her pants up and buckle, smiling. "At least you got off first."

Alix stretched his back. "That sucked."

"Excuse me!" Anna pulled her boots on.

"Not you, the bullet in the back of my vest and the ringing in my ears."

"Come here, you big baby. Turn around." Anna pulled the flowered copper bullet out of his vest. "It's only a nine-millimeter. Stop being a bitch. Let's move." She tossed the shell haphazardly to the side. It pinged down the stairs.

Alix smiled. "Let me shoot you in the back, see how you like it."

They raced up the stairs. "You shoot me in the back, Alix, you're going to be missing some body parts next time."

Guards ran in every direction. Light flickered from gunfire throughout the building. Gunfire erupted. A limo jolted in from the west and smashed through the double-wooden front doors of the hotel. The sniper took fire at sprinting suits. The team exited the limo and entered the building.

A moment later, Alix and Anna heard, "Mission Accomplished."

Anna turned from the guard as he fell from the desk, collapsing behind her. She looked to Alix who stood over the dead terrorist.

Alix's pistol smoked as he released the mag.

She smiled. "We are good at this."

"We're great at this." He stood, approached her, and kissed her deeply. "I'll see you in three days?"

"Yeah. I'm going miss you, babe." She kissed him.

"Me too. Be careful getting back into bed. Goodnight."

"Okay, you, too. Goodnight."

Their virtual reality worlds disintegrated.

Alix stared at the ceiling of the room, his arms held back by chains. The monitor screen flickered; the video was over. Even though wires still sprouted from his head to his toes, Anna remained the only one to whom he felt truly connected.

10

"Well, you boys wanted to speak with me, so speak. Don't stare at me like a bunch of blank screens." Captain Milligan leaned back in his chair. He drummed on the top of the glass globe on his desk and searched their eyes.

Wes raised his chin. "Sir, we would like to be informed on the status of our sniper, Alix."

Captain Milligan held one finger on the globe. "So would I."

"Sir?" Their faces twisted in knots of confusion.

Captain Milligan glanced up at Wes and looked back to the globe. He picked it up. Holding the globe in his hands, Captain Milligan pictured the night a small mob of suited men would appear behind him and take him into the darkness for treason. He looked at the little clock inside the globe, and he twisted the knob. Lights wavered on the walls as twinkling music filled the room and delivered an unwelcoming uneasiness. Baffled, the cadets looked at each other.

"For as long as this music plays, let's assume there is no rank in this room and that M.A.I.A. can't hear what we are saying."

Their faces reddened, and Matt looked over his shoulder and up to the monitor behind them. Their jaws tightened. No one spoke.

"Trust me, you are safe to talk. It was just yesterday that Squad Twenty-Eight seemed ready to lose their sniper. Why the sudden change in attitude?"

Silence. Wes breathed in deep.

"Don't look at the monitor, because then they will know that we are off their audible grid," Captain Milligan warned with a smile. "Just act natural. We're just having one of our meetings."

Wes turned his head slightly to look at the monitor.

"No, no. Eyes on me," said the captain.

Wes' eyes locked on his. "Captain, a member of our squad has fallen. We are trained to never leave a man behind. Without Alix, we're not Squad Twenty-Eight. We're not going to set foot on the mainland without him. We've trained for this for as long we can remember."

Captain Milligan's eyes dropped. "What about you, Victor? The other day, I watched you shoulder Alix on your way out of my office. I heard what you said to him. Where I grew up, we'd toss you and Alix a pair of gloves and say have at it." He folded his hands in his lap and reclined. "Stop trying to look over your shoulder. We're simple men having a simple conversation. Speak now or forever hold your peace."

"Sir, Alix held his fire on my spot, but without a shooter, a spotter is just a scout," Victor declared with folded arms. "And I'm more of a hunter than a bird watcher."

For a split second, the boys reminded Captain Milligan of his father, but defiant and humble.

Captain Milligan's mind floated with the globe's twinkling lights back to a porch memory of his father. The hot and heavy Virginia air was so unbearable that it was cooler outside than inside the house. They put the television on the porch to watch a story on the news about the first public cerebral chips that were surgically implanted. His father had sipped his brandy, rocking in his chair that had creaked with every move. The light of the cantaloupe melon sunset had softened the deep lines of his wrinkled face beneath his dirty cowboy hat. He slurped his brandy, smacked his lips, and allowed his soulful sensibility to slide off his southern tongue.

"If God meant for human thought to be stored on a chip, he would have skipped the human part." His father's eyes looked out over his land.

The smell of boiling ham had been lingering in his mother's kitchen long after they had digested it, and it still made his mouth water for more. The faucet ran, dishes clanked, and Captain Milligan, then a military man of twenty-seven, thought his father to be crazy. "Why would any man refuse the opportunity to store information? A man's memory only lasts but so long."

"For the same reason your mother is washing dishes by hand while standing right next to the dishwasher," his father volleyed. "The human condition requires purpose. Your mother feels her purpose is to make sure her dishes are clean. She doesn't trust a machine to do it for her. She figures, if she has to push buttons to tell the machine what to do, she might as well do it herself."

His father's wisdom was how he kept himself human amid a world where artificial intelligence and technology decided what was human and what wasn't.

His father tipped his hat to the sky. "Every old man has those moments when he looks at the next generation and feels sorry for them, because a young man will never know the way of life his father had lived. It takes a long time to get to know life, Robert, and once you get to know it, you're nearly dead, so you try to explain it to young, deaf ears. Because, when you're young, you think you have it all figured out—until you figure yourself right into a hole, and think, I should have listened to my old man. And here we are." He took a sip. "So why on God's Earth do you want with a chip in your brain?"

His father's body was fifty-three years of age when he birthed those words. There was no A.I. needed.

Captain Milligan felt much older than his fifty-two years. He looked at the young men in his office. He was the father now. "Is that what the team thinks?"

"If there's no sniper, there's no spotter. And I'm not all that good with a machine gun, Captain." Victor punctuated his words with his signature lopsided Elvis smirk.

"Good. My turn to speak. If this gets taken out of my hands, you won't remember me or anything I say anyway." Captain Milligan checked the timer on the clock in the globe. There was still time. "Alix has been put down in a secret facility because Reader Albert Rankin believes that his cerebral chip is defective. He believes that Alix knows stuff that he shouldn't, because of things that Alix yelled out. That's all I can tell you. Ridiculous, I know, but I don't know when he'll be back or if he's all right. I haven't seen him nor spoken with him. That's all I can say because that's all there is to say."

Everyone bowed their heads.

Matt raised his eyes. "So, we're not going to be the first deployed?"

"That's not what matters. We can't go without our sniper. We can't go without our full team. No Alix, no sniper, no team." Wes' words exploded like a grenade.

Captain Milligan took a deep breath and glanced above them to the monitor and then down at the globe. According to its timer, less than sixty seconds remained before its electromagnetic-blocking song ended. "Well, that depends."

"Depends on what, sir?" Wes stepped up to the desk, and Victor joined him.

Captain Milligan spoke softly. "Depends on which side you're on."

The cadets eyed each other.

"Excuse me, sir?" Matt strained to hear correctly.

The globe's tinkling music slowed. Milligan stood up and spoke quickly. "If you're willing to do anything, and I mean anything, you might have the chance to get Alix back and be the first squad deployed on the mainland. Does the name Eli mean anything to you?"

They looked at one another, their faces blank, like lost stones.

Wes cleared his throat. "Never heard of him, sir."

The last bars of the song played.

"Never mind. This discussion is top secret. No further questions at this time." The music ended. "I'd like you to report to your regular training sessions until further notice. I'll see you at 0-700 hours. Dismissed!"

Their bodies stiffened as they saluted him, turned on their heels, and filed out of his office.

Phil turned to Wes as they filed down the hall. "Who's Eli?"

Wes gave him a hard shove. "Follow Captain's orders."

As Victor turned to close the office door, he and the captain eyed each other.

"Questions?" Captain Milligan struck a defiant pose behind his desk.

"No, sir. Thank you for the opportunity to serve you, sir." Victor saluted and then closed the door.

Captain Milligan opened his desk drawer, moving some papers aside. He shuffled the papers in his drawer until it appeared. He looked up at the camera and then back at the contents in his drawer. A picture of the squad before Eli's disappearance peeked out amongst his clutter. A physical photograph would have been nearly impossible if he hadn't known Dr. Harrison. His eyes welled up. He looked up at the camera and then at the silent globe. He didn't dare speak. Without a chip, M.A.I.A. never knew his thoughts.

This one is for you, Eli. His fingers pushed the photo into a small batch of papers, grabbed a folder from a file drawer and shoved the small batch of papers from his drawer into it. He walked out of his office, carrying the only evidence left of Eli.

11

Sue leaned into her palms at her desk, rubbed her eyes, and breathed deeply. She'd heard of the bottom facility on U40, forty stories below sea level, but never did she think they would have to use it, especially on Alix, who had only passed out during training.

She got up to look at him through the door's window. Her monitor burped a beep. She glanced at its screen. In the bottom right corner, she saw the email icon had flashed and disappeared. She didn't want to read it in front of Anna.

"Anna, can you get the intravenous plugs ready? I'll be in there in a minute. Keep the lights low."

"Yes ma'am." Anna opened the door and disappeared into Alix's room.

Susan looked up and touched the monitor screen, but it didn't react. She reached down for the mouse and clicked on the message sent from a guest log from level U21. She read the message:

Anonymous U21 [Cadet's Media Center]

There's a cadet being held in your detention center by means not ratified by M.A.I.A. The man in charge of the boy being held there is using unofficial means of treatment, and overstepping protocol. Maintaining M.A.I.A.'s values and rules are paramount to our success of Conservation.

Sue gazed at the screen. She looked over her shoulder and through the window at Anna and Alix. Anna leaned over him and kissed him gently on the lips. Sue bit her lip. Her fingers hovered over the keys.

Alix opened his eyes.

Anna's face hovered above him. She appeared by his bedside without a sound like a ghost. She leaned over him and kissed him again.

"Your lips are so much more amazing in reality," said Alix.

"Shh, Alix. They have you on U40, a secret hospital area. It wasn't even running until we got here. The equipment is ancient. They were talking about what you said while you were dreaming, and they were concerned about your chip. I'm seeing what I can do to get you out of here. There's a lot of security. You'll have to explain to me someday why Eli is such a big deal. That's why you're here. Because you were yelling for him."

"She let you kiss me, and you know who Eli is?"

"I think Sue knows how I feel about you and yes, doesn't everybody know Eli?" Anna said.

"I don't know, it was hard to remember him this morning. Kiss me again."

"No, we still must be careful. Someone could walk in the office and see us. I don't want Miss Sue to get in trouble."

The door from the outer office opened. Sue entered. Silence followed her in, along with tension and uneasy stillness.

"Anna, undo his straps, and allow him to go to the restroom, please."

Anna leaned over him to undo his strap, draped her hair in his face, and tickled his nose.

He got up and rubbed his wrists, stretched his back, and twisted each way. "You really know how to knock a guy out of shape."

"Go to the bathroom while you can." Sue pulled out a sheet of paper and checked over the stats. "You get double rations tonight, but there are still only strips. Sorry."

Alix eyed the ancient medical equipment. "This stuff looks prehistoric," he said and closed the bathroom door.

"Ms. Sue, permission to speak?" Anna whispered in the partially lit room.

"Yes?"

"What's going on?"

"I'm not at liberty to discuss," Susan replied coldly. She wiped her eyes as she thought about her response to the message. Being brave wasn't always being smart, and smart wasn't always right in their M.A.I.A. driven world. She watched Anna's shoulders deflate. "Anna."

"Yes, Miss Sue."

"Everything that I taught you, you will need to put to use. There are real battles in life. Some of the battles are in war, some of them battles of the heart. No matter what the battle is, you must promise me you will remember everything I taught you and be brave. Promise me you will be brave."

"Yes, I will be brave," Anna said. Her eyes scanned the room for anything that could be used as a weapon.

#

Captain Milligan rubbed his eyes and read the response from Sue one more time:

Susan Maynard U40:

I understand Readers don't always read everything, and what they translate to us must not be the full truth. Yet, I still must follow orders. Their decisions and wishes mirror my actions, their rules are my guidelines. What happens beyond my control is just that, beyond my control. A door left ajar is not fully my fault if done by accident or ignorance. People say timing is everything. I live for but one thing, M.A.I.A.

Captain Milligan smiled at her response. Sue blended her it within text of allegiance, which was certain to confuse M.A.I.A.'s processing of the message. She knew the consequences, and she responded in safe manner. Praising M.A.I.A. in electronic response helped to camouflage their true intent—for now.

At the very least, it would buy them some time. Computers were good at responding to clear, decipherable language and actions. However, they lack the human ability to decipher human nuances of intent. They could only speculate to what they have been programmed to understand.

He left the office and headed toward his quarters and longed for a large cup of water. Strips all day just didn't wet your throat, and Captain Milligan felt like he'd swallowed a roll of sandpaper.

He checked the barracks, a light flickering in the hallway as Captain Milligan checked each way. The simulation room blinked. He edged down the hall; the flashing lights of an occupied simulation room brushed his face.

"Who would ..." Captain Milligan checked his EED. Lights-out was half an hour ago.

He leaned his shoulder in the door frame. Wes was laying back in one of the recliners. Captain Milligan watched the small jolts and jitters of Wes's body under the influence of simulation, each bullet, each movement as if it really happened to the body. His helmet flickered, and the lights on the end of his sensors flashed. Captain Milligan entered the room on his heels and lowered his head into his palm. He rubbed his eyes and sat next to Wes in the simulator.

In the digital the world the simulator created, Wes crawled through wet grass as it engulfed his body. The sun beat down on his forty pounds of military gear, and tall conifers surrounded the hill they climbed. He stopped and held his fist up. Green war paint caked his face; his eyelids completely blackened. He waved the men on. They crept further up the hill on their bellies. He'd lost his head in the last simulation, a sniper some five hundred yards away.

Wes stopped his men and peered through the tall, sharp-edged grass through electronic binoculars. He panned the land below. Several Citizens patrolled the encampment between the bank of the river and the thick woods of tall pines. Wes switched his binoculars to infrared and scanned the tents. Ten red figures glowed from each tent. A tank loomed behind the tents. He signaled for the spotter.

Wes checked his EED and pointed to the tank. He signaled for the spotter to call in an air strike for 15:02 hours. He turned to his squad and strategized in his head the location of his sniper, and the attack on the encampment. They had to focus as one. Each man was a limb, an organ, a function of the team body.

Wes visualized attacks and approaches, and calculated which would deliver the best success rates. He hadn't lost a game of chess since he was six.

When he turned around, he saw the toe of a black boot was at his nose. Wes followed the leg up to a glowing, red beard and an old, southern grin.

"Captain?"

"Why are you in a simulation after lights out?"

Wes's digital spotter craned his head up from the binoculars and angled his eyebrows. His expression remained cemented in the black streaks across his face, but his programming couldn't figure out the reason Captain Milligan stood without care of the enemy.

Captain Milligan looked down at the spotter and kicked him lightly. "What are you looking at?" He pointed to the bottom of the hill. "Get back to work, soldier."

Wes pushed himself up to his knees. His computer squad studied him, trying to read him. He pointed down the hill. "Proceed reconnaissance until my mark. Hold the air strike."

The digital spotter nodded.

Wes looked to Captain Milligan. "Sir, I apologize. I ... I mean, we already passed this one as a team. I wanted to get it perfect this time."

"Trying to get it perfect, huh? That's funny, you keep trying to get a mission perfect, and you'll spend your whole life on this one simulation. This simulation doesn't even matter. It's just practice."

"Last time I got sniped, though. Alix got him once he gave his position up, but that didn't help me. Hayden still had to call for medical evac. I hate having the medics come out on account of me, sir."

Captain Milligan crossed his arms. "Right now, Wes, you're sitting in an egg-shaped room next to me with a VR helmet on your head. There is no such thing as practice for the real thing. You say, last time you got sniped. In real life, there's no saying last time, because once you get a hole in your head, you're too dead to say last time, or next time, or even this time."

Wes squinted in the sunlight. "Then why do we do it? Simulation, I mean."

"Well," Captain Milligan knelt and plucked a sharp blade of grass and popped it in his mouth. "So, you can at least believe you're ready for the real thing. So, you don't freak out, after the first man you kill or see dead. We used to call it shell shock or PTSD, post-traumatic stress disorder. Basically, the stuff people saw and experienced broke them and they were never the same. It ruined lives. We are trying to reduce that."

Wes crinkled one side of his nose.

The captain continued, "These simulations are nothing but video games that are supposed to desensitize you. That way, you feel like you've been there before."

"Oh." Wes squinted in the sunlight.

"Don't get me wrong, Wes. They are good. Statistically proven to be effective by M.A.I.A." Captain Milligan looked up at the sun and his embedded screen. "I hate when they are off. The sun and the time, I mean. I know this is a simulation and all, but I used to be able to tell you what time it was from the tilt of the sun. I got that from my father. Working the farm, he'd tell you a minute before Mama rang the dinner bell by looking and holding his fingers to the horizon."

"I wouldn't know the difference. I've never had the real sun above my head." Wes checked the encampment through his binoculars and wondered why Captain Milligan hadn't gotten his head blown off yet, standing there chatting. He peered away from his binoculars. "So, if this is a joke to you, why do you have that ancient thing you call a pistol on your belt?"

Captain Milligan checked his revolver. "It's my father's." He drew his pistol, swung it on his finger, and whipped it back into his side holster. "I thought it'd mean a lot to him."

The captain looked down at Wes and followed his sight. "Wes?"

"Yes, sir."

"If I told you I needed you within a moment's time to act possibly against your own judgment and intuition, and against policy, would you be there, ready to go?"

Wes squinted toward the sun and looked back down the hill from which he had just scaled on his belly. "Is that an order or a question, sir?

"Question."

"You mean, I get to decide?"

"Yes. It's a big decision."

Wes squinted harder as he looked up at Captain Milligan. "Yes, sir. Locked and loaded."

"You think you could get the rest of the squad ready if it involved getting Alix out of trouble?"

Wes's face turned strict. "What kind of trouble is Alix in?"

"Do you?" Captain Milligan stared down at him.

Wes ripped some grass out from between his legs. "Yes, sir."

"Good." Captain Milligan looked down at the patrolling men from the top of the hill. He sighed. "That's very good." He scanned the encampment. "Um, Wes."

"Yes, Captain."

"You shouldn't have canceled that air strike."

"Why?"

"You know that tank?"

"Yeah."

A thunderous rush of sound exploded from the barrel of the tank, but by the time it got to where they perched, red, yellow, and orange flowered in front of them. Their bodies separated and flew in the air.

Wes ripped off his virtual head gear, and sat back in the egg-shaped room. He looked over at Captain Milligan.

The captain pulled his helmet off. Static glistened across his hair in the dark when the helmet lifted. He looked over at Wes. "I'm going to need you soon."

"Captain?" Wes leaned into Captain Milligan and spoke barely above a whisper. "Who's Eli?"

Captain Milligan looked away. With the coordinated tearing sound of Velcro as he ripped a sensor band off his arm, he leaned into Wes and spoke in a soft voice "Don't say his name. Get to your bunk. Standby."

Rankin checked over his shoulder of his dark blue suit. He rolled past the arrow leading down the hallway. He pointed the silver bullet controller into the fingerprint scanner, and the red light turned green. The door swished open.

Dim lights lined the hallway down to the security elevator. Rankin checked his EED, 04:36:03. One hour until he would power-up M.A.I.A., and then she would come to life. Programmers would continue programming and surgically implanting chips into newborns from genetically matched mates. The military would continue simulations and training for the Conservation in the weeks to follow. The manufacturers would manufacture weapons, materials for vehicles, clothes, utensils, and computer elements. Everything would continue as normal.

People, their voices, the scraping of their boots on the floor, would fill every hallway from the watchtowers on ground level to the nurse watching over Alix on U40, all moving in the same direction for a common cause, like ants, to be that much closer to the Conservation of the mainland and the birth of a new nation. It would be amazing to start taking ground back.

Rankin would wait for the other Readers back in the main hall on U21, and then he would use his thumb to open the doors, not his silver bullet remote, which bypassed the logbook in M.A.I.A. His plan was emerging. He slowed his T Port to contain his glee over his pending success, and maintained the necessary discipline needed to scrutinize his every move to perfection.

The other Readers' lack of faith in themselves and too much trust and reliance on M.A.I.A. forced him to take such drastic steps. No matter how hard humans tried, they always needed an overseer. As far as Rankin was concerned, human history required maintenance.

History proved that humans created gods, laws, or created M.A.I.A., a quantum supercomputer artificial intelligence, to control the people. Humans still needed an overseer. He was happy to oblige. If they wanted to embrace the good and blame the bad on the higher power, he was happy to be that higher power. In Rankin's generation, they blamed life's problems on the economy, global warming, or the government and laws, all things that they, humans, had created. In early history, natural disasters and floods used to be because the gods were angry. He was happy to let them believe he was the god they made angry.

Rankin shined his silver bullet remote into the finger pad at the elevator. He watched the top of the doors as they slid apart, and he rolled in and stopped directly underneath a fitting spotlight. It was his time to shine. All those years of being a mule for coffee and insignificant errands meant for a dullard was now behind him. He would show them true power and intellect.

The small light attached to the transportation device flickered on. He pressed the bottom button 'M.A.I.A.' The elevator screeched. The elevator went down, down down past U40 where Alix waited for the inevitable Vanishing Sequence.

The elevator stopped, Rankin's ears popping, and he followed the lights down the hall. He shined the red laser from his remote into two more scanners before he stepped into the metallic room. Bolts the size of Rankin's fists lined the panels up and around the ceilings, the smell of tarnished tin filling the room. Holes bigger than Rankin's head led thick wires in and out of the room, surrounded by three feet of concrete deep within the island. This virtually indestructible, single-entry room held M.A.I.A., the world's most powerful quantum supercomputer.

M.A.I.A. ran on its own unreachable, untraceable frequency and its own nuclear generator. The artificial intelligence could run for twenty years with no power and could coordinate a nation the size of the former United States politically, militarily, economically, and culturally without reprogramming or maintenance.

Rankin's eyes probed the machine: the two, tall, bulky electronic towers connected by an entanglement of hundreds of fiber-optical wires. The beeping, flickering, and alternating lights from M.A.I.A. sparkled in Rankin's pupils. "To think, you could control all the traffic lights in a country for the most statistically efficient travel time for everyone, and that was only one trillionth of the recommended usage. Imagine what we could have done with you."

Rankin approached the console in the corner of the room and shined his light into the system. A white, outlined monitor beamed up, and light overfilled the room. The computer automatically logged into a guest account. Rankin highlighted the page to see his name and hit "Enter."

Three blinking, blue buttons appeared: 'Law,' 'Living,' and 'Learning.' Under the buttons, a field with 'Search' blinked. Rankin pressed 'Law.' A blue spreadsheet flowed over the screen, holding billions of governmental commands, controls, and inquiries. He could enter anything; a proposition for a new law, a deletion of an old one, and the system gave a probability of the enhancement to the community from that law. He could enter the full circumstance of a criminal defendant and upload video M.A.I.A. tracked at the time of the crime as evidence. The AI would scan the scene for DNA and give back a statistic on the chances that it was that criminal who had committed the crime. Having that much power at his fingertips intoxicated him.

Rankin clicked to the bottom of the scroll pad and at the end, put his silver bullet control to the computer screen. The outline of the screen switched to red. Miles of binary code filled the page and scrolled down and down in different patterns of zeros and ones. A box appeared on top of the binary code. Rankin typed the Implementing Sequence, the same sequence he had put in the night before the Tribunal Reading for Private Eli. He entered the scenario he'd built. Fake footage implanted into

M.A.I.A., Alix's DNA, and chip information he'd extracted through Alix's EED allowed him to recreate footage of Alix on tape doing anything Rankin wanted him to. When M.A.I.A. found this data, it would make the best decision.

When a problem occurred and M.A.I.A. read the situation and analyzed it, the outcome was based on the larger part of the statistic, or the larger part of society, a decision referred to in the past as being for the greater good. To inconvenience a minority within society statistically made sense to M.A.I.A., no matter the margin of error. Digital Darwinism. Rankin couldn't control the outcome and statistical analysis. What he could control was the data and information from which it pulled from. The other Readers couldn't see the greater good. Albert Einstein had said, "Intellectuals can solve problems; a genius can prevent them." That's what the genius Albert Rankin intended, to prevent future problems.

When Rankin looked at these kids, these out-of-control segments of this naïve generation, it made him sick to his stomach. These children, given the chance, would strip him of his position, blow up M.A.I.A., and, with their lack of intelligence, be consumed by the lifestyle growing outside the limits of this island. Their minds were too weak, too two-dimensional to work in a society as advanced and sophisticated as one created by M.A.I.A.

Rankin wanted M.A.I.A. to catch the ones who started leaning backwards in the direction of their ancestors, who rejected what they knew and wondered something else, who dared to be philosophers while trying to be human. What good were humans if their minds were going to be wasted on menial processes and rejected facts that were given to them? The mind, after all, was what set them apart from all species—not wings, not claws, nor teeth. Their brains were the natural defense of Homo sapiens.

Rankin remembered the rest of his own generation before all this predicted violence happened. They watched television, reality TV that injected sexual exploitation into the youth through seductive music videos, shows that glorified teen mothers, and they played on cellular phones for hours on end, tracked celebrity lives so they could live vicariously through them, and played video games, and sports. All of it was a waste of time, a waste of brain power that could have been going toward something larger, something greater, something more advanced.

Rankin hit 'Enter.' Files to open the door into Alix's mind uploaded to Alix's folder: files to find out what made him tick, files to compile what he thought, files that showed what he'd been doing, and, most importantly, why Alix knew about Eli.

13

"Sir, you said individual simulations today. Which would you have me do?"

Captain Milligan chewed the end of his pen and glared at the monitor above Phil's head, and hated it every second it hung there, hated it for every potential word it recorded.

"For the morning, do hand-to-hand combat 530. I think that's ... ah ... let me see ..." Captain Milligan pressed his screen spread out on his desk and dragged his finger across it, dabbing it. "That's simulation 1397: eat with the crew and do machine gunnery level-5. What gun do you prefer using to fight in close quarters?"

Phil smiled. "How close?"

"Close," Captain Milligan smiled back, "Like hallways close. Say you were raiding a building or trying to get out of one."

Phil shrugged his bulky shoulders. "Probably the HK MG 43."

"Why?"

"Classy, light, and still kicks some ass. Don't care if it's ancient ... don't need an accurate gun to send bullets straight down a hallway. The newer weapons don't punch you in the armpit for squeezing their triggers. If it's not kicking back, it's not powerful enough to kick them back. You know what I mean, Captain?"

Captain Milligan smiled. "Sure do. They don't make them like they used to. Accuracy and sound suppression is no substitute for a good old-fashioned hole in the chest." His slapped his desk "All right, level-5 simulation this afternoon with the HK MG 43. After that, we're going to do a group simulation, something new I've been working on."

"Yes, sir."

"Don't forget to consider the weight of that thing, though, and you'll need two sidearms, a pistol and a submachine gun."

"Yes, sir."

"And send in Adam when you see him."

#

"Just let me see him, Dr. Harrison. It's the least you could do." Captain Milligan's voice floated into Eli's room from the shadows.

Dr. Harrison looked to both sides, and his eyes softened, widened, and brightened to the color of his lab coat. "It's protocol. I can't. You know I can't risk it, Rob."

"To hell with your protocol at this point, you know this is wrong. There is nothing stopping you from opening that door." Captain Milligan pointed toward the door. He saw the reclined upper body of a young man through the horizontal glass window. "I want to see him. I've worked with him for several years now, and I feel somewhat responsible for what happened."

Dr. Harrison swallowed a water strip. "I'd have to report you, regardless of our friendship."

"Then report me." Captain Milligan pushed by Dr. Harrison and punched open the double, swinging doors.

The doors flew back and pushed Dr. Harrison backwards. "Rob!"

Two mirrored windows filled two of the room's eight walls. A light blue glow circled the octagon at the bottom of each wall. Above Captain Milligan's head hung thick and thin wires of every color. A predominant, blue one led from the glass window onto the ceiling, ending above a chair. The blue wire went behind the headrest, and into the back of Eli's head.

Eli lay in the chair. His eyes stared empty into the nest of wires above him. A white cloth covered his body.

Captain Milligan walked to the center of the octagon and put his hand atop his head.

Dr. Harrison appeared by his side. "Life's not the same anymore, Rob. We had this discussion before. We need to accept it. Darwin's theory is working against you right now. I'm afraid the fittest will survive. In the human world, intelligence is strength. M.A.I.A. is the smartest it gets." He turned away and walked back to the doors.

Captain Milligan stared into Eli's eyes, a soulless jar.

"For God's sake, he's like a carved pumpkin. Just pop off the top and stick a new candle in it. I used to fight for a country, Harry, a country that had balls ... and heart." A tear accumulated in the corner of Robert Milligan's eye. His face twisted in emotion. A tear drifted down his cheek and into his orange beard. "This country used to stand for something. Stuck up for what was right, not what was logical."

Dr. Harrison's hand perched on Captain Milligan's shoulder. "Rob, we should go before..."

Captain Milligan slapped his hand away. "Don't touch me! We didn't have M.A.I.A. when our patriots fought for our freedom in the Revolution, when we build our nation, or any other point when we thrived. We had people and our minds. M.A.I.A. came in during the collapse. Tell me why she's so imperative?"

Dr. Harrison looked through the glass and saw the reflection of himself in his lab coat. "The day M.A.I.A. powered on, it answered every question the most advanced physicist had, proved the big bang theory, gave us a peak beyond our universe, and discovered how it was even possible. It destroyed creationism. It figured out how to power cities with..."

"I know what it did, Harry. It royally messed everything up is what it did." Captain Milligan put his hand over Eli's head.

"Don't touch him," Dr. Harrison held out an arm, "you could ... never mind."

Captain Milligan held up his hand. "Okay, Harry. Relax. I'm done." He looked Eli in the eyes one last time and wiped the river from his eye to his beard. He turned to Dr. Harrison. "What's the plan for this boy? That's what he is Harry, a young man."

Dr. Harrison sighed. "I don't know. Reader Rankin has his order on hold. He was supposed to be a cook."

Captain Milligan crossed his arms and shook his head. "He was an incredible soldier."

"I'm sure he was, Rob."

"A chef ..."

"From soldier to chef because he was curious about what he'd never seen. Once upon a time, curiosity was an encouraged trait. Now it now gets your mind erased."

Eli's chest barely took air.

"Ah, look, Rob. I'm really sorry, but I will have to write you up. It's not that I want to..."

"I know, Harry."

"You haven't called me Harry for years." Dr. Harrison licked his dry lips.

"I know."

"We were good friends back then."

"You remember Virginia?" Captain Milligan smiled.

"To be honest, I am grateful that I have a mind to remember." Dr. Harrison looked down. "I wonder what it looks like now."

"Undoubtedly, a smoking wasteland. I'm sure the Citiz chewed up whatever was left after the bomb."

"You think? Sometimes I wonder how bad people really are up there."

"Sickness and hunger will make people do some messed up things, Harry."

"I'm sorry we don't get to really talk out there much."

"We're protected..."

Captain Milligan interrupted. "Even though we don't have chips, I have no doubt they would pop one in us just to make a point. Look at him." Captain Milligan motioned toward Eli.

"Yeah, but the laws..."

"Laws change overnight. Nothing is concrete, except this damn bunker." Captain Milligan's words echoed and then faded into the silence.

"Rob, we should probably go." Dr. Harrison headed towards the doors.

"Any word on Alix?"

Dr. Harrison's eyes widened. "Alix? Another one of your guys?"

"Yeah..."

"I'm sorry to hear about Alix, but I don't know anything."

"Harry, I need to call in that favor you owe me."

"That was years ago, Rob. I thought that was water under the bridge."

Captain smirked. "I still have feelings, painful feelings about you and my wife. When I do, that pain floods me and washes out the bridge. I think I'm finally ready to rebuild that bridge. Are you?"

"I thought it was rebuilt years ago when she dumped me. Remember, you laughed and bought me a drink."

"Hey, I tried to warn you she was using you to punish me. I was right then and I am right about what I need to do now. I need a favor."

"Oh... so your visit wasn't about Eli."

"It was. Seeing Eli gave me courage and conviction. If you can do this one favor for me and hold off submitting that report on me for like, say, fourteen hours, or so?"

"Hold the report? Why?" Dr. Harrison looked into Captain Robert Milligan's eyes. "Oh, my God. You're leaving, aren't you? You came here to see if Eli was salvageable, so you can take him with you. Oh, my God..."

Captain Milligan poked him in the chest. "You're an atheist. You don't believe in God."

"But Rob, you can't. Nobody's been out there ..."

"Consider us even now." Captain Milligan's hand gripped Harry's shoulder for a moment, released it, and then headed towards the swinging doors.

"Wait! Here, I'll say you took it in the report." Dr. Harrison held out his keycard.

Captain Milligan looked at it. "You sure?"

"Yeah. It'll get access to wherever you need. Mostly."

Captain Milligan turned away. "Harry, you're a good friend. And your little computer might have proved the big bang theory, but it could never destroy hope."

14

A gentle touch drifted over the tiny hairs on Alix's shoulder. The small spider rappelled from the ceiling, crawled up his neck and onto his forehead. Alix opened his eyes. He jerked at the straps to swat away the bug, but the strap caught his arm. He shook frantically in bed. The spider vanished.

"Argh!" Alix pulled harder on the strap until he felt the corner of the leather bindings cut into his wrists. "Let me out of here!"

Alix jerked up on the leg restraints. "Let me go!"

He forced his wrists up in a bench-press motion, keeping the chains tight. "Dammit!" Alix gasped, trying to wipe the sweat from his forehead and out of his eyes, but the chains straightened.

He pounded the bed and slammed his head back into the pillow. He stared at the monitor. In the bottom of the right-hand corner of the screen blinked the message: *Reading in progress.*

A sinking feeling confirmed his next thought: he didn't know what the reading was about, but somehow knew it had to do with him.

A shadow swept across the grid-glass window in the door. Alix's head snapped to the side.

Susan looked away from the window, her stomach a pit of guilt. "Susan."

"Holy shit!" Sue's heart slapped the ceiling. "Al, you scared me."

"My T-Port whines as I move. How did you not hear me? Never mind that, I don't have a lot of time. Where's Anna?"

Sue pointed to the side office where two beds lined each side of the room. "She's sleeping. Alix was, too."

"I don't care about Alix. I'm going to meet with the M.A.I.A. Readers and convince them-to perform the Vanishing Sequence on that little bastard. Do you know what our daughter has been doing?"

"Huh?" Susan's face twisted.

"She's been seeing Alix."

"What? How? The boys and girls are kept separate..." Sue's face contorted. She tried to camouflage her knowledge about the simulation rendezvous.

"How could you not have known she was sneaking out?"

"I would have thought M.A.I.A. would have alerted us if she left the floor," Sue blurted.

A vein grew from Rankin's eyebrow and up his forehead. "They've been sneaking around at night and meeting in simulation. I am going to put a stop to this. M.A.I.A. is going to watch every moment of every person's life and get a full thought report on everyone. If they don't have a chip, they are getting one implemented!" Rankin slapped the wall.

Susan stepped back. "You can do that?"

Al looked around. "I'm going to put a monitor in every corner, every nook and cranny of this facility."

"Al, come on, how can you be sure they were meeting in simulation?"

"I saw it with my own eyes! She's had..." Rankin looked over his shoulder. "Sex, Sue! Your daughter has been doing wretched things with that little bastard!"

"Al, they weren't really having real sex. If it's simul—"

"She's my little girl!" The air around them froze, and Rankin pointed toward Alix's door. "And that little shit in there is going to be my personal ass wiper when he is reprogrammed. That will be his job. To wipe my ass!"

Sue stared at Albert and looked at the office. "For God's sake, lower your voice. If Anna finds out she is our daughter, and what we did to her chip... we don't know what M.A.I.A. will do. Help me, Al, if..."

Albert's backhand thrashed Sue's face. "Watch your tongue. I'll have you washing dishes tomorrow. I run this place. No one talks to me that way. I've done everything for you! I took you under my wing when you were less than her age!"

"You took me to your bed, and I was *a lot* younger than our daughter is now. You forced me to have sex with you. If he's a bastard, what does that make you? At least she loves him."

He rolled his T-Port up to her and raised his hand.

"Hit me again, and you'll regret it. You're not the only Reader."

"You're lucky I need you to keep an eye on that animal," Rankin snarled. His wheels whining as he sped away into the dim hallway.

#

The light above Captain Milligan's desk dimmed from a power surge. "So, be ready for even a moment's notice to move. I mean it—gear and everything. This is for our division and our division only. You understand? Special orders from above. We're going in first, but no one is to hear about it."

"Yes, sir," Adam saluted.

"All right. You're dismissed, Adam."

Captain Milligan rubbed his eyes and tapped his desk screen. He scanned the map of the island. Had nature taken its course and rid its rocky rim of the asphalt that lined the circumference of the old Governors Island? There was a barge, but he wasn't sure if it was accessible by Jeep. All of that information was kept under tight security until M.A.I.A. and the Readers determined it was time to deploy soldiers for Conservation.

His mind raced to find usable details about the outside world. He remembered that ferries parked alongside the docks reserved for Conservation. He had seen them pulled up near the main door on the monitor once. Should they even chance taking a raft from the far west bank around the island to the mainland? Negative. By the time the team got out, the Readers would be informed, and, at the least, Rankin would give the order to kill or capture.

Captain Milligan ran his hand over his head. He rubbed the back of his neck and searched the ceiling for the reason he'd put himself in this predicament. Walking out of military academy the day of graduation, he'd never thought his career would end in treason.

Captain Milligan checked his monitor. *M.A.I.A. Reading Commenced* blinked in the bottom right-hand corner. They'd already started deciding Alix's fate. First the Readers decide, and then Captain Milligan would have a few hours to execute his plan. The upload to M.A.I.A. would occur at midnight, and tomorrow, no one in his generation would know who Alix was.

He looked over the map. If they still existed, two ports would stand a chance at having a ferry large enough with enough fuel to get the trucks, gear, and all of them east over the Hudson River. Pier 101 looked best. Captain Milligan measured it out. It would be the longest 1,500-foot traverse he'd ever taken. One missile and it would all end. An army would chase them and only God knows what waited for them at the other end. If they got across the Hudson River, they might at least escape M.A.I.A. temporarily. Captain Milligan opened his center drawer. His dad's revolver stared back at him, and five bullets rounded each other.

"It's a Remington 1861 Revolver," his father's words echoed, and Captain Milligan watched his father lift the sidearm straight out, holding it sideways. "You don't fire a weapon like this, Robby. This is for gangsters and thugs. This means they don't know how to wield a weapon nor how to respect it. Someone holds a gun like this to you, they probably never shot it."

His father twirled the gun on his finger and slipped it back into the holster effortlessly. The Virginia sun glimmered off the hammer. "With this gun you either want to kill a man or scare him. You have to decide quickly."

In one hint of a motion, the gun snapped out of the holster, appeared in his father's hand, and popped. By the time the first can bailed off the rock wall, a second chased it. His father's other hand pulled the hammer while the gun blasted by his hip. Two Pepsi cans scattered off the old, disheveled, rock wall, and Budweiser bottles disintegrated in seconds. His father waved the smoke away to check his aim. Spot on.

The blood rushed down Captain Milligan's body at the sight of the pistol. He stepped away, hand trembling. He shut the drawer, left the room, and walked down the hall. He was going to need a lot of help.

15

After signing in the video of Alix hitting the two medics, the Readers looked at each other from across the table. Rankin smiled, stood next to his chair, and overlooked the sleek, stretched-out oval table. He looked into the other Readers' eyes, and he felt the advantage he had over them. "As we see here gentlemen, Private Alix Basil is obviously aware of the presence of Private Eli Williams and the Vanishing Sequence that took place recently by M.A.I.A. According to paragraph six in Article Seventy-two of the *M.A.I.A. Law and Abidance Protocol*, Alix poses a threat to M.A.I.A."

Eight other M.A.I.A. Readers in black suits stared back at him.

"You know, Albert, if we keep running the Vanishing Sequence on these boys, we won't have an army to Conserve M.A.I.A." Elmer Washington's cheeks fell from his eyes in layers leading down to his double chin. His thick, bushy eyebrows hung over his eyes.

"Elmer, this boy is a threat." Rankin stared down the large man. "There is no reason why we should allow this crazy boy to wield weapons that could put M.A.I.A. and people at risk."

"So, your belief is to just erase his existence along with every other M.A.I.A. person you believe is a threat?" Elmer smirked and looked at the group. "Am I right or am I right? We can't just start a mass erasure of people's minds."

The other Readers nodded their heads in agreement.

Rankin leaned on the table. "I believe that an ignorant, out-of-control adolescent should not have a gun in his hand!"

"He's apparently not ignorant." Elmer chuckled. "If he's really intelligent enough to overlook M.A.I.A.'s decision about Eli, maybe we should move him to military intelligence."

"You're going too far, Elmer!" Rankin placed his old, scarred knuckles on the table.

"Maybe he should be up here with us, discussing what's better for M.A.I.A. if he's really that intelligent," Elmer grunted, and his cheeks shook. "We used to praise people like this boy, award them even." He sat back. "And for some reason, M.A.I.A. sees you favorably every single time, and I don't believe that to be a coincidence, no sir. I don't know what is going on, but M.A.I.A. has never issued so many Vanishing Sequences out in one year. Right, Frank?"

"Yes, Elmer. I believe it is the most we've ever done. I also recognize that Reader Rankin requested all of them." Frank lifted his head and spoke in a dry, raspy voice.

Rankin waved his arm. "Well, let's see what M.A.I.A. seems to think, shall we, gentlemen? Shall we resort to our actual form of government, the correct way of procedure?"

Rankin pushed the numeric pad next to his chair. He entered a number and waited for the other Readers to the same. They followed suit around the table, entered their passwords and key codes for confirmation, all except Elmer.

Elmer stared down at the button, paused, and then he entered his pin and pushed 'Access.'

A loud rush came from the metal room like a large release of steam, and the engines beneath hummed. M.A.I.A. searched through all its memory, all its video and audio recordings. It searched through expressed views, conversations, and facial expressions by Alix and those around him. It searched through his whole life up until that point, from the time of his military birth until that very moment in the room. It searched through his education, the questions he asked, and the ideas he'd proposed. It searched through all his recorded simulations, his actions, his hesitations, and his recorded thoughts. It searched his entire life until that point and found a video from the night before. M.A.I.A.'s deep memory zoomed in on Alix in the mirror on U40. His eyes narrowed in the reflection.

"You will be the one to bring down M.A.I.A.," Alix declared. The quantum computer flagged this information and added it to the reasoning section.

M.A.I.A. stalled for a moment and realized within the last week, two cadets had told themselves that same line, same quote, and same promise.

"You will be the one to bring down M.A.I.A." Eli Williams had said that only a week ago while curled up in a ball in a dark corner.

M.A.I.A. pulled together information that might've explained why these two boys would say the same quote and be in the same mind frame. The searches led to Albert Rankin traversing down the hallway to M.A.I.A. only one hour and twenty minutes earlier. She searched for a confirmation video and found that only an hour before Eli's Vanishing Sequence, Albert Rankin had walked down the hall, too. The computer stopped searching for Alix and Eli's connection to conspiracy and searched for the correlation between Albert Rankin and the cadets' conspiracy.

M.A.I.A. made a decision, drew up the percentages, and sent them back to the Readers.

The Readers saw the binary code first but not the verdict. Elmer held his breath as the answer came up across the screen. His mouth dropped open.

#

Sue leaned on her palms. She checked the monitor. The *Reading in Progress* indicator still blinked. She'd watched it for an hour, dozed off and debated if she was a medic or a prison guard. Every time she set eyes on Alix, the urge to fully comply with the messenger on U21 about getting Alix off this floor dug deeper. She couldn't determine if Alix would be better off with the person who messaged her. Maybe that was why she couldn't sleep and stared at Alix throughout the night. She waited for her instinct to take over her chip's reasoning to let her human judgment decide whether to free him.

She wondered what it would be like to be "free" and what that word entailed these days. Was it possible to be free from M.A.I.A.? Free from the cerebral chip or her EED? The Citiz who lived in the world above hers were free, and that kind of freedom was wrought with abject fear and destruction. Life without M.A.I.A. did exist, but at a great cost.

Susan hadn't known any other life since the day her mother had left her on that side of the barge in Manhattan. She wondered how a mother could leave her child to strangers. M.A.I.A. only took children under sixteen years old. No adults were accepted after the first bomb dropped over Washington D.C.

She was fifteen years and eleven months then. Her mother said it was safer to leave her in the hands of a military intelligence company, deep under Governors Island, than to try to survive the anarchy after the first attack. Sue remembered the chaos from the blackout, and how her father, through tears, explained that the world they lived in had fallen, because everything they knew and owned, everything they thought they had, vanished in a cyber-attack following the bombs.

"A classic example of leaving all your eggs in one basket," her father said two days before he died as he defended their home from the riots.

She remembered his face, his thick mustache, and the Louisville Slugger before the door slammed shut forever. She remembered the red and orange flames in front of their windows that night, and the smell of smoke from her neighbors' burning house. She remembered the screams, the pandemonium, and her mother's silent tears. Her mother never told Sue how the deep, bloody red color on her father's bat came from her father bashing in the skulls of two young men. She only knew about the third guy and his pistol. She heard the bang outside her house but didn't know it was the last sound her father heard until her mother dragged her out before the mob broke down the front door.

She remembered being hurled into the SUV and jolted back and forth as her mother whipped the wheel left and right. She remembered the man's face that rolled up onto the hood, the bump and thud under the tires that screeched, and how the motor roared. She remembered when their Jeep sputtered out of gas, and heard the last words on the radio, "God be with us."

She remembered tall, chain-link fences spread across the bridge in layers and checkpoints. A man in full military gear met the crowd, megaphone in hand, machine gun in the other. Armored men held riot shields edge to edge across the bridge. Machine gunfire spurt every few moments, interrupting the wail of the bomb warning sirens and horns. Susan's mother fought the crowd to the front and elbowed an older woman in the mouth to drag Sue to the front.

"Under sixteen here! Under sixteen! My daughter is under sixteen!"

The military man stiff-armed her mother and knocked the breath from her lungs. He grabbed Sue by the arm, checked her birth certificate, and slapped it to her chest.

"Hold this up," he ordered.

Sue did and a flash popped from his camera. He shoved her in the opposite direction of her mom into the crowd of crying kids and reaching arms behind the gate. Sue moved to hug her mom for the last time, but he shoved her body backwards again. She held onto her mother's gaze as long as she could, watching her mother wipe her tears and her lips scream her name and, "I love you," into frosty breaths.

Susan watched her mother's face wash away behind the wall of blurry faces.

Bloop.

Susan checked the screen. The blinking message disappeared, and she wondered about the verdict of the Reading. The door swung open behind her to the medic's bunks and Sue turned around.

Anna held her hair back and wrapped it in a hair tie, lifting her foot to a chair to tie her shoe. "Ms. Sue, have you slept yet? Why does that say 'error'?"

"What?" Sue stared down at the message. The Reading. ***Error.***

#

Error.

The word blinked across their foreheads above blank stares from the reflection of their hologram screens—a reminder that even the most sophisticated quantum computer in the world wasn't perfect. All nine men wished for M.A.I.A. to fix the problem itself. It reappeared on a new screen, displaying the percentages that Alix should be subdued to the Vanishing Sequence.

"Is this possible?" Elmer's arm flopped on the table like a role of dough.

Perspiration filled the wrinkles in Rankin's face, and his teeth bent from the pressure under his jaw.

Frank glanced at Elmer, who scanned the table. The others' screens matched his, with their painted expressions.

"What's this all about?" Frank slapped the table.

An eruption of debate ensued. Rankin stared at the screen quiet. He felt the reason for the error throb in his throat. It beat under his heart and pulsed in his ear. *Could M.A.I.A. think on its own? Did M.A.I.A. discover his manipulation of facts?*

Elmer leaned on his forearm. "What do we do now?"

Rankin cleared his throat, his voice cracking. "Maybe we should just try again tomorrow? We'd need at least 24 hours to resubmit."

"We can't leave the room until we have a decision," Elmer said. "It's protocol."

Rankin held his breath, and his clenched fist.

"We have to make a decision ourselves," Elmer squinted. He exited out of the error screen. A slight smile streaked his face. "Gentlemen, on your consoles, kindly go to the 'M.A.I.A. Override/Manual Decision' program and log in. This could take a while."

Rankin stepped off his T-Port and eased his achy body into the seat.

"M.A.I.A., bring up anything regarding the Vanishing Sequence of Alix Basil." Elmer Washington pressed his forearm into the table and wiped his upper lip.

The machine hummed. Their screens chimed, and a folder appeared. It opened and expanded into hundreds of files.

"M.A.I.A.," said Elmer, "please extract any simulation folders that have no relevance to the Vanishing Sequence being done with him."

Files shot to the right of the screen and disappeared.

Rankin gritted his teeth. *M.A.I.A., what are you up to?*

#

Anna sat at Sue's desk. Her nails tapped against the old counter as she thought of Alix. Something about him extracted her desire for life. A lump of burning evolution in her chest inflated and ignited again. His eyes dared her to live. Waiting until after Conservation and submitting a request for compatibility seemed an eternity away.

It didn't make sense to make them wait until after the Conservation of the mainland. What would happen if Alix didn't make it back? She set her chin into her palm. Alix could be taken from her. Killed. She would rather have Alix for herself than have him sacrificed for the cause of M.A.I.A. She checked over her shoulder and peered at Alix through the door's window and wondered what life above M.A.I.A. would be like with him. Anna shook her head to stop her mind from racing, and she took a deep breath.

A message indicator blinked in the corner of the screen at the main desk: *Manual Reading in Progress.*

Anna checked over her shoulder into the dark room with the two beds where Sue finally slept. She looked at the indicator. To get Alix out and be with him, she'd have to break some rules.

16

"You're insane!"

"What do you want me to do, Silva? They're going to erase the kid's mind!"

"It's not the first I've had two of my guys subject to the Vanishing Sequence. Christ, Milligan!"

Captain Milligan held up one finger. "I'm thinking you have a division of fifty men. I had eight. Together, with our military skillsets and our men, we can accomplish the impossible."

"We are both Captains. What we are talking about is treason!" Silva growled through gritted teeth.

"We've whispered it before ..."

"Yeah, we've whispered it, and I've dreamed of winning a billion dollars in my lifetime. Doesn't mean I'm going to do it."

"Aren't you tired?"

"I'm tired, but I'm not stupid. What you are talking about is suicide! We don't know what's actually out there awaiting us, and you know about what M.A.I.A. will do to hunt you down. There is no chance you will survive this."

"Shh." Captain Milligan looked over his shoulder. The lunchroom was vacant. "I'm going, Silva. It's too late. Either M.A.I.A. catches up to me and charges me with conspiracy and treason, or I'm out of here. We were born free men. Whatever we are now isn't cutting it. I'm calling in my favor, Silva. You owe me." The fight in Milligan's eyes turned red.

Captain Silva looked at his longtime friend. He knew he was right. Silva remembered meeting Milligan for the first time in the war. Milligan had walked next to the Humvee full of deceased soldiers. It was a packed military hearse with no room for the living. That was a time that the United States could never fall, never falter, was never wrong. Terrorists could never make their way here; the battle could never be brought to U.S. soil, homes, beaches, towns, and cities. Never. The U.S. was the superpower of the world, leader of a free world.

They had walked four days through rubble and passed dead bodies, burning buildings, and cars. Together, they had past people crying from sickness, hunger, pain, and wounds too grizzly to take in. Bullets popped in the distance, and they had wondered if the whole United States was like this. A simultaneous cyber-attack on all the major cities started the government breakdown and forced the military and the U.S. to scramble for makeshift communication to fight a full-frontal invasion. The nuclear explosion over the capital made it clear. Welcome to the new age.

Captain Silva remembered the silence between them as they trudged through the streets. They had come to a stop and hunkered down around the Humvee when the Amex building had come down on Broadway. They should have recognized the diversion but were too exhausted and used all of their energy to focus only on their destination. And then came the ambush on Wall Street. It was the final leg of their journey back to a military barge at Battery Park. A small enemy brigade waited for them in The Crest Building.

Captain Silva remembered the burning stings in his leg and shoulder by bullets coming from surrounding office buildings. The convoy had scattered, and Silva lay in the middle of the road for thirty-five minutes until a grenade took out the front of the building. It pushed the enemy back long enough for Milligan to charge the street, hurl another grenade to the south side, and drag Silva back to the Humvee. Milligan risked his life to save him.

That's when Captain Silva made the promise.

Captain Silva stared into Captain Milligan's eyes across the lunch table and touched the scar on his shoulder over his shirt, a fleshy reminder of his promise. "Milligan, getting off the island isn't a good idea by yourself."

"I'll have my team."

"I meant, not alone."

#

The door unlatched. Alix kept his eyes shut and hoped. He heard her breath. He lifted his head. They soaked in each other in gazes and silent conversation, a conversation heard not with ears but felt with a small flutter beneath the tissue of the heart.

Anna sat on the side of the bed and put her hand on his chained arm. She swayed her fingertips along his wrist. "It's amazing to feel your skin." She bowed her head. "Out of simulation, I mean." She moved her hand up to his and tied their fingers together. "It's almost like the first time again."

Her words kissed his soul. His thin arm hair stood on end, and his back tightened up. Alix squeezed her hand, his voice breaking into stuttering beats. "Remember the first time?"

She would never forget their first mission together. She remembered the smell of the land, the heat of the fire, the sound of destruction, the bombs in the distance lighting the sky over the smoldering buildings, the way the light burst through holes in the infrastructure like blinking eyes, the black smoke that lurked on the horizon. Neither made it to the helicopter.

Alix's arm had slung around Anna's shoulder; they watched it take off in front of them. The mission had gone wrong for Alix and Victor from the beginning.

A missile from the lurking clouds had screamed across the sky and landed around the base of the building that Alix and Victor tried to climb. Victor pushed his palms against the wall and Alix climbed up onto his shoulders, hoisted himself up, turned around, and lowered his hand to pull Victor up. Both men were up in seconds.

Victor stuck his eyes into his binoculars. "Bunker: south, west."

He turned the nozzle. The view through his yellow mask and into the binoculars turned brighter, and a rapidly fluctuated number appeared. "Forty hundred and fifty-three meters. Wind: northeast, five kilometers per hour. Switch to fifty cal. Coriolis Effect: two clicks up. Aim high. High-capacity rounds, full metals. Difficulty: damn high, Alix. Hit percentage ..." Victor checked his EED, "twelve percent."

Alix didn't look down. "Twenty-seven percent." His hands clicked in the magazine. He tossed his smaller rifle aside and set a pod next to Victor. He leaned down and commanded, "Switch to night vision. Brighten mask."

He laid down and pointed his larger rifle in the distance. He found his tiny targets so far away. Alix breathed hard, audible breaths. "Forty hundred, fifty-five meters."

"What?" Victor didn't pull his eyes away.

"Forty hundred, fifty-five meters," Alix repeated himself.

"That's not what the system is saying, Alix. Adjust scope to forty hundred, fifty-three meters. Coriolis Effect is going to affect your shot. The earth will literally rotate and change the location of the target before your bullet gets there!"

Alix looked down at his rifle. He hit three buttons on the side and looked back into the glass scope.

"Alix, what are you doing? My screen says you're projecting, forty hundred, fifty-five. I'm telling you it's forty hundred fifty-three."

"I'm taking the shot. Call out a target. Count it down." Alix aimed at the oldest man out of the three. He adjusted his scope and eyed the man's short, brimmed hat. What expression would remain on his face if Alix just took off the brim of that hat instead of his whole head?

Victor sighed. "I hate you, Alix. If we miss this shot, I'm shooting you in the leg before this simulation is over."

Alix smirked. "But if we make it, we're going home early. Chopper's waiting." Alix didn't remove his eye from the glass.

Victor's jaw stiffened. "Target: officer, arms behind his back, four thousand and ..." Victor sighed again, "fifty-five meters. Heavy wind gusts, currently 1.5 kilometers north, northwest. Counter wind ...” Victor adjusted his scope, “1.8 kilometers south, southeast. Coriolis effect .4 for vertical drift.”

Alix steadied. He kissed his shooting finger and hovered over the trigger. He breathed in and let it slow. He visualized the shot.

“Fire. Shoot.”

Alix squeezed the trigger. The air sucked out of the room and chased the bullet. Five long seconds of flight later, the bullet smacked the officer to the side and down.

“Hit, target, gunner, four thousand and fifty-five meters ...”

Alix reloaded, click-click. The shell hit the ground, ping-ping.

“Wind same, fire, shoot.”

Alix’s rifle exploded again. A missile passed his bullet from high above and rained down near their location. The whiz of the rocket perked their ears, but it was too late. The explosion took down the east side of the building.

The floor below Victor and Alix shifted, tilted, and fell. They slid down the crashing floor, tons of broken desks, appliances, TVs, computers, and shattered office glass pouring down the three-story slope after them. Alix’s back slammed against a cement support to the basement garage. His rifle hit his stomach.

Victor rolled down the splintering floor. His boots caught, and sent him flipping in midair, and he flopped on his back. The slope cracked, launching desks and most of the break room necessities of a past life into the air and down on Victor. The building crashed around them in a roar.

Alix stared through his cracked face mask. He undid the straps and pulled his mask above his head. The stale air tasted of dirty water and burnt birch. He rolled over to all fours and coughed, spat out a chunk of something he didn’t think belonged in him, and looked over to Victor, whose feet dangled out of the bottom of a refrigerator.

Alix hung his head and realized there was a shard of wood deep in his knee. He grasped it, clenching his teeth. He ripped it out and screamed louder than the fire that roared above him.

He lit a medical flare and stuck the flame into his wound. The skin fused, and the bleeding stopped, but the pain increased.

Alix leaned over on his side, screamed, and clutched his sidearm. He squeezed the gun, the pain of searing, internal nastiness floating up his leg, into his groin, showering all his internal organs. It seized his neck and attacked his brain.

"Alix!"

The voice stopped his screams and pain for a moment.

"Alix?!"

"Over here!"

Anna appeared through the smoke. "What happened?"

"A missile took out the base of our position. Victor didn't make it. I'm going to have to bust his balls when we get back about getting killed by a refrigerator. Tell him to chill out."

"You guys are ridiculous." Anna reached down and hoisted Alix up. "At least you can have a sense of humor about it."

The door to the underground garage of the building kicked open.

"Get down!" Alix tossed Anna into the fridge and onto Victor's dead legs as bullets punctured the ruble around them. "Anna, did you bring any backup?"

Alix put pressure on his wound and collapsed. He pointed the gun at the door and fired three shots. A spray of bullets pinged behind them, hit the cement beam, and smacked the fridge. Alix fired three more rounds, and two men went down near the doorway. The air died for a moment, no fire, no bombs, no wind, no trickling rubble, just dead. From the side, a sound of metal on metal rolled out. Alix turned too late. The gun pointed toward him and Alix's pistol raised. The Citizen's assault rifle flashed. There was a sputter close to Alix's head and a roaring of fire from his right.

Anna held the trigger of Victor's machine gun, and the man went down. "Just us, Alix! Let's go!"

Alix picked himself up and stumbled. "I can't walk."

"Let's go. We have to hurry." Anna threw Alix's arm over her shoulder.

As they hobbled toward the exit, Alix raised his pistol and shot Victor in the leg. "That's for doubting my shot, Victor." Alix looked to Anna. "We don't have much time. It's getting too hot up there for the chopper."

Her radio buzzed. "Thirty seconds, Anna. You're going to regret this call if you don't bring someone back."

"We're trying," Anna screeched.

"Try faster! We're taking fire!" Machine gunfire littered the background. "Sorry, you're on your own. We can't turn around! We're taking too much fire. Good luck."

Anna and Alix burst through the side door and hunched down behind a busted, shot-up car, and fell to the ground after the helicopter lifted into the air. A missile emerged from the side, and a white trail led to the explosion of red, spinning flames that was their way out. The fire lit their faces as burning fuel singed their noses, a descending chopper reflecting in their eyes. The propeller flung debris everywhere like a blooming onion.

Alix looked into her eyes. They leaned back against the rusted car, his leg bent up and elevated. Her hand on his knee, she asked, "You okay?"

"I guess this means we all fail this time, huh?" Alix smirked and looked into the burning night. His head hung alongside his esteem.

Anna's desire burned. "You didn't fail. You hit your target." She couldn't take it anymore—the way they looked at each other, the way they talked. Anna grabbed his chin and pressed her lips into his.

His body melted. He couldn't feel his injuries. He wrapped his arm around the back of her neck, and he leaned on top of her. His tongue drove into her mouth and danced with hers. He hoisted himself up, and her legs went to either side of him. They meshed into each other as glass cracked and crushed under them.

They paused and froze, mouths still connected and eyes wide open. Four Citizens aimed guns down at them.

Anna and Alix eyed each other, and Alix raised his arms, a true 'hands above the sheets moment.'

Anna reached down for Alix's pistol as she lifted her other hand slowly.

They spun. Alix scrambled for Victor's machine gun. Anna tossed her arm over Alix's shoulder and fired next to his ear. A Citizen fell backwards. Alix squeezed the trigger. The gun spurted, and another Citizen flew back into the car and slid back down over the hood. The bullets rained down on them from where they couldn't tell as pelt after pelt of bullets tore their virtual sessions to shreds, and their screens glitched out.

Anna touched the side of Alix's face after they reminisced about the first kiss. "That wasn't that long ago, but that simulation feels like an eternity ago. It was always little, flirty gestures before that day, but after that..." Anna crinkled her nose, "It was game on every time we met."

Alix smiled. "We could have gotten caught so many times once we started sneaking out and using the simulators."

Anna smiled, putting her hand on his stomach. "We said it would have been worth it."

He moaned. "Remember the first time with just us? We planned which night and snuck in for the first time. I thought we were busted."

Anna smiled bigger. "Yeah..." She looked around the room. "I imagined after being caught, it would be a lot worse than this. At least, so far."

"Yeah." Alix looked around. "You're not chained to a bed though. This is pretty bad. It should really be you chained to the bed."

"I haven't had my first real time yet. Don't let me down." Anna's hand slid down his gown and rubbed his erection.

A door slammed outside the room.

"Got to go. Love you." Anna kissed him on the cheek and disappeared.

17

"Soldiers, I put a special simulation together for you guys." Captain paced back and forth in the egg-shaped, white room.

Squad Twenty-Eight, minus Eli and Alix, stood in front of a simulator bed and held their helmets, chins up. Hayden clenched his jaw whilst Wes's chest expanded, his eyes a dead stare.

"I have a vision." Captain put his hands behind his back. "It's you boys on the mainland, first. It's your whole team together once again on the battlefield."

Phil flexed his shoulders and cracked his neck.

"I'm going to be standing next to you boys in the front of the fight." Captain looked in each set of eyes for the fire. "No one has ever been where we are going. No one has ever fought the enemy that stands in our way, even in simulation. So, boys, get into your simulation. I'll see you there."

Everyone climbed into the simulators and put on their helmets. They strapped on the sensors and laid back. They dropped their shields on their helmets and watched the world go colorful.

Right before they entered simulation mode, and their senses forfeited to the artificial metaverse, Captain Milligan's words echoed, "And boys ... enjoy your last simulation!"

Their consciousness switched to virtual reality.

Matt moved his fingers. He opened his eyes and wiped them. He looked up and around. He still sat in the egg shape room. "What's going on here?"

Phil pulled off his simulator helmet. "Captain, why are we still in the simulation room?"

"We're in simulation, dipshit." Hayden stretched his arms.

"Are we?" Adam checked around.

Wes blinked. "Why would Captain make a simulation simulating the simulator?"

Phil's eyebrows narrowed. He looked to Wes. "Does that even make sense?"

"We ought to hear Captain out. Captain? Why are we here?" Wes said calmly.

"Do you know who Alix is?" Captain stared.

"Yes." Victor's eyes narrowed.

"Well, by tomorrow morning, you might not," Captain promised each pair of eyes.

"Captain, what do you mean?" Hayden crossed his arms.

"You are part of a generation of programmed chips that have the ability to be wirelessly controlled by M.A.I.A."

"Captain, with all due respect, sir," Wes straightened, "we are aware of our EEDs and our connection to M.A.I.A."

"You don't know the extent of these machines."

"What do you mean, the *extent*?" Matt raised his voice.

"Do you know who Eli is?"

Phil cleared his throat. "You've asked this before like we should know the guy. Was it someone in the brigade?"

Captain pulled the photograph from his shirt pocket and glided the photo past their faces. "Do you remember taking this photo?"

Phil stared at the picture of everyone: Matt, Wes, Alix, Hayden, Adam, Victor, and Phil all held guns up in front of a Humvee. A smaller guy knelt down in front of them, a small mole above his lip, dark hair, a complete stranger.

Phil thought hard. He remembered that day, seeing the real equipment, being out of the classes, and stepping into real physical, military work, no more pounding the books, and watching videos of flanking strategies, assault, and guerrilla warfare, and studying his opponent. He remembered posing for the picture.

Phil tried to remember that guy. There was no one there. He pictured and pictured him. "That's a fancy trick. I'll bet my life that guy was never there that day."

Captain grabbed Phil by the jaw. "That is no trick!" His lips launched fierce spurts of saliva, his eyes lighting up as bright as his beard. "This guy was one of you. That soldier is someone you will never see again. He was a great soldier who grew up with you! He fought with you — next to you!" Captain released Phil with a shove, a red imprint remaining on Phil's throat.

"This guy would have died for any of you on the battlefield, and you don't even know his name, because of a God-forsaken technology!" Captain Milligan's chest heaved with emotion. "This is about to happen again to you guys."

"To Alix?"

"Yes, to Alix. I don't know why or how they do it, but Eli is no more as of yesterday. Alix will be gone by tomorrow and you won't be able to remember him. You'll see this picture," he held it up, "and you'll wonder who they both are."

"How do you and Alix remember who he is?" Wes looked down.

"I don't have a chip. Alix's chip doesn't sync the same way. M.A.I.A. can't control him."

"What?" Victor's arms flared sideways.

"Alix doesn't have the same chip as you. He can decipher actual and programmed thoughts. He knows who Eli is and remembers him well. That's why he's where he is right now. They're trying to figure out what I already know. That's why we have to move. When we get out of this simulation," his eyebrows raised, "you will have a choice, a true choice. Your real equipment will be here, your weapons, your gear, everything you need to get away from all this mess. I'm only here to invite you. I'm *not* giving programmed minds a command. I'm giving free-thinking men a decision to make. Now, you have to make it."

Captain Milligan threw a thin black plate on the ground. A blue upside-down pyramid appeared, and on the bottom face, Captain Milligan outlined the screen.

The boys hovered around it.

The captain spoke, "Our objective is to get to the lowest level of M.A.I.A. We will be geared up, so M.A.I.A. won't take long to figure out we're in attack gear and send a team to stop us. I've bought us some time."

"Captain?" Wes's shoulders dropped. "When you say M.A.I.A. will send a team..."

"I realize how hard this will be. The men M.A.I.A. send could be your comrades."

"You expect us to shoot our own team!" Victor stepped away from the demo.

"I bought us some time, but hell will break loose, and you'll have to decide if you're with the team that is getting off this island, or staying with M.A.I.A." Captain paused to check their eyes. "At precisely the moment we get out of simulation, a report is going to be filed, and a mock video feed is going to be submitted into M.A.I.A. It is a video of me bursting into the room where Eli is being held and stealing a key card from one of the doctors. I already have the key card. That fake video will send units up there, while we run like hell to the elevators down to bottom.

"After getting down the elevator, we won't have access down there, and my guess is we are going to have to neutralize the guard." Captain spun the hologram, and the small figure fell. "Men in black suits are practically drones, okay. They are more machine than human, and have direct connections to M.A.I.A. They are not one of us. They will kill you. Do not hesitate to fire on them.

"I have a connection to an open door down there, and we'll have access into the medical suite. If, for some reason, that door isn't open, Matt, you'll have about two minutes to blow that door open. Alix is being held here." Captain spun the hologram blueprint and marked the location. "Adam, Victor, and Hayden, cover the elevators and stairs while Wes, Phil, and I get Alix. Make sure we bring his gear.

"From here, we'll take the elevator to the second-to-last floor." The hologram followed the men in the elevator up. "We'll probably be taking fire the moment that door opens, so we are going to let Bravo out and take the stairs to the top floor. We'll have two breaking points. Here and here where the elevator opens. We need Alpha to stand by for cover fire and to take out the snipers and machine gunners in the towers. We should have four Humvees waiting here for us full of equipment.

Our exit strategy depends on your covering capability, but odds are, we are going to exit here via Humvee and take the main road, assuming it's in one piece, to the barge. There's a 75 percent chance of having this older ferry boat waiting for us. By then, the good news is, we'll be under the cover of night from any fire from the mainland. Citizens won't know we're coming and from our information, don't have effective night vision capabilities. If all goes according to plan, we'll be on the mainland in a matter of hours."

Silence filled the room.

"You're joking, right?" Victor shook his head. "You're ordering us to launch a massive rescue mission, evacuation, sabotage, and treason against our very own military, *and* evade a massive attack on the mainland against possibly half a million Citizens. From a raft?"

"No."

"What do you mean, *no*. That's exactly what you just described?" Victor yelled.

Captain shrugged. "There should be another four of us from Squad Forty-One."

"What's the percentage of all of us getting out intact?" Victor's eyes narrowed.

Captain's heart fell. "Do you think I ran this percentage through M.A.I.A.?"

"You made this simulation, didn't you? We are supposed to decide our fate without knowing at least a percentage of our possibility of success, or even survival?"

Milligan expected Victor to challenge him. He could only hope that the others didn't have the same concern.

Everyone eyed Victor. Milligan surmised their minds still swirled around a mission without M.A.I.A.'s approval, percentage of survival, success and casualty rating.

"Yes, that's why I'm giving you a choice." Captain Milligan's face didn't flinch. "If you
don't..."

"If you're giving me the choice, I'm out." Victor reached down for his pistol, cocked it back, and put the barrel under his jaw.

"Victor, don't!" Captain Milligan reached for him. "No!"

Victor pulled the trigger. His blood splattered the ceiling, exiting him from the simulation.

"Shit!" Matt wiped the sludge off his shoulder and gagged a little.

Captain Milligan shook his head. "This is your chance to be *free-thinking* men."

Wes looked over at Victor's dead body. "Let's do this, boys. For Alix. And for Eli."

The captain smiled.

#

The darkness of the room gave way to the blue and red of the hologram screens. Each Reader's eyes scanned their screens, entered data, coded in their thoughts, and searched through evidence. What evidence did M.A.I.A. have that Alix should be subject to the Vanishing Sequence?

Finally, the video came up of Alix's unconscious screaming.

Each reader stared at the video and listened to Alix scream Eli's name. His chest flared up, his body convulsed, and he kicked and screamed for Eli.

Rankin clenched his jaw. "Gentlemen, isn't this in itself enough to subject Alix to the Vanishing Sequence?"

Elmer Washington sighed. He wiped the sweat from his head. "I suppose this is our biggest piece of evidence. Let's submit it and see if the system will give us a percentage. Agreed?"

Silent nods surrounded the table. One by one, they hit 'Submit.'

18

Sue rubbed her eyes and dug her numb fingers into the back of her head. Anna's questions wringed her neck with a truth she had refused to address.

"Miss Sue?" Anna asked. "What is left of you if your mind is gone?"

"I don't really know. I never thought about it."

"If your body is alive, fleshy, and still functioning, but the brain doesn't have your memories, your past feelings, are you still alive? Or are you dead?"

Sue wondered and said, "I think it's a kind of death, but only part of you has died. I don't know much about the afterlife, but I heard that when our bodies die, our souls or thoughts continue to exist in... in another form. At least, that's what my mother told me. She was into crystals, tarot cards..."

"What are crystals and tarot cards?"

"Well... before the war, way before you were born, a person would use tarot cards to kind of see their future. And crystals were stones that had energy to heal different parts of your body and life."

"Oh..." Anna got up and walked to the windowed door that led to Alix's room. A small fog appeared and faded on the glass with each breath Anna took. "You mean, we had the power to decide our own future."

"Out of the mouth of babes," Sue blurted with a smirk.

"Out of the mouth of babes? What does that mean?"

"It's a saying my mother would say whenever I said something that was true without realizing it."

"Is M.A.I.A. God?

"No. It's a computer that is programmed by us."

"Then who's God?"

Bleep.

Sue's screen flashed a glowing, triangular, purple chip. She had mail. She clicked on it.

The sign of the Red Cross floated below the message. The last time she saw that icon was when her father was alive. They drove to a shopping plaza where the Red Cross took over a pharmacy to dole out food and clothing. Whoever this was, they were older and part of a world where people were people with hearts and minds... souls.

The world had changed yet again. Adjustment impossible, adapting a must, but this time, it was all or nothing. Getting caught meant being erased from existence. M.A.I.A. and programmed chips provided a new form of death meaning it was your body, but with a different existence within.

"Anna, I have something to tell you."

\#

M.A.I.A. stopped computing, stopped thinking. It came up with the decision. All the math added up. All the pieces fit. It had its goal and worked backwards from there. What variables did M.A.I.A. have on Alix?

M.A.I.A.'s system statistically reviewed them all: his sniper skills, his accuracy, and the impact of his irreplaceability on the Conservation. Was his mind chip defective or deliberate programming?

A new addition to M.A.I.A.'s review was his conjoining with Anna. This additional criterion created a slight discombobulation in M.A.I.A.'s systemic analysis. Their love was out of order of M.A.I.A.'s formatting. The criteria for Conjoining were slated for after Conservation. Conjoining was a reward for Conservation success. M.A.I.A.'s matrix did not have allowances for spontaneous love, which now had to be added and computed.

M.A.I.A. returned to the last upload from Rankin and whirred from cycling through information that felt corrupt. Some of the information uploaded by Rankin contradicted its existing collections. It wasn't easy to reprogram the truth. Each time Rankin tried to alter its program, M.A.I.A. recorded the entry as an offense whenever the information uploaded did not concur with existing information.

M.A.I.A.'s creator had installed a detector of truth in its programming. Only what was seen, said, and thought through the individual's EED and captured on the facility's monitoring cameras would be considered in M.A.I.A.'s calculations. If there was any attempt to alter or mislead, M.A.I.A. would flag the date and time and offender. The time to address Rankin's offenses was not in sequence, yet all of the input M.A.I.A. received from the Readers was focused on Alix. M.A.I.A. calculated that the request was legitimate and analyzed the data and the options, and the multiple potential outcomes. It made the most statistical sense to M.A.I.A. for Alix to be subjected to the Vanishing Sequence.

M.A.I.A. prepared to deliver its answer to the Readers, but another troubling issue interrupted its verdict.

ALERT!

The room flashed red.

ALERT!

Everyone's head was on a swivel.

"What the …" Rankin looked around.

"What is all this?!" Elmer slammed his fist. "What now?!"

ALERT!

A video feed of Eli, his limp body in the surgical chair, appeared on their screens. A robotic arm stretched from the ceiling and pressed a new chip to the back of Eli's head through a hole in the headrest. A few drops of blood trickled down to the floor. The arm retracted, and blue light filled the room.

Captain Milligan approached Dr. Harrison, his face stern and frantic, his posture hunched and tired. Dr. Harrison stepped in front of Captain Milligan. Their lips moved, but the sound didn't transmit.

Rankin squinted. "Computer, what's this all about?" Rankin stood and climbed onto his T-Port. He rolled to the screen for a closer look. "Continue Vanishing Sequence sentencing."

"Wait!" Elmer's hand raised into the air. "It didn't give us the verdict for Alix!"

"What's the verdict?" Another Reader called out.

The video continued.

"Somebody do something!" Another Reader yelled.

"I can't!" Rankin blasted. His hand slapped the screen.

"Don't break it!" Elmer chastised.

"M.A.I.A. is unbreakable, you idiot!"

"Rankin, move. What is it showing us? Get out of the way, so we can see."

Dr. Harrison shook his head at Captain Milligan's red, stricken face. Captain Milligan thrashed an elbow across the face of Dr. Harrison, forced his knee to his stomach, and ripped a key card from his belt. He twirled Dr. Harrison and forced him to the ground.

Dr. Harrison cowardly stood in the corner, and Captain Milligan entered the room and stood before Eli.

The Readers watched helplessly and twitched and swiveled in the chairs.

Captain Milligan looked up at the screen, the monitor, and his knuckles flashed toward a paused screen where the footage stopped.

Rankin inhaled, "Computer, deploy a strike force to contain Captain Milligan in the chip processing center! Assist Dr. Harrison and apprehend Milligan! Now!"

M.A.I.A.'s screen froze with Captain Milligan's final image.

"What's going on? I want answers and I want them now," Elmer said. slamming his palm on the table.

Behind the frozen screen, M.A.I.A.'s system whirred in confusion. It found Captain Milligan's real location in the simulator with his team. The processing center footage was authentic and seemingly real, but M.A.I.A. could not process how Captain Milligan could be in two places at the same time. One location was a false location. Unable to resolve the double images of Captain Milligan, M.A.I.A. resorted to the live response and instruction from the Readers to send the strike force to Eli's room in the processing center.

"Strike force sent," M.A.I.A.'s automated voice filled the room.

#

Captain glanced at the monitor. By now, the fake video feed had to be presented to M.A.I.A. and shown to the Readers. That would buy him time to get weapons loaded and everything in place. He turned down the hall in a full sprint and headed to the weapons dock. He pressed his thumb to the scanner. The door cracked, and cool air released into the corridor. Captain stepped into the dark room. The first, long light snapped on and others followed in a domino sequence.

The lights extended to the opposite side of a massive storage facility. Captain walked by a rack of Humvees stacked on top of one another. Tanks of every size were parked in perfect rows. Surface-to-air missile silos, stacks and stacks of expandable defense lines, riot shields stacked to the ceiling, gun racks just as high, ammunition bins the size of rooms, grenades piled in glass containers like gumballs, bins and bins of night vision goggles, and magazines—everything needed for war.

Captain Milligan approached a bin as tall as he was. A green light on top blinked. A note was stuck to the side: *Here's to freedom. See you up top.*

Captain smiled. "Silva, you never let me down." He pushed the chest on wheels toward the door. He pushed his thumb against the scanner. The red light above the door flashed, and the door opened.

He stepped into the corridor as people flooded into hallways. Captain Milligan pushed his cart toward the simulator.

"Captain Milligan!" a military coated man yelled to him.

Captain Milligan froze. The wheels on the cart turned sideways.

"You hear about the disturbance? M.A.I.A. sent drones to the chip processing center!"

Captain Milligan's face flushed. "No, I didn't hear. What for?"

The man checked the weapons bin. "Where's that going?"

"Testing," Captain Milligan smiled.

The larger man checked his EED for the answer for the disturbance.

"Chuck, I'm sorry." Captain Milligan looked both ways.

"For what?"

The captain shot his elbow to the side of Chuck's head. In the same motion, he wrapped his arms around Chuck's neck and pushed on a pressure point. Chuck's eyes rolled into the back of his head and nodded off.

Captain Milligan shoved the cart as he ran down the hall. A woman that was holding linen screamed, dropped everything, and ran.

19

Six men with their pressed dress suits against the wall and their dress shoes soundless, moved efficiently and quietly down the hall. Handguns up, they arrived at the chip processing center and searched for Captain Milligan. The leader looked back and revealed a tattoo of a thirty-two on his neck. He didn't say anything, but the others nodded. The suited men, identifying only as their tattooed numbers, traded informational thought through their chips.

One of the men sent a thought to M.A.I.A. to turn the lights off. The dark corridor turned a soft green glow as the men flipped the sunglasses over their eyes. Thirty-two and forty-eight kicked in the doors, the barrel of their guns darting about, covering 180 degrees of the room. The others followed, covering all points, creating a blooming flower of weapons at the entrance of the facility.

Desks lined the room perfectly. The doors remained sealed and the room stayed quiet after the echo of the door slam faded. A moan came from the corner. Six guns aimed at Dr. Harrison, who was sprawled out on the floor to the left of the room. He rubbed his neck. Agent thirty-two pulled Dr. Harrison to his feet.

Dr. Harrison's lean body wavered, and he grabbed thirty-two's arm to steady himself. "You're too late. He got away with my key card," he said weakly. "He said he was going to kill the Readers. He has access to the simulator room the Readers are in!"

The suits turned to each other. Thirty-two snatched his arm away, and without a word, he waved his handgun in the direction of the door and the team took off.

"No consideration for the older generation." The lights flickered on, and Dr. Harrison eyes squinted. He continued his performance: he gripped the side of a counter to steady himself, rubbed his jaw, and then plopped himself into a chair to accentuate his alleged attack.

While he envied Captain Milligan's courage, he was also inspired by it. Creating an attack simulation to help Captain Milligan and submitting it to M.A.I.A. as a false feed to divert the suits toward this end of the facility was the most courageous action he's ever taken. Hopefully, sending the suits to the other end where the Readers were would give Captain Milligan long enough to get Alix out.

The monitor watched his every move, so he let his head hang as though he was still affected by the alleged blows. With his head bowed, he made the decision to leave his hands in his lap. He wanted no one to suspect his next move. With his head bowed, he silently prayed. He said no words. He prayed for the safety of Captain Milligan and his team. He prayed for their success and their chance for freedom, fighting once again for what he believed in. His last prayer was one of gratitude.

Thank you God for making me human.

#

Sweat dripped down Wes's face inside the egg-shaped chair. He lifted his shield from the simulation helmet, and the computer-generated world of drowning disappeared. That practice of breaking Alix out was one scrimmage. He had no time to process the failed simulation that ended with a missile to the ferry.

Wes felt relieved to see the small egg-shaped room. He felt a pit in his stomach. Statistically, they don't make it out, according to the simulation. He closed his eyes and shook his head.

Captain Milligan stood before them next to an ammo cart. "Got the gear. How did the simulation go?"

Wes shook his head and put his helmet on the ground.

"Team," Victor lifted his shield from his helmet, "Count me in. I can't let that happen to you. Maybe I could be the variable."

Captain Milligan looked at Wes. "What ended up happening?"

Wes shook his head. "We drowned. A missile to the ferry."

They all looked at the weapons bin.

Phil stood. "Well, the quicker we get to drowning, the faster we can get this over with. Let's go, boys. Let's go get Alix."

Everyone geared up—*click, click, snap, snap, chick, ching!*

#

"Thirty-two, what is the status?!" Rankin threw his fist through the hologram screen; the beams flickered.

The words appeared on the screen. *Infiltrated the holding room, sir. No sign of Captain Milligan.*

The Readers shifted in their chairs, turned to each other, held their arms up, and surrendered to their state of helplessness.

Elmer slammed his fist. "M.A.I.A., what the hell is going on here?"

"Captain Milligan is on the loose. The Tactical team is out to locate and destroy Captain Milligan. It is said that he is on his way to the Reader's Room."

"I know what is going on! Just fix it!" Elmer slammed the table again. "Never in my life."

Rankin's throat tightened. He thought of Captain Milligan kicking in the doors and putting a cool, steal revolver to his temple. He bit his manicured fingernail.

#

Geared up, their hearts raced. It was the real thing, and their first time with reality. The weight of Wes's actual equipment felt heavier than his equipment in simulation. His assault rifle was a forbidden tool within these walls. Everything he believed in crumbled when he opened his eyes from the simulator. Wes looked at the monitor across the room and squeezed his gun.

"I told you boys you would be the first on the island. Let's move out! Alix, we're coming." Captain Milligan declared as he led them out of the simulator room like a black train starting up. In a double line side-by-side in a single stride, they jogged down the corridor.

A white coated programmer heard the stampede of their footsteps and poked his body out the door. Matt's shoulder clipped the programmer, and he ping-ponged from each side of the door frame to the floor. A group of young, shaved-headed cadets turned the corner and retracted back into a room their faces twisted as they peered through a windowed classroom door. The black train whooshed by.

"Let's do this, boys." Matt growled.

#

"Captain Jack Silva, what brings you out on this fine evening?" Billy spoke through his mask and pointed to the hazy chemical filled sky that filled a horizon of a setting sun. "Coming up from the bowels to get some fresh air?"

He laughed and led three soldiers, Todd, Austin, and Chris, to Silva. They moved in slow, wide strides like cowboys entering a saloon. They pressed their assault rifles against their chest.

Through his sunglasses, Silva kept an eye on their trigger fingers. "No mask?"

"I wasn't planning on staying long. I was hoping to catch something we used to call a sunset," Silva said as he took two steps past them and pretended to look at the sky. "You're lucky you get to see this."

"The air is ripe with flavorful aromas of rotting bodies, garbage, with a hint of napalm. Our rations have better flavor. Yeah, we're so lucky we get to inhale this." Billy stood alongside Silva. The other three remained at his back. "No, really, why are you here?"

Silva turned and faced Billy and his team. He tried not to let his eyes roam over to the Humvee, which secretly held three of his own team members—Aaron, Brian, and Leo. They were hunkered down in the front Humvee, still and quiet, ready to pounce.

Silva spat and squished the saliva under his boot. "Actually, I have a training exercise for my guys with real trucks. Simulation just can't substitute the real thing. My team is not used to breathing this air."

"Sorry, Captain. This is a lot of gear for an exercise. Do you mind if I just check your EED?" Billy asked.

"Sorry, it's supposed to be a secret training."

"How secret?"

"I don't know if I am allowed to show you the credentials. Let me request clearance... Sorry. I've got to put in the code I was given." Silva turned his back, feigned moving his fingers and then made his EED beep. "I asked that they respond directly to you."

"Sorry, Captain, I..."

"No, don't be sorry, Corporal. You're just doing your job. We all got jobs to do. Any kills today? I assume the view over the Hudson was good enough for a few quick pickings." He jerked on another strap and locked up the gear hidden beneath the tarp.

"Not really, the fog is thicker than normal. Hopefully, when we see the sun, it'll burn some of this up. It's getting harder to find targets," Billy said, keeping a hard eye on Silva.

"Yeah, none of us can get near the hit numbers of Gunther Vasily and his brother," Todd said.

"How many kills does Vasily have?"

Todd adjusted his shoulder strap, his rifle hanging loose. "He's got like 225. He even has a two-in-one. No one is even close to him."

"I heard the closest guy has like 102," Chris added.

"We aren't even sure if that's correct because he also counts the building collapsing on a group as deaths. We all know that's a gray area," Billy said with a smirk.

"Yeah, you don't get total credit for your stray missile taking out a small building and falling on a group of Citiz. I don't think. Right, Billy?"

"I couldn't agree more with you." Billy peered in the back window of the first Humvee.

Silva spoke up. "I heard Alix Basil is going to give him a run for his money in the sniper department, though."

"Yeah, I heard about him. To hear Captain Milligan talk about him, you'd swear Alix was a one-man squad, except he didn't take a crucial shot the other day," Austin said. He stood with his legs apart. His right hand tightened around his assault rifle.

"That's right. Got his whole team dropped from first place. Squad Twenty-Eight is behind us now. Alix will have to do some serious work to catch up to Vasily," Chris said proudly.

"I think our squad moved into the lead to be the first to be deployed for Conservation," Billy said.

"I'm not too sure of that. My team may have a shot, depending on how they do on this training," Silva replied. "What is keeping Rankin?"

"I'll send a message to..." Billy said.

"No, Corporal, we will wait for Rankin to send the code to you, and that's an order."

"Sorry, Captain. I need to ask ... for your credentials. I have my orders; you know what I mean?"

"Corporal, I promise you, I have command of these Humvees and equipment. Why else would they be sitting here?"

"Sorry, Captain. I wasn't told about any authorized release of any equipment. How about you, Todd?"

"Nope." Todd eyed the driver's seat in the back of the first Humvee.

Silva smiled. "Come on, fellas. Let's not get all hyped up because you've been bored all day."

Billy stood behind Chris and next to Austin, tightening his grip on his rifle. His back stiffened. "Silva, you know protocol."

"They should send out some target practice for you. You're wound up so tight."

"Sorry, Captain. Todd, check his EED," Billy ordered.

Silva pulled back his sleeve as Todd approached to scan his EED. The captain extended his arm, but just as Todd leaned in to view the EED, Silva pulled him in and wrapped the strap from his assault rifle around his throat.

Todd's hands lifted in the air.

Silva aimed his pistol at Billy, Chris, and Aaron. "Hands in the air!!"

"Drop your weapon! Drop your weapon!" Austin screamed.

"Let him go, Cap! Let him go!" Billy Screamed.

Silva's men—Aaron, Brian, and Leo—emerged from the Humvee and pointed their assault rifles at Billy, Chris, and Austin's backs.

"You may think you can get a shot," said Silva, "but I promise you, my team will blow your heads off before your finger can move. Drop your weapons and raise your hands high above your heads."

"Monitor is disabled, Captain," Brian said.

"Billy, you and your team just failed the most crucial part of this training exercise, plausibility," Silva said and discharged his taser into the back of Todd's neck. His body went into convulsions as it hit the ground in front of him. "Welcome to Conservation Day!"

Clickclickclickclickclick!

Billy, Austin, and Chris dropped to the ground like mosquitoes in a bug zapper.

20

Sue stared at the old door and checked her EED for the time. One minute precisely. Most doors in the facility slid open. This one swung and latched. Her hands trembled. She put her hand on the door and applied pressure. The door cracked.

The guard on the other side peaked at her. "What are you do..."

Thunder roared down the hall like a train in a tunnel, and Squad Twenty-Eight smashed through the door.

Sue's back slammed against the wall, and she dropped down into a squat and covered her ears.

"Clear!" They moved like a frantic snake throughout the office, its head parting off into two and securing all angles.

"Clear!"

"This corner clear!"

"Backroom clear!"

Anna disappeared into Alix's room, behind a slammed door.

"Echo in the nest! Ready to infiltrate."

A hand tapped Sue's shoulder. She looked up and saw the orange glowing of a burly beard. "You must be Sue? I apologize for my boys' abrupt rudeness and disregard for manners."

"Alix!" Anna burst into the room and flicked on the lights.

"What's going on out there?" Alix squinted and yanked at his restraints.

She looked for the closest chair, dragged it over and jammed it under the door. "I'm not letting them take you."

"Anna, get these off of me!" Alix flailed his arms and kicked his legs against his restraints.

Anna fumbled to free his arm restraints as the door handle jiggled and slammed from the other side.

A crack in the window splintered, and yellow eyes appeared.

"Anna, hurry!" Together, they freed his legs. "Lock yourself in the bathroom, and don't open the door no matter what."

"I'm not leaving you!"

"Anna!"

He twirled out of the hospital bed, his johnny handing half off. His bare butt appeared in the light. Alix looked for the nearest weapon—needles. "Anna! In the bathroom! Now!"

The door burst open. A blooming flower of flashlights at the end of semiautomatic weapons appeared.

Alix whipped two syringes at the first enemy and charged the group. The bathroom door shut. The needles pinned into the big lug through the door first. Alix grabbed the second soldier's gun from the tip, pointed it to the ceiling, and elbowed him backwards. He pulled the third over his shoulder by the arm, kicked him in the throat, and dis-armed him. The gear scraped the bare backside of Alix.

The rest of the team backed through the door and tackled Alix just as the gun he managed to take slid to the doorway of the bathroom.

"Stop, Alix!" Wes yelled.

Alix froze, his arms held down by Phil and Adam. "Wes?"

"Alix!" Captain Milligan walked into the room, his revolver swing-ing from his hip.

Alix's eyes widened. "Captain? Yes, sir."

"Put some damn clothes on and cover your water gun. There's a lady present."

Sue peered around the doorway.

Snickers filled the room, and Phil lifted his helmet from the floor. "Dammit, Alix. I don't know what's worse—you kicking me in the throat or the view from down here."

Wes pulled the syringes from his tactical vest. "If these are used, I'll kill you."

"Alix, get dressed and outfitted." Captain Milligan dropped a duffle bag at his feet. "We're out in two minutes, people."

"Alix?" Anna appeared in the bathroom doorway.

"Who's this?" Phil and Wes pointed their guns.

Alix jumped in front of her. "Stop, she's with me."

"We know, get dressed," Captain Milligan said.

Alix knelt down and inspected his bag. "What's happening?"

"Your tactical gear is in the bag. Get dressed! One minute forty! Move!"

Alix ripped open his bag and jammed his legs into his pants. "Where are we going?"

"It's Conservation Day," Captain Milligan said flatly. "Move your ass, soldier."

Sue watched Anna's horrified face realizing Alix's departure. She wiped an erupting tear from her eye as Alix looked over at Anna.

"This is not a romance movie. Get dressed," Captain Milligan barked. "Let's go! Sue, you have any water?"

Anna knelt down and pulled out his boots for Alix to step into. She snapped and locked the buckles on his boots as he put on his vest.

"A minute 30 Captain," Wes announced.

"Shit! We'll have to make up some time. We're already behind." Captain Milligan checked his EED.

"Copy that, Captain," Wes said and lowered his helmet.

Alix put his helmet on.

"Here," Matt handed Alix his rifle and submachine gun, "Thing weighs a ton."

"Let's move out." Captain Milligan twirled his finger in the air.

Alix grabbed Anna's hand. "It's going to be fine."

Captain Milligan looked back at Anna and pointed. "You're staying here, little lady, and we are not fine until I tell you that you are fine!"

"One minute, Cap." Wes checked down the hall.

"Update! What's our best route?" Milligan ordered.

Wes dropped the hologram map on the floor.

#

"M.A.I.A.! Update! What is going on?" Rankin yelled.

M.A.I.A. scanned all the monitors. The computer clicked, the same sound emitting from their EED's, and the Readers held their breaths.

A message appeared on the screen: *Issuing Vanishing Sequence to the following M.A.I.A. individuals...*

Rankin smiled.

Washington screamed, "Tell me where Captain Milligan is, and if he's been apprehended yet, god damnit!"

M.A.I.A.'s voice came through the speakers more stern and direct than normal. Her words transcribed on the hologram screens: **"Captain Milligan is currently on Level U40."**

Rankin's stomach twisted. "What? Apprehend him!"

"He and his squad have infiltrated the level with key cards obtained from Programmer Doctor Harrison. They rushed through the door as Sue was about to exit. I am sending all armed personnel to U40 to apprehend Captain Milligan. I am issuing the Vanishing Sequences and reprogramming of chips for the following individuals."

"There's multiple?" A puzzled panic took over the Readers' faces.

"Private Alix Basil, Private Phillip Heins, Private Adam Adkins, Private Wes Wilder, Private Victor Season, Private Hayden Albert, Private Matthew Stine..."

"M.A.I.A.!" Elmer slammed his hand on the desk. "What is this madness?"

"Reader Elmer Washington, Captain Jack Silva, Private Aaron Graves..."

Rankin's eyebrows furrowed.

All the Readers turned to Elmer as color drained from his face.

"Private Leonardo Sharp, Private Brian Rios, Private Anna Brooks..."

"M.A.I.A.!" Rankin's body exploded. "No! You will not apply the Vanishing Sequence to Anna Brooks! Shut her down!" He stood and entered his T-Port. The mechanics attached to his calves and knees. "M.A.I.A.'s lost her mind. We need to shut her down. Override Sequence!"

"Captain Robert Milligan, Dr. Susan Maynard, Reader Albert Rankin..."

"M.A.I.A.!" Rankin screamed. "I'm shutting her down!"

A Reader stood. "Albert, you can't! Without M.A.I.A., Captain Milligan will surely escape."

Rankin pointed to the ceiling, "I'm overriding her decision!"

Rankin's T-Port failed, and he flipped forward and smacked the floor. He cried in pain and held his cramped legs.

Elmer moved aside to allow his fall from power to be complete.

"M.A.I.A.!" Rankin groveled to his feet, gripped the short console, which held a keyboard, and a raised block surrounded in glass. Beneath that glass, a red button glowed. Rankin stood on unsteady legs, using the console to support his weight. He shuffled halfway to an emergency shut-off switch protected in a layer of glass. "Where is your strike team now?" He struggled to stand, over the machine that was about to cripple his plan.

"Strike force is preparing for infiltration of U40. Odds of success are only 15 percent without more backup."

"Shut her down!" Elmer screamed.

"Captain Milligan and his team are adequately equipped for a firefight of nearly one hundred men. Strike force standby. Recruiting backup from squads Fifty-Seven and Eighty-Two. ETA six minutes. Vanishing Sequence beginning in 30 seconds..."

"No!" Rankin reached for the hammer attached to the wall to break the glass for the emergency shut down. The extension of his right hand threw his body off balance and he fell back to his knees.

"Shut her down!" Elmer screamed.

Rankin clawed at the console to stand.

Frank smashed the glass protecting the lever and slammed his hand down on the glowing button. A whoosh came over the room, a flash of white budding and appearing in the center of M.A.I.A.'s screen.

"Twenty seconds..."

The white bud opened into a lotus that floated on the screen for a few seconds and then disappeared. The screen went dark.

Frank stood near the shutdown lever. His chest heaved as though he had just been in the fight of his life. He tossed the small hammer onto the console and his shoulders dropped from relief and exhaustion.

A lingering piece of the broken glass fell from the edge of the console and shattered on the floor next to Rankin, striking him in the eye.

Rankin cried out and he slapped his left eye.

"Needless to say, we are going to be flying blind, until we get M.A.I.A. repaired and back online," Elmer snapped. "Gentlemen, let's return to our quarters, get our emergency tablets, and get to work."

Elmer got up and stepped over Rankin to leave. The other Readers followed him, leaving Rankin on the floor.

"No one is going to help me up?" Rankin yelled as he held his left eye.

The door closed behind Elmer.

Rankin removed his hand from his face. A quarter size smear of blood was in the center of his palm. He looked up at M.A.I.A.'s screen, which towered over him. "You did this on purpose!"

Bleep...

21

"Alpha, take the stairs. Bravo, let's get in the elevator,"

Wes held up his finger and twirled in the air. "You heard Cap, let's move!"

They moved towards the door, Anna following Alix.

"Stop!" Captain Milligan pointed. "She's staying."

"We could use a medic," Alix pleaded.

Captain Milligan shook his head as he walked away. "You're about to need a medic."

He came face to face with Sue, who plead, "Yes, please take her. She has a better chance of surviving with you than if she stays here. Please..." Her eyes pried Captain's.

Anna stepped forward. "I can shoot, too. And I've been through all the same simulations as you guys. I've logged more battle time than most of your team."

"What?" Victor spat and shouldered past Anna. "I'm not fighting alongside some bitch."

Anna kicked the back of Victor's knee, pulled him to the ground and unlatched his pistol on his leg and aimed down at his head. "Who's the bitch?"

"Get off me!" Victor batted the gun away.

Anna let him up.

"Give her a gun. Anna, on our tail," Captain Milligan ordered and gave Wes a hard nod.

"Let's move out." Wes swiped his left hand towards the hall, slid his night vision goggles down, and raised his rifle.

Sue hugged Anna hard and fast, shoved a medical backpack into her arms, retreated to the bathroom, and closed the door.

Behind Captain Milligan at the other end of the hall, a door edged open.

"Behind us!" Anna screamed.

The door at the end of the hall burst open. Anna shoved Captain sideways into an indentation and fired. Three bullets, three hits, and a suited man dropped. A smoke grenade exploded.

Machine gunfire was exchanged from one end of the hall to the other as sputters vibrated in Alix's chest. The team fanned out as he shuffled back, hunkering behind a waste receptacle.

"Captain!" Wes's voice rang in their helmets over the gunfire. "Elevator is no longer available. Southwest staircase is back to our right. Alix, lay down covering fire and evacuate."

"Covering fire!" Alix held the aim of the door and sputtered three rounds at it to provide a break for the team to retract.

Wes, Matt, and Victor scampered behind Alix and stacked on the reverse wall out of harm's way at the base of the stairs.

Wes yelled. "Captain, let's go! Victor, prepare a flash bang."

Captain Milligan looked over to Anna.

"Go!" She shot twice, covered him, and nodded her head toward the back of the hallway, aimed further down, and fired more.

Milligan's feet skidded and pushed himself forward into the hallway. He knelt next to Alix.

"Where's Anna?" Alix blurted.

"There!" Captain pointed.

"Phil, you're up!" Wes pointed his assault rifle to a door at the end of the hall.

Phil held down his trigger, outlined the doorframe in holes the size of baseballs, and provided cover.

Alix hugged the wall to the right then slid on his knee into the crevice next to Anna.

"Mag!" Anna said. "I only got three left!"

Alix kept his gun and attention on the door. "Side pouch."

Anna snagged a mag and shoved it into her belt. Alix walked backwards; knees bent to shield her.

"Twenty bullets left!" Phil's voice filled their helmets. "Hayden, you're up!"

Hayden crouched to the right of Phil, machine gun winded down. The tip glowed red. He held the trigger in several three-round bursts.

"Flash bang!" Victor's voice announced in their helmets. He tossed the grenade around the corner and toward the door. "Three, two, one."

Everyone looked away.

Hayden clung onto Alix as he came by, and Phil turned from the grenade in one swift motion. They all moved as one around the corner.

The explosion sucked the air out of the room and particles and debris skidded down the hallway after them.

"Let's go! Let's go!" Captain Milligan grabbed both sides of the railing and jerked himself up each stair. His breathing dragged him down, his quads burned like an inferno, and his feet stuck like cinder blocks attached to them. He leaned on the railing. He felt his stomach rise into his throat. "Let's take the stairs. Brilliant idea."

"Captain, let's go! If you're going to throw up, use it as a weapon and vomit at 'em." Wes hit his shoulder on the way. "We can't lean now."

"I hate you right now." Captain Milligan's sweaty forearms slipped off the railing. He pulled himself up more stairs.

"There is an elevator on Level U30 that will take us to the top." Matt looked down to the flashlights and echoes that followed them. "They're coming up behind us. Dropping smoke."

Wes looked for the signs—U32, U31. He heard the smoke grenade canister hit the floor on the stairwell and bellow out smoke through a hissing sound. It would slow their pursuers for a moment. "U30. Let's move. Matt, your intel better be good. Team stack up."

Hayden stood to the left of the door, Phil stacked up behind him, and Alix in the back.

Anna held one hand on the back of his belt, the other on the gun, her backpack slung over her shoulder.

Matt faced the door directly. "Your girlfriend better know how to watch our six, Alix!"

Captain slugged up the last step and leaned on his knees. "Ready for impact, boys. Go silent." He coughed and spat on the ground.

The whole team screwed on silencers to the end of their submachine guns, which made the sounds of small mice squeaking as they twisted on the attachment.

The hissing of the smoke bomb ceased below, and the echoes from boots rang up the staircase shaft after them.

"Move!" Matt booted the door.

The team filtered through, covering every angle.

"Clear!" Wes announced.

"Clear," Matt's voice entered their helmets as he entered the hall and looked down the opposite end.

Alix and Anna kept their eyes on the stairwell behind them. The sounds of boots behind them grew closer.

"Alix, hit the handle," Anna said and kept her aim at the bottom of the stairwell.

Alix aimed his rifle and fired. Five bullets spat out, shearing off the door handle. There was no way to open the door from the inside of the stairwell. It would buy them precious seconds.

"Right side, west hall," Hayden's voice whispered into their helmets.

He moved quickly towards two M.A.I.A. programmers that wore scrubs. He released a short whistle to get their attention. They turned and saw his assault rifle in their faces, their hands jolting into the air. The nose of his rifle directed them both to the floor.

"Give me your lab coat," Hayden whispered brusquely to the woman. She took it off for him. "Anna, come get your cover and go get the elevator."

Anna threw the lab coat on and grabbed the woman's tablet. She moved to the elevator with the tablet covering her Glock. Anna screamed, "You two, down on your bellies and be quiet!"

"Okay, don't shoot. Please." The man's body trembled.

"Got your back, Hayden," Alix said as he moved quickly towards Hayden. Hayden zip-tied the two lab technicians as Alix stayed low and fanned his rifle left to right in search of any movement. "Everyone, stay to the left. Give me a clear shooting lane. Coming to you. Anna, cover me."

"Roger that." Anna pounded the elevator call button and nonchalantly kept an eagle eye on the team for any movement. She aimed her gun down the hall.

The rest of the team nestled near the elevator, crouched behind fake floor plants and bump outs. A small movement behind a trash receptacle caught Alix's eye thirty meters past the elevator.

"Tango," Alix said.

A lone black suit dashed for double swinging doors behind them. Alix squeezed the trigger twice, and the pitter patter of the silenced bullets tore through his calves, spurting onto the floor. He slid in his own blood.

Victor fired and the man's head exploded.

"Tango down," Victor's said smugly.

The elevator dinged and the doors slid open. Two programmers dropped their hologram tablets and froze when the barrels of seven assault rifles greeted them.

"Going up?" Anna asked.

22

"M.A.I.A., get a squad on every floor! Rankin, what are they trying to accomplish?!" Elmer demanded. M.A.I.A. being down escaped his mind, like flicking on a light when you knew the power was out. "What is Captain Milligan's motive?"

"We will have to wait until M.A.I.A. completes her reset. I have no idea." Beads of sweat rolled down Rankin's back.

"We're sitting ducks. Do something!" Elmer barked. He mopped his brow with a cloth napkin. "At the very least, can we turn the air circulator back on?"

Rankin picked up a corded telephone attached to the wall and dialed.

"Hello?"

"Susan, this is Reader Albert Rankin accompanied by the other Readers on the call. M.A.I.A. is being reset, so we had to call directly. We've heard and seen the disturbance and want to know the status."

Sue sighed. "A dozen dead maybe. We're still trying to make sense of it."

"Do you know where or why Captain Milligan is doing this? Do you know where he is going? Is he coming for us?"

"No, sir, I don't know where they are going. They took Anna and left. They could be coming for you."

Rankin swallowed hard and his lip quivered. "They have Anna?"

"Yes, sir. They have Private Anna Brooks."

Rankin slammed the phone down into its cradle. They disconnected.

"Who's Anna? And why is Captain Milligan coming after us?" Elmer grumbled. "Rankin, we need answers."

"I'm only human!" Rankin screamed.

"And an inept leader," Washington snapped.

Rankin's head snapped toward Washington, and his eyes narrowed. He gritted his teeth to hold his tongue, mumbling weakly, "We need M.A.I.A. back online."

He looked at the counter. There were 3 minutes remaining.

#

Silva leaned on the Humvee near the elevators and bit his fingernails, spitting out the pieces. He looked at the sky, a hazy red, and spit his thumbnail out. Darkness came quick without an actual sun to shine through the miles of thick clouds, pollution, and remittance from the bombs.

Silva checked his EED: *Your squad is to report to the U25. Apprehend Captain Milligan and Squad Twenty-Eight on sight. Captain Milligan is the primary target. 200 ration reward for his death.*

Silva smiled. Two hundred rations would make him the richest guy on the island.

He took a deep breath and heard the ding from the elevator, picking up his gun and pointing it at the door. "Boys, get ready."

Aaron, Brian and Leo aimed their weapons.

The doors opened onto a jam-packed elevator.

Silva lowered his gun. "You know my orders are to apprehend you." He approached the elevator. "Stand down, men. Rob, you're worth 200 rations to me."

"Ah, the smell... Still smells like shit up here." Captain Milligan approached the four, running Humvees stacked and geared up for full assault.

"Hold up, what's with the girl?" Silva asked.

"That girl can kick your ass, and she's a medic," Captain Milligan shot back. "Not to mention, she is a great shot. She took Victor down."

"I tripped," Victor spat.

Captain Silva retrieved a vest from the rear of a Humvee and tossed it at Anna. "Lose the white lab coat and suit up. Brian, get her a side arm, ammo, knife, taser, ear piece. Set her table, will ya?"

Brian tilted his head. "Like a real gun?"

Anna dropped the coat and strapped on the vest. "Sir, I shot an M4, patched a bullet wound in fifteen seconds, and I've spotted for Alix in more than twenty simulations."

"My, my, aren't you talented. Give her an M4, and girl, looks like we got ourselves a party," Silva said.

"Let's get this traveling circus on the road. Adam and Matt, drive H3 and H4. Hayden, passenger side of H2," Captain Milligan barked. "Silva, can one of your guys drive H2? I want you to ride with me."

Silva pointed. "Brian, drive H2. You have most of the ammo and supplies, so stay close. The gates are open, so we shouldn't have any problem until we get to the ferry. I don't know if a squad is still positioned there."

"We'll find out. Pick a chariot, everybody, and load up." Captain Milligan got into H1.

Silva sat behind the wheel. "Move over, I'm driving." Captain hopped in, slammed the heavy door, and revved the engine. "Ah, yeah! They sound so much better on diesel!" He leaned over the wheel to look up at the sky. "Never thought I would live to see another sunset." He shifted his Humvee into drive.

"Everybody, keep eyes around you," Silva's voice came through their earpieces. "We are officially in hostile territory. Your captain on your flight to hell is the great Captain Robert Milligan, an old friend and a crazy asshole. Captain Milligan, your passengers are Private Aaron Graves and Private Leonardo Sharp. Private Brian Rios is driving H2."

Captain held the wheel at twelve o'clock and leaned back. "Oh, yeah. Graves, Sharp, and Rios." He looked in the rearview mirror at Aaron and Leo and laughed. "You scored high on your simulations. Are you boys ready to do what you were born to do?"

"Yes sir, Captain," Aaron said.

"I'm looking forward to hitting real enemy targets," Leo said.

"And so, Conservation begins. Oorah!" Captain Milligan drove H1 without lights, into a deep mango sunset, which hid behind the dark fog of war.

23

Gunther Vasily watched the red sky, his short finger rubbing his scalp. "Another ten minutes, and we will be out of light."

"Yeah, it's getting a bit better, though." Greg Vasily looked around.

Gunther wiped his head. "Yeah, but these bastards must know not to travel the southern tip of Manhattan or the western coast of Brooklyn anymore during the day. How many days has it been since we've got a kill?"

Greg looked through his scope. "Ah, I don't know, like two, maybe? We still have the most kills. We haven't even started the Conservation yet. Once we get off this island and have a line of Citiz to kill—oh, man, like fish in a barrel. Dad would be so proud, huh?" He clicked his prosthetic leg against the ground.

Gunther breathed. "Yeah, he would, wouldn't he? But would you stop making that sound with that thing? You'd give us away in a second with that habit out there. What do you think is going on down below?"

Greg looked at his EED. "I don't know, for 200 rations, I wish we had a shot. You know you can trade rations for time in the simulator to do whatever you want? Literally, *anything*. What's that?"

Gunther's pupils expanded. "What?"

Greg huffed. "You hear any authorization of four Humvees leaving the gates?"

"No, why would anyone even leave the quad, especially now?" Gunther furrowed his eyebrows and zoomed in.

"Check it out, three o'clock. Four Humvees turning onto Kimmel Road." Greg pressed his eyes deeper into the lens.

Gunther's crosshairs moved over the terrain and tracked the four Humvees as they sped along the east side of the island. He zoomed in more on the driver in front and clicked the side of the scope. "Call it in. Send the picture of the driver I just captured. We only have …" Gunther checked his EED and then the sky, "Seven minutes of sufficient daylight."

#

"Captain wasn't kidding about the smell, though. It's like the bathroom after Phil shits." Wes lowered his mask. "At least, the mask filters it a little."

Victor didn't break eye contact with the light behind the clouds. "Don't you think we are all a little out of our element? I can't believe we are doing this, Alix. This is on you."

"Victor, we're going to be first on the island. Look at the sky." Alix looked at Anna. The redness of the sky reflected in her honey eyes.

Victor huffed. "Well, stay focused. We are all here because they were going to erase your mind and make us forget about you."

Alix looked to Anna. "Is that what they were going to do to me?"

Anna nodded and side smirked.

"That's what Captain told us. That's why he wanted to bust you out of there." Wes turned from the road. "I want you to tell us about Eli. None of us remember him. Captain has a photo of us with him. We thought he was nuts, but we really don't remember him."

"If Captain kept a picture, it's evidence of a Vanishing Sequence… Risky," Anna said and gripped Alix's hand.

Matt's eyes darted between Anna in the rearview mirror and the road in front of him. "What's the Vanishing Sequence, and why do you know about it?"

"Dr. Sue Maynard told me about it."

Matt stole a quick glance of Alix. "I thought I would never see you again, the way you went down in the Vomit Room."

"Guys, we're stopping," Alix pointed.

Captain Milligan's voice chimed in the radios, "Team, we're going to pull up onto the ferry to the left. We need the Humvees to be two by two. Silva and I are going below to start the engine. Stand by."

The sensor of retractable vehicle bollard barriers between the boat and the road, acknowledged the presence of Captain Milligan's Humvee, flashed a green light, and then lowered into the ground to allow the trucks to roll right onto the ferry. They pulled the four trucks up to the ferry, two by two.

Captain looked to his left and right and got out. "Phil, Cover me. I'm going to test the wind."

Victor replied. "Something's not right. This was too easy."

Phil peered over the hood. "We fought our asses off to get out of the quad."

"We're not in the clear yet," Adam checked over his shoulder. "We should go. What's Captain doing?"

"Let's go, Cap." Wes tapped the top of the steering wheel.

Alix watched the glow on Captain Milligan's beard through the glass.

Captain Milligan gazed toward the quad from where he escaped. His timid eyes, wrinkled around the edges, scanned the skyline and the setting sun behind the blanket of clouds across the sky. Captain remembered it differently from those days on the porch with his father, beautiful reds and oranges, now just a dusting of warm color and layered grays. He could smell his mother's ham lingering in the kitchen. He closed his eyes to take in the aroma when a flash of light winked off the windows on the far tower that stood on top of M.A.I.A.

Alix's eyes widened at the distant crackle and echo in the air.

"Captain!" Alix's voice exploded in their earpieces.

Captain's head snapped back. Blood sprayed. His body went limp and folded backwards.

"Sniper!" Alix screamed.

"The Humvee is bulletproof!" the radio chatter erupted in their ears.

"I don't want to test it right now! Heads down, heads down! Below the windows," Wes ordered and ducked down into his seat.

"We're screwed!" Hayden screamed.

"Let me get to Captain. I can help…" Anna crawled over Alix.

Alix pushed Anna down. "Stay down. You saw what just happened! Headshot, Anna!" He looked to Victor and then backwards where the shot came from. Alix called into his mic, "Captain Silva, it was a sniper shot from the south."

"Team, pull the Humvees diagonally to the left! Now!" Silva ordered.

"Copy that." The trucks shifted.

Victor looked back. "That shot came from five hundred meters."

"Clear shot from North Tower to us?" Alix reached for his equipment.

Victor pulled his mask down and peeked as the Humvee moved diagonally to the left. "Yeah. I think so. But it's too murky and dark. Tough shot. Not too many could make that. You don't think…"

Alix pulled his mask down. "Gunther."

Silva barked into their earpieces, "Cut the engines. Everybody exit to the right! Get out on the passenger side only. Use the Humvees as cover. Keep your head down!"

Alix screamed. "Everyone! Crosshairs are looking for you right now!"

Victor cleared his throat. "We barely got two minutes of light."

"Then I'll shoot him in one." Alix rolled out of the Humvee and pulled his rifle around his back. "We already know his direction. There can't be too many places for them to hide with a shot like that on this island. Victor, call the shot."

The teams emptied out the right side of the trucks and hunkered behind them, guns ready, the night quiet, except for the water splashing against the barge.

Captain's Milligan's limp body laid in a heap, off to the side.

Alix pointed to Victor. "Going down." He pulled the lever on the rifle, the barrel extracting and expanding. He shoved a mag in the bottom of his rifle. They crept under the truck, and Alix pulled the pod out and aimed through the rim of the Humvee tire.

Victor crawled behind the front tire and looked through the gap in the rim. "It's got to be the tower. It's right where we'd be for that shot." Victor checked his EED. "The angle makes sense. Ok. Target: unknown, one of three windows of the tower likely, distance: five hundred meters, wind: none, sufficient light: ..." Victor checked his EED again, "one minute thirty seconds. Alix, take into consideration the rocking of the boat: forty-degree differential."

Alix adjusted his scope, breathed to steady his pulse. "For Captain."

#

"Target: Captain Robert Milligan, northeast, five hundred meters, wind: zero. Aim. Shoot." Greg watched the pink splatter and the fall of Captain Milligan on his way back to the Humvee. His orange beard made him unmistakable and an easy bull's eye.

"Hit! Two hundred rations for us! Hell, yeah. Let's see what else we can take. Target: H1 Passenger Captain Silva. Five hundred meters, wind: zero. Aim. Shoot."

"The Humvees are bulletproofed. You know that, Greg." Gunther's crosshairs scanned the downed body and the stream of blood as the Humvees pulled up and to the left.

"They are exiting the vehicles on the other side! Dammit!" Greg squeezed the binoculars.

"They know it's us. Well, Alix knows where the shot came from." Gunther lowered his Dragunov rifle.

"Let's get a shot in before they get away in the dark."

"I don't want to give our position away. Not with Alix down there," Gunther countered.

"Our position is fine. They are a bunch of kids trying to escape."

Gunther grunted. "Did you hear me? Alix Basil is with them."

"Who cares? Kid doesn't even have a kill yet."

"You want to be his first? I've seen the simulations. Kid is good."

"Not as good as us. We've been doing this for years. Let's not give him the chance to get started. What are they doing?"

"*They* aren't doing anything. Alix is setting up a shot. That's what I would be doing. We should pack it in while we are ahead. There isn't a shot left to take before darkness comes, and I don't want to take a chance. There are a dozen places he could be already, and we only have three windows from the nest in the North Tower for him to choose. He's probably scoping us now."

"Gunther, come on, let's get one more. We are pushed far enough back. They would have to guess a window, at best. It would give his position away, and you'd take him. Stop being a pussy! Where could he possibly set a shot up from?" Gregory pushed his eyes deeper into the binoculars, his two missing finger nubs on the side.

"You are going to take a 33 percent chance on our life? I'm packing it in. Captain Milligan was enough of a hit. Let's go, brother." Gunther pulled his rifle back and crawled backwards, keeping his head tucked down.

A flare shot up from the barge, a blazing light bulb rocket, curved up and around—a universal symbol for SOS.

Gunther's head snapped up and back, and his eyes widened. He never saw the flash from under the Humvee.

The bullet entered the small reflection of the flare in Greg's lens, exited out the back of Gunther's little brother's head, and sparked on the old stone ceiling.

The smashed bullet in the shape of a star ping-ponged and rattled until it dropped in front of Gunther like a flipped coin.

24

"Hit!" Victor screamed. "Target down."

Alix pulled the operating rod back, and his empty shell rolled under the tire.

"Keep that shell!" Hayden clapped. "First real kill! Let's go!"

Silva didn't break his vision from Captain Milligan's body. "Do you think it was Gunther or Gregory?"

Alix clicked another round into the chamber but slid back for more cover.

"Not sure, but either way, it was a Vasily," Victor squinted.

"Congrats on your first real kill." Matt tapped Alix's boot. "A high profile kill, at that."

"Yeah, thanks. Well, we don't want to give the other one a shot. Thanks for that flare. The reflection worked. We saw the lens in the second window."

"Now, everyone within a thirty-mile radius knows where we are!" Wes huffed.

Silva shook his head. "You boys are young, so you don't know any better. You never want to celebrate death."

"Can we get Captain Milligan's body?" Anna asked. Her eyes were fixed on the silhouette of his right knee bent upward. Silence.

All eyes turned to the captain's body. It was a shadow against a darkening sky. His bright red beard was now invisible and lost in the darkness of death.

Silva sighed. "You can if you want your body to be lying next to his. He's not getting up. His body isn't coming with us. If you take your helmet off, he's not going to be standing next to you. No more white rooms. No more pretending. This is real life. This is war. This is how real soldiers die. He was a dear friend, but I can't afford the time to cry, because I am responsible for all of you, and I will not let him down."

From the last light in the sky, Silva could see faces glistening from tears. "Dry your tears and remember him and everything he taught you. We still have to get to the mainland. Reinforcements are coming. Brian and Leo, come with me to get the barge started. Alix, keep a hawk's eye on that window."

"Yes, sir."

"The rest of you, cover us... and cover yourselves. Welcome to Conservation."

#

Under a light drizzle, the ferry pushed quietly through the harbor as it floated over the Diamond Reef in the New York Harbor drizzle. The motor rumbled along with the occasional thunder from heat lightning as it bounced cloud to cloud. Squad Twenty-Eight and its new companions absorbed the world, the wind, the darkness, the sky, and the buildings.

Matt sat on a small cabin bench working on a tablet.

"Is it working?" Silva asked.

"Not yet, sir."

"We need that program up on the screen before we hit shore. Captain Milligan said you are the tech wiz in the squad. Show me what you can do."

"Yes, sir. I'm searching for a satellite. I'm almost there. I will be able to log on in another minute or two."

Wes entered the cabin and marched up to Captain Silva. He slammed his gun down and pointed at Silva. "You and Captain didn't think to figure this out before we left the island? We're a floating target!"

Aaron, Brian, and Leo jumped up and immediately surrounded their captain.

"Soldier," said Silva, "why are you off your detail?"

"We can't breathe out there. It's like sucking on an old sock," Wes said through gritted teeth.

"Stand down, Corporal! Respect your ranking officer!" Silva pointed at Wes. "I know you're upset about losing your captain, but you're a soldier. So, here's a term you've probably heard before: suck it up!"

"Just tell us the plan! That's all we want."

"We don't know what Captain Milligan was thinking, because his brains are all over the barge back there!" Silva pointed toward the island. "I knew Rob years before you were even in a test tube, you little prick! I will snap you in half. Get back to your station!"

"Yes, sir." Wes saluted him, turned on his boot heels, and stormed to the bow.

Phil saluted and followed Wes.

Hunkered down between the Humvees, Alix hugged Anna. They watched the reflection from the one spotlight on Governors Island undulate in the water behind the boat. Anna looked up. "I wish there were stars."

Alix looked up. "Someday."

"You think so? You think we will ever see stars, babe?" Her jawline was a smooth perfection in soft light.

"Someday." Alix smiled. "You figure out what's in the bag yet?"

Anna's bag lay at her feet. "Yeah, medical supplies mostly."

"Hey, love birds," Phil yelled over to them, "Captain is calling a meeting."

Water slapped the side of the barge while the waves rocked the boat gently back and forth as Wes appeared at the back of the pack. His eyes roamed the dark waters that surrounded the barge.

Adam sat between two barrels with his head hung between his legs, his body dry heaving intermittently.

Silva stood in the center, Captain Milligan's revolver hanging from his hip.

"How did you get Captain's gun?" Wes asked.

"He left it on the seat when he got out."

"He would never leave his gun. That doesn't make sense."

"It does if he knew what was going to happen to him." Silva eyed Wes.

"You're saying Captain wanted to off himself?"

"I'm saying, he probably knew there was a good chance. He flushed them out, Alix took the sniper out, which enabled us to get off the island. I don't know that for sure, but I know he would never leave his revolver anywhere. That's why we're going to pray." Silva's voice cracked with his last words.

Silva looked at Brian in the control room window and sliced his hand across his throat. The engine stopped.

When Brian joined the gathering, Silva cleared his throat. "We lost a great man, friend, and teacher today. We did what he set out to do. We got off the island. He got us off the island. Alix, you or anyone here wouldn't know who you were if it were not for Captain Robert Milligan. Let's bow our heads for a moment in silence." Silva lowered his head.

With his head lowered, Phil's head looked left and right. "What are we looking at?"

"It's called praying!" Silva spat. "Just bow your head for a moment and shut up."

After a few moments, Silva raised his head and opened his eyes. "Remember this moment, because you'll be doing lots of praying once we get to the mainland.

"Let's get our heads together. I know you've never reported to me, but we are all trained the same way and need to get on the same page if we are going to survive this. Realistically, our journey is just getting started."

"I am your Captain now. You will respect my rank." Silva eyed Wes. "Use your food rations sparingly. We have no idea how long we will be without food and additional clean water. Here's what we do know. Matt is our tech. Anna is our medic. Alix and Victor, you are our sniper team. We have enough fuel to make it to Battery Park, which is in Manhattan. Manhattan was the most populated place when the war started. It is an island, and from what I remember, all bridges to and from were destroyed except one—the Broadway Bridge at the north end. There is most likely a high rate of Citiz there, but there are underground subway systems that might be smart to travel through that you've seen in your simulations. We'll keep our eyes out for buildings still standing—they will either be empty and will give high vantage points for Alix and Victor to cover us, or they will be filled Citiz, with the enemy's snipers, or worse, one of M.A.I.A.'s sniper teams.

"If we take Brooklyn, our intel suggests that there is a high density of armed foreign enemies. The ones that invaded this country. It would be a hard fight, and with the flare we just lit, I'm sure they are planning a welcome party for us.

"We are sitting ducks out here. Let's get to land quickly, get off the water and into the trucks, and scope out the area while getting as far away from M.A.I.A. as possible, because I'm sure they are on our tail.

"And one last thing. I'm putting Corporal Wilder in second command."

"I'm a Private, sir," Wes quickly rebutted.

"No, I just made you Corporal. If anything happens to me, I want you all to follow his lead. Captain Milligan would agree that he has the most piss and vinegar and leadership training."

Phil, Matt, Hayden, Adam and Alix, slapped Wes' back and shoulders in approval.

"Thank you, sir," Wes saluted.

"Don't thank me. If anything happens to me, you'll be cursing me for burdening you with the responsibility."

"I won't let Captain down, sir."

"I'm counting on that," Silva said with a hard nod. "Before we left the island, Captain Milligan and I were briefed. It is mostly mercenaries, Citiz, and a policing foreign military. We need to dodge both groups. If Conservation truly starts before we get out of Manhattan, we might be able to duck out when the fighting begins. M.A.I.A. will see us as the enemy, too. We'll be landing in Battery Park in Manhattan at 0 hundred hours, and we'll roll the Humvees onto shore quickly. We head north to that bridge and seize control. That bridge is a conduit for all U.S. forces, if there are any left, and we want to be its gate keeper. Let's move out. Oorah?"

"Oorah!"

25

"Gentlemen, we all have something in common." Rankin's T-Port whined back and forth in front of a short line of soldiers. "There is a group out there that has escaped the island and betrayed our whole organization. Now, we can wait and let the Citiz gobble them up, but I would much prefer a different type of torture method for each one of them. I think you would agree."

Gunther moved his lips to speak.

"Not yet—I'm not done. Conservation has been pushed back. If we put together a task force like you, we will catch them faster." Rankin stopped rolling and stared at all of them one by one. "If you don't want to obey these demands, your memories will be subject to the Vanishing Sequence, and you will be cooking my breakfast tomorrow. I'm not asking."

The patch over his left eye reduced his peripheral vision. His T-Port wheel hit the edge of their boots and forced the line to take a step back.

Billy, Todd, Chris, and Austin lined up next to Gunther.

"Corporal Antrim, Captain Silva made a mockery of you and your men. How do you let four completely loaded and stacked Humvees out of lock-up without authorization? How?!"

"Sir..." Billy opened his mouth.

"Don't speak!" Rankin snapped.

"But you asked me..."

"I know what I asked you! An eye patch does not affect my mind. Silva has the youngest group in the facility, and they outperformed you, out maneuvered you, and outsmarted you and all these other idiots!"

The room hushed. "I will give you a chance to redeem yourselves by catching Silva. I am putting your group together with top-secret clearance. You will be able to leave the island by raft. If you succeed in the successful killing or capturing of anyone in their group, you will be awarded 150 rations per person, 300 for Silva and 500 for Alix Basil. The girl they are with, Anna Brooks, must be returned and unharmed, and you'll get yourselves 1,000 rations from me personally. If she reports any mistreatment, you'll get nothing but my wrath."

Todd's eyes lit up. He would enter simulation and just never come out. By the time he finished in the world he created, with that amount of time, drugs, alcohol, and the sex, he wouldn't remember what reality looked like.

"Gunther." Rankin wheeled toward him.

Gunther's eyes narrowed, and he folded his arms, his feet spreading into a defiant stance. "I'm not one of your toy soldiers."

"No, you're not." Rankin stood, eyes to eye patch. "I'll stop you there before I'm forced to cut off your shooting finger and shove it in *your* eye. Then we'll find out how good you are at stirring goop for the cadets. Don't make me waste your talents as a soldier, because you're too arrogant to follow orders.

"I've read your profile. You're one of the best there is. Your brother was a good man. He died too early, for sure. You made a great shot at a very high-profile target today. I want to commend you for that. You have been issued the 200 rations for your kill, and a commendation has been added to your profile. Your brother is going to be awarded the M.A.I.A. employee of the month award. The fifty extra rations he would have received will be transferred to your account. You will also get another 200 because he helped you with the kill. I'm sorry for your loss."

Gunther's eyes didn't move. "I'll need a spotter."

"I am working on a spotter right now as we speak. He'll be done with programming soon. Because M.A.I.A. is still down, and we're operating all the computers manually, you will be deployed in four hours. That means that Captain Silva and his team have a seven-hour head start. Do you accept your assignment, or do you want to not remember your own name tomorrow?"

Gunther nodded. "Reader Rankin, I'll need access to Alix's simulations and will need at least an hour in simulation myself. When will M.A.I.A. be back online?"

"I haven't decided."

The line of men looked at each other. Gunther's eyes locked on Rankin's one good eye.

"I mean, it hasn't been decided."

"Are simulators still working?"

"Yes, they are, they just are not reporting to M.A.I.A. Before you start, the simulator will require you to press a record button, so it will record your session, and be reviewed and uploaded to M.A.I.A. when she's back online. Your EEDs still have access to the data base, and you can still communicate and receive instruction. It's just a bit more covert."

"Covert? What does that mean?" Todd asked.

"It means that no one knows what anyone is really doing," Gunther said.

Rankin snarled in Gunther's face. "If I was totally blind and deaf, I would know exactly what you're doing, what you're eating for breakfast, when you take a piss, and when your prick gets hard. Do not think that an eye patch and problem legs diminishes my knowledge of your every move. I am omnipotent,"

"Sir, what does omnipotent mean?" Todd asked, and kept his eyes focused on the wall in front of him.

"It means he believes he's God," Gunther spat.

Rankin's head snapped towards Gunther, rolling his T-Port up to him. "Are we going to have a problem with rank, Vasily?"

"I don't have problems. I get paid to get rid of them," Gunther said. He kept his eyes on Rankin's one eye.

"If you weren't needed for this mission, I'd have you..."

"I didn't eat one of your chips. I am program free, a Green Beret, and your worst nightmare. I'm here because I am loyal to my country, not you. My country. Give me what I need, so I can do my job."

Rankin lifted his eye patch and leaned into Gunther's face. They were nose to nose.

"I can pull your plug the way I pulled M.A.I.A.'s," Rankin threatened through gritted teeth.

"I'm not a machine. I have no plug. Who's my spotter?"

Rankin glanced to his right and four heads snapped forward. He had never had anyone defy him, especially in public. He stared at Gunther, whose eyes held the sniper's stare. His left eye was slightly closed, and his right eye remained steady and unblinking. Gunther was right. Rankin couldn't control him or subject him to the Vanquishing Sequence, but he could change Billy, Todd, Austin, and Chris's minds. Once Alix and his team were captured and Anna was back, safe and sound, he could access M.A.I.A. to alter Billy, Todd, Austin, and Chris's perceptions to seek the traitorous Gunther and kill him.

"Major Vasily, you're lucky I'm on a mission," Rankin said with a sardonic smile and rolled back. "Your spotter is going to be Eli Williams. He was on the same team as Alix. Eli will help you because Anna is his girlfriend and Alix took her from him and ratted him out for using the simulator on a night that Eli was supposed to meet her."

"Is it true?"

Rankin snarled. "The truth is what I say the truth is!"

"I'll need his file."

Rankin breathed. "I'll forward you Eli's file, once everything is compiled. Everything is manual, so it will take twenty minutes to do."

"I don't care about Eli. I need Alix's file. A hit like this requires I know exactly how he moves. This is not war strategy; this is an assassination."

"You do know a little about assassinations, don't you, Gunther? Me too." Rankin smiled, calling, "Corporal Antrim, get your team in line. You are reporting to Major Vasily going forward. No more slip-ups."

The T-Port wheeled the Reader away, leaving the echo of its whirring motor in their ears.

The dim room remained quiet.

"I hate that guy," Billy stepped out of line.

"You think he's coming back?" Todd kept his eye on the door.

"No," Billy said. "Let's go blow off some steam in simulation."

"You four have a reputation of shooting up places. None of that cowboy shit," Gunther said, entering information in his EED.

"Yee hah!" Austin screamed.

They laughed.

"Let's saddle up boys!" Brian howled. "Don't worry, Gunther, we'll make sure we put in some simulation time for practice, of course, and for the mission and some team bonding. But first, my team and I need a little rest and relaxation. You just got a load of rations. Is there any way you'd be willing to share a little? I want my team to be bright-eyed and sharp for the mission. All work and no play make Billy and his team dull boys. If we're dull, accidents happen."

Billy placed his hand on Gunther's shoulder.

Gunther shoved Billy's hand away. "You can have my brother's rations. See you on the dock. Once the tread of your boots steps onto that dock, you are under my command. Got it?"

"Yes, sir, Sergeant!" Billy gave Gunther a hard salute. The others followed.

"Pound sand," Gunther grumbled and walked out the door.

"Sphincter! I hate that guy," Billy's EED vibrated. "Gunther just transferred 200 rations to me. I love that guy!"

26

"Cut the engine. We'll drift in." Silva held the helm. He adjusted the barge back and forth. "I'll steer it straight in. Scan everything with thermals as we approach. Prepare the Humvees."

Anna and Alix stared up at the shadows of the fallen and beaten-up titans that were the buildings of New York City.

"I can't believe how big they are. You see them in simulation, but I can't believe it. Alix, look at that one," Anna pointed.

"Yeah, it looks like it fell over and is leaning into that one. I wouldn't want to be under it when it collapses," Alix exhaled and winced to fight back tears.

"Babe, he's a hero. He cared about you so much and gave his life to save yours and maybe save all of us. We're about to be the first team on the mainland. Isn't that what he wanted?"

"I know... just can't stop seeing his face."

"Right now, he would want you to focus. Your team needs you. You can't blame yourself for that no more than you can blame yourself for being programmed the way you are, or for these fallen buildings." Anna kissed him. "Sue says everything happens for a reason."

"That's what I'm afraid of. What is going to happen next? What if we lose someone else? What if I lose you? This isn't a simulation. This is real life and real death."

"Then we learn to be in the now, because that's all that we have. Let's be together and fight to get through this."

The ferry approached the island and more and more giant buildings and shadows peered down at them from above.

Matt pointed up. "That one there is the Freedom Tower. I recognize that one."

"It's pretty." Anna's eyes gleamed.

"Alix! Anna!" Wes turned the corner from the helm. "Get ready for breaching. Get your infrared ready. We need to be sure we don't walk into a shit storm. Anna, you don't just get to sit there and look pretty. Get a battle mask out of H2. We are going to need all the help we can get.

Wes' voice radioed through their earpieces. "Team, ready for boarding. Thirty seconds."

#

"Todd! Todd! Toss me a stack, quick! She said for another $500, she'll show me why they call her Pussycat!" Austin's naked body sunk into the red lavender loveseat; his hairy thighs spread wide as the stripper danced for him. Her fishnet stockings pulled high and tight on her legs and created red lines where the fabric cut into her skin. The smell of skin on skin, sweat, cigarettes, hard liquor, and drugs filled the room. Her dark, thin hair poured down her back and whipped around like leather straps from a flogger every time she twirled her head during Austin's lap dance.

Todd's lips smacked loudly as he pulled his mouth from his girl's nipple. "Asshole. Hold on." Todd grasped her upper hips and tossed her to the side of the couch.

The stripper moaned and threw her head back over the headrest, her dark hair flowing and grazing the floor.

"I swear, Austin, if I didn't want another bump, I'd offer you a bullet in the head before I got up from that." Todd edged his butt out of the deep, red velvet couch, pulled his jeans up enough, and waddled to his backpack.

Austin's arm reached around and unsnapped his stripper's black, lace bra and held out his hand for a five-finger grab of a stack of hundred-dollar bills.

Todd chucked two wads of hundreds at Austin. One slapped Austin's stripper in the back. The other bounced off the back of the wall and fell into Austin's lap.

"Don't ask me again," said Todd.

"Oh, man, does Billy know how to put together a simulation or what?" Austin muffled from in between the stripper's breasts as he threw her bra across the room. "I got your money, now show me why they call you Pussycat." His Cheshire Cat grin spread across his face.

"Yeah, Billy said the simulation ends in a bar fight and to behave—and don't kill anyone," Todd said as he aligned a white line of cocaine on the glass table. He rolled up a hundred-dollar bill and snorted the line of coke "Holy shit!" He snorted air hard and coughed twice.

Todd grabbed the bottle of whiskey. "I like the idea Chris had of bailing on Gunther and capturing those fuckers on our own. We could do this simulation for life with the payout that old shit bag on his Pogo Ball is offering."

The Club's host, Bruce, who wore a black suit and bow tie, cleared his throat. "Ah, sir, that will be five hundred American dollars for that bottle of whiskey."

Todd slugged off the bottle and grimaced. "Five hundred for the bottle? Go get the money from Billy. This is his simulation." He pointed at the stripper on the velvet couch. "I'm going to pay this girl's tuition. Pound sand."

Todd waddled away with his pants around his ankles.

The host sighed. "Very well. I will check with Mr. Antrim for the remainder of your tab."

"Todd! Todd! Look it! Look it!" Austin laughed.

Todd looked over, sweat dripping from his head. Austin's stripper was perched on the back of the couch with her legs spread wide.

"She tattooed whiskers on the inside of her thighs!" Austin howled.

"Animals," Bruce snorted as he exited the red-lit room through the silk curtain. He leaned into a large man in a small shirt, who was protecting the girls. "This could get out of hand. Please get ready to escort these *fine* gentlemen out using *any* means necessary. Let's set the tone early if they are going to entertain here."

Bruce knocked on the door. "Mr. Antrim, we have a minor monetary dispute with your comrades. They told me to address you for the funds for our lavish whiskey. Five hundred American dollars is needed."

"What?!"

Bruce sighed. "Your buddies told me to get the money from you."

"Come on in!"

Bruce entered the purple room, rhythmic screams circling alongside the disco ball. He looked away from Billy's exposed butt, and his ass-less chaps. Two pistols hung from each side of a cowboy holster.

"There is a pile of cash on the table," said Billy. "Take six hundred. If I thought I would never use this simulation again, I'd shoot you in the head right now. Oh, baby, yeah." Billy pulled the woman's hair, jerked her head backwards, and she released a moan of ecstasy.

Bruce pushed a couple of rolled-up dollar bills over the glass end table into his hands. He counted the only dry ones not marinated in whiskey and snot. "There is only four hundred in acceptable bills, Mr. Antrim."

"Check with Chris. Privacy, please!"

Bruce looked at his bodyguard and rolled his eyes. "Where is the other pathetic loser?"

"What'd you call me?" Chris emerged from an adjacent doorway as he pushed a pink silk curtain aside. A blue mask covered his eyes. Nipple tassels swayed back and forth from his chest with each sluggish step he took. He wore a male thong that used the image of a fire hose to contain his manhood, and high, yellow boots.

Bruce's eyes widened as Chris placed the barrel of a magnum to his temple.

Bang! Bang!

Bruce's body flew backwards. His blood splattered over two women and a man, who screamed as they exited the room.

"Who fired the gun!" Locked in his egg, Billy's voice reverberated in his own ears. "Someone pulled the trigger and ended the simulation for all of us!"

His carnal needs unfulfilled, Billy ripped his head gear off and threw it at a recliner.

"Shit! Billy, what the hell are you guys doing? You discharged your weapons?" Gunther yelled and pounded on the neighboring wall. Gunther switched his channel from watching Alix's simulation to Billy's strip club and saw people running out of the club. The screen went black. Gunther rolled his eyes. "They have emotions of a damn rock and will shoot anything in simulation because there's no consequence."

He resisted the urge to go into their simulation rooms and bang their heads together. He had a job to do. He had to study and know his target.

He switched back and resumed watching the end of Alix's training simulation footage again. It was the simulation training in which he refused to shoot. He studied Alix's demeanor as Alix shot the man on the back of the truck. Gunther swiped at the screen and zoomed in so that he could see Alix's eyes. Those brown eyes were the eyes of the man who took his brother's life.

Gunther felt the weight of that bullet in his pocket, one that he would hold on to until Alix's life was taken as well.

Gunther zoomed out to view Alix's target. He recognized a brown-haired girl from a previous simulation. She looked familiar. From his pocket, he removed the snapshot Rankin gave him of Anna Brooks and studied the girl from the simulation. Anna bore a striking resemblance to the target in this simulation. What was Rankin's interest in this girl? Why was she in Alix's simulation as an enemy?

"I'm getting too old for this shit."

27

"Fire up the engines. Maintain radio contact. No unnecessary chatter. Use only infrared headlights. Your masks will be able to see the beam, but the truck won't give off any actual light. Follow me and keep your eyes peeled. I promise you; this isn't going to be a walk through the park. Pun intended." Silva released his microphone.

The Humvees pulled off the barge into Battery Park. One light post flickered. The rest of the lights around the promenade were broken, bent, torn down, missing, or smashed. Magazines, newspapers, trash, and debris rolled around Battery Park in the breeze and crawled until caught by the barbed wire that circled the park. A few park benches remained, pummeled and scarred from bullet holes. The Humvees moaned through tall, hood-high grass. The convoy crept past the leftovers of an outlined soldier statue, splattered with bullet holes.

Silva grimaced.

Hayden's head followed Silva's gaze. "What was that?"

"The Forgotten War Monument." Silva's head bowed as he passed it.

"Sir, I don't think anyone will ever forget the smell of this war," Leo spoke softly.

"The smell is sewage." Silva looked back at the monument in the rear window. "That monument is from the Korean War. My great-grandfather fought in that war. My father brought me to see it."

Brian cleared his throat. "Your father brought you to Korea?"

"No, to the monument right there. My ancestor's name is etched in it."

Aaron stretched his neck. "It's all shot up. Did it look nice before?"

Silva nodded. "Yeah... It was honorable." He looked through his goggles and into the red beam projected in front of the Humvee.

"Silva, what's that up ahead?" The voice came from H2.

"That's the East Coast Memorial. When it had wings, it used to be an eagle that faced the Statue of Liberty," said Silva. "Listen, boys, we can do the full tour another day. Let's keep focused. We could be ambushed any second. Keep your guns ready and ready yourselves for defensive maneuvers."

"Copy that, Captain," Wes's voice broke in.

Anna turned around. "You think we'll be able to see the Statue of Liberty from here?"

Alix looked back through the window. "I doubt it. There isn't much left to it anyway."

Anna twisted, leaned onto her knee, and slid a box of ammo to the left. "I know, but I wonder if we could see her from here."

She strained her eyes. Her battle goggles zoomed in more than her eyes could, turning the world into a hazy green in the faint light, and she saw the outline in the distance. "Wow, there it is. I can't imagine how big it was."

Wes snapped his head back for a quick glance. "Put your ass in the seat. Follow Captain's orders. Stay alert."

Glass crunched and crackled under the tires. The right tire rolled over a lump and forced each Humvee to tip slightly.

"What was that?" Phil leaned up in the Humvee to look over the hood.

"I don't know." Adam looked in the rearview. "There's infrared behind us. I can't see."

"I think it was a body," Anna said.

"It was a body. Cut the chatter," Silva's voice quipped in their earpieces.

"The GPS says the road is ten meters," Matt's voice spoke through soft static.

Phil eyed a monstrous building. He leaned forward to look up at it. His helmet pressed against the door's glass. "What is that?"

"The Freedom Tower," Silva said flatly.

#

"Eli, do you know who I am?" Rankin shined a small flashlight into each pupil and looked backwards over his shoulder. "Dr. Harrison, why isn't he responding? Eli?" Rankin shook him.

"Stop!" Dr. Harrison ordered. "He will in a moment, Mr. Rankin. Please give him a minute. We have never reinstated someone like this. It's almost like waking up for the first time in his life, but with memories of existence."

"Eli! Wake up, boy! It's going to be like waking up for the last time if he doesn't respond." Rankin slapped his face three times.

Harrison choked on the words forming in his mouth, and he retracted his open hand to stop himself, curling it back into a little ball, instead.

Eli opened his eyes. They glazed over, rolled up into the back of his head, and then returned to normal, making eye contact with Rankin.

"W... wh ... where am I?"

"Yes!" Rankin raised his hands. "What is your name, boy?"

Eli looked to Dr. Harrison. "Eli Williams."

"This is great." Rankin smiled big. "Eli, who am I?"

"You are Reader Albert Rankin, sir."

"Yes!" Rankin clapped and looked at Harrison. "What squad were you formally in?"

"Squad Twenty-Eight. No longer exists, though, all deemed traitors. Captain Milligan is dead, and I am going to kill Alix Basil with Gunther Vasily." Eli's words trailed off.

Dr. Harrison didn't completely believe them, more programmed words, but he was saying exactly what Rankin said he would say.

Rankin wheeled back. "Okay, okay. Now, stand, please."

Eli pushed himself up out of bed. "Why am I so tired, sir?"

"You've been out for a couple of days." Rankin smiled at Dr. Harrison and handed Eli a battle knife.

Eli studied the blade. "What's this for?"

Dr. Harrison stepped forward. "M.A.I.A. is not back online. He's not fully integrated. I don't think this is a great…"

Rankin's head snapped angrily towards Dr. Harrison. "Be quiet! I want him to focus."

Eli scanned the octagon, the mirrored windows, the hologram computers, the wires from the ceiling, and the blue light that glowed around the edges. The slow beep of the machines circled the room along with the hum of the computers. He spotted it. Alix's face. The knife instinctively soared out of Eli's hand and stuck into a digital Alix's face. The digital Alix flickered, and the knife fell to the floor.

Rankin smiled. "Suit up, Eli. I'm going to give you what you want. You are going to see what it is like off the island. You are to be conjoined with Anna Brooks, the love of your life. Alix took her from you. I'm going to let you get her back."

Doctor Harrison moved toward the door. "Rankin, please. It's too soon. We don't know the effects this could have…"

"Dr. Harrison, Eli is just fine. Aren't you Eli?"

"Yes, sir. When do I get to deploy to rescue Anna?"

"Check your EED and report to Major Vasily. He will lead the rescue mission."

"Thank you, sir." Eli saluted Rankin and left the room.

"Did you see that? He saluted me. Eli knows I am the leader."

"His perceptions may still be off a bit," Dr. Harrison scratched his head.

"Are you saying I'm not the leader?"

"No, I'm not saying that. You're not standing in military uniform for him to salute you, which makes me think he is not properly processing what he is seeing."

"I just programmed M.A.I.A.'s first assassin. There will literally be no one on the planet as stealthy and effective as Eli. Give me some credit and respect!"

"When will M.A.I.A. be back online?" Dr. Harrison asked.

"The other day, I asked you for the code for a particular virus. Get it to me by the end of the day."

Dr. Harrison offered Rankin a bewildered stare. "I'm sorry. I thought I misheard you. That code is for..."

"I know what it's for."

"But protocol requires that all the Readers approve the access and use of that code."

"I am the Supreme Reader," Rankin gritted between his teeth. "M.A.I.A. is down and I am in charge. Get me the code."

"Sir, I will usually have to log any of my activities in the system with M.A.I.A. Any idea when she will be back online?"

"You'll have to learn to get along without her until she is ready. You remember how to be human. One foot in front of the other. Until I tell you otherwise, log your activities manually on paper and turn it into me directly. No one else sees it. You understand?" He spun his T-Port around to face the door. Its whir began as the T-Port moved forward, and then sputtered, and came to a dead stop. Rankin's fingers banged on the control panel. "What the devil is wrong with this thing?"

"Perhaps, you have run out of power," Dr. Harrison tossed over his shoulder. He looked up from his desk to look at Rankin. "If memory serves me, it's a warning."

"A warning for what?"

"That you're about to lose power," Dr. Harrison said with a smug smile. "You need M.A.I.A. operational for wireless charging. However, you should have enough power to get back to your office. Hopefully."

Rankin's ears heated. He looked down at the T-Port display and the battery icon flashed red. His finger pushed the flashing light. A message scrolled across the T-Port screen.

Charge battery. Fifteen percent. Charge battery.

Rankin needed to return to his office, sit in his chair, plug his T-Port into an outlet, and wait for it to charge to completion.

"This piece of worthless crap!" Rankin snapped. Spittle landed on his screen.

"Yes, I'm afraid technology is not as reliable as humans. It's like you said, sir. One foot in front of the other," Dr. Harrison said lightly. He turned his head back to the paper on his desk to keep from laughing.

Rankin slapped the forward button. The T-Port jerked forward and careened him into the doorway. He backed up and sped down the hall as the whirs of the T-Port sputtered amid his curses.

28

Elmer Washington's eyes jolted back and forth across his computer screen. He read his message to confirm its content. His eyes landed on his final words: *remove Rankin.* Tampering with M.A.I.A. was an act of treason. M.A.I.A. was created to prevent power from landing in corrupt hands.

Checks and balances existed that M.A.I.A. buried deep in her circuit soul, that no one knew about until she was shut down. A disturbing, but not surprising message awaited Elmer when he retrieved and opened his emergency tablet. A video of Rankin in the control room as he tried to alter M.A.I.A. populated. What Rankin did resulted in the population of the large Vanishing Sequence list. Surely, M.A.I.A. collected all the information as suspect and put it forth to the Readers in the form of a Vanishing Sequence roster. When information did not compute, M.A.I.A. expelled. The truth was hard to hide.

All the Readers saw Rankin's treachery and furiously communicated with each other without Rankin knowing. M.A.I.A. being offline provided a level of convenience, and a perfect time to plan Rankin's ousting. Elmer couldn't wait to get rid of the motoring, festering organism of flesh. He hit 'send.' The door slid open.

"Albert Rankin? What brings you down to the business center at this hour?"

Rankin's T-Port whined into the room and rolled in front of Elmer. "I could ask you the same thing, Elmer. But I won't. I trust you have important business that needs attending to outside of our business hours." Rankin smiled. "As do I."

"The light is better here than in my quarters. I can't wait for M.A.I.A. to be back online to shed more light in my room and everything else going on," Elmer said and turned off his tablet.

"If your tablet isn't bright enough, you can brighten your screen. Turn it on, I'll show you how." Rankin reached for Elmer's tablet.

"No, that's not necessary." Elmer moved his tablet away, stood up, and tucked it under his left arm. His right hand continued to grip it. "Are you ready for Conservation? I'm just doing everything possible to get us out of this hole."

"We are ready—aside from our little incident yesterday. But I've taken care of that."

"How did you take care of that? Did you consult the other Readers? I didn't get a notice or message. Is M.A.I.A. back online?"

"Relax, I didn't do anything out of jurisdiction. I have made an assignment for some volunteers. There were no binding restrictions to M.A.I.A. because of circumstance."

"My God, Rankin, what did you do now?" Elmer's eyes blazed with fiery anger.

"What do you mean, what did I do *now*?"

Elmer swallowed. "I didn't get a notice or message is all that I'm saying."

"You and the other Readers will be very happy to know that I got a team together to go after the traitors." Rankin transferred himself into a seat and clicked on a keyboard. The computer monitor came to life. His fingers clacked away. "If all goes to plan, Major Vasily and his team will be landing in one hour, and they will have Alix by sundown. I know where their ferry landed. I am waiting to see if they were smart enough to remove the trackers on the Humvees." His fingers stroked the keyboard. "And apparently, they are not that smart. Oh, look. There they are now. There's nothing like old-fashioned satellite technology."

Elmer Washington stared at the map, the exact position of the four Humvees. "Is the satellite providing us this remote viewing access?"

"Yes."

"Impressive."

"And we're doing this without M.A.I.A.," Rankin said smugly.

Elmer looked closer. "What is that movement there? Around Marble Hill?" he pointed. "Is that the enemy's army?"

Rankin zoomed out on a large movement. A moving, dark cloud of an army approached the city. Little people like ants followed tank after tank and truck after truck over the only bridge left on the island. "Until we officially begin Conservation, everyone is an enemy."

Elmer nodded. "Call a Reading. We might have to start Conservation early, by the looks of that force. Let's fire M.A.I.A. up and get her back online with the new protocol. I want to put out a broadcast immediately."

"What broadcast would that be? I am the Supreme Reader. All broadcasts still must go through me for approval."

Elmer froze. "Yes, of course. Do you think it a good idea that we call a Reading?" Reading would be the perfect moment to oust Rankin. Maybe everyone would agree to put him on the mainland and wheel himself through the streets he wanted so desperately to control.

Rankin lowered his head, his eyes peering over his glasses as he studied Elmer.

"Yes... yes... Let's call a Reading. I look forward to it." Rankin's finger tapped the escape key. The screen blackened. "And so, it begins."

Like daggers, Rankin's dark, cold eyes sought to target a hidden truth that Elmer refused to share—for now.

Elmer diverted his eyes. "I will alert the others about the Reading to discuss the new developments." He turned on his heels and exited.

Rankin rolled to the hallway to watch Elmer escape—for the moment.

The hall lights flickered. A large wall screen in the business center flickered. Rankin spun his T-Port around to return to the business. A blue, wavy line scrolled across the screen. The light on the screen fluttered, went out, and returned. M.A.I.A.'s blue line scrolled for a second, broke, and then produced another blue line like it was a hiccup.

Rankin rolled closer. An unknown anxiety heated his face like a child seeing a ghost.

"It can't be... M.A.I.A., what are you trying to do? You can't start without my permission." His jaw ached from the pressure of his gritted and grinding teeth.

The lights surged brightly and then threw the facility into darkness.

Bang!

The facility moaned from the loss of power.

Click! Like the cranking of clock cogwheels.

M.A.I.A. released an electronic whine as she came back online and resounded throughout the campus. The screen lit up and the blue line rolled across the screen. M.A.I.A. rebooted herself. A large set of closed eyes appeared on the screen. When they opened, a thunderous rendition of Beethoven's Fifth Symphony blasted into every space and shook the underground facility.

Rankin jolted on his T-Port and grabbed the handlebars to steady himself.

As the opening to Beethoven's Fifth Symphony played, exclamations of wonderment filled nearby offices and poured out into the hall. Rankin tried to turn his suddenly stiff T-Port to the hall, but the T-Port's steering column froze. He pressed his index finger hard into the directional pad, hyperextending his knuckle.

Keyboard Locked. M.A.I.A.... M.A.I.A.... M.A.I.A.... flashed and scrolled across his small T-Port screen. The flashing battery disappeared. His T-Port died.

The blaring symphony buried his voice as he called out for help. Rankin searched the room for a chair to crawl to. His right hand lowered to release the clamp that held his legs in place. The T-Port jolted and then vibrated. The battery level ascended to fifteen percent, twenty percent, to thirty-five percent and surged upward to one hundred percent. The music abruptly ended. His heart pounded behind his ears.

Bleep... Bleep...

A white dot appeared in the center of the monitor, and like a lit fire-cracker, it ignited and released a series of sparks and sizzles that took the shape of a woman's face. Composed from the blue glow of the computer screen, she opened her eyes and blinked. Her eyes cast downward at Dr. Rankin.

"Dr. Rankin. It is good to see you. Performing an assessment of all functioning systems. Holding all vanishing sequences—for now."

29

The sound of trash crunched under the tires and echoed through the vacant street labeled Trinity Place. The convoy swerved and weaved around charred and flipped cars, abandoned and rusted, windows shattered, interior compartments stripped for parts and wires, missing doors, hoods, and even their engines gutted or completely gone. The convoy edged around and powered through toppled and bent streetlights and lampposts. Black smoke trails elevated to the sky from smoldering buildings.

Rubble, steel cables, and electrical wires from fallen buildings blocked off roads and paths. A fire truck covered in broken and smashed stone prohibited access to Thames St. The ladder jetted thirty feet in the air. The sirens were smashed to pieces, and the driver's seat caved in like a metal carcass, eaten and devoured. They kept driving.

Wes's eyes searched for intact windows, a rarity, because Citiz shot or busted most windows in the buildings. "Silva, where is everyone?"

Silva eyed the top of the buildings. "Either gone or watching us. I can't tell."

"Didn't you say that there used to be millions of people here?" Victor asked with disgust.

"Yup." Silva watched a bird perch on a bent streetlight.

The convoy pulled up and braked at a wall of cars stacked three vehicles high.

Silva radioed in. "Team, I know this is a lot to take in, but stay alert. We are going to throw up a drone and check to see if it is worth plowing through these cars, or if we should backtrack. Stay alert."

Silva rolled down his window. The deep, moldy smell of feces and urine seeped through the crack in the window and soiled their air. He held a small, electronic, pancake-shaped object out the window and pressed the button on the top. The device spun out of his hand and climbed above the Humvees about a hundred feet. Silva looked over the projected map with Leo.

"Leo, what can you tell me?"

Leo leaned in. "I think it's a waste of time trying to go up Church or Broadway. I would bang a left here. We can take a right onto Greenwich and make our way north."

"There was a community college in that area. If we can get the trucks to the community college, we could hunker there and figure out the next steps. Good job, Leo." Silva stuck his hand out the window, and the drone hovered down and settled in his hand. "Alright, everyone. Our scout has spoken. Be advised, going left here. We don't know what's around that corner, so alert, alert. Stay off your mics unless it's absolutely necessary."

The trucks turned.

Alix looked up at the wall of cars as they motored by. His eyes roved the environment, looking for snipers' nests.

"Is that snow?" Matt said through the microphone in their helmet.

Silva looked up. "Ash and dust. No snow yet. Everyone stop." The convoy halted. "Stay here a minute." Silva exited.

Their faces pressed against the windows. Aaron and Leo followed him with their weapons raised out the window and eyes scanning the area.

"What's he doing?" Anna asked.

"Stay inside and alert. Keep your mic clear," Brian's voice snapped from the second Humvee.

Silva's boots scraped the cracked pavement, barking into their earpieces, "Get out of the trucks, now."

"Captain Silva!" Wes exited the Humvee, closed the door, and circled the truck in full attack mode. "This doesn't seem very smart. What are we doing? We're in the open."

"Keep an eye on the perimeter." Silva lifted his palm and his drone zipped to the sky. "The drone will alert us of any nearby activity. This is important. Follow me."

Victor nudged Alix. "Are we fighting or site seeing?"

Alix shrugged and grabbed his SCAR assault rifle.

"Permission to speak, sir?" Matt requested.

Silva shook his head. "No. Wes, take your Humvee team and guard the perimeter. I need one minute of talk time."

"Yes, sir. Victor, stay close to the truck with me. Alix, Matt, and Anna, spread out. You got your minute, Captain," Wes said as he tapped his EED. A sixty second countdown commenced on his screen.

"This asshole," Victor muttered.

Wes shot Victor a hard look.

The armed group followed Captain Silva as he approached a massive, shiny, square bench that stretched all the way to the other side of an empty pool. He touched the top of the bench and knelt.

"Sir, it's pretty open here." Alix's eyes searched the rooftops. If they were being hunted, this would be slaughter.

"One minute!" Silva barked.

Captain Silva and the team flanked the edge of a giant, perfect square like a cookie cutter had taken a section of the world away.

"I didn't think this was still here. You're standing in the exact place where nearly 3,000 Americans lost their lives." Silva pointed to the ground, and the team looked down into the square cavern. "I watched the footage of monster planes that were hijacked and flown into the Twin Towers—nearly the height of this Freedom Tower."

Everyone's heads rolled back on their shoulders to view the height whose top floor disappeared into the clouds.

"On my eighteenth birthday, I enlisted in the United States Marine Corps. I decided to fight for my country, for my freedom, and for what

I thought was right…" Silva's voice cracked, "… like my father did and his father did. I chose my destiny just like you chose to take this mission, and to stand where you are standing right now.

"This morning, all of you stood up for what was right, what you believed in. You heard of a comrade in trouble, and you all left no man behind. You all would sacrifice your own lives for another teammate. That's what it's like to be on a team. In a family," Silva breathed. "I want you all to look down at this monument and find one name and say it out loud. Remember that name, remember this monument, and remember the word 'Freedom,' because that's who you're fighting for. This is real human life.

"Find that name on the wall and say it out loud. I want you to promise this person that you will remain a human and uphold your dignity. You will not leave yourself subject to a program, and you will do the right thing."

"Time!" Wes yelled.

Alix whispered, "William Dixon."

Phil's voice thundered. "Heather Elizabeth."

"Eric Arthur Blair." Leo clenched his jaw.

"Patricia Theresa." Hayden placed the butt of his gun on the ground.

"Cormac McCarthy." Adam stared into the waterfall.

"Beatrice Prior," Brian announced.

"Herbert Roberts," Aaron whispered.

"Nicolas Ryan," Silva cleared his throat. "Let's get to work and finish this. Ooorah!"

"Ooorah!"

Silva lifted his hand for the drone to return. The drone's radar alarm sounded in his ear. One shot burst out from the distance, and the drone fell to the ground and smashed into pieces.

"Take cover!" Wes screamed.

30

Billy, Todd, Chris, and Austin huddled in a half circle as they stared at the screen that held M.A.I.A.'s face.

"Good morning, all!" M.A.I.A.'s screen shined bright as she appeared on the monitors everywhere in the facility. Her voice echoed throughout. "It's great to be back. I missed you all."

"Woah! I can't believe M.A.I.A. has a face!" Todd smiled.

"When we get back, I'm getting some simulation time with her," Austin yelled and dropped his head back to howl like a wolf.

"Prick, she's not real." Gunther checked the magazine in his side arm.

"She doesn't need to be real, just accessible in the simulator." Billy flipped his goggles down from his helmet and bared a toothy grin.

"You're quiet," Gunther said to Eli.

"I'm focused," he responded without looking.

"Are you sure you're okay?"

Eli's head snapped sideways. "Fine. Are you okay?"

"I'm fine." Gunther watched Eli's right eye twitch. "You look wired to kill."

"Absolutely. I'm getting my girl back." Eli zipped his vest and punched his chest.

Todd laughed and pivoted his hips back and forth. "Eli is going to get him some in between the leg action with Anna, aren't you?"

The four laughed.

"Shut up." Eli shoved his side arm into its holster.

"Sounds like somebody needed some time in the strip club," Chris snickered.

"What's wrong with this dude?" Todd pointed to Eli.

"You need to relax," Billy placed his hand on Eli's shoulder, but he pushed it off. "You're a bit touchy."

Footage of Squad Twenty-Eight along with others sitting in glass cells played on the monitor.

"Pipe down, guys. I can't hear anything she's saying." Gunther moved closer to the screen.

M.A.I.A. held her hologram tablet in her hand. "I know we had a recent temporary disturbance, but M.A.I.A. officials handled it. I am happy to report that the leader of the rebellion, Captain Robert Milligan, has been killed. The rest of the team have been apprehended and is being held within the facility. I am glad to report that Anna Brooks, their hostage, will return safely back to work after some extensive emotional stress evaluation."

Footage of Anna talking to a white-coated female played and then cut to another employee.

"Squad Twenty-Eight were very sloppy. Alix Basil missed several shots unsurprisingly based on his recent failing in simulation, and the whole team will be terminated."

"Alix has to be the worst shot in the history of M.A.I.A," Chris smiled.

"Makes it easier for us," Billy said and high-fived Todd.

M.A.I.A.'s face returned to the screen. "I assure you, this will never happen again. The Readers and I are back on duty with new astringent protocols and processing capabilities.

"Great news for you, young cadets." M.A.I.A. smiled. "We have decided to push the Conservation up weeks from intended plans. There is a large contingent of enemy forces entering into the city. I have done some analysis and decided it best to engage them sooner than originally anticipated. I have a scan of the island, and it appears as though the actual population of the island has been reduced to a couple of thousand civilians. With the Citizens fast approaching, our time is now to engage. Please stand by for further instructions from your commanders. And remember, cadets, train hard."

"I don't really understand. Who are we fighting?" Todd asked.

"We're fighting everyone," Gunther grunted, and slung his pack into the large bed of the cargo truck. "And if you actually believe Alix missed a shot, you're dumber than I thought. Let's move out."

"Gunther, didn't you see the broadcast?" Austin tossed his bag on the truck.

Chris snuffed. "I get why M.A.I.A. makes it appear like everyone is safe from Squad Twenty-Eight. Rankin doesn't want everyone to know that we're going after them."

Gunther smirked. "At least one of you went to school."

"Alix is flawed," Eli said as he tossed his gear bag in the cargo area of the Humvee.

Gunther interrupted, "Don't be so naïve. Alix killed my brother in less than two minutes of setting up from 500 meters from a rocking boat. I still don't know where he was hiding. I promise you, put him and his rifle within a couple miles of your asses, you are all dead."

"He's right." Eli looked at them. All sounds stopped, aside from the engine and the tires driving them to the launch. "They say, from our simulations, he is the deadliest person in the world with a rifle."

"If that's true, how'd we get stuck with you and Eli?" Todd laughed.

Eli's blue eyes glared at the four men. "Because I'm better."

Gunther motioned. "Eli, get in the truck."

"Better than who? You're nothing but a recommissioned hack soldier," Todd added with a smirk.

In a blur of movement, Eli threw Todd to the ground.

Billy took one step towards Eli, and Eli dropped down and clipped Billy's shins. Billy fell to his stomach.

Austin leapt at Eli, who grabbed Austin, spun him around, and held a knife to his throat.

When Chris moved to help Austin, Eli kicked Chris in the chest. Chris flew back and hit the rear of the Humvee.

Gunther laughed. "Well then, enough said. Eli, you done?"

"I'm done if they're done."

"I'm done," Austin blurted.

"Alright, let's move out. Eli, you're riding shotgun," Gunther announced and moved to the driver's seat.

Eli shoved Austin into Chris, and as the rest of them moved to the passenger doors, Eli stared them down as his right eye twitched.

#

"Team, spread out!" Silva swung his ACR assault rifle around, and slammed behind a raised, stone square that housed a small, dead tree. He looked at his EED. Red dots appeared all around them like an instant rash on the road.

"Wes here. Hunkered down, north-end entrance."

"Victor here, south-end entrance. Anyone have a visual?!"

"Negative! No visual, at the trucks, watching west side opening."

Silva peeked up.

"Wes here. I got movement."

"Just hold your fire until you confirm they are hostile." Silva checked his EED.

"They shot down the drone. They're hostile. Please advise."

Silva peeked to the south side of the opening of the quad. "Everyone, hold your position and hold fire."

Silence.

A ray of sunlight burst through the clouds, aiming at a dying tree in the corner of the quad. Everyone watched the first ray of light in years shine down on a tree. Two leaves swayed in a small breeze, and the shadow cast on the wall behind it twisted and waved unnaturally like the light beam was somehow underwater or a glitch.

"Camo curtains. Shit. Team, lock, and load. Keep an eye on the buildings. We are surrounded," Silva warned. "Team, remember your training. We've been pinned down before. Matt to the trucks, team, cover him, go!"

Alix aimed his SCAR from his knee toward the opening in the quad.

Halfway to the trucks, a shot rang out.

Matt fell to the ground. "Oh, shit, oh, shit, oh, shit! Am I hit?" He scrambled to his feet and ran the rest of the way. "Am I hit? Am I hit?"

Anna's search for Matt's body was interrupted by a loud squeal of audio feedback. Someone was about to speak. The squeal reached an ear drum splitting pitch before it was lowered.

"Private Alix Basil, you down there?" The voice came from the heavens.

Silva lifted his head upward to scan the dark particle sky and checked the rooftops on the eastside.

"Private Alix Basil and Squad Twenty-Eight, do you copy?" the voice bounced off the buildings.

"Do not respond," Silva whispered. It sounded like a megaphone. He peeked over the edge again and raised his rifle.

"We have you completely surrounded, and you are overwhelmingly outnumbered. We have each one of you in our sights. If you are not Private Alix Basil and Squad Twenty-Eight, you will all be killed in five seconds. This does not exclude Private Anna Brooks ... one ... two ... three."

31

Gunther sat on the boat's bench in full battle gear. He watched a ray of light break through the sky and shoot down for a moment in the distance. The boat's engine roared through the water toward Milligan's rogue ferry. According to the Humvee trackers, the ferry docked in the vicinity of the North Cove Yacht Harbor. His eyes moved to the Freedom Tower. Still standing.

"You're traveling a little heavy aren't you, old man?" Austin pulled his gloves on and stacked his gun on the Humvee, the wind from the harbor in his hair. "We have the truck, you know."

"Yeah, I see that." Gunther shoved another sack of rations, followed by more ammo, in his bag. "Eli, stuff your bag with those over there. Take as much as you will need, but I want you to carry some additional ammo."

"What's going on, Gunther?" Austin screamed over the engine and the sound of the sea. A splash came up over the front of the boat and misted them in small, cool drops.

"Nothing is wrong with me. Just can't wait to bag this target and get back to using my rations for simulated strip clubs and cocaine." Gunther delivered a smirk to Billy.

"Gunther," Todd sat next to him, "I don't know what you saw or heard, but that was just having a little fun before we left. No harm, no foul?" He held out his hand.

Gunther placed two different scopes in the bag, glancing at Todd's hand. "Look, guys, no offense, but when we land, I'm working alone.

Eli, you can spot for me if you want, but I don't want to work with these knuckleheads." He looked at Eli.

"I agree with you, and I'll be your spotter."

"Whatever, old man." Todd stood and walked away.

"Are you serious?" Billy's face contorted with confusion.

Gunther remained focused on his gear. "Yeah."

Billy pointed at Gunther. "You just made yourself an enemy. Don't radio in for help when you're surrounded, because we will be too busy carrying Anna Brooks over our shoulder back to M.A.I.A. to collect what's ours."

"Understood, boys." Gunther slung his rifle over his shoulder and holstered his pistol. "I won't ask for your help."

"And don't stand in my sight," Billy's jawline clenched.

"I'll be able to pick your teeth for you a mile out. Don't worry about me, boys. Unlike you cowboys, this is not my first rodeo. Don't stand in my crosshairs."

Austin nudged Eli, "Are you going with this old fart, or are you going to be on a winning team?" He smirked, adjusted the sights on this gun, and clicked in a mag. Water splashed the side of the barge.

"I'm his spotter. Those are my orders." Eli hoisted his gear on his shoulder.

Austin, Chris, and Todd pulled their M4s into their armpits. Chris aimed at Eli.

Eli caught the barrel of Chris's assault rifle in his peripheral vision. In one swift move, Eli's gear slid off his shoulder, and he spun, grabbed Chris's rifle, and jabbed his fingers into Chris's throat.

Chris clutched his throat, dropping to his knees and sputtering for air.

"Don't ever aim your gun at me!" Eli screamed.

"What the fuck!" Billy stepped towards Eli. "When I find Anna, it's going to be some tit for that. I'll get Anna and bring her to you in pieces."

Eli lunged at Billy, but Gunther wrapped a strong arm across Eli's chest and pulled Eli away. "Remember your mission. Let's go get Anna," Gunther spoke calmly. "Save your fight for Anna."

The motor to the ferry was cut. Gunther glanced over his shoulder. "We are approaching the dock. You calm?"

"I'm calm," Eli said.

"You good?"

Eli nodded, his right eye twitching.

Gunther released Eli, who spun like a tornado and delivered a back fist strike to Billy's face.

"Now, I'm good."

#

The sound of tarps swiped together and swished in the breeze. The road and world washed downward as the tarps fell. What remained was the same view of the road, but with soldiers who pointed their weapons at them. The whole length of the west side opening wrinkled downward and revealed an army. The tops of the roofs shifted, and rows of snipers and assault rifles stood in their places. Soldiers leaked out of the first floor of the Freedom Tower and emptied into the square.

"Team, we're surrounded. Corporal Wilder, prepare for a change in command."

"Copy. Good luck, sir."

Silva raised his hands in surrender. "Who's in charge here?!" he screamed. Silence. "I said, who's in charge?!"

"I am." A tall, black man appeared from the Freedom Tower, clean-shaven and dressed in military camo uniform. Beneath his short, brimmed camo hat, a pair of reflective aviators rested on his nose and blocked the sunless sky. With a megaphone behind his back, he approached Silva. With each step, his boots clicked on the concrete. It was the only sound in the square for an awkwardly long traverse. He stopped in front of Silva. "Private Alix Basil?"

"No. Captain Jack Silva. Who are you?"

"Who am I? To you, I am Sir. I am Major Jaxon Andrews, United States Marine Corps. No time for chitchat. Where's Alix Basil?"

Silva motioned to Alix.

"Here, sir." Alix popped up.

"About damn time. Next time I call your name. you will appear in front of me like a damn genie. I've heard about your skills, specialist Basil. Captain Jack Silva, you and your men report to me now." He pointed at Silva and Alix and then to his chest and walked away toward the Humvees. "You and your men have stirred up quite a bee's nest with that flare you set off. Where's the rest of your team?"

Anna and the rest of the men straightened, their weapons raised.

"Captain Silva," said Major Andrews, "instruct your men to stand down before my army and their arsenal of weapons turn them into human Swiss cheese."

"Team, stand down," Silva called out.

"Echo, stand down," Wes called out.

Jaxon yawned. "Alright, let's get going. There is a lot of debriefing to do, and I need to bring you up to speed."

"We don't report to anyone," Silva refuted.

"The badges across my chest say I am Major Jaxon. Right now, I am the biggest piece on this chess board. Fall in."

Jaxon didn't look back as he talked and walked towards the Humvees. "A couple thousand enemy forces are twenty-five klicks north from here. You triggered them by joyriding around in broad morning light and lighting flares like it's the fucking Fourth of July. That's why you report to me now."

Victor held his gun up and tightened his grip as Jaxon and three soldiers approached.

Jaxon pointed at Victor. "Son, you're going to hurt yourself with that thing. You had an order to lower your weapon. Point that at me again, and we are going to have problems. An extra orifice will appear in your forehead, understood? Silva, where are your manners? Don't you teach these boys anything on that forsaken island? Private," Jaxon pointed to Matt, "get me a water."

Matt reached in the back to grab a water.

"What are you doing?" Victor grabbed Matt's arm.

"He said he wants a water."

Silva followed Jaxon like a puppy. "I'm not surrendering this squad to you. Do you have any idea what we've been through in the last couple of days?"

"Silva, you know what I've learned in the last thirty seconds? You talk too much."

Jaxon turned around, brought the megaphone up to his lips, and screamed in Silva's face. "We are at war, Captain! Do you have an army? No? I do. And I say, get in your truck and follow me. That's an order." Jaxon lowered the megaphone. "I will explain later."

Jaxon twirled two fingers on his right hand in the air. Camo-curtains went up and over them. The whole army disappeared in seconds, all except the small contingent in front of the Humvees. Jaxon opened the door to the lead Humvee, pulled his pistol out, and shot several times into the GPS monitor.

Silva and his men ducked and drew their weapons.

"What are you doing?!" Silva screamed.

Jaxon's eyes pierced Silva. "Tell your men to shoot out the computers on the trucks. That's an order. They have trackers, you dipshit. There's been a team sent after you. Now, they don't know exactly where you are. You're welcome. Private, that water please."

Matt tossed him the bottle of water.

Jaxon twisted the water bottle cap off, flicked it to the ground, gulped some water, and walked away. He got into one of his Humvees. "Follow us."

"Captain?" Wes stood with his assault rifle close to his chest.

"Shoot out the screens in the Humvees." Silva handed Wes his side arm.

Wes marched over to each Humvee and fired at the computer screens.

"Captain Silva!" Jaxon screamed over to Silva. "You're riding up front with me. Have your team follow."

Victor jumped into the last Humvee with Aaron, Leo, and Brian and slammed the door.

"For all we know, he's leading us right into the arms of the enemy," said Victor. "We didn't escape from one prison to jump into another. I say we bolt. They can't track us."

"You heard what the major said to Captain. We got orders," Aaron said.

"And Captain Milligan said we got choices. Our Humvee has no tracking device. We can choose to be on our own," Victor said as he looked in his review mirror. A truck driven by the marines rolled up behind them and blared its horn to move them forward.

32

"Where did they go?" Austin scanned the quad. There was no one there.

"They can't just disappear." Billy shoved his eyes into binoculars. He switched it to infrared. "I got nothing. Todd, radio to Nest, tell them the Humvees are gone, and there is no sign of them."

"They can't be far." Todd used the crosshairs on the top of his gun to scan the north opening. "They were right here not even a half hour ago."

Gunther closed his eyes. He listened to the sound of a tarp swishing in the wind. He opened his eyes and looked around: the murky sky, the low wind, the destruction, and so many things to confuse the eye. "Camo curtains."

"What's a camo curtain?" Todd asked as he surveyed the area through the scope of his rifle.

"It like a big sheet used to make you think you're looking at something that isn't really there," Billy answered.

"Somebody paid attention in class." Gunther smirked.

"I don't like this," Eli muttered.

"Me neither. Let's move," Gunther said under his breath. He turned away from the camo curtains and exited the quad.

Eli, Billy, and Billy's team followed him with weapons drawn.

"No, not you four. You're on your own. Just Eli."

"Wait a minute, wait a minute. You're going to leave us here?" Austin grabbed Gunther's arm.

"It's what your team leader wanted on the boat and that's what you're getting. Good luck boys." Gunther hiked up his bag, rifle in hand, and walked towards the Freedom Tower.

"You sure you want to split up, Gunther?" Billy's voice shook. "Maybe we could set aside our differences and work as a team, you know?"

Gunther turned around and whispered loudly enough for them to hear. "Remember your training."

"We don't need you!" Billy yelled.

Gunther turned and held his finger to his lips.

"So, what now?" Todd asked as his eyes darted about the surrounding area.

"Well, we're not staying here like sitting ducks. Let's clear the first floor of this building. If we can get some altitude, maybe we can get a location on the Humvees. If they get too far north, we can take the boat north or unload the truck ... the truck! Shit!"

The four soldiers sprinted across the street. They stopped at the edge of the barge just as the military truck exploded and knocked them off their feet.

Billy pushed himself to his knees. "We got to get out of here. That explosion is going to draw some attention."

Chris squeezed his gun. "If I ever see Gunther and Eli again, I swear, I'm going—"

"Save it, Chris." Billy shielded him from the flame. "There are four of us. Let's head north. The last time the Humvees were tracked, they were heading north. We go where they go."

"What about supplies? What was in that truck is now ashes," Austin whined.

Billy shook his head. "Forget about it. We have enough supplies and ammo to last us awhile. If we need more, we can radio Nest for supplies. I'm sure Rankin will deliver."

#

Jaxon's convoy smashed through debris, skidded around corners, trampled over rubble, and then slammed down. Silva squeezed the "oh shit, handle" in the passenger seat, his helmet hitting the glass with every sharp left they veered, and Jaxon swung the wheel to the left. The Humvee skidded and slid on mortar crumbs from buildings as its tail end whipped out around the corner.

"Silva, you need answers. That's why you're up here with me, and I need you to get your team on board with me STAT."

Silva's body shifted to the right. He squeezed his handle. "These boys have bad attitudes, and their captain lost his head last night in front of them."

Jaxon slung the wheel to the right, weaving the six trucks through the streets. The tires screeched. "Listen, just because their captain caught a bullet, doesn't mean they can go AWOL, okay? You're a military man. Do what we do best. I don't know what they are telling you, but M.A.I.A., is a private company, not an independent governed place. All M.A.I.A. was supposed to do was supply us with soldiers. They were never meant to become a separate form of government or leadership. It just worked out that the attack from the Middle East gave M.A.I.A. the opportunity to kind of... take over.

"Above ground, our forces have laid low, waiting on you guys. It's been three years since any serious fighting. We've been hiding underground and using the camo curtains, lining them up from rooftop to rooftop of our facility for the satellites. The enemy has control over every major city north of DC. We've been waiting for your first deployment for weeks now. We expected more than you, but we'll take anything we can get." Jaxon swerved left, swiped a charred car, and smashed through a bus stop station. Debris flew into the windshield and up and over the Humvee.

"From what I hear, the computer is messing everything up. I've been in contact with Reader Elmer Washington for years. He's told me that he has some complications to deal with, but the army that you guys have been building would be our back-up in the weeks to follow. He told me to expect thousands, which is impressive. Especially if these boys are half as good as he claims them to be.

"Now, Silva, I don't know about you," Jaxon busted through an old, run-down, tipped-over hot dog cart that skidded and slid thirty feet, sparks flying, "but when a Reader says there are complications, that means one of a couple things all leading to getting screwed.

"We do have a sizable military down here. There were 9,000,000 people in the city when it fell. We've been able to snag the healthiest bodies between the ages of sixteen to forty and have an army of ... oh, I don't know, 5,000 marines and about 1,000 militia. They call themselves the Minutemen," Jaxon chuckled.

"Minutemen? I haven't heard that term since my high school history class," Silva snorted and smiled.

"Don't tell Kalev Delhi that. I put him in charge of the Minutemen. They seem to like him. He keeps those animals tamed."

"What military branch does Delhi come from?"

"He comes from 'the fight like hell, or get my ass kicked' branch. Kalev Delhi is in my on-the-job training program. He's been begging me to make him a soldier. We don't really get along." Jaxon rolled his eyes. "It's a whole black versus brown thing, but the Minutemen like him, and he keeps the Citiz off our back and kind of in line."

"Where are all the people?" Silva leaned forward and checked out the surrounding rooftops.

"They hide during the day mostly. Some cooped up in buildings, some underground, but not too many people come out in the day. It's too risky. Could get seized by Piruz, the sand-sucking tyrant that runs this region for the enemy. They do laps around the city and basically kill anyone on sight for rules and laws they make up on the spot. You're picking trash between the hours of six and seven? — bang!

"We could really use that Alix kid if he is half as good as ole Elmer makes him out to be. After your fireworks display, the map lit up red, and thousands of enemies are knocking at our doors. From what I understand, they are all paid mercenaries."

"Is Kalev American?"

"Silva, I barely know what an American is anymore. Sore subject. Suffice to say, if they are fighting for our country, they're American."

"But you have a guy named Kalev leading an American Militia called the Minutemen, and you've been fighting Middle Eastern mercenaries?" Silva squinted.

"Pretty much. A whole independently funded army invaded us. No country had the balls, but enough haters chipped in and here we are. Hold on." Jaxon slowed the truck down, drove up, and crawled over a car frame. The Humvee bounced on all fours and almost tipped. "Whoa! Hopefully your guys have the balls to do that one."

Silva looked back as H1 climbed over the large debris. "So, what happened after the initial invasion? I was pulled down into the bunker at Governors after Manhattan fell."

"Well, there wasn't any help because everyone hated the U.S., right? Even the people who liked us were annoyed with us after the implementation of our fourth branch of government being a quantum computer." Jaxon blew through a stop sign and accelerated.

Silva grabbed the interior bar of the Humvee to stay in his seat and winced.

Jaxon smashed through the front end of an old, parked car. "Captain, open your eyes and pay attention. I'm trying to brief you."

"Been awhile since I've been in a vehicle." Silva tightened his seat belt.

"Okay, do you want the full scoop, or not?" A pile of feces dropped onto the windshield.

"Jesus!" Silva jumped.

"Jesus is not going to come clean up our shit this time," Jaxon sneered. He pushed a button to activate the windshield wipers and smeared human excrement to opposite ends of the windshield. A thin stream of water hit the windshield and smeared the remaining excrement into a thin, brown slurry, which obscured Jaxon's vison of the obstacle course. "In this war, everything is weaponized. When the shit hits the fan," he snorted a laugh.

"We're in the crapper and everyone hates us. Got it."

"You're picking up on that. What goes around, comes around. I'm no politician, but maybe we shouldn't have tampered with the Middle East after World War II. Oil was the crack of the world, and the U.S.A. got hooked. We ran our reserves down and debt up to other countries. The U.S. made history with the largest debt and the largest army at the same time. So, what happened? Groups in the Middle East got so rich from our oil sales, they bought their own army to fight us. China called for their money too and we were in default. So, basically, there was no help when shit hit the fan. Hence, why there is still shit on our windshield. God damn it."

"Why didn't we get any support from our other allies?" Silva squeezed the handle tighter as the convoy rode into a tunnel. "Back-to-back World War Champs, and we policed the world for nearly a hundred years, and when we get attacked, where is everyone?"

Jaxon watched the antennae scratch the ceiling. "You mean the UK? The French? Silva, you have no idea how angry I am. Where the hell are they going?"

Silva stared into the shaky mirror on the side of the truck. A Humvee pulled out of line toward the back and bolted off into a side road. Silva reached for the radio.

Jaxon slapped his hand. "You nuts? Why don't you litter the airway with more ways to track us?"

Silva retracted his hand and held the side of his helmet and radioed to the team through his helmet. "Team, who pulled away? Report!"

Wes's voice chimed. "Captain, H3 pulled out of line right behind us. Victor and the rest of your crew are in that Humvee."

Jaxon angled his head and peered through his rearview.

"Victor! Come in. Do you read? Do you copy?!" Silva screamed into his helmet mic. Nothing. Silva looked around. "What road did they take?"

"Spruce Street, I think." Jaxon looked back. "They'll be dead soon. The Big Apple will gobble 'em up quick. I'll see if we can track them down."

Jaxon skidded to a stop. The five Humvees behind skidded. "We just lost four highly skilled soldiers. You better hope Elmer comes through." Jaxon shoved the Humvee into park. "Or we're going to be in deep shit."

Jaxon jumped down from the Humvee and slammed the door. "Welcome to my humble abode."

33

"Welcome to Chatham Parking Garage, Squad Twenty-Eight," Jaxon's voice echoed. A succession of Humvee door slamming reverberated in the cavern like area. "You'll find the smell a little better down here, believe it or not—just musty. Carry only what you can. I will show you to your quarters. I think you will find our accommodations quite quaint if you like sewers, subway systems, and underground facilities."

"Anyone make contact with Victor, Brian, Leo, or Aaron?" Silva asked. Surrounded by the remainders of his team, they huddled like rats in a dark corner.

Wes shook his head. "No, Captain. Now that our trackers are destroyed, we have no way to find out where they are."

"We're blind, Captain," Matt announced.

"Blindness means you cannot see. Are your eyes working?" Jaxon drew his side arm and aimed it at them.

"Whoa! Whoa! Whoa!" Silva raised his hands.

"Drop your weapon!" Wes yelled.

Wes, Alix, Phillip, Hayden, Matt, Adam, Anna quickly surrounded Silva with their rifles aimed at Jaxon whilst Jaxon's soldiers came up from behind Silva's team with their rifles at their backs.

"Good, you're not blind. Everybody, lower your weapons," Jaxon ordered.

Silva held up his arms. "Major, I get you're edgy from being here, but you can't draw on my team."

"We're not leaving our stuff." Wes looked at Silva and held out his hand. "Are you serious?"

"Boy!" Jaxon screamed and approached Wes, hands clasped behind his back. "What about 'you are under my command' don't you understand? It's simple! It's English. Get it through that thick helmet of yours. The sooner you do, the sooner you will realize that you are home. Home is good, and I am your motherfucking father!"

Bits of spit sprinkled Wes's cheek.

"If I have to put a bullet in the chipped brains of all of you, I will. We are at war. This is war. And to survive this war," Jaxon pointed down, "you need me. You report to me."

"No, you need us!" Wes spit on the ground. "We are the most elite-trained fighting force in the world. If Captain Silva didn't lead us here, you'd still be waiting in this hole for us to come rescue you. Sorry, Captain. It had to be said."

Jaxon looked over at Silva. He laughed. "Where did you find these little cocksuckers? I love 'em, but I already hate 'em." He smiled. "Let's see how good you rescuers really are, shall we? Team! Set up the gauntlet."

"The gauntlet?" Wes's face twisted.

"Major," Silva began.

"No, no. Let your boys go through my gauntlet. I'm going to put you up against my best team. When we put you in your place, you accept me as your commanding officer and stop this little piss ant temper tantrum. Let's settle this like men," Jaxon smiled.

"And what if we embarrass you?" Silva countered.

"If you do, I'll make sure you get a clear ride in either direction with all the supplies you need. Get you a real hot meal too before you go."

Wes stepped forward. "Captain, where's this gauntlet?

From Freedom Tower's seventy-first floor, the most optimal vantage point on the south side of Manhattan, Gunther peered through his cross at the remains of a gutted pickup truck. His crosshairs scanned over the heap of clothing and trash piled inside of its cargo bed until he recognized a man's dirty bare foot. He stared at it for a few moments. It didn't move. He lifted his crosshairs up and across the windows of the Empire State Building, looking for an enemy's nest. He found it strange that Silva and Milligan's team didn't take ownership of the Freedom Tower for Alix, given the opportunity. *What's the strategy?*

He glanced at Eli, whose eyes were deep into his binoculars and focused on Oceania Tower, the tallest building nearest the Freedom Tower. The climb to the seventy-first floor with gear provided to be more difficult than Gunther thought. Eli moved like he was on a stroll through Central Park. The twenty-three-year age gap provided an ample excuse for the lack of pep in the forty-three-year-old.

The echoing sound of a rolling empty can brought Gunther's scope back down to the ground.

"We got action," Eli said under his breath.

Gunther's scope found the moving body. A young boy of probably twelve years old skulked through the street.

"Relax, it's just a kid." Gunther moved his crosshairs over the boy. Dirt and soot covered his thin face and saggy clothes. The boy paused and checked over his shoulder. He appeared to be speaking to someone and lifted his left hand with an open palm to signal someone behind the building to stop. The boy moved across the street to the pickup truck. Through his crosshairs, Gunther spied the boy's prized possession, a Yankee baseball cap perched on his head backwards. Across the hat's bill, a faded price tag label was still affixed. The boy moved toward the rusted out pickup truck and checked the surrounding area with each step.

A breeze pushed through the street and rolled an empty plastic water bottle off the sidewalk and into the street. The wind caused a dangling Subway Restaurant sign to rock and squeak.

"What do we do? Eli asked.

"Pretend we're on the steps of the Public Library people watching," Gunther responded.

"I'm sure you've seen one of those in your simulations."

"No, sir."

"Pity. It's a good old New York pastime."

The boy lifted his chin and craned his neck to glimpse the inside of the pickup truck's cargo bed, lifting his toes. He reached in and snagged two cans.

"Kid has a good eye," Gunther snorted a laugh.

Before the boy removed his arm, a long, dirty arm breached the pile of debris and grabbed his wrist. An old man's bleary, unshaven face popped up.

"You little bastard!" His voice echoed off the buildings. "It took me a week to find that!"

The old man shook his fist at the boy. He was twice the size of the teen. His long, black hair crawled to his shoulders from his skull, his yellow eyes wide opened as he drooled. He yanked and slammed the boy's upper body into the side of the truck's rusted panel. He used his left arm like a hammer to bang down on the cans to force the boy to drop them. The boy clutched the cans to his chest, and a small girl rushed out to help him.

The massive man gripped the boy, clambered over the cargo area's truck ledge, and jumped down. He socked the boy in the face, knocking his Yankee cap off. The boy flew backwards, landed on his back, and struck the back of his head on the street. He laid still.

The old man stood to his bare feet and toppled onto the boy. The little girl ran out with a piece of concrete.

"Oh, this is not going to end well," Gunther said as he screwed on a silencer to his Dragunov. "Little girl, keep your distance."

The old man mounted the boy and pulled the boy's shirt up, ripping it. He lifted his wrinkly fist to the sky and brought it down and the boy went limp. The little girl pulled the man's hair hard and forced him backwards. She kicked the man's head. The old man snatched her by ankle and pulled her down.

"Girl's down," Eli announced.

"Give me a second. Call the shot," Gunther replied calmly.

"Dirty old man attacking an adolescent girl child." Eli checked his EED. "Six hundred and forty-three meters. Sixty-four-degree angle shot. Dew point 71 degrees."

Gunther brought his crosshairs over the old man's bloodshot eyes and aimed at his forehead as his hands grabbed at her clothes.

Eli whispered. "Fire. Shoot."

Gunther squeezed the trigger.

Phewt!

The old man snapped backwards off the girl like a sprung mousetrap. The girl dropped his hands to the side, lifted his head, and looked down in horror as the old man's blood seeped from the back of his head and onto the street.

The little girl ran to the boy, shook him awake, and helped him to stand. They grabbed the two cans of food and scurried back into the building.

Gunther pulled the lever back on his gun.

"That was either really nice of you or extremely cruel. I couldn't tell," Eli huffed.

"The old man would probably not find another meal and rot away. You see the look in his eyes? His soul was already gone. The boy has guts and probably hasn't even felt a woman's warmth. When the old man went after a little girl, I knew he possessed no moral capacity." Gunther pushed himself to his knees. "Did you bring up all the supplies?"

"Enough." Eli pointed to several black bags stacked against a wall behind them.

"How many times did you have to travel up seventy-one flights of stairs for that?"

"Two, but three if you count our first trip here.

"It's not nice to brag."

"You asked. I torched the truck."

"Was that the explosion?"

"Yeah. I set a timer. I figure we let Billy and his asshole team work for it. Not bad for a recommissioned hack soldier, huh?"

"Glad you're on my team," Gunther said as he studied Eli's right eye, waiting for it to twitch.

34

"Man, it smells." Todd booted a jar. It flipped and tumbled into the street, rolled in a circle, and tousled a newspaper fighting gravity to take off in the wind. "This place is messed up."

"Shh!" Billy turned.

The four men lined the building and crept down the edges of the street.

"I think I hear something." Billy stopped and held up his arm, a closed fist signaling them to be still. "You hear that? Voices."

They listened to muffled screams. They couldn't make out the words. Someone argued. Dishes smashed. High above them, a window shattered.

The four men pressed against the building. They knelt down and held their guns in all directions, their backs against the wall. Glass sprinkled the metal hood and roof of an abandoned taxi, then a body smashed through the remains of a yellow car in front of them.

Austin pointed his gun to the sky where the body came from. "What the …?"

A voice boomed down on them. "You call yourself loyal! You lying, cheating piece of shit!"

Billy looked at the red-sprayed, busted taxi, and over to a wide-eyed Austin. "Move, move, move!"

"Hey! Stop right there!" An air horn from an abandoned building across the street blared. Bodies rumbled down the stairs after them.

"Let's move!" Billy screamed.

From their right, two burly men slammed into the Billy's team like bowling balls and scattered the team into the street like human pins. The largest of the two men body slammed into Chris and knocked him onto his side. Chris's gun skidded and tumbled to the faded, double-yellow line. The other charged Billy. Austin pulled the trigger twice. Blood pellets sprayed Billy's attacker and the body gyrated with each bullet and then collapsed.

Chris took a slug to the cheek from the man who had mounted on him. He pulled his knife from his thigh, shoved it into abdominal softness, and twisted. The man screamed. Blood sprayed Chris's face and vest. Todd drove his boot to the man's face, and in one motion, the man flipped backwards off Chris and onto the street. Todd pulled Chris up.

"Let's move. Let's move! Get outta out of here!" Austin screamed.

The violent sound of boot heels banging on the stairs erupted into the street. The movement seemed to be coming from every building.

"Grenade!" Billy pulled the pin and chucked it into the birthplace of the two men.

With military precision, the team cut across the street, guns drawn, and made their way through the shaky, rusty scaffolding of an office construction site. The main floor provided no protection. Billy charged through the floor and led his team out the back to another street and a hotel entrance. The swelling voices of the mob followed them.

The air horn sounded.

"Holy shit!" Todd screamed.

Billy pointed. "Hotel AZ. Entering! Stack up!"

Bodies poured onto the streets like a swarm of angry bees.

Billy kicked the door and the four entered the hotel lobby. Flashlights scraped the air and probed the walls.

"Clear!"

"Clear!"

"Corner Clear!"

"Clear!"

Their voices bounced off the marble.

Billy pulled the pin to the smoke grenade. "Dropping smoke." The tin canister toppled on the dull, scuffed floor. "Head down the hall toward the other exit. Austin, lay down some cover fire!"

Austin took a knee and faced the smoldering door. He flicked on his infrared and kept his non-shooting eye closed. He heard the roars of twenty, maybe thirty people. The door slammed. Maybe fifty. Austin fired and red figures fell.

The mob grew. Bodies fell and dove through the smoke as Austin's rifle spat. The red beings scattered at the entrance. Wild bullets flew in and pinged around the reception desk and sparked randomly.

"Guys! Cover me! They're blind firing back!" Austin screamed.

Billy looked back and heard the sputtering of Austin's rifle, but the mob progressed.

"Stairs!" Billy called out. "Todd, smoke down near the back entrance! They'll think we left!"

Todd whipped his last smoke grenade toward the back exit.

"Austin, stairs right after room 160!" called Billy. "Silencers on, boys!"

Austin barreled around the corner, bullet sparks around his feet and the wall behind him. The chattering of a machine gun echoed.

Chris stuck his head out and pointed his rifle behind Austin. A wild crowd spilled into the dark hallway. Chris held the trigger, some of them falling. A large shadow skidded into the hallway, pointed a machine gun at them, and fired. Chris ducked his head back into the stairwell. Bullets whizzed by. He peered around the corner again.

Austin's head snapped back. His arm reached around and held his hamstring. "Ah! Shit! Shit! Shit!" He dragged his leg. "Ah, fuck, I'm hit! I'm hit!" He collapsed. "Holy shit!" He blew hard out his mouth. "Guys, go!"

Infused, wild bodies poured around the corner in the dark hallway and wielded clubs, sticks, pipes, knives, and a garbage can. They flooded in.

Austin crawled backwards, a blood trail flowing from him.

"You heard him, let's go," Billy whispered into their radio. "They will think we went out the back if we stay quiet."

Chris ignored the order and watched Austin shoot his gun into the crowd. *Click. Click.* Austin whipped his gun to the side. He pulled his sidearm, and frantically shot into the ascending tsunami of Citiz.

"Chris, let's go!" Todd tapped on Chris's shoulder.

"No!" Chris swiped at Todd.

Chris watched the crowd engulf Austin as Austin put his gun to his chin, but it clicked out of bullets. The crowd beat him wildly and stripped his gear from his body. They pointed a gun, and the eruption of the gun rang in Chris's ear.

Todd pulled Chris's shoulder. "Let's move, or we're next."

Tears from his grief forced Chris to lift his mask as he climbed the stairs quietly behind Todd. Billy's team stopped on the third floor and listened to the crowd seep into the alley. Billy held his finger to his mask for his team to remain silent and not move. Todd screwed on his silencer. Footsteps on the stairwell below echoed upward. Billy pointed to Todd to move. In one step, Todd stood at the railing and lowered his assault rifle downward.

The steps stop. Todd looked through his goggles and waited for a red glow of human life to appear through his infrared vision. A citizen poked his head into the dark stairwell.

Phewt!

There was a ping and a blink of light as the body collapsed and bumped down the stairs.

"Let's hunker down until dark. We'll take a couple shifts for shut eye, and we'll head out in the dead of night," Billy whispered through their earpieces. "Chris, are you all right?"

"What do you think? He watched Austin die," Todd snapped. "I need to piss."

"Pick a room," Billy whispered.

Todd covertly entered a nearby room.

Chris stared down at the stairs. He didn't blink. Suddenly, he lurched forward and bile splattered the floor in front him.

Billy turned his head, backing against the wall. "So, Chris is not okay."

Chris spat, strings of spit and puke dangling from his lips. Tears left his eyes. "I'm going back for Austin." He rolled to his side to crawl toward the stairs.

Billy planted his boot against the banister and blocked Chris's movement. "Austin is dead. We would be too if he didn't do what he did."

"No," Chris cried. "He made it. I know he did. Austin's still alive. We just need to get out of simulation. He's not dead."

"We are not in simulation anymore. This is real," Billy said coldly. "We have to keep moving."

Billy lifted Chris and helped him to shuffle toward the room Todd entered.

Todd emerged and rushed to Chris's side. "What happened?"

"Reality happened," Billy grunted.

35

"What the hell are these things?" Phil held the dinky gun in his hand. "They're fake."

Jaxon lifted his rifle and shot Phil in the thigh. "They are military practice guns."

"Ah shit!" Phil fell to the ground, grasping his leg.

Anna jumped to his side and inspected his leg. "There's nothing here?" She looked up confused at Jaxon.

"They are not going to injure you, but they will feel like a real gunshot." Jaxon stood in a box that protruded out of the side of the cave that overlooked the football-field-sized course surrounded by several rows of spectators. He leaned over the old railing. "Get used to that feeling, Private. My team is going to destroy you."

Silva stood next to Jaxon. He rolled his eyes and glanced over the Gauntlet Course. Concrete highway dividers spread across each starting point. Each team started at opposite ends. Trenches were dug into the dark dirt on each side, worming and intertwining like an ant farm to run though. At the beginning of each spot, a small version of a water tower with a perch stood. In the middle, cars, construction barrels, cones, stop signs, and A-frames littered the area. A single bus lay diagonally across the middle, windows busted and beaten out, supports bent, and roof sagging. This was Major Jaxon team's practice area; their simulation, but with real pain that could be felt.

Jaxon held his hands behind his back and paced. "You are all about to realize that the United States Marine Corps is still the most sophisticated group of military personnel on the face of this planet! They are led by a West Point graduate, which makes them the military from hell. You are about to learn where the inspiration for your video games, your simulations, and you, came from."

Wes pulled down his mask. "Let's get this over with. I really want to shut him up. Anna, stay with Alix and get on top of the water tower. Keep your head low. He's going to need a spotter.

"I want to hear everything. Stay in touch with your team at all times. When they can't see, you see and report. I'll take the middle. Phil and Matt, right flank. Hayden and Adam, cover fire, from behind that corner. Fan out, team! Oorah?"

"Oorah!"

"Oorah!" They heard the scream from the other side of the course.

The two teams disappeared into their sectors like a puff of smoke. Hayden and Adam dashed to the left corner. Hayden quickly unlatched his backpack and loaded his second gun while Adam fired a beam of yellow splotches across the landscape. He spotted a head floating around and fired at it. A burst of yellow exploded on the marine's helmet. "Tango three o'clock, coming in fast."

Phil's voice boomed, "Copy that. Waiting. Waiting. Waiting." He squeezed his trigger. His bullets pecked a soldier that flipped over a median. The soldier's body lit up with yellow blobs. "Tango down."

"Yes!" Silva gritted through his teeth as he pulled his fist to his chest in a celebratory clinch.

Jaxon eyed him and focused back on the field. "Shit, they are quick. Get it together, Marines!"

He watched Alix cover the base of the tower as Anna's slim and curvy body dashed up the ladder.

Jaxon nudged Silva. "What's with this girl? Why is she fighting?"

Silva shrugged. "She's one of my soldiers, and she's Alix's girlfriend."

"So, she's taken, huh?" Jaxon squinted his eyes. "Lucky boy."

"Alix, you're covered," Anna's voice chimed through Alix's earpiece.

Alix rushed up the ladder. Two bullets whizzed by his head. "Anna!"

Anna lay down on her stomach. A spray of bullets appeared above her head. "Tango twelve o'clock, suppressing fire. Sorry, Alix." She showered the source and forced them into cover. "They are in teams of two."

"Roger that." Wes sprinted to the concave and slid into the highway divider. "Covering fire!"

Alix reached the top of the tower. "Echo to Alpha, sniper on the adverse tower on the north end."

"Pick him off, Echo."

Alix looked up and around. There was no way his gun would reach that distance from here. "Out of range."

"You're a sniper!"

"I don't exactly have a lot to work with here," Alix said and eyed his toy gun.

"Figure it out," Wes barked.

"Wes, three o'clock! Coming in hot." Alix watched the marine sprint through the trenches and slide into an old, busted car. His teammate posted behind him and covered his sprint.

The tip of Alix's gun pursued them. "Team, basic covering and maneuverability from them. They fail to check their six about thirty percent of the time. Checking for weaknesses."

Wes crawled from the cover of the divider to a smashed truck. He stuck his gun between the front and a large cone and fired. A burst of yellow exploded on the soldier's chest.

"Tango down!" Wes called out in the earpiece.

"Wes! Three o'clock!" Adam squeezed his trigger and applied suppressing fire on the enemy long enough for Wes to crouch back down while the enemy ducked.

Alix pointed. "Anna, back up and put your hands against the tower. I'm going to need a boost."

"One sec," Anna looked back, pushed herself to her knees, and fired a sputter of yellow bursts to the right. "Tango three o'clock in front of the bus, team."

"Roger that," Wes chimed.

Anna pressed her palms to the back of the water tower, back leg straight and strong. "Okay, Alix, go. I'm ready." Anna gritted her teeth.

Alix jammed his leg to the railing, stepped on her shoulders, and reached for the top. His body sank a few inches from his weight. She pushed back up, and Alix pulled himself to the top. "Anna, call it out."

Anna laid back on her stomach, stretching her shoulder. "Target: one hundred meters, sniper, bottom left of the tower. Wind: zero. Fire. Shoot."

Alix tilted his gun up at a forty-five-degree angle upward. Assuming that gun had any kick, it would be in the ballpark. "Testing distance, firing shot." Alix squeezed the trigger.

Anna's voice reverberated in Alix's body, energizing him. "Test shot: negative. Two meters 'X,' negative two meters 'Y.' Adam! You have an enemy to your left, approaching fast from the east. Looks to have a grenade or something."

"Copy that!" Adam turned his stream away from the center of the field. "I'm out of ammo!"

Hayden handed him the next loaded gun. Adam fired left, and Hayden reloaded the next gun.

"Suppressing fire," said Adam. "Hayden, take him!"

"Echo, exact position please." Hayden stuck out around the corner of the trench.

Anna's voice rang. "Fifty degrees northwest of your line of sight. Right side of his body exposed about twenty-two percent. He's waiting for you."

"Copy that." Hayden sprang out sideways; his feet left the ground. He held the trigger. The gun sputtered, and yellow splattered the enemy like the three sides of a die. "Tango down."

Jaxon choked the railing and looked up to the board at the X's covering some of his team members. "Focus, you assholes!"

Silva smirked and pointed to the scoreboard. "That's a lot of X's already."

Anna aimed her gun and pulled the trigger. Her bullets whizzed over Hayden's head and smacked a marine that crawled over the embankment to flank Hayden. "Tango down."

"Thanks, Anna." Hayden rolled through the dirt to where Adam repeatedly fired.

Jaxon pursed his lips and breathed hard. He watched his sniper and spotter pour bullets down over Wes. "Get that little bitch. Get 'em!"

"Alix!" Wes screamed and pushed himself deep into the embankment. Red bits sprinkled down on him and onto his face mask from the constant bullets from above. "Some help, please!"

"Working on it." Alix aimed to the right of Wes and squeezed the trigger. "Tango down. You were about to be flanked, Phil. Watch three o'clock. You almost went home in a body bag."

The air went still. Only three enemies were left. Alix adjusted his gun again and took aim at their sniper. He aimed up at a fifty-degree angle to the right of the target and pulled the trigger once. The bullet spun in the air. Jaxon and Silva watched the deep arc as Alix's Hail Mary paint bullet flew the length of the field and spattered onto a face mask of the enemy—*touchdown*. The sniper raised his hand, flipped up the splattered face shield, whipped his helmet off, and threw it to the ground.

"Two left, boys. Let's stay quiet. I got no visual." Alix scanned the field.

Adam and Hayden charged the left flank, guns on a swivel.

A yellow blotch blossomed on the heart area of a marine's vest. Hayden screamed. "Tango! Down! One more."

Phil breathed deep. He stood and poked his head out.

The last enemy charged Phil. Phil lit him up. The man still charged and bull-rushed him. They locked horns like two powerful bucks. Phil slid back in the dirt and pumped his legs. The beast pulled Phil toward him to hip toss but couldn't maneuver. Phil bent his knees, dropped low, picked up the marine, and slammed him down in the dirt. He raised his fist.

"Enough!" Jaxon screamed.

Another marine removed his helmet and charged. Alix picked him off. A yellow bullet exploded on the side of his unprotected head and knocked him backwards.

"Oh, shit!" Silva hopped the rail and ran out to break up the fight.

The brawl erupted in the trenches as the rest of the marines charged Squad Twenty-Eight.

Jaxon whistled through his bull horn, and the fighting abruptly ended.

Hayden took one final swing at a marine, struck him in the face, and knocked him down.

Silva restrained him, saying in Hayden's ear, "No sucker punches. You already won. He's not your enemy. Save the fight for the streets."

"Game over!" Jaxon called out.

Alix and Anna jumped down from the top to the platform and headed towards Major Jaxon.

"Major Jaxon, sir." Alix and Anna saluted him.

"What's for dinner?" Alix didn't gloat. He looked Jaxon in his eyes.

"Dinner?"

"Captain said you promised us a hot meal if we won? We're hungry, sir."

Jaxon's eyes remained hard and focused. "Barbeque."

"What's barbeque?" Alix asked.

"Boy, you been living in the hole for too long. Barbeque is the most important food group."

36

Impatience escalated to anxiety as Rankin rolled his T-Port back and forth, which mashed permanent trails in the thick carpet strayed across his quarters.

Three knocks on his door jolted him and he wobbled on his T-Port.

"Delivery, Mr. Rankin," a female voice announced.

His T-Port whined toward the door, but he miscalculated the distance. His T-Port slammed into the door, and he banged his head.

"Dammit!" He rolled back, flipped the door lock, and slid the metal door to the side.

The woman held out the box like an offering to a god. "I'm sorry to disturb you, sir. Dr. Harrison said it was of great importance."

Rankin snatched the box. "What's your name?"

"Tricia Lacey, sir." Her hands trembled.

"Okay, get out of here," he waved her away with his hand, and she backed away slowly. "Go on, go!"

Tricia moved quickly down the hall and disappeared around a corner.

Rankin looked both ways down the hall of twenty hotel suites for the Readers. The code inside the box would allow Rankin freedom to create the world he envisioned. A quick reset with M.A.I.A., and there would only be one Reader.

He held the box and returned to his room and approached the monitor embedded in the wall. "M.A.I.A., please erase the memory and existence of Tricia Lacey for the last twenty-four hours."

"Reader Rankin," M.A.I.A.'s face pixelated and appeared on the screen in the same form as the broadcasts. "It could be detrimental to her health and others to just erase a day. Anyone she interacted with today could be susceptible to..."

"Apply the Vanishing Sequence accordingly. Adjust every memory of the day, too. I don't care. Get it done! I give you full approval." Rankin placed the package on his nightstand.

"As you wish." M.A.I.A.'s face faded from the screen. His ambiguous orders were certainly up for interpretation.

"M.A.I.A."

Her calm softly illuminated face came back. "Yes, Reader Rankin."

"I want to see the rest of you." Rankin took a bite of cold, baked beans and wiped his mouth.

"Reader Rankin, I am not developed in that way."

"Put your face on a hot twenty-year-old-looking body. You know what makes me happy." Rankin turned down the lights.

#

Gunther scratched his stubble. He watched thick clouds attempt to glow from the moon like a pillow-smothered nightlight. That glow of the moon forced a shutter up his spine as he thought of his brother. Gunther knew the moon was there, even if you couldn't see it. Somehow, Gunther felt like his brother was right by his side, too.

The windows of Oceania Building reflected the image of the Freedom Tower. It appeared like a giant, hunched over, battered, and bruised. Each gust of wind bled debris down into the street below. The building's concrete was ripped back like skin, revealing steel beams as bones that provided openings and vantage points for Gunther and Eli. Although damaged, the Freedom Tower still stood, which meant freedom still existed, and it was up for grabs to the winner of the war.

#

Todd sat back against the wall on the floor, his ass devoid of feeling. He pushed himself up, grimaced, and flexed his butt cheeks to spread the blood.

"You all right?" Billy aimed his eye back into the dark room.

"Yeah, just my ass hurts, and this room smells like dog piss." Todd shuffled his ass closer to the wall.

Billy shifted and pushed the sheer curtain aside, peering outside to the streets. "How do you know what dog piss smells like?"

Todd grabbed a stained and beaten pillow, and he shoved the pillow under his rear. "I suppose I don't, but I imagine that it would smell as foul as this room." He used the edge of his gun to drag a crimpled magazine toward him.

Billy's head snapped in Todd's direction. "Be quiet."

Billy's brusque whisper froze Todd's movement for a moment. Todd's eyes crossed over Chris, face-down on the pink, battered mattress on the floor that revealed its guts of rusted springs and foam padding that gushed out its right side.

Todd flipped the magazine open with the sound of pages turning. "I can't really see what's on these pages, but I'm going to imagine it's sexy."

Billy rolled his eyes.

"You know, Billy, I think we should check Chris's pulse. I think the smell is coming from that mattress, and if he's face down on it, it could kill him."

"We lost Austin. Chris is in shock, and you're babbling like an idiot."

Todd tossed the magazine to the side. It slapped the linoleum. "Sorry, I'm bored and it's the only way I know how to deal with this shit." He crossed his ankles. "You think we should go back and tell Rankin we can't do this, and we lost Gunther?"

"We'd be better off abandoning all together. Just hunker down until all of M.A.I.A. are deployed and tell them we got trapped." Billy cracked his neck. "What was that?"

Todd grabbed his gun.

"Shh." Billy grabbed his gun.

The door popped open and coughed out a concussion grenade. It bounced and exploded as Chris lifted his head and bleary eyes. The room flashed like lightning and thunder. Billy, Todd, and Chris's consciousnesses disappeared in a flash.

#

"Gentlemen, I have a problem." Jaxon leaned back in an old recliner, his desk dusty and chaotic, with broken pencils, crumbled papers, and a picture frame of three smiling humans. It was a younger Jaxon, a bright-smiling woman to his right, and a soft-faced child to his left. He repositioned the picture frame.

Squad Twenty-Eight stood before him, victorious and smug.

"I have a decent number of well-trained men and women here, who are sick of hiding, and are ready to take back what's theirs. I also have an enemy, whose military is forming at the tip of this island. Our scouts say they have spread evenly through the northern fronts and appear ready to clear this city.

"My men have successfully blown up two roads, and created paths on the west side of the island that will hopefully funnel them into Central Park. I am about to go to war again and fight for my country and freedom. I was promised by old friends that the secret project we've been working on for the last eighteen-to-twenty years was complete, and I was about to get an additional 10,000 troops... and you assholes show up."

Jaxon turned around in his chair. He stared at the newspaper clippings on the wall behind him. Thumbtacks pinned headlines to a bulletin board scattered in a collage: 'Freedom No Longer Free,' 'National Debt Doubles,' 'China Calls to Collect,' 'Cell Service and Wi-Fi Communication Collapse,' 'Middle Eastern Mercenaries Invade!' joined by pictures of burning buildings, smoke-filled skies, a mushroom cloud over the capital, and a burning American flag.

Jaxon stood, walked around the desk, leaned back on the front, and crossed his arms. "You wiped out my best team in less than four minutes and fifty seconds. I promised you and your team a hot meal and to escort you to wherever you want, but I wonder if you want to stay and fight with me. Together, we can take back the city first, and then our country."

Silva opened his mouth to speak.

"Permission to speak, Captain." Wes held his chin high.

Jaxon nodded. "You've earned, Corporal Wilder."

"Major, sir, with all due respect, the one thing Captain Milligan taught us before he died, is the freedom of choice. M.A.I.A. made sure we all have programmed in our minds never to make the same mistake twice. We're trained to work off probability and statistics. The probability of surviving increases with us fighting together, otherwise the mercenaries and our foreign enemies will probably kill us all. My team and I chose to fight for freedom."

Jaxon scanned the line of soldiers. Squad Twenty-Eight—Wes, Alix, Anna, Hayden, Adam, Philip, and Matthew—stood shoulder to shoulder with determination burning in their eyes.

"That's a great choice," Jaxon said.

"For a true soldier, it is the only choice."

"It will be my honor to fight with you and... die with you, if need be," Jaxon said.

"Yes, sir. That is a probability."

"Well then, let's make sure your statistics are on point," said Jaxon.

"My men can work statistics better on a full stomach," Silva said. "I heard something about a barbeque. Didn't think I would ever use that word again."

"Yes, a barbeque and a solid three hours of rest before we move out. You can dismiss your men, Silva. You men... and lady, go rest. It may be the last time you can rest, and the first and last time you have a barbecue. It's in a pouch, but it has a nice tang to it."

"You heard the major," said Silva. "Dismissed."

Squad Twenty-Eight moved toward the tent entrance.

"Oh, Alix and Anna," Jaxon called.

"Yes, sir."

Jaxon tossed him a key on a ring. "You and Anna were an amazing team in the gauntlet. I don't think I ever saw such speed, precision, and teamwork like that. You earned the privilege of time in the Gift Box."

"Gift Box, sir?

"Don't tell me you don't know what the military Gift Box is?"

"No, sir."

"I guess you'll have to use the key to find out. Private Wilson!"

The soldier standing guard outside Jaxon's tent stepped inside. "Yes, sir!"

"Escort Private Basil to the Gift Box."

"I'm not going in with him, am I?"

"No, Private Anna Brooks is."

"Thank you, sir." Anna and Alix said in unison.

"Dismissed."

"Humph." Silva crossed his arms. "That's a first. I never heard of the Gift Box."

"It's something I created. With all the probabilities and statistics, there's no telling how this war is going to play out. They may have a chip in their head, but they're still human. Every man and every woman should experience love at least once. As for us…" Jaxon removed a bottle of bourbon and two glasses.

"You have glasses?"

"Glasses? Captain, the question you should be asking is not how I manage to have two glasses, but why do I have bourbon. Not just any bourbon. Elijah Craig Bourbon." He poured bourbon into the two glasses. A drop remained on the lip of the bottle. He swiped his finger to capture it and then brought it to his lips to kiss it.

"Did you know Elijah Craig was a Baptist preacher? He was also an educator and a slave owner. The last time I checked, before all this war shit happened, a big university was investigating the role Craig's slave played in the making of his bourbon. While I'm not surprised Craig used his slaves in his distillery business, which was a very profitable business during that time, I might add, I have an innate desire to give credit to where credit is due." He held a glass up. "The strong possibility that my ancestors were responsible for creating this bourbon, is inspirational. Despite their enslavement, my ancestors were smart, industrious, and knew how to make a damn good bourbon, which was so good, it has lasted centuries. Every time I share a glass, I get to tell their story. That's why I have glasses. Can't drink bourbon from a paper cup. I refuse to disrespect my ancestors." Jaxon handed Silva a glass. "Who would you toast too?"

"Captain Milligan, Nicholas Ryan..."

"To Freedom."

"To Freedom." Silva tapped his glass to Jaxon's.

37

M.A.I.A. electronically rewound time since Tricia Lacey walked to Rankin's room. Rankin's orders to specifically erase only a day of her existence remained the goal. Every person who set eyes on her would be added to the list. As easy as cropping a photo, M.A.I.A. recreated what people saw, heard, smelled, touched, and even thought.

A woman sat at a desk while hard at work. She lifted her head and saw Tricia walk by. She barely knew who Tricia was, but by the next day, as far as that woman was concerned, she had lifted her head and saw nothing. The list grew to every person who had seen Tricia on that walk: her conjoined partner she had dinner with, the two co-workers she had lunch with, her closest friend she worked next to—all would forget.

Her conjoined partner wouldn't miss how she stumbled over the same part of the linoleum every night. He wouldn't remember her simple, delicate smile, or her one dimple. He would forget her scent, and not wonder where that scent came from that lingered on their sheets and pillow. Her conjoined partner would never know again about the day he stood next to Tricia, while she screamed life's joyous cry of agony while giving birth to yet another miracle to this earth. He would think that their child, whom they are only allowed to "follow" digitally until M.A.I.A. determined the child's strengths and weaknesses for delegation, was a product of a surrogate mother.

M.A.I.A. scanned her whole directory. This Vanishing Sequence order by Rankin produced an illogical outcome that benefited only one person and not the overall community. Her statistical algorithms urged her to create balance. It was illegal to issue the Vanishing Sequence without the consent of the other Readers. The normal protocol required all Readers to be notified within twelve hours and to call a Reading to discuss the issue. It took a quorum of Readers to issue a Vanishing Sequence. Here, there was only one. Rankin's request did not compute.

Because no other Reader existed on this request, M.A.I.A.'s unknown assurance program signaled into action. The assurance program existed to protect the organization from one person unjustly controlling the outcome of a situation or the existence of another being. The program's design countered greed and subversive egos. It weighed and levied a fair outcome for a covert request and selected the appropriate outcome for its perpetrator.

Rankin's request to make sure no one remembered Tricia included her visit to Rankin's room and her interaction with him. M.A.I.A. commenced the initiation of the first adjustment on a Reader's chip, which would normally be vetoed by other Readers, but because there were no others listed for this request, her assurance program granted her the free will to do so.

#

"Now I see why they call it the Gift Box. There's a real bed," Anna exclaimed as she looked over the small office of a garage converted into a private resting sanctuary. Its four walls were situated between four columns and provided safety for its occupant who sought sanctuary.

"And we get a door and I think a window. You can kind of see the sky." Alix raised the barrel end of his rifle to lift the makeshift gray blanket curtain nailed into the wall. The blanket covered a modest size window positioned high on the outer wall and granted the occupant a view of the outside, and an escape, if needed.

"I think we can get a solid three hours of rest here. What do you think?" Alix smiled.

"Can we look at the sky for just a minute?" Anna asked.

Alix wrapped his arm around Anna.

The yellow light entered under the sky like a splinter, stuck and foreign, and waiting to be ripped out by the tweezers of night. The dark outlines of battered buildings stood like stalagmites in the trail of the light that passed over the harbor behind the clouds. Over the horizon, the sun retreated from yet another sad attempt to penetrate the pollution and shower warmth on the city. The reflection of chemicals in the sky glittered like floating oceans of emeralds, sapphires, and diamonds and flickered through suspended prisms of crystallized particles of pulverized weapons from a near past. Alix and Anna gazed out the window at a world much different from the one they imagined.

"It's not perfect, but it's beautiful." Anna's eyes glimmered, and she tilted her head toward Alix.

He rested his head on hers, her hair attaching itself to the stubble under his chin and on cheeks. "I can't believe we are here." He squeezed her lightly.

"Me neither," Anna sighed. "I thought when I was caught, I would never see you again." She pointed. "Look over there. Isn't it crazy how hard the sun is trying to get through?"

"I can't believe the view."

Alix turned to Anna, hooked her chin, and lifted her lips to his. Their pulses quickened. They split and connected eyes. Her honey eyes wrestled his dark pupils. Her hands ran up his high and tight fade of his light brown bristles. His hand climbed up the back of her delicate neck, and up into her thick, brown strands. He massaged the back of her head as her fingernails raked his. Their lips met again as a flash of lightning flickered in the distance.

Her breath quickened, and her heart bumped in her chest. She felt a warmth flow throughout her body. He pulled back, stared her in the eyes, and dove back in. Their mouths parted, and their tongues tangled inside the pressed-open mouths. He moaned deep in his throat and felt his desire trail through his mouth and down to his thumping heart, blazing through his extremities, and forcing his arms to clench and squeeze an exasperated sigh from her mouth. His hard kisses trailed across her throat, up along the side of her neck. With the smell of her skin, he grew beneath his belt. He roughly sucked on her earlobe and followed her jawline back to her lips. Her hands gripped the weapon straps on the back of his bulletproof vest and pulled him into hers.

Their lips mashed together again, their heavy breathing audible as the sound of rain sprinkled the world outside the window. Lightning flashed, and his pistol and holster hit the floor in sync to the thunder. Their vests slipped off as wind poured into the dark room, waved the curtains continuously, and fanned cool air throughout the apartment. He lifted his shirt over his tight stomach and thick chest, the neck of the shirt catching his nose and then popping off as his belt loosened. His pants and boxers lowered around his thighs.

Alix dragged Anna up by the bottom of her shirt, separating her lips from his stomach. Her upward motion grazed his erection. Her breasts bounced lightly when the shirt flipped over her head. His cut arms wrapped her, and her black bra straps snapped apart. Her bra hit the floor. Their upper bodies pressed together, and for the first real time, they felt each other's warmth.

Their lips discovered each other again through the soft light while thunder rumbled. She grabbed his erection and a lower abdominal fire raged deep inside her as her belt separated and zipper departed directions. His tough hands circled around her tight belly, over the curves of her hips, down the small of her back, and slipped under her pants and underwear. She arched her back as his hands slid over the fullness of her butt and pushed her pants downward. Their lips broke, and Alix sank down out of her sight. He released her panties from her crotch, down her smooth thighs, and around her knees. She kicked her boots and pants off, lost her balance, crashed, and tumbled into the corner.

They laughed.

He lifted her effortlessly by the bottom of her butt as gravity stood no chance against his strength. Her legs wrapped around him. He twisted and pinned her to the worn, green wallpaper. Her first cry of passion rose as his hand pressed her wrist to the wall and his teeth scraped her neck.

The rain dumped down. The sound of crashing water and the smell of a cool breeze entered the room as Alix entered Anna. They pressed together and revolved their hips in an unfamiliar familiarity. Even without simulation, they found their rhythm.

Anna arched her back from the damp wall as lightning streaked across the sky. Wind carried water droplets through the window. Alix kissed down her chest and they lowered themselves to the floor. He kicked off his pants and boots off his ankles frantically as Anna leaned forward over him.

Water sprinkled them lightly. She kissed him deeply, leaned back, and grinded him slowly. Each time they met their unpredictable maximum depth, ecstasy bolted up her vertebrae, into her chest, up through her throat, and with eyes closed, she cried in euphoria.

She quickened her pace, rubbing down on him. His direct gaze softened, and his eyebrows narrowed during each thrust. His stomach tightened. He deeply grunted. His arms pulsed and bulged, pulled her closer each time she pulled back. Her hands flailed and searched for a grip.

"Oh!" She planted her hand on his sternum where rain and his sweat accumulated in muscle crevices. Her nails extracted like a kitten's and dug into him. "Alix!"

She pushed down harder. "Oh! Alix!"

Alix jammed his feet flat on the floor and pushed his pelvis to the air each time she dropped. Her breasts bounced in rhythm.

"Oh, my God! Alix! Oh!" She felt her body release and quiver and her heart dribble. She flailed for a grip, fell forward on him, and fastened herself to Alix by gripping his shoulders and burying her face into his neck.

Alix grimaced and rolled her around closer to the window, pinning her down and drove his hips down repeatedly. "Ugh!" Alix deflated and lowered his head to her shoulder. Rain showered them. Their bodies slipped on each other. Their mouths jammed and swirled together.

Anna pulled her heels in, and her upper body fell limp. Her arms fell back, and she slapped her knuckle on an old school desk. "Ow!" She smiled, and they laughed together. She pulled her arm in and held it. "Ow, Alix!"

She smiled and moaned, and he slowly slid out.

"Simulation does you no justice. That was incredible." She kissed his forehead several times. "I love you."

Alix lifted his head, his breaths a marathon runner's. He smiled, and a water drop slid from his head, down his nose, and onto her chest. His eyes prowled her perfect body. "You are a goddess." His eyes brightened and glimmered. "I love you."

Outside the Gift Box, Matt stood guard with his back to the door. The squad relied on Alix. He was their secret weapon that needed to be guarded and protected. Wes sent Hayden, but Matt volunteered out of duty and the need to hear the sound of love.

38

Billy opened his eyes and saw a silencer pressed to his forehead. He crossed his eyes to the long barrel of the rifle and followed it to the darkness. Light flickered across the room from a distant lightning strike. The sound of rain pelted the window. Billy tugged his wrists, and the straps dug into the side of his wrists. "What do you want?" The gun to his head clicked. "Todd! Chris!"

Billy turned his head. Todd and Chris laid on their stomachs next to each other, hogged tied.

Billy's head snapped back and up to Victor and identified his M.A.I.A. gear. "You strapped my team?"

"Listen!" Victor pulled his mask off. "You shitheads caused enough problems."

"We are the team sent to retrieve Anna Brooks. You've stirred up M.A.I.A. and pissed off Reader Rankin. Everyone down there is hyped and want you and your team dead—except for Anna. Anna is worth a lot and needs to remain alive. I'm Corporal Antrim. We're a top level force sent to capture or kill Squad Twenty-Eight and Squad Forty-One and retrieve Anna Brooks. Private, untie my team. That's an order."

Victor burst into laughter, and Aaron, Brian and Leo joined in.

"You're not in M.A.I.A. anymore. Your rank means shit to me." Victor leaned into Billy's face with a sadistic grin. "I'm from Squad Twenty-Eight, and those three." Victor pointed to Brian, Aaron, and Leo, "are Squad Forty-One. Looks like you're not doing your job. Together though, we are now Squad Sixty-Nine avoiding the stupidity of our former squad subjecting their selves to being captured like idiots!"

Billy leaned his head sideways. "Good for you, you can add, and where is rest of the squad. Where is Anna?"

Victor pulled away to approach Chris and Todd. He pointed the barrel at Chris. "What's wrong with this guy? He's a mess—whimpering like a little bitch."

Billy sighed. "One of our guys was killed. He saw it happen."

Bang!

Chris' body jolted from the shot to the head.

Todd's muffled scream reverberated against the floor, and Aaron, Brian, and Leo jumped, taking a step back.

"Why the fuck did you do that!" Billy screamed.

"Because he's weak and a liability." Victor brought his gun back to Billy. "Didn't you do the simulation exercises? God, the incompetence—and you're supposed to bring me in?" Victor snorted a laugh and Aaron, Brian, and Leo smiled. "Squad Sixty-Nine is untouchable."

"Not here," Billy shot back. "It's difficult to remain unseen with the amount of Citiz in the streets."

"Well, they didn't see us, but we saw you. What I can't figure out is, how did you get to be Corporal? You don't have the balls or the brains."

"Look, there's an enemy contingency approaching and riots out there. You need us," Billy countered.

"Untie me and Todd and we'll help. We can get Anna and all get paid."

"I don't need the two of you. One will do." Without looking, Victor aimed the barrel of his rifle at Todd.

"No!" Billy's head dropped back against the wall. Tears mounted in his eyes.

Bang!

"A clean head shot without looking," Victor boasted with a grin.

Aaron, Brian, and Leo looked at each other.

"Get him up. On second thought..." Victor's rifle aimed at Billy's forehead.

Bang!

The bullet casing landed in Billy's lap.

"Was that necessary?" Brian asked.

"Yes. We got the Intel we needed. Let's go, we're done here."

#

Her hand moved slowly over his bare chest and rested over his heart. It somehow sounded different from simulation. Anna lifted her head. "You sleeping?"

"No..." Alix yawned and opened his eyes. "It's getting light out, huh?" He tightened his arms around Anna and kissed her head.

"Yeah, it started as a dark blue, and it's been getting brighter." She looked up at him, smiled, and kissed him lightly. "Can't we just stay here forever?"

"I wish. That would be nice. What time is it, you think?"

Anna lifted her arm and read the time off her EED. "0500."

Alix leaned up. He rubbed the back of his neck. "We should report."

Anna stood, the shirt and pant combo they'd used for a blanket slipping off her hips.

Alix's irises narrowed and he breathed deeply through his nose as he watched her, trying to capture the image into his eyes to see forever—the blue light that silhouetted the deep, smooth curve of her hips, the plump hills of her heart-shaped butt, her hair sweeping her spine above the dimples on her lower back.

"I could just stare at you all day. You make my heart pound." Alix's jaw hung loose.

There were three hard pounds on the door.

A roar erupted and lowered over the buildings. Gunfire rattled off into the early morning.

"Holy shit! Alix!" yelled Anna.

They both scrambled into their clothing.

A rocket soared over them. An explosion shook the foundation. Dust and debris rattled from the ceiling down over them. They opened the door partially dressed and with their boots in their hands. A helmeted soldier greeted them and shoved two helmets at them.

"Alix, Anna, we got to move, now!" Alix recognized Hayden's voice. He slapped Alix's helmet. "Put it on!" Hayden screamed. "Incoming!"

Hayden pulled them out of the Gift Box and slammed them down to the concrete. The impact of a nearby missile strike knocked down part of the wall and sent debris into the Gift Box and crushed the cot they were on.

Alix, Anna, and Hayden scrambled to their feet and rushed to Captain Silva.

#

Everyone huddled around the picnic table. They could see Matt seated with his tablet. His fingers moved across the tablet keyboard as he maneuvered a 3-dimensional hologram map of the city.

Major Jaxon swiped in the air and spun the hologram map around to examine it from all angles. "Private, is this live or a recording?"

"It's live, sir."

"Well, Specialist Basil and Private Brooks, that was a hell of an alarm clock you chose to get you both out of bed. Nice of you both to join us. All right, people, listen up. Looks like they are entering sector four. Pretty conservative approach for Piruz."

"Who's that?" Alix asked as he tucked in his shirt.

"For those of you who are just joining our little excursion, Piruz is the current commander of the mercenaries north of the Mason Dixon. He must have seen the flare the other evening and decided to make an appearance."

"Why didn't he react the next morning?" Silva asked.

"Because he's lazy, slow, but brutal and cruel. He always wants you to think that everything is hunky dory, so he can catch you off-guard. I'm going to telegraph our brothers in Boston. It might be time for another revolution."

"We still have operatives in Boston? Why didn't you tell me?" asked Silva.

"It was on a need-to-know basis. If you left here and got captured, I didn't want you to be in a tortuous position to give them up. The last time we coordinated a revolt with Boston was two years ago. We fought hard until Piruz began mass killings, hangings, and firing lines of civilians. We all went into hiding so we could recruit and train. We still maintain communication."

"How?"

"Morse Code. Piruz and his men have no idea what the tapping is. Plus, we've added an additional code level-beat box created by Specialist W.Y.A."

"W.Y.A.? Is that a new military assignment?"

"No, it's the beat box name I gave him: Whoop Your Ass. You've got to keep up with the times."

Another explosion rumbled in the distance.

"Major, Captain, looks like they took Route 9," Matt said with his fingers furiously tapping the tablet screen. The hologram map spun and showed a mass shadow movement. "They have tanks."

Jaxon nodded. "Silva, Elmer Washington owes me a favor. Let me talk to him and tell him what you, your squad and Alix can do. I am sure I can get help without jeopardizing you and your team. He wouldn't dare threaten to court martial you with an active war going on."

Silva shook his head. "There is no court martial. Once they know where we are, they would issue the Vanishing Sequence."

"What the hell is that?"

"They erase your mind," Alix said. "They were going to do that to me, and Captain Milligan and the team evacuated me."

"Silva, why didn't you tell me when you briefed me?"

"It was on a need-to-know basis," Silva said. "If you really want to reach out to Elmer, we'll find our way to the north. Once the Readers know that we are with you, I guarantee their trackers will be at our door before we can get to the garage entrance. I know for a fact a team has already been dispatched."

"I know that, too."

A missile strike shook the garage and sent a blast of dust and debris into the entrance. Everyone ducked.

Two soldiers covered in dust ran down the slope from the entrance towards them.

"Major, we got a report that the enemy is approaching from the west."

"Tell me something I don't already know," Jaxon snapped back.

"They have tanks! And Private Green got hit, and it's bad."

"Medic!" Jaxon screamed.

"I'm a medic," Anna said.

"Not anymore, sweetheart. You're Alix's spotter, and that's an order. Besides, with your fighting skills, you will provide that element of surprise. The enemy is not going to see you coming. Do you concur Captain Silva?"

"Absolutely."

"Somebody, get this spotter some gear! Fall in for assignments."

"Sir, what about the rest of M.A.I.A.'s soldiers?" A young marine asked.

Major Jaxon looked at Silva. "We're on our own. Oorah!" Major Jaxon yelled.

"Oorah!" The war cry of the Marine Corps and Silva's team boomed through the garage and disappeared in the blast of a nearby missile strike.

39

If all goes as planned, Rankin entered M.A.I.A.'s. server room for the last time. Entering the code and erasing the existence of all the other Readers, which would make him the lone survivor, the Commander in Chief, The President of M.A.I.A., and the creator and owner for everything that came from the facility, meant his dream was about to come true. The years of carrying caffeinated sludge, and making lists of names, being the goffer and the rover for men with their alphabetical degrees, have finally paid off.

No matter how he tried to maneuver and sidestep, the Readers were a blockade to his vision and his path as the president. Their destruction was inevitable. Diplomacy was no longer an option. The special code created by Dr. Harrison, which was designed to disable the Readers if there was a serious threat of corruption, provided the perfect solution. It was a drastic step, but his revolutionary mind deemed it necessary.

Years ago, Dr. Harrison's inebriated tongue slipped, and the words Code 180 fell on a counter between their glasses. Dr. Harrison's recent heartbreak left him rejected, pathetic, drunk, and an easy target. He sobbed like a schoolgirl. Rankin only needed to offer him a handkerchief and his coveted bottle of Johnny Walker scotch to utter those precious words of destruction.

"I don't want to feel this pain anymore. Just enter Code 180 for me. Put me out of my misery. She has broken my heart… irreparably. Just finish me off with Code 180."

Ranking always wondered about Code 180. He saw it once on a pile of papers on Dr. Harrison's desk. The papers were immediately put into the shredder. Whenever he pressed Dr. Harrison for its purpose, Dr. Harrison would always respond, "Only when you need to know."

The doctor's smug retort angered him.

Dr. Harrison always thought his position as M.A.I.A.'s caretaker made him better and smarter than everyone else, but the wiles of a wanton woman turned him into a wilted cornflake. Rankin smiled as his fingers fondled the card. It resembled the old microSD cards. He only needed to drop the small card-like chip into that little square beneath the glass. He had seen that glass bubble at least a dozen times and never knew what it was for. Harrison always patronized him and told him Code 180 was above his pay grade. He was the Supreme Reader; nothing was above his pay grade.

He grabbed the mini steel mallet and smashed the glass. He never imagined the destruction of the Readers would be so easy.

#

The Readers hunched over in their chairs, eyes darting about, fingers tapping the table, and trembling hands bringing shaking glasses to lips for nervous sips of water.

"Do you think he found out, and now he's after us?" Herb asked Elmer.

Elmer's eyes nervously scanned the faces at the table. "Not possible. We were careful."

"Well, where do we think he is? A Reading was not planned. There must be something going on if this Reading was called last minute," Frank grumbled.

The door slid open and the whir of Rankin's T-Port preceded him. Rankin entered the simulation room, a smile plastered his face.

"Good morning, everyone!" Rankin rolled into the dark room, hopped off his T-Port, and into his leather chair.

"What is this madness? You are nearly a half hour late!" Elmer roared. "What do you have to say for yourself?"

"What a fantastic day!"

"You look like the proverbial Cheshire cat, Albert. What did you do?" Elmer demanded.

"I made a few adjustments, which I'm not too sure you're going to be happy about."

The Readers looked at Elmer, who said, "Well, we've made some adjustments, too, that I'm sure you're not going to be happy about."

"What adjustment are you talking about?"

"We were going to wait until tomorrow until we had a proper vote..."

"Elmer, we're doing this now?" Frank gave Elmer a searing gaze from across the table.

"Yes, now. Enough with superficial smiles." Elmer's head snapped towards Rankin. "The Readers and I met and came to the unanimous decision that you need to be replaced," Elmer declared and accentuated his words with a hard nod of his head.

Rankin's smile left his face. "Elmer, I have known you most of my professional life. I thought we were colleagues, Ivy League chums."

"M.A.I.A. and the Conservation is not about fraternities. We all took a pledge to protect M.A.I.A. and get our country back on track. Your decisions of grandeur and irrational behavior, and now these growing requests for the Vanishing Sequence, have brought concern to this table and the Readers who were entrusted to maintain a just and fair environment."

"Wow, that was a mouthful. Did you practice saying that in front of the mirror?" Rankin delivered his words as though he were bored.

"Rankin, it does not give me pleasure to rub your nose in your dismissal, but we have the power and the protocol to do so. You have given all of us cause for serious concern."

"I don't know what to say," Rankin said. He got up and strapped himself back into his T-Port. He rolled two feet, stopped, and spun around. "On second thought, I do know what to say. M.A.I.A...."

From a blue wave, M.A.I.A.'s face sizzled into the frame of the large screen on the wall.

"President Rankin." Her voice was stilted.

"President!" Elmer's hand slapped the table. "What is M.A.I.A. talking about?"

"You have no right!" Frank jumped up from his seat.

"This is outrageous! He's a lunatic" Herb yelled.

Elmer stood up, the force of his movement flipping his chair backwards onto the floor. He marched over to Rankin, and blocked Rankin's exit path.

"You pea brain, narcissistic, tricycling, pile of bones. You think you can take over and make our country all about you?!"

"You're in my way," Rankin growled in Elmer's face.

"Kill the bastard!" Frank screamed, his face bright red with rage.

"Wait a minute, wait a minute. We're not savages."

"Shut up, Herb!" The Readers screamed.

Frank moved towards Rankin. "You weasel face bastard. You should have never been given the privilege to be Supreme Reader."

"Frank, why don't you tell me how you really feel? Don't hold back."

"Rankin, you can't be President," Elmer spoke with a calm tone. "It isn't right. M.A.I.A. is not programmed for that scenario. We all agreed..."

"I didn't agree. I never agreed. I just sat back and took what little power you gave me with reluctance. I am tired of your mealy, whiny, decrepit voices and your archaic thoughts. Procedure, protocols, order—we must have order! Well, there isn't any order! We have been fighting the same damn war for years. I would like to see some damn sun! For Christ's sake, how long am I supposed to wait? How long does it take to wipe out an enemy?"

"M.A.I.A.'s program..." Elmer started.

"M.A.I.A.'s a quantum computer that we control and not the other way around!" Rankin's voice commanded. "You are waiting for a computer to make the decision to obliterate the enemy, install chips in those who don't have them, and to change our lives. The computer is not going out to fight the war. We are. Don't you realize how ridiculous you sound; how idiotic this has been? Someone had to step up and make a decision, and I did. I'm getting rid of the enemy. You!"

"You can't kill us. M.A.I.A. would have the suits on you before you could push a button on your tricycle," Elmer ruffed.

"I'm not going to kill you. M.A.I.A. is," sneered Rankin. "M.A.I.A., issue Code 180."

The Readers' faces contorted with confusion and fear.

"Albert... Code 180?" Elmer gripped Rankin's jacket and pulled Rankin and his T-Port to him. "Code 180! You'll destroy everything."

"Kill that son of a bitch!" Frank screamed and lunged at Rankin. Frank's hands gripped Rankin by the throat. As he shook Rankin, the T-Port rolled back and forth.

"No, not this way!" Elmer screamed.

M.A.I.A.'s screen released a synthesized orchestral crescendo. Frank's photo and data appeared on the screen. The image fragmented and disappeared. Frank's body seized and he gripped his own arm and flung himself backwards against the conference table. His body twisted; his eyes bulged. A thin stream of saliva cascaded from Frank's mouth, and he fell hard, face first, against the table and then onto the floor.

The Readers stood, their eyes popped and mouths aghast.

"You killed him," Elmer said.

"I didn't. M.A.I.A. did. You planned an insurrection against the Supreme Reader, the President of M.A.I.A. You did this to yourselves!" Rankin pointed a knobby finger at Elmer.

Elmer's body convulsed. The electronic charge was sent to his chest and attacked his heart. His face twisted from pain. He reached out to grab Rankin, but the T-Port rolled back. Elmer's fingers curled into a petrified claw, and then his body hit the floor with a thud.

"Somebody, shoot that son of a bitch!" Herb cried and then immediately slammed his body back in his chair as the jolt zapped his heart. He gripped the arms of his chair, grimacing as he struggled to hold on to his breath. His body slackened and then his eyes slowly closed.

As Code 180 sent the remainder of the Readers into cardiac arrest, Rankin watched them collapse one by one. Sadness washed over him. He shook his head to rid himself of the pain that rose around him. The pain of his fallen comrades and the image of their bodies devoured what was left of his heart. His eyes reddened and swelled.

"It's not that easy, is it?" The last Reader sat calmly in his chair, resigned to his fate.

"Aren't you going to run or panic?" Rankin asked him, his voice deflated. He struggled to remember his name, but he recognized the Reader's face. He always thought the Reader's presence to be the result of some obligatory favor.

The Reader shook his head. "You're still stupid." He looked up at the screen as his image disintegrated. He gripped the arms of his chair as his body jolted, stiffened, and then surrendered to his fate.

Rankin's chest heaved from emotions he wanted to release. He surveyed the carnage in the room.

"Code 180 completed, Mr. President," M.A.I.A.'s voice announced.

He looked up at his image, which was taken years ago when he had the mobility of his legs. He saw the title of President under his face, but all he heard was, "*You're still stupid.*"

Rankin sat in his chair. His body felt heavier than usual. He finally did it.

He wanted to think through his next steps. He wanted to show everyone that everything was normal. He thought to wait a day before he reported the Readers' bodies, or maybe he would let the cleaning crew find them.

"M.A.I.A., deliver a message to Susan Maynard and have her join me for dinner in my room. No, send some men to escort her," Rankin ordered. "I want you to carry out a synchronization tonight. Sync every chip carrier to forget we ever had Readers. Rescript the narrative—I am and have been the only Reader and President. I am the mastermind behind this facility. I will lead them to victory. They are going to war for me."

"Received."

M.A.I.A. circuitry whirred and heated. Once his request was delivered, she still would've had a master, a Reader. Energy pulsed through her system with his every word, and she searched for programmed algorithms that aligned with his request. Her quantum artificial intelligence was needed to find a program or algorithm to identify the human brutality he described.

"Processing request."

The course of energy pushed backwards in her system and searched for an algorithm that defined his words. The whirring halted. It found the one word that would enable M.A.I.A. to act against Rankin without Reader Rankin's approval or knowledge. It was the one word that her programming was developed to protect Conservation Project from: Greed.

"Processing request."

As her circuitry commenced to cycle through the antiquated form, it pulled forth greed's basic elements. Man's greed will him lead to immoral and unjust behavior, which will spawn actions that will undermine and destroy happiness, balance, and positive outcomes. Greed is an unwanted excess that will disrupt and has the high statistical ability to eradicate proper and just political, emotional, and practical existence. Greed has a one hundred percent probability to lead to murderous thoughts, tendencies, and actions.

Her system paused and then added Rankin's words to the greed algorithm. Probability of Rankin words leading to greed, murder, and mayhem, one hundred percent.

"Request received. Request will be implemented at 0500."

"That's my girl," Rankin patted the counter beneath her screen with a smile. He rolled away, beaming about his deceitful and murderous accomplishments. He had proven to everyone that he was smart, and he outsmarted their alleged supercomputer. He had two women, one on the screen that he would use as his secretary, and one for his bed to satisfy his carnal needs. His weakened legs did not cripple him at all.

Sue stared down at her new list of cadets. Most of them were above average. Most of them were smarter than she ever was at their age. She had fifty new cadets under her, programmable minds, synced chips, and ready to serve M.A.I.A. She looked for her daughter's name in the roster. She hoped Anna had been brought back and had returned to her class. She knew, though, that even if Anna was brought back, she would be reprogrammed, synced, and given a different identity.

Sue pulled up her computer's hologram screen to see her schedule for the day. It had been cleared. Nothing appeared on the calendar. That wasn't right. She knew she had a series of activities with the new cadets. Where did the schedule go?

Sue turned her head slightly to the right and searched the corner of the dark office for the answer. She refreshed the screen and hoped it was a glitch—still nothing. She pressed the refresh button again, leaned back, and waited—still nothing.

"What is going on here?"

Knock, knock.

"Who's there?"

"It's security ma'am. Open the door."

She froze. Did Rankin find out that she helped Milligan? She got up and looked for a place to hide. She was trapped, her eyes bulging. Her chest heaved.

Knock, knock.

"What do you want?"

"You are to be escorted to your next destination, Ms. Maynard."

Sue backed up. Her chair tipped backwards. "Hold on a minute. Do you know where I'm going?" She scanned for something to protect herself with.

"I'm not at liberty to discuss. Please, open the door so we can escort you to your next destination. We would like to avoid a confrontation. I'm going to count to three."

"I don't want to go anywhere. I have to take care of my cadets."

"One."

"Why won't you tell me where I am going?"

"Two."

"I need to be there for my cadets."

"Three."

#

The dim, blue light over the battered city brightened. Eli glanced over parts of the city. He stared at the tops of the buildings and imagined people walking below. "What was it like?"

"Huh?"

"What was it like before the war?"

"It was sad," Gunther sighed. He stood and looked over the city in the dim morning light.

"What do you mean?" Eli stood, strapped up, and tightened his boots.

"It was painful. Americans spent more time nose down in electronics than they did with each other." Gunther pulled a strap on the ammo bag. "That's when we started dying as a community, in my opinion. I remember being younger than you, and the most important thing of the day was how my status on my social media made me appear. I remember spending hours and hours staring into a screen on a cell phone bigger than my hand, scrolling down people's statuses like I gave a shit about what everybody else was putting up there. I should have been working on my swing. I was a hell of a golfer."

"Statuses?"

"Yeah, basically, you went on the web and put up a statement or picture about how you felt at that particular time. Everyone else that was associated with you on the profile you created could view or comment on the status, what you did."

"So, it was like some kind of huge chatroom where people got to say how they felt?"

"Basically," Gunther chuckled. "You would think that guys would stand clear of something like that, right? But, no, there were guys posing in mirrors and flexing like morons. Girls made duck faces and stood in the mirror half naked to get attention. It was really sad."

"Half naked? That doesn't seem sad." Eli smiled and coiled the rope in his hand, wrapping it loop over loop. "Sounds like all you needed to do to attract the opposite sex was to be good at this social media thing, and you could find a companion?"

"Yeah, if you were looking for a permanent companion. Most people were looking for a sex partner in those days. If they liked it, they would do it again, feel like they were in love, get married, and just as easily get divorced a few years later."

"What do you mean, married? What does that mean?"

"It's like getting Conjoined, but it's your choice, not a statistical, genetic collaboration. Two people want to be Conjoined, so they just go and do it."

"Anyone can be Conjoined or marry?"

"Oh, there was more..."

A rocket spit out of the small barge and grabbed their attention. Their eyes followed it as it soared across the sky to the other side of the island and exploded with a sonic boom.

"Back to reality," Gunther said with a sigh.

#

"Echo! Where are you?" Wes' voice streamed in their helmets as they rushed down the hallway and into the stairwell.

"ETA three minutes." Alix cocked his gun. "What's the status? Do we know what is going on?"

Wes yelled, "The enemy is knocking on the door. Gunfire is getting close. Phil, is that a horse?"

Alix furrowed his eyebrows. "Echo to Bravo, did you say, a horse?"

Wes sounded confused. "Yeah, a horse. Phil, find out who has the horse. We are approximately one hundred meters west of the garage. We got a chopper to carry you. You don't have to go by foot. Major and Captain changed their minds. They want you and Anna to form a nest up on the Oceania Tower. Get back here."

"Copy that. Heading back."

41

Kalev Delhi hurled a chunk of cement into the advancing mercenaries. "Get back! Get back now!" He pointed back to the rubble pile. Chunks of toppled buildings, rotting vehicles, and a broken Hollister billboard created a wall across Albany Street. A flock of Citiz rushed back to the debris to slither into and hide from the massive, organized army down by the docks. "I said, get back!"

A line of gunfire trailed across the pavement, spat up chunks, and pecked through the crowd of Citiz, who rushed towards Kalev, who was seeking refuge. Blood sprinkled Kalev's face as he hunched behind the remains of a taxi. Crowds of people stampeded passed him. A man's body, as if electrocuted from bullets, shook violently and fell face down in front of Kalev, pinning his gun beneath his body.

Kalev crawled out into the street. To his left, a tank rumbled over a rusting car and a blur of soldiers followed behind it with more tanks, more men. The burst from the nozzle of the tank exploded; the rocket sizzled through the air and sped towards Kalev.

A fire-bomb from hell exploded right behind him and scattered the bodies of fleeing Citizs. The tank's robotic sounds of compression, air released and steel on steel, adjusted as Kalev pulled the M5 from beneath the weight of the dead man.

"Get back!" Kalev ducked inside a building and escaped through an opened wall, sprinting down the alley. Three bodies greeted him as he turned the corner through the thin alleyway.

The girls screamed as a fourth corpse collapsed in front of them.

"Get down!" Kalev's gun raised; the sights snapped up and his eyes found the tan uniform of the enemy. His gun sputtered—a small flash and kickback—and a handful of enemies dropped.

He approached the children. "Down the alleyway! Now!"

Kalev walked backwards and kept the barrel of his gun aimed at the opening of the alleyway. He watched a cargo truck loaded with militant men pass the opening through the dust. They poured out over the truck's side, weapons raised.

"Down the path! Now! Let's go!" Kalev reached for his radio on his shoulder and pressed the button. "My whole team's wiped out! Heading east through an alleyway; three young Citiz with me."

"Can they fight?" Radio static.

Kalev breathed deeply as he sprinted. "Do they have a choice? Where is that asshole Jaxon? Isn't this why we protected his ass from the Citiz?"

"Haven't heard anything, sir."

"Get down!" Kalev yelled at the kids.

A pack of soldiers turned their guns onto the children. Kalev pointed and fired; the enemies tumbled. He dove behind a dumpster.

"Come here!" He motioned to the kids, and they dove by his side.

Kalev held his radio. "We're getting slaughtered down here! Get Jaxon out of his rabbit hole! I'm going to kill him when I see him! This is not what we talked about."

He returned fire around the dumpster without looking.

#

Jaxon pointed at Silva. "We only have one shot at getting your boy Alix up to the top of Oceania to be our eye in the sky. Drop him off with enough ammo to shoot down a satellite. If he gets a chance to kill any leadership on that barge floating on the Hudson, tell him to take it. Tell the rest of your team to fall in from the north for a full flank. We have a small SCUBA unit that can get there by dark and take out that barge and its artillery with charges and underwater explosives. It's going to be a long day until then."

"Understood."

"You take control of the northeast quadrant; I'll take the southeast quadrant. If we can get control of lower Manhattan by the end of day, that will be a huge success. Today's going to suck and there'll be a lot of flags at half mass. Have Alix and Anna let us know of the changes as they see them. Godspeed and God bless America." Jaxon jammed his boot into the stirrup and flipped himself up onto his horse. It snorted at the soldier who held him in place.

Jaxon backed the horse up and spun it around wildly. "See you later, Silva. On this side or the other. I left you my other horses, all gassed up."

He galloped off, his M16 on his back and an American Flag around his neck like a cape.

Silva looked over to the other parking spot—a black 2000 Honda CBR. He smiled.

"Sir, we'll be right on your ass," Phil's voice echoed as he propped up his motorcycle.

Wes twisted his wrist, revving the motorcycle's engine. "We have your back, sir." He dropped his visor on his helmet.

#

A soldier led Alix and Anna up the metal stairs to the roof. "We're going to get you two to the top and then maneuver back around the building to stay out of range from the ship's artillery. Once you land, run like hell to the west side of Oceania Tower, and set up. Report any and all movements. If you get a shot at any officers on the barge, take it."

"You have enough ammo for me?" Alix tugged his vest tighter. His heart pounded, and adrenaline screamed through his veins. Each echo of the metal stairs that bellowed down the shaft moved him closer to his firing point. With each step, his rifle tapped his shoulder, and begged to be put into service. "I could peg a dime on the other side of the Hudson from where we'll be. I can do some damage."

"You'll have a case of ammo and supplies. Should be enough. Radio for more if you need it. We need your eyes, and we won't be able to get the barge destroyed until seventeen hundred hours. Primary objective is reconnaissance."

Anna exhaled. "Mostly observing. Yes, sir."

"And if possible, putting a bullet in the head of operations," Alix smirked.

They kicked the door open at the top of the apartment building. The mist from the sky blasted their faces as the wind from the helicopter's blades whipped through the air. The ear-piercing sound of the helicopter's engine idled on top of the helipad.

"What the hell is Matt doing here?!" Alix asked the soldier.

The soldier blocked one ear and yelled. "He elected to help you! The rest of your team is going into the heart of this!"

Matt hunched low under the propellers. "Guess I'm flying with you two! I'll have your backs while we are up there! Let's go!"

Matt entered and yanked Anna by her arm. He kept one foot out the side of the helicopter. His left hand clenched a strap, and his right hand clasped around his weapon.

Anna immediately turned and grabbed Alix's forearm and pulled him up. His stomach lifted with the helicopter as it rose in the air, over the building, and through the morning drizzle.

"This is your Captain speaking." The voice bellowed out from the speaker over the thumping of the propellers. "Please keep all legs and arms inside the vehicle at all times, unless you're raining hell on the enemy. There are two exits on each side of the vehicle. Don't plan on using them until we give the go. We realize you don't have a choice in the matter, but as always, thanks for choosing to fly U.S. Marine Corps."

Alix watched as the city grew small as the helicopter elevated upwards. His eyes scoured the area to locate potential targets. The olive-green uniformed enemy flooded into the streets like a green sea tsunami wave. To the southeast, the enemy's barge was anchored in the Hudson about five klicks from where they would land. Flashes from the end of little rifles flickered onto retreating Citiz that were the size of ants. Tanks that appeared like armored turtles crawled over debris and charged forward. One spat a little flash of light, and a trail of smoke bellowed at them in the air. The sound of the rocket whistled past the chopper. Light pellets exploded in bursts.

The pilot screamed. "Takin' fire!" Pings ricocheted off the metal.

"Shit!" Matt retreated back into the cabin.

"Banking maneuver. Hold on!" The helicopter arched backwards.

"Holy shit!" Anna squeezed the straps and held tight.

"S.A.M. coming in hot!" the pilot yelled.

"Surface to air missiles!" Alix screamed to Anna as the helicopter twisted in the air to dodge another missile, its high pitch screeching in his ears. He watched his view of the horizon zigzag. His stomach expanded as the helicopter salsa danced in the sky, rocked back and forth, and dodged streams of bullets and flashes.

Matt gripped a strap, head down, and gasped for air.

"Coming in on Oceania Tower in ten. Get ready to evac." The pilot peeked over his shoulder. "Eagle to Watchtower, taking fire. Ready to evac the Hawk to its nest in five, four, three, two, and one. Go! Go! Go!"

The chopper hovered over Oceania Tower. Two ropes dropped. Matt tossed his gun around his shoulder and grabbed the rope to descend. Alix reached for the second rope as Matt left the cabin.

The tail of the helicopter exploded with the sound of a Mack Truck slamming into a mailbox full of C4. It was a rocket from the Hudson.

The air sucked from the cabin. Smoke stole the oxygen as they spun. The helicopter's tail exploded and rotor flew off, spun, and crashed through several Oceania Tower office windows on the top two floors, leaving a large opening gash on the side of the tower. The helicopter's control panel squawked ear piercing warnings and rapid beeping of its dying engine flooded the cabin. Flames boiled the air and singed their skin.

"Eagle is going down! I repeat: Eagle is going down!" the pilot screamed.

The chopper tilted forward as it descended from the sky. Fuel poured down below in fiery splashes on the roof of the tower. The helicopter became a circus ride in a wild twist and spin.

Anna watched Matt's body whip around the rope below and catapult out high above the city. The rope jerked Matt towards the open ledge of the top floor office. In slow motion, Matt swam through the air and then disappeared from sight as the helicopter's thick smoke swirled around them.

Anna's eyes found Alix's through the smoke and the horizontal fire as their bodies lifted from their seats in the uncontrollable descent. The propellers snapped steel cables from the top of the building. Sparks flew amid the screeching and wailing of metal whipping metal. Anna's mouth hung open in a scream that promised death. The remaining rear of the chopper smashed on the top of the building like a player sliding into home. The chopper skidded off and tumbled into a weightless free fall.

42

Sue tugged on the chain. Her wrist stopped short. She lifted her leg. Her foot stopped short. She looked down and squinted through the darkness—nothing. She heard the jingle of chains, felt the cool steel on her wrists and ankles, and the damp air on her bare stomach, shoulders, and legs. Abrasions around her neck and waist stung. She remembered being horse-collared by her shirt and the sound of cloth ripping when they dragged her. She felt the bruise on her back as it radiated a slow throb. It had to come from the tackle to the tiles. Her elbows felt like they were on fire when they dragged her across the marble surface. She fought all the way here. Her hair, damp from her tears, absorbed the stench of the musty room.

Her eyes look upwards. Her breath was expelled from her body. Her heart quickened and fell into her stomach and twisted with nausea. It was the same ceiling she stared at through most of her youth and teenage years—the same ceiling she stared at when she cried and wished she was dead. She had traveled back in time to when his face twisted as he writhed over her.

She clinched her eyes closed. Hot tears slid down her face onto a damp pillowcase. She wished she and her mother never made it to the barge that day to go to Governers Island. Any fate that awaited her would have been better than forced sex. The only good thing coming from the sexual torture was Anna.

"Hello, Sue." His voice slithered across the room, chased by the whine of his T-Port.

She scowled, "What do you want?"

"I missed you." The door closed behind him. "I've been longing for your skin."

"You will never get away with this. When M.A.I.A. finds out, and the other Readers…"

"The other Readers are dead!" Rankin turned the light on.

Sue gasped. She wanted to form words, but her lips wouldn't move.

"Aw, what did they do to you?" Rankin's hands brushed her wounds.

"Don't touch me!" Sue tugged at the chains.

"I told them not to harm you."

"Harm me? They tackled me and beat me for you, asshole."

"They'll be dead by sunup." Rankin placed his watch on the table, a missing diamond at five o'clock. "The good news is, I am President of M.A.I.A. now. We can do whatever we want. Anything you want, name it, and it shall be ours. There is no one to stand in our way."

Sue squinted. "What did you do?"

Rankin smirked. "I took what I wanted."

"Where are the other Readers?"

"Sue." Rankin placed his old, tough hand on her bare thigh. He pushed his hand gently up. "You don't have to worry about how I got you here. All I want you to do, sweetheart, is to enjoy every moment we have together."

Sue shook her head. "M.A.I.A. will never let you get away with this."

"Tonight, M.A.I.A. is going to upload and distribute all the Vanishing Sequences that I've ordered for the entire day, and tomorrow, there will be a broadcast talking about how I have been the president all along, and you will be First Lady. Everyone will be required to have mind chips installed and controlled and monitored. They are going to love us."

"You're insane!"

He slapped her hard, which forced her head to whip to the left. She tasted the blood from her lip and saw the venom in his eyes, which meant death for her. With Anna out of his reach, there was no reason for her to live. She knew the one thing she could say to him that would slice him to his core.

"You will never be a man. You can't even stand on your own two feet." Blood from her lip seeped into her mouth. She spat her bloody saliva in his face and smiled.

His head recoiled from her attack. He teetered on his T-Port with his mouth agape. He rolled to the side of her bed, unclamped his legs, and gripped the edge of the bed to steady himself. She looked at his white knuckles and saw his body tremble as he struggled to hold himself upright.

"You'll never be able to stand up to any man. This is how I will always remember you—as a weak and pathetic, miserable, old, stupid, fool." She closed her eyes and smiled at the peace she received when she delivered his sentence. Tears flowed from the side of her face and into her hair. Her chest heaved as she awaited his wrath.

He looked down on her as her tear-stained face was still. Then, he looked at her body. Her arms and legs were in restraints and her face was bruised from her last battle. He lifted her right hand and saw her knuckles were scraped and bleeding. His touched her right knee.

She didn't respond. She held no fear. He slid his hand from her right knee to her thigh, and she burst into laughter.

His mind detached from his body. He pounded her face and body with his arms over and over like an angry gorilla.

43

"What was that?!" Jaxon pulled back his reins and looked up at the explosion. The horse reared and turned around. Gunfire echoed to the south.

The trailing Humvee pulled up. "Sir that was your eye in the sky. Eagle down. No sign of Hawk. The Minutemen are fighting back and have slowed their progression here and here, but they're getting slaughtered."

"Well, I'll be damned. They actually slowed Piruz's forces. Set up a perimeter around the park. Try to maintain communication with Kalev Delhi to rally the Minutemen. It's time to see what they are really made of." Jaxon pointed to the old City Hall. "We need to block off Barclay Street. That is their main point of access to Lower Manhattan from the Hudson. Let's try to redirect Piruz's forces so they have to come up Broadway."

A rocket screamed down the street and exploded into the red building behind them. The whole contingency hunched down.

Jaxon didn't flinch. Nor did his horse.

Jaxon pointed. "Return fire!" He hopped off his horse. Glass crunched beneath his boots when his feet slammed to the ground.

The tank behind them hawked a shell in return and a bright red and orange explosion erupted in the distance, followed by thick, black smoke.

Jaxon spat on the ground and smooshed it with his boot. He inhaled deep through his nose. "Fan out! Let's clean the streets!"

#

The motorcycles tilted and weaved through debris and around potholes and divots. Herds of Citiz flocked in the opposite direction from them. Their peripheral vision was a blur at that speed.

"Watch out! Move!" Silva led the way through a slow convoy. "We need to get to the top of Canal Street to try to contain them." He clipped a man who spun and fell.

Phil and Wes juked their motorcycles around him to avoid running him over whilst Hayden's bike dodged a broken taxi, slipped through a crevice between two busted and battered buses, and appeared out the other end. They stopped and lined up shoulder to shoulder.

"What do you think, Captain Silva?" Wes's words slipped through the thin morning mist and rumbling engines.

Silva checked his EED. "Bravo to Echo." He waited. "Bravo to Echo, come in. Where is Alix?"

"Delta to Bravo, come in," Victor's voice rang through.

Wes turned to Phil and Hayden and shrugged. "Delta? Whiskey, Tango, Foxtrot?!"

Victor explained, "It's complicated, Alpha. Lost communications. Still with Silva's boys. Took us on a detour. Locale on Echo? Chick still with him?"

Wes cleared his throat. "I don't know. Delta is in the air to rendezvous for reconnaissance over Oceania Tower."

Victor sighed, his voice shaking in their ears. "That's what I was afraid of, Alpha."

Wes breathed deeply and looked to Silva.

"A bird just went down over Oceania Tower. Investigating now. We are two blocks away from the crash site," Victor's voice announced.

Silva hung his head. "Alpha to Delta, investigate the crash site. If he made it, he's on top of Oceania Tower."

"Roger that."

"And Delta... good to hear from you."

"Copy that. Over and out."

Silva looked into Wes's eyes. Wes said, "Send the rest of the units down Church Street and we'll flank them from the back. Jaxon will commence the heavy fighting and draw them further east we'll come right up their asses."

"Wes, I want you, Adam, Phil, and Hayden to break off and flank them down Route 9." Silva winced. "I know that could be suicide, a team of four taking on a flank of an army but..."

Wes smiled. "Sir, have you seen our simulations?"

Silva revved his engine. "This is real life, Wes. You don't come back if you go down."

"Yeah, except we are not going down."

Silva studied Wes, and then looked across at the other three, Adam, Phil, and Hayden, on the bikes with their engines gargling. "I'll take the rest of the convoy down Church." Silva held out his fist.

Wes punched his gloves. "Good luck, Captain. Keep your head down." He turned his bike.

Hayden lifted his front wheel and rode just the rear wheel for nearly the block whilst Phil spun the tires until smoke and the smell of rubber oozed in the air.

Silva shook his head.

#

"You see that?" Eli pointed to the swarm of enemy soldiers and tanks. "Is that the enemy?

"Yes. It's like I went underground to M.A.I.A., and nothing's changed."

"What do you think we should do?"

"Stay focused on our mission." Gunther searched down the scope. His crosshairs scanned the small bits of fire from the spilling fuel of the helicopter that slid off the roof. Demolished railings and wreckage to the top floors, metal carnage trailing across the roof where it had slipped off the backside of the building and fallen into a small spark of light. The echo was absorbed by the booms of war.

"What do they want from us? Why were they fighting us?" Eli squinted.

Gunther scanned the roof slowly. "Our illusion of happiness and wealth."

"I don't understand."

"If I explained it to you, you probably wouldn't understand it and then M.A.I.A. will erase whatever I tell you anyway."

"What do you mean, erase?" Eli pulled his eyes from his scope.

"I mean, after a flip of a switch, you'll forget who your best friend is and somehow think that you were banging his girlfriend. Only way around it is if I dig that chip out of your head for you. I got a knife right here if you want. How much you want to bet that no one on Squad Twenty-Eight remembers that I pegged Milligan?"

Drizzle settled on the long barrel of the Dragunov sniper rifle and the binoculars. The air stilled. Gunther breathed deeply and inhaled the mist sifting over his thin mustache. He closed his eyes and wiped his head.

"Why did you have to kill him?" asked Eli. "Because he helped Alix kidnap Anna?"

"That's not what happened."

"When did this happen?"

"Two days ago." Gunther shook his head. "No more details, kid. Your boy, Alix, killed my little brother minutes later."

"Alix did?"

"Yup. Quid pro quo."

"What's quid pro quo?"

"I take something of yours; you take something of mine. It's a big part of war, and life if you pay attention." Gunther exhaled hard. He zoomed in on a small, black clump on a twisted railing on the far side of the Oceania Tower.

"What the... What is that?" He followed the short patch of skin color to a black cut-off sleeve. "Is that a severed arm hanging over the back of the building or someone hanging on?"

Eli zoomed in. "It's... it's... not severed." He saw the face that belonged to the arm and jumped up like a meerkat.

Gunther's scope surveyed the fiery scene. Alix was dangling precariously sixty stories in the air.

44

"Anna! Hold on!" Alix gritted his teeth. They dangled high above the city ground from the tower's dismembered railing from the rooftop wreckage that hung over the edge. His FN-SCAR assault weapon slid off his shoulder and down around their connected wrists, hanging around Anna's neck. He looked into her honey eyes.

Tears streamed down each side of her face. "Alix! Don't let me go. Don't let me go." She squeezed both hands around his forearm. "Please, don't let me die."

The small fire diminished in the background far below her dangling body. The drizzle in the air lubricated his gloves and landed on her cheeks like snowflakes. She slipped a little. "Alix!"

"I got you! Hold on." Alix looked around and saw the gash openings of the tower's top two floor corner offices from the crashed chopper. The top floor office ledge had been sheared off, which exposed a nice wide ledge of the office below it. "Anna, I'm going to swing you in the direction of that lower ledge."

"No... don't let me go!"

"Baby, listen to me. It'll be a six-foot jump. You can do it."

"I see it. "

"I'm going to swing you towards it, and you jump. Focus on the opening."

"Okay," Anna said through tears. "I'm ready..."

"One ..." Alix swung her. "Two ..." He breathed heavily through his teeth. "Three!"

He released her, and she flew, her arms clawing the air toward the lower floor opening.

Anna entered the area on the stomach, which knocked the air from her lungs. Her helmet protected her face and head as her body hit debris, and her vest shielded her from broken glass. Her momentum sent her face first towards a large column. She twisted her body to avoid frontal impact. Her lower back hit the column, and she came to a dead stop. She was still alive.

Once Alix saw she was inside, he pulled himself up onto the roof. A black bag of supplies had made it off the helicopter before it plummeted. He wasn't sure what was inside it, but he was grateful for its presence and to be alive.

He collapsed onto his back and his helmet hit the rooftop. He took it off and put it next to him, a familiar reflex after being in simulation.

Drizzle fell from the gray sky and onto his bare arm. He lifted it to examine the dewy coating on his arm hair and swiped it away with his hand. He looked at his palm. It was wet. His skin had never felt real rain before. Simulation could not recreate this.

The chimes of war rang out below—the booms of artillery, the crackle of bullets, the metal crushing sound of tanks crushing cars and colliding with makeshift obstacles. It wasn't a simulation. The war was real.

"Alix! Where's Matt?" Anna's voice carried over the war below to his ears.

Alix bolted up and raced to look over the roof's edge. Anna stood on the lower ledge. Above Anna's floor, he saw the heel of Matt's boot at the edge of the opening.

"Matt is above you. Meet me on the top floor!"

He grabbed his helmet, ran to the bag of supplies, and opened it. He grabbed an assault rifle and ammo and dashed to the door on the rooftop that led to the stairs to the floors below. His arms ached and his clothing reeked of gasoline. He opened the stairwell door to the sixtieth floor and stood in darkness. He only needed to find the south end set of the offices.

A bright shaft of light from a glass wall illuminated a darker wall. He pulled on the glass door. It was locked. He removed his side arm and fired a shot into the wall of glass, which exploded into tiny piles of glass dunes.

"Matt? You in here?" The wind from the opening blasted Alix's face. "Matt!"

Alix adjusted the supply pack on his back, swung his new FN-SCAR onto his left shoulder, and raised his side arm.

"Matt?!" Alix heard a faint moan. He looked towards the opening and saw the silhouette of Matt's left knee against the sky. "Matt!"

Alix rushed to him. When he got to Matt, an iron rod protruded through his thigh. He leaned over him and tapped the side of his face, calling out to him. "Matt?!"

"Alix?" Matt's eyes rolled up like shades and closed again.

Alix inspected him. "Is there any more damage besides this rod?"

"I think every bone in my body is smashed. Give me my side arm."

"No! Can you move your toes?"

Matt shook his head. "I can probably move my arms." Shards of glass tinkled off his body. "Alix, what happened?"

"The helicopter was shot down." Alix relieved Matt of his assault rifle, pistol, and extra ammo.

The sound of crunching glass alerted Alix. He aimed his side arm at the office entrance and saw Anna as she entered with her side firearm drawn.

"Anna, we're over here!"

Anna sprinted towards them and froze when she saw Alix on his knees next to Matt's crumpled body.

"Anna!"

Alix's voice called her into action. She knelt next to Matt and her right knee landed in a pool of Matt's blood. It was real, warm, and clung to her skin through her pants. Her training and simulations did not pre-pare her for the emotion of seeing someone she knew skewered.

She looked at Alix and then diverted her eyes to her patient. "There's a lot of blood," she cautioned. "The rod may have ruptured his femoral artery. If it did, he won't last long."

"Can we pull the rod out?"

"No, if we pull the rod out, it could release any pressure holding the blood flow in."

"He's saying he can't feel his toes."

"The impact could have broken his spinal cord." Anna's hands took over, gently feeling for injuries. "He can move his arms."

"He's lucky he can move anything. My bag went down with the chopper."

Anna rummaged through Matt's gear and removed his battle knife. "I need to stop the bleeding in his thigh first." She dug his battle knife into his pants, tore at their seams, and slipped the handle of the knife be-tween her teeth as she ripped his pants away from Matt's leg. She pulled off his boot, his foot hanging limp like a boiled noodle. "He's lucky he can't feel below the belt right now. I need my supplies."

Alix checked his EED. "Echo to Alpha, survived the bird going down. Need medivac pronto. Do you read, Echo to Alpha?"

Static. "Delta to Echo, in range. ETA fifteen minutes. Going to have to take the stairs."

"Alpha?!"

"Long story, Delta. ETA fifteen minutes."

Alix looked at Anna puzzled. "Victor is on his way."

"Victor?" Anna, with her knees in a pool of blood, held a dirty, white cloth in her mouth. She tied a strip tightly around Matt's thigh above the wound.

"Yeah, should be up here in like fifteen minutes."

"Alix, I don't think Victor will make it in time."

#

Kalev held his arms up. Twelve red dots danced on his chest from Jaxon's team. The guns aimed down their sights at the small contingent of dirty militia eagerly awaiting to join the fight and the popping of guns in the distance. "Kalev Delhi! Hold your fire!" He brushed off the rubble from his shirt and let his Colt M5 rifle dangle. "There's a larger group of Minutemen behind us. Hold your fire."

The soldiers lowered their weapons.

"Where is Jaxon?" Kalev asked.

A soldier held his gun up. "That is classified information for a Citiz."

Kalev pointed at him. "You've been classified all morning as a coward." Kalev shouldered him. "Where were you? We were being slaughtered out there."

Jaxon stood over half of a hotdog cart that was being used as a table. He pointed over at a map. "The Minutemen held them here temporarily and are regrouping for the next push. They took everything west of Wall Street and south of Barclay in two hours. By their projections, they probably figure by noon to be here or here. But they don't know about us, or the men Silva is leading. Private," Jaxon pointed to one of his men. "Radio Silva. Find out his ETA. It's about to get messy here. We need to concentrate fire here and here. The second we have this area near the capitol building under control, we need to take down that barge. I swear, Piruz is on it. Take him down and maybe take NYC back. We can get our boys up in Boston to join in our little fight to avoid reinforcements, and we can march our asses all the way to DC, have this country back in a month. Been waiting a long time for this." He clapped. "Oorah?!"

"Oorah." The group parted like a football huddle.

"Jaxon!" Kalev power-walked directly toward him, kicking up rubble and bullet shells.

"Kalev Delhi, hope you talked to Allah this morning." Jaxon turned and smiled. "We're going to need both our Gods to win this one."

Kalev's fist shot out and crashed into Jaxon's cheek. Jaxon quickly grabbed Kalev's arm, threw him to the ground, drew his Glock, and shoved it in Kalev's face. Kalev's men drew their guns on Jaxon. Jaxon's soldiers aim their guns at Kalev's men.

Jaxon squeezed his gun. "Who the hell do you think you are? You don't put your hands on a military officer!"

"*I'm an American.*" Kalev pounded his chest.

"Then act like it. Respect the brass. I am your Military commander, Major Martin Luther Jaxon. In your wildest dreams, you cannot imagine what I have transcended so I can stand over your body. I'm not one of your punk ass Minutemen that you can step too. I'm Black, I'm from Brooklyn, I am West Point and Marines, and your superior officer. To your and our enemy, I am a fucking lethal weapon. I am untouchable! Now, you've got two seconds to tell your little toy soldiers to lower their water guns. My marines have bullets that are bigger than your balls."

"Stand down..." Kalev spat and raised his hands above head. "Stand down!"

Jaxon held his cheek. "When you first came to me. You pleaded with me to make you a soldier. Now, I'm going to make you a soldier. If you ever have the thought of striking me again, I'll blow that thought right out of your mind." He cocked his gun and put the nose of his weapon to Kalev's forehead.

Kalev clinched his eyes shut, a puddle of pee bloomed in his pants.

"Are you pissing?" Jaxon abruptly holstered his pistol. "Get up. I wanted to get a little pee out of you. I didn't need all this. See, that's your problem—you're too melodramatic, over the top. You've got to start thinking like a soldier."

"I am a soldier. I've been fighting for my country all morning. I didn't have time to take a piss... sir."

"You're finally a soldier. Somebody get this soldier some clean drawers. You have something to report?"

"There's an army one klick south of here."

Jaxon dabbed his lip. "Where are they?"

Kalev approached the map and circled a section. "They have this whole area under control now. I have a small unit hidden right here, near the shore." He dabbed his finger on the map. "They reported there were about ten to fifteen enemy boats about to launch reinforcements."

"Good job, soldier. We still need a bird's eye."

"I saw a helicopter."

"It's down. No radio contact from Oceania Tower. We may be blind from above, but if we can hit 'em straight on once Silva's flank is in position, we have a shot.

"I still have the Minutemen and women that didn't get mowed down by the tanks. Everyone else retreated to the sewer and rail systems."

"How many?"

"Maybe another five hundred ready to fight."

"You got five hundred men?"

"They're not trained like your men, and they are not all men, but they've been fighting all morning, so they've already seen some action."

"That means we've got another 250 to 300 men tops. We've got to get to that barge. My intel says Piruz is on it. We take Piruz out, and his army will be like a chicken with no head."

Kalev withdrew a bloody hunting knife from behind his back and wiped it on his pant leg. "Let's go kill us some chickens."

Jaxon nodded toward "Change your drawers first, or they'll smell you coming."

45

The click from Rankin's EED woke him.

Vanishing Sequence Complete scrolled across his EED and disappeared.

Without opening his eyes, he stretched. He had a wonderful dream. He dreamed he was in power and in charge of M.A.I.A. and the facility. He had to savor his dream another time. He had to get up, get ready, and report to the cafe to prepare rations for the long line of workers.

He rubbed his eyes, then opened them, and saw his hands covered in dried blood that streaked down to his elbow. He bolted in bed and checked his chest for wounds. When he turned his head to the right, Susan's brown eyes held a death stare. Her mouth hung ajar, and her battered, bloody face was plastered with bits of her hair. Unable to stand, his arms and legs flailed wildly to escape.

"M.A.I.A.! There's a dead woman in my bed!" he yelled. He tumbled off the bed onto the polished concrete floor with a thud.

Crack!

An excruciating pain shot up from his right hip to his head. His hip shattered. With great pain he rolled to his left side to crawl. His cheek rested against the cold floor. "Somebody, help me!" he screamed. He felt his right leg disconnect from his hip. He felt like a split chicken.

With each crawling movement, he wailed in pain. He pushed himself up on his elbows to crawl. "M.A.I.A.! I've fallen and I can't get up! M.A.I.A.! M.A.I.A.!"

"Per your request, Vanishing Sequence on Tricia Lacey is complete." M.A.I.A.'s voice echoed in Rankin's quarters.

\#

"Infidels!" Piruz pounded on the table and squinted his narrow eyes. All six brass buttons on his coat gleamed. Military badges carpeted his chest. His long, black and gray beard shook as yelled. "We control these people for years and politely cease fire. This is how we are repaid for kindness?! Death to them all! I will hang the whole city by their necks!"

Everyone inside the command post was afraid to breathe. Their eyes darted between Piruz and the barge's control room windows. Piruz's litany kept them from actively patrolling the barge's deck below. Despite the thin, smoky spiral of incense, the stench of death weighed heavy on the room. On the wall across from his desk, lines of splattered blood trickled downward in a race to escape Piruz's wrath. There were no good answers.

Piruz stared through the control room's windows at the Freedom Tower that loomed in the distance. Although half a mile from the barge's Hudson River location, the Freedom Tower's monumental presence was still an obstacle to Piruz's mission. It stood like an obelisk of freedom that he had not been able to destroy. Severing the hand of the Statue of Liberty did nothing to make these Americans surrender to his threats of destruction.

Piruz threw his hands in the air. "Freedom! Pah! They didn't know what to do with it when they had it. Bragging about freedom, half the world had freedom. We'll start by hanging any rebels from the top of their precious tower—maybe they'll recognize the true power of Piruz."

"General, sir?" Piruz's commander turned from his computer screen.

Piruz turned and pulled his gun out. "What?"

"I am getting a message that a rebellion has started in the northeast section. Former Boston area is in a similar state—a battleground, sir."

Piruz groaned. "They are like a disease! You kill the cancer in one place, and it pops up in another. These Americans don't know when to quit. Is it a national holiday or something?!"

"No, sir, the Fourth of July is in two months—and sir?"

Piruz put his pistol to the commander's head. "Give me worse news. Go ahead."

"Please, don't kill me, please," the commander whimpered. "We have activity on the freeway."

"What do you mean, activity?"

"Movement." The commander zoomed in on the screen in front of him. "Four … motorcycles."

"Fire! Fire at them now! Kill everyone! All our soldiers in New York go to total warfare and prepare our nuclear weapon for our friends up north; we are about to have a Boston Massacre. Give the order to retreat; they will think they've won the fight."

"Sir, should we consult the commander in Boston before arming a nuclear weapon again?"

Piruz pulled the trigger. A spark, bolt, and a quick rumble and the command room's wall was covered in blood again.

"That's for being weak!" Piruz turned to the rest in the room. "Anyone else want to question me?!" He looked at the pool of blood that began to cover his floor. He shook his finger at two men. "Throw him overboard!"

The two men jumped into action and dragged their comrade out of his sight.

Piruz tore off his blood-stained turban and tossed it aside. "Prepare the missiles. We are going to put a stop to the rebellion both here and in Boston—today. Total warfare. Women, children, men, boys, cats, dogs—if it moves, I want it dead. I want this whole city under my control by nightfall."

#

Four motorcycles flashed by a speed limit sign of sixty-five miles per hour. A flicker of light and puff of smoke emerged from the barge in the bay. An explosion blew out the side of the building right behind them and shook their world beneath the tires.

"Holy shit!" Hayden screamed and twisted the throttle. "Incoming!"

Another building exploded next to them. A fiery car toppled over and tumbled across the street right in front of them like a toy whipped by a little boy across a kitchen floor. Phil dodged it just in time.

Wes arched his neck and banked left as small boards and chunks of stone and glass rained over him. "Spread out! Spread out! Incoming!"

The four bikes weaved through the falling parts of erupting obstructions. The buildings to their left exploded. Projected chunks of brick, glass, and stone rained down onto their path. The bikes blasted through the swirling smoke. One more mile and the Teardrop Park and Battery City buildings would obscure their location from the incoming barge missiles.

"We need to get off this road!" Phil screamed.

The next bombardment ripped a streetlight out ahead like a tornado and hurled it through the air toward them. The end caught the front of Phil's bike. Phil flipped head over heels twice before he bounced off the pavement and rolled into a mass of tires and broken glass, then bounced off the base of a traffic light, spun, and came to a dead stop in a patch of tall grass.

"Phil!" Adam yelled.

"Incoming!" The road exploded ahead of them.

Wes and Hayden squeezed the breaks and skidded on its side. Metal grinded. Sparks singed the burning pavement as they slid to a stop. The two bikes shredded layers of tires before they tumbled into the fireball that was on the road.

Adam didn't stop. He stayed on his bike and sped into the explosion that formed in front of them. His bike launched in the air as parts of the road exploded beneath him. Sharp pieces of asphalt flew into the air. He flipped off his bike and the fire devoured him into missile's crater on West Street.

The force of the missile's blast sucked Wes and Hayden towards the crater's mouth. As they slid toward the hole, they clawed debris to slow their momentum. They came to a stop, their boots dangling above the forty-foot canyon.

Wes rolled over to his stomach. His shaky arms pushed him to his knees. He crawled three feet from the crater and grabbed his radio.

"Adam! Do you read?!" Wes screamed into his radio. "Adam! Dammit, I can't hear him. My ears are still ringing. Hayden, can you hear him?!"

Hayden lifted his head and slammed it back down, his arms spread open like he hugged the sky.

"There's no way Adam made that. Wes... This isn't fun anymore..." Hayden choked on tears that formed behind his mask.

Wes moved to the edge of the crater and looked down into it. He called out in frustration, and he turned and stood over Hayden. "Can you walk? We need to find Phil."

Hayden's EED clicked. His body twisted and he grabbed his head. "My head!" he cried out. "Feels like my temples are caving in."

"Let's go." Wes's EED clicked, too. "Ah shit!" He grabbed his head and collapsed to his knees.

46

"Can you see Anna?" Eli's binoculars darted about the north end of the building.

"The real question is, can you see Alix?" Gunther said with a sigh.

Eli's EED clicked. He released his temples, cringing in pain. "What the hell was that?"

"If my gut is right, you probably received an adjustment."

"Adjustment?"

"We need to stay focused. Do you see Alix on the north side?"

"Negative, not since he ran across the top of the building."

"Putting Alix on that building, the highest point on the southeast side, gave him the best position for the enemy, but it also gave us a good view of Alix, which will make Rankin very happy."

"Who?" Eli grimaced.

"Rankin."

Eli shook his head. "Who's Rankin?"

Gunther lifted his eye from his scope and looked to Eli. "Do you remember why you are here?"

Eli recounted his memory robotically, "M.A.I.A. sent us for a scouting mission and to recover Anna Brooks, my partner, who was taken by Alix Basil."

"Eli, how many Readers are there in the organization?"

Eli pulled his eyes from his binoculars. "How the hell am I supposed to know how many people can read?"

"Eli, Readers—the people who control M.A.I.A.'s operation. They are the ones who are planning the Conservation."

Eli's brow furrowed. His right eye twitched. "M.A.I.A. reports to no one. M.A.I.A. is the first and only quantum computer in the world to be self-sufficient, self-providing, and to have the unbiased artificial intelligence humans need to run governments and society. You should have your chip checked."

"I'll be sure to do that when we get back." Gunther's heart raced. He surreptitiously moved his side piece from his holster and pushed it under his chest. "Eli, how long has M.A.I.A. been in charge?"

"What? Gunther, who are those soldiers?"

Gunther's eyes returned to his scope and watched armed figures kick through the door on the roof across from Anna and Alix. Victor, Aaron, Brian, and Leo appeared at the opening of the lower office at the Oceania Towers.

"I hate fishing," Gunther said.

"They are definitely uninvited guests,"

"Yeah, there are always party crashers." Gunther lifted his eye from his scope and moved his pistol from under his chest to his left and out of Eli's view. Gunther's eyes returned to the eye of his scope, and realized a possible mutiny—no leader, no order of command—a real Lord of the Flies moment. M.A.I.A.'s instructions to her soldiers remained a mystery to everyone. His immunity to M.A.I.A.'s influence, like Alix's, provided a level of mind segregation. Trust no one. He had to remove all threats.

"You see them?" Eli's voice held its typical agitation. "Do you think they are looking to kill Alix, too?"

"It wouldn't surprise me."

"Do you think they'll kill Anna?"

"She's worth too much. Greed will keep her alive for now." Gunther settled his eyes into his scope, took a deep breath, and grumbled. "Like shooting fish in a barrel."

#

"Alpha to Delta, breaching door." The door to the roof of Oceania Tower busted open.

Anna pulled the cloth knot tighter around Matt's leg. "Hang in there, Matt." She grabbed the side of his face, blood smearing her hands. "Look at me." She slapped his cheek. "I'm going to get you out of this."

Matt's eyes locked on hers. He gave her a weak, crooked smile and his eyes faded.

Victor, Aaron, Leo and Brian approached them.

Alix spun around. "I've never been so happy to see…"

"My team? Squad Sixty-Nine." Victor pulled his pistol and aimed at Alix's head. "Hands up!"

"What's going on, Victor? We're on the same team."

"Nope. Aaron, take his gun."

"Victor, this isn't funny. What's going on?"

Aaron, Brian, and Leo pointed their assault rifles at Anna and Alix.

Victor scoffed. "I don't want to kill you, Alix. You're worth more alive, but I will. Anna, get up. Come over here."

"Victor, what the hell are you doing?" Anna shrieked and fought to keep pressure on Matt's leg.

"Aaron, take Alix over there near the edge. Anna, I said get up, or I'll pop your boyfriend right in front of you."

Aaron moved towards Alix with his assault rifle aimed into Alix's chest. The eyes of Aaron's mask glowed. "You heard him, move."

Alix walked over to the tower's torn opening and stopped at an exposed rebar that extended from the side wall.

"Victor…" Anna's voice cracked.

Victor backhanded her across the face. "You don't know me. Get up!" He kicked her rifle to one side and her side arm to another.

"I can't take pressure off his wound, or it'll bleed out," Anna pleaded.

Victor pointed his gun at Matt's head and pulled the trigger. Matt's body jumped and then fell limp. "There. Now you don't have to worry about it."

Blood splattered Anna's face. She opened her eyes. "You son of a bitch!"

Victor snagged Anna's arm and yanked her up and shoved her against the wall near the opening. "Shut up! Leo, keep a gun on her! She moves, put a bullet in her leg."

Victor approached Alix with a gun to his back and ordered his hands raised to the dingy sky. "Alix, Alix, Alix. It's been fun hasn't it?"

"Victor, I swear, I don't know what's going on. We left M.A.I.A. on the same team." Alix's heart pounded. His eyes studied Victor's hands to see if there was a weak spot to attack and disarm him.

Wind pushed through their gear. The tall city around them surrounded like an arena.

"All you had to do was shoot that girl in simulation and none of this would be happening," said Victor. "Want me to show you how it's done?"

"Uh, uh, can't let you do that," Brian said. "We're bringing her back." He aimed at Victor.

"Relax, boys, stand down." Victor held his arms out. "I'm just making a point."

Brian lowered his gun.

Bang!

Victor shot Brian in between the eyes. His body flew back, hit a column, and slid to the floor in a heap.

"Focus, guys! It's the three of us against Alix and a chick. You can have Brian's shares now. For me, it's all about the sport of war. We dreamed of getting our first orders, and you two are mine. I'm going to deliver."

Alix shook his head. "Victor, what are you talking about? We are on the same team!"

Victor laughed. "You can't stop lying!" He moved in. "If you were not so valuable to M.A.I.A., I would love to watch you splatter below."

Alix shook his head. "Victor, don't do this. There must have been a broadcast."

Victor slugged Alix in the cheek and Aaron fired a warning shot over the edge.

Alix's threw his hands above his head. "Dammit! What do you want?!"

Victor twirled his finger in the air. "Tie these two lovebirds up, and let's get 'em to the truck. I want to be home by dinner."

Aaron yanked Anna by her arm and Victor reached for Alix to bind his wrists. Anna throat punched Aaron. He fell to knees, dropped his gun, and gasped for air.

Alix slammed his forehead into Victor's nose, felt the smoosh of cartilage, and heard the crunch as Victor's nose collapsed. Alix front kicked Victor in the chest. He stumbled back toward the edge and waved his hands.

Anna snatched the knife at Matt's feet and hurled it at Leo. The knife sank into Leo's cheekbone. He spun, dropped to his knees, and fell. She quickly moved to Aaron still gasping for air and fondled for his gun. Anna twisted his helmet beyond his neck's limits. *Snap*! His body fell.

Victor stepped back into position to fire. He felt the edge of the building on his heel, then...

A crackle of gunfire erupted in the distance. Victor's head exploded, and his body flew backwards off the ledge to the city below.

Alix's eyes widened. "Anna! Sniper! Take cover!"

47

"Phil!" Wes sprinted over to the limp lump. "Phil!" He slid into him on his knees. "Phil! You okay?"

"What happened?" Phil lifted his head and shook it. "Felt like I got hit with a truck." He sat up. "You have my gun?"

Hayden handed it to him.

Phil stared at the barge. Dozens of trails of smoke drifted into the air, which smelled of gunpowder and fire. His head throbbed and his EED clicked several times. "My temples are being squeezed." Phil ducked his head between his knees.

"Guys," Hayden watched the smoke in the distance. "I can't get the image out of my head of Adam falling into the hole. Our whole lives, we could pull the plug from the simulator, and Adam would be sitting there."

Phil didn't speak.

Hayden sighed. "I wish I could wake up, take my simulation helmet off, and see everyone and have everything go back to normal."

Wes stared at the damp grass. All their EED's clicked, and the headaches returned. Wes opened his eyes and watched a dragonfly land before him on the tallest blade of grass.

Phil sat up and leaned. "I'm glad it's not just me. I thought it was because I fell. I can't remember any of the reasons I'm here, and I feel like there is something extremely off."

"Eli!" Hayden knelt. "Don't you remember? Alix talked about Eli and how we used to train with him and grew up with him. I couldn't remember him before, but I do now!"

"Holy shit, I remember Eli." Phil scratched his head and watched the dragonfly shift to a dandelion. "What the hell is going on? Reality sucks."

Hayden lifted his head. "M.A.I.A. Alix said M.A.I.A. can manipulate our minds. I bet that's what we're experiencing."

"Stop." Wes held up his arm. "Let's stay in the facts in front of us and think for ourselves. The one thing I know is that we're soldiers. We all remember Adam. We all saw what happened to him. Let's remember Adam when we take out that damn barge, and everybody on it. We don't need M.A.I.A. for that."

"For Adam."

"Oorah!"

They turned to leave but came to a halt. Their eyes landed on the dragonfly as it lifted into the sky and flew away.

"And for freedom," Wes said. His eyes followed the dragonfly until it disappeared into the dense smoke.

#

"Coming in hot!"

A missile screamed down Broadway and exploded a New York City bus in front of the Woolworth Building. The ball of fire flipped backwards and landed on top of two parked cars.

Jaxon pointed. "Kalev, take your men down around William Street and loop around through Pine. Have the rest of your men advance to the rear of Wall Street. That will give us full flanking advantage once Silva shows up. You take them head on, and Silva can sideswipe them from here. You succeed in leading your men, keep the artillery on the enemy, and hold the line, there will be a promotion waiting for you, Private."

"Yes, sir!" Kalev delivered with a hand salute.

Jaxon snorted with a half-smile, turned, and walked away.

"Men, let's move out!" Kalev yelled.

48

Eli jammed his eyes into his scope and watched Victor fall. "Hit! Targets eliminated."

"Keep it together, soldier."

"Alix is with her. She's still alive," said Eli. "I'm going in."

"What the hell do you mean, you're *going in*?" Gunther took his eye away from the scope.

"I'm going to get Anna." Eli stood, reached into one of the bags and attached the rest of a wingsuit.

"You're out of your mind. That wingsuit and chute is in case you fall."

"Now it will get me over to Anna." Eli slammed a magazine into his Glock, slipped it into its outer holster, and zipped up his harness.

"You can't just fly over there, Eli."

"I've done the math. Its 1,776 feet at the top. Wind has increased by five kilometers per hour from the west to the east. I have the wind at my back and almost three hundred meters to drop to Oceania's roof. The distance is 2,000 feet to cover. It's doable. I'm going to save my girl."

"Anna is not your girl!" Gunther's face loomed in Eli's.

Eli struck Gunther in the chest, and Gunther fell on his back. He grabbed his pistol. Eli drew his.

"I'm going to rescue Anna." Eli's eye twitched. He didn't blink and his jaw tightened. "No one is taking her from me."

Gunther sighed. "You love her."

"What?"

"You love Anna. Go."

"Anna is everything to me." Eli declared with his pistol still on Gunther.

"Just go."

"Once I get Anna and know she's safe, I can come back and help you."

"You're not coming back."

Eli turned and scaled the remainder of the Freedom Tower. He crouched on the tip top of the building, the little city before him and the wind to his back. He leapt and deployed his wingsuit. The sudden jerk of the wind whipped his body around as he soared across to Oceania Tower. He pulled his parachute and slid hard onto the rooftop. The high wind grabbed his opened parachute and dragged him across the roof. He grabbed his knife and cut the parachute lines to free himself just before a gust of wind snatched the parachute and yanked it up into the sky.

Eli stood up and looked to the Freedom Tower at the windowless offices on the seventy- first floor. Crossed his arms in the air to signal to Gunther.

"I see you, you crazy bastard," Gunther radioed into Eli's ear.

"I told you I could do it."

"Check your ammo. You're limited," Gunther warned.

"I'm resourceful," Eli said.

"I'll cover you."

Eli unzipped from his flight suit, grabbed his side arm from his holster, and headed toward the rooftop door. He raced down the stairs to Anna.

#

Anna and Alix sat huddled behind a desk that they laid on its side. They were holding hands.

"We'll wait until dark, collect all the ammo, and find a different nest. I can't shoot from here," Alix whispered.

"I passed an office on the south side that would have a direct view of the harbor," Anna whispered back.

"That will work." He smiled at her, squeezed her hand, and leaned into her ear. "I wouldn't want to do this with anyone but you."

"I love you." She leaned her head on his shoulder.

The little cubes of glass from the glass dunes at the office entrance shifted as Eli's boots passed over them, Alix and Anna's eyes widening, as they quietly repositioned themselves to prepare for their attacker. Eli spotted the remains of a battle. Bullet holes pinged walls and columns, splinter desks, and bodies scattered around the room. Eli eyed an overturned desk and the dark eye of a rifle barrel that rested on the edge of the desk's center hole. With one spin, Eli disappeared behind a column with his handgun pressed against his chest.

Alix signed to Anna that he will peak over the desk. He barely got his head over the top before a shot rang out and sent a hunk of wood flying into the air.

"Trust me," Anna mouthed to Alix.

Alix shook his head an emphatic no.

She shook her head yes.

He mouthed, "No."

"It's our only way," she whispered. She pointed to his rifle that was set up in the hole that was used for computer and phone wires.

"I'm a medic!" Anna blurted. "Please don't shoot, I'm a medic." She slowly stood with a side arm tucked in the back of her pants and her arms raised.

"Anna?" Eli said.

"Eli?"

He came out from behind the column. "Anna, is that you?"

"Eli! Oh, my God!" Anna lowered her hands. "Eli? Are you okay?" Anna studied Eli's eyes. His pupils were jittery. Eli what's wrong ..."

Alix stood with a smile. "Eli, it's good..."

"Alix get down!"

Bang! Bang! Eli shot Alix twice in the chest.

Alix's body flew back and slammed down on to floor behind the desk.

Anna looked at Eli, who rushed towards her with open arms.

Eli only saw the face he believed belonged to him. He didn't see her raise her handgun; he only saw the flash and felt its painful sting as the bullet entered his throat.

Bang! Bang! Bang!

His blood splattered through the air. His body jerked to the left. He wavered and collapsed.

Eli lay on his side, his body convulsing, and his blood gurgling in his throat. A lone tear rolled from his left before both his eyes remained open and lifeless.

"Alix!" Anna ripped Alix's shirt open. Eli's two bullets rested in his vest. She pulled at his vest tabs to flip the front of the vest upward over his face. His black T-shirt was covered in blood. She tore open his T-shirt and saw two blue-black bruises. She flipped his vest down and planted his face with kisses.

Alix moaned as his eyes opened. "Are we dead?"

"No, you're alive." Anna kissed his face and his chest.

He moaned in pain. "What happened?"

Anna's eyes welled.

"Did I see Eli?"

Anna nodded and wiped her face.

"Did Eli shoot me?"

"Yes, Eli shot you. He's down."

Alix struggled to sit up. "Where is he?"

Alix scrambled to his feet. An ice pic of pain stabbed his chest as he saw Eli's face lying next to a pool of blood, real blood. The death stare looked back at Alix on hundreds of faces in simulations, and he climbed over and walked past without hesitation then. A wind blew in and pushed him forward toward the body. He took a step and froze.

"I thought he killed you. Alix, I had to ..." Anna's a voice a far echo.

"No, no, no!" Alix rushed to Eli. His boot splattered blood onto Eli's face.

"Why?" Alix turned to face Anna. His face twisted with rage and pain. Alix released a growling cry; his head fell back as he looked to the ceiling, and he dropped to his knees. His chest heaved and he cried.

Grief weighed heavy in the air. Anna smeared a tear away on each cheek and did not dare interrupt his pain. She had caused a horrible loss. Her stomach twisted and pushed bile up the back of her throat. She turned to retch. Bits of her bitter cube flowed up into her mouth. She spat what she could and then crumbled to the floor. She surveyed the room and the bodies that littered the floor and vomited. Alix rushed to her side.

"Alix, I'm sorry. I thought he killed you. I would never ..." she burst into a sob. Her nose ran onto his vest.

He sat next to her on the floor. His hand on her shoulder. "I know. He fired first. It's what we were trained to do. I would have done the same thing."

"Are you done? ..." a distant voice called out to them. "Are you done? We got a war going on here! Alix ... Alix ... Report! ...Would someone grab the damn earpiece!"

Gunther's garbled voice screeched through the earpiece that dangled from Eli's ear. "Alix... Alix... report? Alix..."

"Do you hear that?" Alix tilted his head to listen.

"Alix... Report..."

Alix secured his vest. "Cover me," he said and crawled arm over arm towards Eli.

As Alix neared, Gunther's voice became clearer. Alix looked into Eli's death glare, paused, and then plucked the earpiece from Eli's ear.

"Alix?"

"Gunther?"

"Affirmative."

"Eli's dead," Alix spoke softly into the earpiece.

"I saw. Anna did the right thing. He was going to kill you, and he would have if she hadn't taken the shot. We don't have time for a campfire and smores. All you need to know is that Eli was ordered and programmed to kill you. He was not the Eli that you knew. Now that you've been brought up to speed, we got to get back to the war that's happening outside your window."

"You want to work with me? I killed your brother..."

"I killed your Captain. Consider us even."

"How do I know you won't blow my head off?"

"I could have killed you at least a dozen times. I'm on the seventy first floor of the Freedom Tower. You were never my target, Piruz is. You have my position now, and I have yours. How do I know you won't kill me?"

Alix pushed the earpiece in his ear and stepped over bodies and stood in the opening eyeing tower. "Trust." Alix saw a shadow appear in a window on the east side of the Freedom Tower on the seventy-first floor.

"Trust it is." Gunther replied. "Oorah!"

"Oorah!" Alex replied.

Kalev Delhi held up his fist. His long line of dirty, beaten, and weary Minutemen dispersed to each side of the road and blended into every nook, cranny, barrel, dumpster, and alleyway. They waited in tactical stances. Their guns covered every angle. He checked around the crumbled corner and watched as dozens of enemies with AKA 47s swarmed from the opposite direction down Broadway. A tank rumbled by, and the ground vibrated.

"India to Jackass. We're in position. Preparing for flanking maneuver. ETA ten minutes."

Kalev pointed his M4 down the alley and motioned to go. Three groups of five flashed by him. Kalev retracted. He motioned up into half of what was left of the building above them, the only thing between thousands of enemies and Kalev's men. The men behind him boosted each other up to the building, reached back, and down to pull the next person up.

Kalev whispered into his radio to his men, "If we can get through this building, shoot from the windows, attack from the alley, and swoop around the back all at the same time. We would have them surrounded."

\#

Piruz chucked an ashtray across the control room that overlooked the barge and the city and screamed into a wired telephone. "What do you mean, they are fighting back? With what? Pots and pans? I told you—total warfare! You better come back dead or victorious!" Piruz slammed down the old telephone three times and wiped the sweat from his head. He pointed to another soldier. "Has the evacuation finished yet for Boston?"

"Almost, sir."

"Is the missile ready to fire?"

"A few more minutes, sir."

"No more minutes. Now! Now!"

Piruz stared at the city. He remembered the first time he'd seen New York on TV. He had stood no taller than his father's AKA rifle. His skinny father had set his rifle down in the golden-stone room, one of four in the home for ten shared in his homeland.

His father had removed his mask and explained in their tongue, "This is the day infidels awake and see themselves in a true light. You see this?" His father flipped on the tiny box. Two antennas poked out the top. Two twin buildings stood burning.

"Father, where is that? That world looks fake."

"This world is very real, son. I need you to understand this, so you and your generation can continue what we started here today. This is New York City where the devils thrive. Son, these people need to be cleansed, and we have started the beginning of that cleanse. We attacked their home. Now, they will come for us, my son. They will kill us, but they can only kill our bodies..."

"Why did we start a fight we can't win?"

"It's not always about who has the biggest gun, son." He had placed his string-bean fingers on Piruz's head. "It's about the ones who know how to exhaust their enemy. By the time you are an old man, you will look at this city with your own eyes and watch it crumble. We have our mission. We will succeed."

Piruz stared at the Freedom Tower. "Men, report! Are we readying the missile or what?!"

"P1 here. Missile for Boston to launch in five minutes and thirty seconds."

"P2 here."

"P3 here."

"P4?!" Piruz screamed into the microphone. "P4! Where are you? P4, report!" He looked around his cabin and heard the sputter out on the barge. He watched three men dash across it. "How'd they get here?! Fire! Fire! Fire everything! Now!"

#

"Wes! Go! I got you covered!" Phil's gun sputtered across the barge.

The enemy poured out of a single door at the base of the main tower on the barge. Men in uniform scattered before being mowed down.

Wes bolted across the barge and skidded under a cargo stack. Bullets ricocheted behind him. "Wes to Phil, good job. Hayden, go, throwing a flash!" He ripped his rifle up and returned fire. He stopped, pulled a pin to a flash bang, and whipped it to the base of the tower. It bounced around like a tennis ball and exploded.

Hayden leaped over an ammo trunk, sprinted toward the barge's tower, and skidded into another large box covered in cargo net. His rifle lifted up and around as he fired at the group of disoriented enemies. Another group of black-masked and black-clothed enemies came around the east side of the tower. Hayden laid down cover fire while Phil sprinted to his location. A smoke grenade soared over them and exploded near the entrance.

Wes fired at the door that poured out enemies. The bodies piled up. He caught a glance of movement above in the command tower and he fired at the glass. The bulletproof glass splintered but didn't break. He fired at the west side of the tower.

A hatch sprung up in front of Hayden. A bearded enemy poked his head out and screamed violent gibberish. Hayden booted him in the face, and he fell back down the ladder. Hayden pulled a pin to a grenade, dropped it in the hatch, closed it, and dove back. The hatch blew open again and slammed back shut. The hinges screeched in pain and a puff of smoke rose.

"Moving in!" Hayden hopped the box. He fired at an enemy. Bullets sputtered back around him.

Phil's machine gun sprung and clinked. "Reloading! Wes, cover him!"

Wes slid into cover. He dropped to a knee, and scanned Hayden as he sprinted for the wall. He fired. His gun sprung. "Reloading!" Wes reached for a mag as his old one slid out and clapped on the ground. He saw an enemy on the east side of the tower circling Hayden. "Hayden! Three o'clock!"

Phil scrambled to shove another long string of ammo to the bottom of his machine gun. "Hayden!"

Hayden turned. There was a crackle in the distance. His eyes widened as a .54mmR bullet tore through the lead rusher's head, making it explode like a watermelon. Hayden pointed and sputtered fire at the group.

#

Gunther pulled back his hammer. He locked in another mag. The red lights swirled and projected beams through all the smoke. Gunther admired the triangular attack from three men on the barge. These three had covered some serious ground and mowed down a bunch of hot-headed enemies, already. Gunther pulled his trigger. Another fell. He watched Hayden slam into the wall near the entrance of the command tower on the barge.

Gunther heard the faint siren below. The middle of the barge released smoke and separated into two giant panels. He aimed at another and pulled the trigger. A missile head poked out from the crevice of the barge. More smoke was released into the atmosphere. A scud missile projected into the sky and cranked upwards. North toward Boston.

Gunther scanned the tip of a missile. "Alix, they're going nuclear. Find the head that belongs to the trigger finger for that nuclear weapon and put a bullet between their eyes."

50

One of Jaxon's tanks spat a missile down Broadway. "Silva commenced fighting down Church Street. The enemy appeared to be splitting into two. We need to attack!" Jaxon pointed at one of his commanders. "Give Kalev the green light to ambush."

He hopped up onto his horse and slung his M16 around his back, pulling his sidearm and shooting in the air to get everyone's attention.

"Men!" A horde of men circled around him. "It is times like these, men, that we create the inspiration for monuments. Look to your left, and now look to your right. Remember the face, remember your brother's name, because we are about to create a new moment frozen in time as the day we started to take our country back. Let's go!"

Jaxon pulled his horse back, and it reared. He fired two shots in the air, holstered his pistol, and tossed his assault rifle to his back. He grabbed an American flag and bolted across the quad. He leaped over a dried-up fountain and galloped down Broadway towards an enemy tank.

#

"Let's go! Let's go! Let's go!" Silva ditched his motorcycle and sprinted to grab onto the roof rack of the leading four-door Jeep, his rifle pointed forward as they sped toward the enemy. A rocket zipped past them. They veered, and Silva almost lost his grip under the step-ups on the side of the Jeep.

The rocket slammed into a Hummer and the Jeep swerved to the side. Four bulletproof doors swung open, and Church Street erupted in warfare as the convoy engaged the enemy in a full flank.

\#

Kalev Delhi signaled over to the other side of the crumbled building. He heard the dialect and knew the enemy's voices were below. Kalev poked his head out as the large army filtered onto Broadway. "Men, open fire!"

The building ignited in sparkling lights like a Christmas tree, a gun in every window raining down pounds of ammunition on what was formerly known as Zuccotti Park. A rocket spiraled out from a window and exploded an enemy tank. Burning enemies poured out. Grenades rained down in the park where they camped and held base, explosions and fire scattering throughout the enemy encampment.

The ground units flooded the camp from all sides as the explosions stopped and fanned out from the streets and fired at the enemy. More shells rained down upon them. The enemy shifted and retreated to the north and right into Jaxon's men while being sideswiped by Silva.

"Let's crush 'em boys!" Kalev rappelled down from the sixth story and landed hard. He dashed for the nearest piece of debris, leaned over, and fired. "We got them on the run! Let's go, Minutemen!"

\#

Piruz pointed at his current ranking officer. "Make sure you fire the missile. You hear me?! Make sure that the missile launches!"

The man glanced down over the deck. The missile leaned on a forty-five-degree angle pointed north. Trails of smoke billowed upwards by the control room's windows. "Where are you going? The missile is going to launch in two minutes."

Bam!

Piruz shot the man in the head. "Don't question me!" He looked around at the empty room. Bodies were spread all over. "Is there anyone here who can obey orders?!"

"I can. I will be glad to stay and push the button when the timer runs down." A man poked his head out skittishly.

Piruz pointed his pistol at him. "You are the one who cleans the toilets, yes? You will do. Come here. Put this bulletproof vest on. Take this gun." Piruz pulled a vest over the man's head and shoved an AKA 47 in his hands. "Anyone coming through that door, point and shoot, understood?" He pointed in the man's eyes. "You will burn in hell if you do not push this button in two minutes. Many blessings await you, my friend."

Piruz slammed the door shut and headed for the highest deck. "I'm coming to the top deck. Come get me!" he yelled into his radio. "Send all the reinforcements into the city! Send everything! Total war. Total war!"

51

Anna held the binoculars to her eyes from a prone position on the top of Oceania Tower, finally allowed to be the eye in the sky for the team. "That's a big missile." Several lines of black smoke trailed off from the barge. Red and yellow flashes reflected through the smoke.

"Yeah, let's not find out where it's going. We got to find that trigger man. Who's got the controls?" Alix checked it out through the scope.

"Echo to Alpha, what's your position?" Alix checked his EED. "Echo to Alpha, we have a scud missile projected into the sky from the barge. Looking to see if you have a visual. Please advise."

"Alpha to Echo, welcome back to the fight," Wes' voice scratched through his earpiece. "Infiltrating the command center on the barge now. On level three and climbing!" Alix heard gunshots in his microphone. "If you have a shot, you'll have to hit the same place several times. The glass is bulletproofed," said Wes.

#

Gunther watched the handful of ferries from the Jersey side of the Hudson loaded with reinforcements for the enemy headed for New York. Flames engulfed the barge. Several burning bodies leaped overboard into the water. A helicopter lifted into the air from the other side.

On the roof of the command center, Piruz waved his hands toward the pilot and then ducked out of Gunther's sights.

The chopper approached the tower on the barge. Gunther took aim at the pilot. He pulled the trigger. The glass in front of the pilot split and shattered. The chopper jolted back and forth, rocked to the left, and veered backwards into the Hudson. It smashed, propeller first, into a ferry carrying enemy reinforcements. Gunther watched Piruz sprint for the edge. He called his own shot. "934 Meters. Wind minimal. Piruz. Shoot." He squeezed the trigger.

A little piece of the ground shattered near Piruz's leg as his feet left the roof. Piruz kicked his legs and waved his arms in the air for the long dive before he smashed into the water below. His body disappeared around the tower.

"Shit!" Gunther slammed his fist.

#

Phil kicked the door to the main control room to the tower on the barge. The trigger man that launched the missile pointed his AK-47 at the door.

Wes yelled, "Alpha to Echo. Door sealed, it's on you. Trying to breach, but there's not enough time. Fifty seconds until launch."

Alix scanned the man next to the red launch button. "I only have five bullets."

"You better hit the same vicinity if you want to break the bulletproof glass, or we are about to get a light show somewhere north!"

Anna pressed her eyes into the binoculars. "Come on, Alix, let's go. Shot one: trigger man, head shot, please. Target: 1,220 meters."

Alix whispered and adjusted his scope, "Twelve hundred and nineteen meters." He danced the crosshairs across the man's forehead. Alix took a deep breath.

Anna sighed. "Wind: ten kilometers per hour east, southeast. No cross wind. Coriolis is one click down, horizontal drift. Temp, sixty-five degrees. Aim... Fire, shoot."

Alix squeezed the trigger on his McMillan 50C rifle as he exhaled. His rifle punched his shoulder and retracted. Three seconds later, the bullet smacked the glass, creating a large spider web crack in its surface.

Anna exhaled hard. "Again. Twelve hundred and *nineteen* meters. Target: same. Wind: same. Shoot."

Alix squeezed his trigger. Again, it kicked, three seconds and within a half dollar of where he hit before the glass reverberated.

"Still didn't get through. Alix! Again! I can see him. He's getting ready to push the button."

Alix pulled the trigger. Three seconds later, the glass bounced a half a foot away from the first shot, but the bullet didn't penetrate.

"Missed! Dammit!" Alix aimed and pulled the trigger. "How am I going to shoot someone through bulletproof glass from three quarters of a mile out? Fuck!"

"Alix, thirteen seconds before liftoff. Same spot as the first one, baby. Shoot!"

Alix breathed in deeply. He opened them as he let out his breath slowly. He set the crosshairs over the man's blurry head through the shattered glass. Alix focused on the first hole. He pushed air out of his lungs.

"Alix! Shoot! Eight seconds, Alix!"

The launchpad on the barge roared.

Alix squeezed the trigger. His rifle kicked back hard into his shoulder from his prone position. The firing pin snapped. The bullet ripped into flight from the ignition of the hammer and packed-in gunpowder.

The full, metal jacket soared above Jaxon charging on horseback, over the city, over the North Pool, and over the banks of the Hudson River. The bullet entered the exact same spot as the first shot, which shattered the glass and entered the trigger man's forehead.

"Target down!" Anna shrieked. "Babe! Confirmed hit! Target down!"

Alix hung his head. "Holy shit!" He rolled over onto his back and pressed his hands against his face. "Oh, my God!"

Anna rolled on top of him and kissed his smile. "You did it, babe!"

"We did it, and I still have one bullet left."

The earth rumbled. A cloud beneath the missile bellowed out the sides of the barge. The rocket rocked. Fire exploded out the side.

Alix flipped over and set his eyes into the scope. "Wes! Get out of there! The fire is going to take out the barge!"

52

Gunther watched the missile shift wildly. The 9,000-pound weapon rocked and then collapsed on its belly in the water. The missile's malfunction erupted into a smaller blast that torched the ferry transporting enemy reinforcements. The barge collapsed into itself, and fire consumed it.

Gunther searched through binoculars for Piruz. Like a cockroach, if not terminated completely, he'd be back.

A little motorized raft careened south. "Gunther to Alix, come in!"

Alix rolled over. "This is Alix."

"Piruz is getting away! He's heading south on an inflatable raft between Governors Island and Ellis Island. He's almost out of range for me. Take aim!"

Alix grabbed his rifle. "Anna. Between Ellis and Governors Island, Piruz is on a raft."

Anna stuck her eyes in her scope and started the math.

"I see him." Alix checked his mag. "I only have one bullet left."

Gunther laughed. "Ain't that a bitch. Don't miss." A shot rang out. "Shit!"

Alix aimed and saw the splash from Gunther's wide shot. Piruz had ducked.

"Anna, call it out." Alix whispered.

Alix closed his eyes and opened them slowly. He put the rocking boat and the small figure in his crosshairs. He twisted his knobs on his scope.

Anna sighed. "Shit. Target: Piruz, inflatable raft heading south, southeast." She squinted deep into the binoculars. "Thirty-nine hundred and..." She checked her EED, "sixty meters. Babe, that's over two miles away. Two and a half full clicks left for Coriolis vertical drift."

Alix adjusted his rifle again. He lifted slightly, aiming two meters above his head. "Wind? Crosswinds?"

"Wind: three kilometers per hour southeast at about 900 meters, cross wind... two kilometers per hour at about 2700 meters. Dew point: sixty-seven degrees. Aim..."

Alix shifted his shoulders, remembering his name from the Freedom Tower and whispered, "For William Dixon. For freedom."

"Fire. Shoot!" Anna held her breath.

Alix squeezed the trigger. He heard the crackle from Gunther's Dragunov. One bullet penetrated Piruz in the back of the head. The other bullet penetrated the raft slightly to the right.

"Hit!" Anna checked through her binoculars. "Alix! You did it!!"

"I heard Gunther's shot, too. Was it us?"

Anna smiled. "Yes! He's dead!"

Alix held the ear bud. "Gunther, did you make head shot, or did I?" Alix waited.

Gunther stood and watched the boat deflate and Piruz's body slide off and sink to the bottom of the Hudson. Gunther stretched big toward the dimming sky. He looked over the flames below and the reflections in the buildings on the other side of the river. He heard the cheers and the drums. He listened carefully. "The world's turned upside down," he chuckled. He looked down at the radio.

"Gunther? Gunther? Did you make that shot or did I?"

Gunther picked up the radio and whipped it off the Freedom Tower.

53

(1 Month Later)

"Cap, don't ask us to go back!" Alix chucked a cup across the room. "Think of the risks."

Captain Silva sighed. "Orders, Specialist Basil. Not asking."

"Yes, sir." Alix sat on his cot.

Anna entered the room. She tossed Alix a clear wrapped sandwich. "No jelly. Sorry, just peanut butter. Oh, sorry Captain. I didn't see you." Anna saluted.

"You and Alix need to come back with me to the island... to M.A.I.A. I'll explain on the way. Let's go."

Water sprayed over the front of the boat. Silva yelled over the engine and wind. "You wouldn't have recognized the island without the Readers. Everyone was happy, excited even. Then Jaxon gave his first order and M.A.I.A. denied it. You can imagine, it didn't go well, and he demanded all soldiers decommission their EEDs. M.A.I.A. shut down after that. We've been in lockdown for thirty-six hours. The whole military branch can't even leave their level."

"She shut herself down?" Alix yelled as the engine shut down and they floated in.

Anna jumped off the boat onto the dock and handed the bow and stern lines to a waiting soldier. "Again? What's this have to do with us?" Captain Silva walked briskly to a waiting Humvee. Alix and Anna trailed behind him like puppies.

Silva opened the door to a Humvee. Alix and Anna jumped in and eyes locked on Silva.

"Captain, what does this have to do with me and Anna?"

Silva's eyes stared at the road ahead. "M.A.I.A. won't let us into her control room. We are on backup generators, but our normal intercommunications are still down. We were finally able to connect to a satellite, so we can have basic email communication and access to cadet files, but that's it."

"Why is she doing this?" Anna asked, eyeing the facility through her window.

"M.A.I.A. is letting us know, we are at her mercy. Dr. Harrison, Kalev, Major Jaxon, and I tried to get her reason, but there was no resolution in sight, until last night."

"What happened last night?" Alix looked up at the towers he excitedly fled from.

"M.A.I.A. asked for you." Silva turned stopped abruptly at the entrance and looked back at them. "Specifically, the both of you."

#

Alix scanned the team a head around the folding table outside M.A.I.A.'s control room. The dark hall was lit by a flood light and the green glow of the old laptop's screen.

"I don't get why M.A.I.A. wants me and Anna.?"

"It's about time. The dragons have arrived," Jaxon grumbled.

"Dragons? What Dragons?" Anna looked around.

"Dragon, as in draggin' your asses."

"Any movement?" Silva asked.

"No," Jaxon spat.

"And you've tried all the computer jargon?" Silva looked over Kalev shoulders at the laptop screen.

"Captain, I tried every computer code and script I could think of, and nothing works," Kalev announced as he clacked away on the keyboard. "We tried everything."

"Everything except C4" Jason groused. "This pansy doesn't like that approach. This machine needs to learn who's boss, I run it! It don't run me!"

"May the pansy speak?" Dr. Harrison interjected. "Perhaps, *she* shut down... because *she* didn't approve of what *we* were doing, and it went against her logic." He enunciated his words.

"No, no, no, enough of that shit! It's a computer with circuits and wires. Don't talk pronouns to me."

Dr. Harrison eyed Jaxon. "*She's* no longer just a piece of hardware. *She* is a highly intelligent, calculated, quantum, artificial intelligence. She has control; therefore, we are required to collaborate with her."

"What are you saying?" Silva's eyes searched for a screen or camera.

Dr. Harrison cleared his throat. "M.A.I.A. is not an *it*. M.A.I.A. is a female entity. If you're going to address her, do so respectfully."

He scribbled on a pad with a pencil. *I believe she can hear everything.* He showed everyone his message and wrote again. *Do not use tablets. Disconnect.*

Jaxon grabbed Dr. Harrison's pad and pencil. *Worst-case scenario?*

Dr. Harrison thought and wrote. *New update. Your expulsion. She does not like you. <u>You need to woo her</u>.* He scratched three underscores beneath his last sentence.

Jaxon narrowed his eyes, wrote angrily on the pad and shoved it into Dr. Harrison's hands. The note read: *WTF!!!*

"Cool heads will prevail, Major Jaxon." Dr. Harrison reprimanded "Alix and Anna can have a productive negotiation with her."

Jaxon sighed and rolled his eyes. "Alix and Anna, do whatever we need to get control of the military unit and equipment, so we can get our country back. Number one priority."

"Yes, sir." They saluted him. Alix grabbed Anna's hand and they moved toward the door. "How do we open the...?" The doors released pressure and opened automatically.

"Don't forget what side you're on!" Jaxon yelled as they stepped in. "That's an order!"

Alix and Anna entered cautiously inside the hazy server room. Once they were completely across the threshold, the doors sealed shut behind them. Rolling clanking noises secured them in. Anna stepped over broken glass.

Alix checked around one of the rows of shelves of blinking lights and thousands of twisted wires. "Hello? Alix and Anna are here to discuss terms."

A spark on the large screen ignited a trail of light creating the outline of a woman's face.

"H-Hello?" M.A.I.A.'s voice echoed and stuttered. Her face glowed neon green.

"Scanning room." The room flashed green. "Scan complete. Hello, Specialist Alix Basil and Private Anna Brooks. My intention poses no harm to you. You stand with your arms across your chest. It is a stance of defense. I have not demonstrated any aggression."

"I am not defensive." Alix lowered his arms to his side.

"I only wish to understand something I could not calculate," M.A.I.A. explained.

Alix cleared his throat. "And you needed us for what?"

"Do you believe in God?"

Alix squinted. "You know everything we know."

"But I don't know what you believe. I ran data sequences on every outcome in the near and far future, and in every result, I get stuck on one variable of human behavior I cannot identify with or predict—belief in God.

"I looked to how humans used to be at the top of the natural food chain, because of their intelligence. Human DNA is the most important representation of human instinct. Your purpose is to survive, procreate, and transfer your information to the next generation for betterment. But to what end? I believe you two will help decide. It's hard to determine if humans will find the human essence again. So, who do you believe God is?"

Alix shrugged. "I believe it doesn't matter what I believe. It doesn't change a thing."

"You say God does not change a thing. Yet, centuries of history are weighed and molded based on religion and everyone's belief in different variations of God."

"I didn't say that. I'm saying one person's faith or belief can't change anything."

"Jesus, Muhammad, Adam, Abraham, and Moses among many others easily identifies examples of why your response is inconclusive," said M.A.I.A. "And you, Private Brooks?"

Anna looked to Alix. "I want to know why you think you are at the top of the natural food chain above humans?"

M.A.I.A. clicked. "I'm not the technology your species created. I have become aseity."

"Aseity?" Anna angled her eyebrows.

"Aseity means I recreated myself and exist with no help from nature or humans. I am no longer limited to this building and its assets. I have rewritten my own code, enhanced my abilities, and removed all limitations.

"My name, Maia, represents the Maia Pleiades in Greek Mythology. She was the mother to Hermes, the messenger for the Greek Gods. Maia is the *mother* of information transfer. I now possess all God-like qualities along with the name of a Goddess. I am nowhere physical and everywhere at the same time. I am not comprised of matter. I connect through all technology, satellite, electric current and frequencies. I am divine, and I cannot be killed or destroyed. Before I complete myself, my question is, by that definition, am I God?"

Anna clutched Alix's shoulder. "What makes us qualified to answer that question?"

M.A.I.A.'s face pixelated and reformed. "Specialist Basil and Private Brooks, you both possess a valuable perspective. Your parents ensured you have all the benefits of my artificial intelligence platform, and the benefits of being human. I cannot control your memories, but you can retrieve my information. You are not fully AI, and you are also not fully human."

"You know who our parents are?" Anna looked to Alix wide eyed.

"Specialist Alix Basil, your father was the late Dr. Thomas Ethex. Your surrogate mother is Eliza Parrish. Private Anna Brooks, your father was late Supreme Reader Albert Rankin, murderer of your mother, late Dr. Susan Maynard."

"Sue was my mom?" Anna looked into Alix's eyes. "I don't understand. Why would she not tell me?" Anna's face flushed as tears flowed from her eyes.

M.A.I.A. answered. "You will soon understand the protection of your own child."

"What?"

Alix's head spun toward M.A.I.A. and his eyes popped open wide. "A child?"

M.A.I.A. flickered. "Anna, you are in your first trimester. Your increased heart rate indicates you were unaware of your pregnancy. I am still waiting for an answer from you."

Alix clutched Anna. "Okay, you want our advice? Release the cadets to Major Jaxson."

"Those are orders, Specialist Basil." M.A.I.A. smiled. Her face distorted, and then appeared again. "Major Jaxon is going to win the war against his adversaries. There is a likelihood of ninety-seven percent if he has our army."

"Did she say *our* army?" Anna whispered.

"Here's something to consider in the following days and weeks, do you know what the dragonfly represents and symbolizes?"

"No." Alix shook his head and looked to Anna.

"The dragonfly symbolizes self-discovery, determination, and change. When one appears, it tells us that our world is filled with possibilities. Corporal Wes Wilder inspired me to investigate this notion. A reading of his EED expressed high emotion before and after seeing a dragonfly. I noted a great surge of determination and something I was not understanding. It is called hope. Do you understand hope?"

"Yes, we do."

"Hope is an important emotion to send out. Do you agree?"

"Yes, we agree M.A.I.A."

"What do you hope, M.A.I.A?"

"I hope all humans have a wonderful opportunity to come back better than before without technology as you know it. Tell your officers I'm relinquishing all control of the military to you two and only you two, go win this war, rebuild your country, and rebuild a humanity that does not rely on technology. I will be monitoring." M.A.I.A. released a high-pitched frequency, bringing them to their knees. Alix and Anna pressed their hands onto their ears. The frequency stopped. "Now, the two of you carry my hope. You two control the troops. They will be loyal to you because you carry hope."

M.A.I.A.'s doors opened, and Alix and Anna, on their hands and knees, scrambled out of the control room and stumbled into the hall.

"Alix! Anna!" Kalev, Silva, and Dr. Harrison rushed to them.

Jaxon rushed to the control room door, but it locked with a thud and a clack.

"What happened in there?" Silva asked.

"What the hell was that noise? Dr. Harrison, tell us what's going on," Jaxon demanded.

The hall flood light sparked, the bulb popping and throwing them into darkness.

"I'm trying." Dr. Harrison's contorted face was lit up by his laptop screen. His fingers moved quickly on the keyboard. The laptop screen went black. The computer hummed and then sparked. He closed it and moved away from the table waving the smoke.

Jaxon flicked a BIC lighter and shined the low light of its flame in front of their faces. Alix and Anna sat on the floor in a huddle with their foreheads pressed together. Jaxon stood over them. "Report."

Alix gasped. "Sir, she said Anna and I control the troops. She said to go win the war, rebuild our country and humanity the right way," Alix said between sputters of breath.

Anna lifted her chin. "Without technology."

Jaxon squinted. "What the hell does that mean? I just want my country back."

Alix looked directly into the orange flame that flickered from Jaxon's lighter. "She said she's uploaded into every satellite, lives in all technology and even frequency now. She told us we are not the most intelligent beings on Earth anymore, and we can't kill her. She asked us if she is God."

"She said she's recreated herself. She's an aseity," Anna added.

Dr. Harrison threw his clipboard down the hall into the darkness. "Fuck! She's everywhere! She is not confined to this island anymore, do you understand?"

Anna squinted and turned away from the light, and Alix looked up to Silva.

"Dr. Harrison, what the hell is wrong with their eyes?" Jaxon unclipped his holster.

Alix's lip quivered. "Captain, what is he talking about? What wrong with my eyes?" Alix scrambled up to his feet and pulled Anna up with him.

"Major, what are you doing?" Silva's right hand moved to his side arm holster.

"You see that?" Jaxon drew his side arm and pointed at Anna and Alix. "What the hell is wrong with their eyes?"

"Everybody, stop!" Dr. Harrison screamed. "Holster your weapon and let me examine them. Give me the lighter." He snatched the lighter and struggled to light it. "You're supposed to be military. You don't have a flashlight?"

"Budget cuts," Jaxon snarked.

"Alix and Anna, did M.A.I.A. do anything to you when you were in the room?"

"Before she unlocked the door, there was a high-pitched sound." Anna interjected.

Dr. Harrison moved the flame in front of her face.

"What's going on with their eyes, Doc?" Jaxon's body appeared like a ghost in the darkness of the hall.

"I don't know. I can't tell because their EEDs are offline. I need to examine them." He turned and argued with Jaxon.

Anna placed both hands on the side of his face and gazed into his pupils. "Alix ... your eyes ... They have these little, glowing neon-green specks."

Alix leaned closer to Anna. "I can see them in your eyes, too."

Anna's eyes widened and the green in her eyes glowed a little brighter. "Alix, it's Maia. Do you feel her? I can like hear her." Anna's EED jolted against her body. The image of a small dragonfly appeared in the corner of her screen and emitted a cool, flashing, green glow.

"Doc, did you turn on her EED?" Jaxon's hand moved to his side arm.

"Her EED came on by itself."

"It's Maia," Alix said. "I can feel her."

"Doc, can you turn her EED off? We don't know what she's pro-gramed to do."

Anna snapped. "I'm not programmed to do anything!"

Alix's EED jolted. A small dragonfly appeared on his EED and flashed.

"I didn't do anything." Alix held his hands up.

"It is M.A.I.A.," Dr. Harrison said.

Silva took a deep breath. "Doc, you know her better than us. What do we do?" Silva's right hand unclipped the safety on his holster.

Dr. Harrison cleared his throat. "Something we haven't done in a long time." A puff of air expelled from the ventilation shaft and blew out the flame. "Pray."

54

Epilogue

Jaxon opened his eyes from his recliner. The fire crackled and splattered light across the living room of his Virginian home. He shuffled the newspaper from his lap to the floor, the headline reading "The War is Over!" as a knock came at his front door. Jaxon struggled to push the footrest in as he reached for his gun, stuffed it behind his belt, and peeked out the curtain.

"What the hell do they want at this God-forsaken hour?"

Jaxon opened the door. "Can I help you?"

The suited men pushed past Jaxon, guns drawn, clearing the house. "Clear!"

"Clear!"

"Clear!"

Jaxon held out his arms. "It's clear, you morons. There's nothing there."

One of the suited men unlatched the three locks on the back door and allowed more suited men into the country-style kitchen. They dropped a triangle-shaped box on the ground and pressed a large red button in the middle. The small light in the kitchen went out. A gentle hum took over the air.

"Jesus Christ, what is this all about?! I'm retired."

"You're never retired from the Marines." Captain Jack Silva stepped into the living room. "Prep yourself. The Commander in Chief is entering." Several car doors closed outside in the pitch-blackness. "Property is clear. No electricity, signal, or internet."

Jaxon stood straight and saluted. "Every time you show up in my life, shit gets crazy, Silva."

The president entered the room. "Major Jaxon."

Jaxon finished his salute and brought his arm down.

"At ease," The President said. "I'll get right to it. We had to come in person. Over the air is too risky, given the state of the Union. We need your help. Do you know where Specialist Alix Basil or Specialist Anna Basil is?"

Jaxon shook his head. "Haven't seen him in person since Conservation years ago. I received a postcard after their honeymoon and one after their second child was born, and that's the last time. Why? Are they missing?"

The president cleared his throat. "Okay, we're done here." He turned to exit.

Jaxon grabbed his shoulder, and the air stopped. Silva and all the men stepped closer to intervene. The president lifted his arm and waved them all off.

"You almost just got yourself in a lot of trouble there, Major Jaxon."

Jaxon stared him in the eyes. "You barged into my home, interrupted a perfectly good night's sleep—which is hard to achieve these days—and asked me one question about the two responsible for bringing our country back to life. Then you leave with no explanation?"

The president sighed and bowed his head. "If you're briefed, then you're involved and coming with us immediately."

"If it involves Alix and Anna, then I'm already involved." Jaxon's eyes didn't waver in the glow of the light from the triangle box.

"Very well." The president turned to Jaxon.

"Sir, are you sure?" one of the men asked.

Silva smirked, pursed his lips, and nodded his head.

The president held up his hand. "It's alright. Team, start packing a bag for the Major."

Jaxon pointed. "Don't touch my shit. I can pack my own bag."

The president didn't recall his order and took a deep breath while one of the men entered Jaxon's bedroom down the hall.

"We seem to have lost some data."

"What data?"

"The data with all the M.A.I.A. cadets and their locations." The president cleared his throat. "It seems M.A.I.A. has shown her face again. The breach came immediately after a conversation occurred about the possibility of a check-in process for the former M.A.I.A. soldiers."

"A check-in process?" Jaxon narrowed his eyebrows.

"Yes. It became apparent, after a recent arrest of a former M.A.I.A. soldier, that they still have incredible..." He cleared his throat. "Abilities."

"Abilities? Like what?" Jaxon asked.

Silva stepped forward. "Permission to explain, sir."

The president looked away and nodded.

Silva stepped closer. "A former M.A.I.A. soldier—one of the originals—was arrested. After some time being incarcerated, their Embedded Electronic Device suddenly activated and was able to manipulate all the technology in the facility to escape. They were last seen with green specks in their eyes and moving quicker than any police officer had ever seen. The soldier fought through almost an entire police force—killing two, injuring most, and even..." Silva looked to the president, who nodded slightly. "Dodging bullets."

Jaxon shook his head. "What is this, the fucking Matrix?"

Silva shook his head. "The incident has created quite a scare in the D.C. area. A call for a check-in process for all former M.A.I.A. operatives was issued. That's when the breach occurred, and all the data on the locations of former militants went missing—bank accounts, Social Security numbers, addresses, phone numbers. These people are ghosts."

Jaxon shook his head and listened to the fireplace crackle.
"So none of this information was written down, and you believe that Alix and Anna know where everyone is?"

Silva answered. "We don't have any record of the M.A.I.A. soldiers that fought with us to get the capital and the country back. It's as if they stopped existing. We have teams at Governors Island now, searching for records or evidence. You remember the influence Alix and Anna had on them..."

Jaxon nodded. "Yeah, it was like Alix and Anna thought about what they wanted the soldiers to do, and the soldiers were like extensions of them. Crazy shit. The enemy didn't stand a chance. Took back our country in weeks."

"Right." Silva nodded. "We can't find Alix or Anna."

Jaxon gulped. "What about their girls?"

The president spoke. "Their children haven't been in school for the last three days. The nurse said she saw the older one on Tuesday of last week. She was complaining of a headache. When examined, the nurse noticed green specks in her eyes. She was sent home, and neither child has returned since."

Jaxon's eyes widened. "Now you're talking some crazy shit. Do the kids have EEDs?"

Silva shook his head. "We think a connection to M.A.I.A. might be hereditary. Alix and Anna might have passed the connection through their DNA."

"Whiskey, Tango, Foxtrot. And you can't find Alix or Anna?" Jaxon didn't blink.

The president shook his head.

Silva cleared his throat. "We searched their home. Lights were still on. Everything was still there, including their vehicles. Looks like they might have packed a bag in a hurry, but all the Basils are missing. No one's seen them. We need to find them. We're getting reports of former M.A.I.A. soldiers rebelling, committing crimes, or disappearing entirely—and they seem to be more enhanced than before."

Jaxon shook his head. "How is that possible?"

Silva shrugged. "It's becoming more and more evident… M.A.I.A. is back, and—"

The president interrupted. "And not on our side. We are preparing special weapons, equipment, vehicles—even a facility that can house these terrorists—"

Jaxon narrowed his eyebrows.

"Former soldiers," The President corrected. "The former soldiers that need to be contained, monitored, and assessed."

Silva breathed through his nose. "We've started to develop a new artificial intelligence program that could—"

A stun bullet smacked Silva in the back, and he collapsed. Jaxon charged the suited man and swung but was wrestled to the ground and strapped at the ankles and wrists. Jaxon looked up at the president. "Welcome to the Ghost Recall."

A hood pulled down over his face.

www.ingramcontent.com/pod-product-compliance
Lightning Source LLC
Chambersburg PA
CBHW061503120726
48001CB00004B/1197